Sue Simpson

After the sudden death of her mother when Sue Simpson was five, her childhood became unsettled. Finding herself in a hostile boarding school environment she struggled academically. Leaving school with no recognised qualifications or skills it came as something of a surprise to find many years later that she had a natural storytelling ability. At the time she was working on a secure unit with the mentally ill in Chester and was constantly in trouble for turning serious reports into humorous accounts of mayhem. She was given the job of writing the work magazine. From there her writing took off and to date she has over four hundred short stories. She hopes to be able to leave the caring profession behind to become a full time writer.

Sue has been writing for the American music/fiction magazine 'Legends' for three years and is the horror/suspense editor for the internet writing and magazine site UK Authors.

Sue's first published work is a children's book called 'Lizard's Leap.'

'Better the devil you know' is her second novel and her third, 'People On The Edge' will also be available this summer

Sue lives in the market town of Dalton-in-Furness on the southern tip of the Lake District and is the mother of two boys, Christopher and Mark. She is currently working on two new novels. Sue can be contacted on sooz.006@virgin.net

Other books by this author:

Lizard's Leap

People On The Edge

Better The Devil You Know
by
Sue Simpson

Better The Devil You Know
by
Sue Simpson

Best Books Online
Mediaworld PR Ltd

First paperback edition published in Great Britain
May 2003 by
Best Books Online
Mediaworld PR Ltd

ISBN 1-904502-34-2

Better The Devil You Know is dedicated to a very special lady who was more like a mother than a friend. She passed away while I was in the process of writing *Devil* but she never stopped having faith in me.

Marion Mawson 1.11.2001 God bless always.

I'd also like to dedicate this to my two sons,
Chris Whiteside and Mark Simpson.
I'm proud of you lads and always will be.

And finally not a dedication but a big thank you to my storyboarding partner Karen Seaman. Kaz is my niece and whenever I have a problem we sit and fight it through. There's her way and my way and somewhere in the middle the perfect way. Without Karen *Devil* would still have been written, the story demanded that, but it would have been half the book it is now. Her ideas bring freshness to the story when mine go stale. She's also the one who kicks me up the backside when I get lazy and tells me to get on with it.
Thanks Kaz the next night out's on me.

Chapter 1

Every novelist knows that it is the kiss of death to write about window gazing in her opening sentence. Evelyn Erikson, age twenty-seven and current resident of Cherry Tree Cottage on top of Beech Hill, didn't know this. In fact Evelyn knew remarkably little about the nuts and bolts of writing, despite having three books hovering in or around the bestseller list. This day held all the promise that only a young day can, and the unpalatable, cooling coffee was her reason for remaining rooted at the dining table watching that promise unfold.

Jake padded in from the garden and sat in front of her chair demanding attention. He looked uncommonly girlie, sitting with his great, big head adorned with lavender blooms and cocked enquiringly to the right. Eve laughed despite her mood.

"You've had your nosy snout in that lavender bush again, haven't you?" She said in a mock reproving voice. "Those bees'll have you and then you'll be sorry."

Jake grinned and chuffed at Eve, he was a clever German Shepherd and he knew the 'Bee' word.

Bees: fat things that don't make sense to a logic seeking dog. They shouldn't be able to fly with that round, furry body and tiny, thin wings. It's not right that they should be able to fly and Jake can't. Hmmm they taste good though and it makes his humans laugh when he pulls funny faces as he tries to eat one. Jake forgets sometimes that he only has one human now. He used to have two. Jake mustn't forget that he only has one human, because Eve gets sad when he goes round the house looking. But if Jake could find her, and bring her back, then Eve wouldn't be sad anymore. Jake thinks she's in that hole where they saw a mouse last year. That mouse went in the hole in the skirting boards and never came out again. It is all very confusing though when the whole house smells of her. Eve doesn't smell her everywhere like Jake does. Eve would whine all night too if she could smell her all the time and had an itch behind her ear. Bees shouldn't oughta fly like that; it's not right.

Eve put her hand down and stroked the dog's head. The strawberries were almost ripe. '*She would have loved that,*' thought Eve; she would enjoy picking the first strawberries of the season for their tea. It was always quite an occasion apparently. The first ones would be ripe for picking next week, but it wouldn't be the same and Eve doubted that they would taste as sweet without Ellie there to enjoy them with her.

"Oh well Jakey boy, we can't sit here all day can we? I've made a momentous decision while you've been having fun without a care in the world. I'm going to start writing today."

Jake cocked his head again, deciphering the unfamiliar words from the ones he knew. There was no 'dinner' or 'out' in them, but sometimes humans disguised dinner and out so that they sounded like something else.

Eve got up from the table, and before she was even upright Jake was bouncing around like a puppy.

Oh yes, oh yes, this is it. This is the out. Out, out, out. Oh I'm so excited. We're going out. Do the round and round thing. Eve likes the round and round thing. Make Eve smile. Round and round. Round and round. Out. Out. Out. No Eve that's the study. That's not out, that's Ellie's study. The front door's this way. Eve, Eve. Out. Look I'm wagging, I'm wagging Eve. Out. C'mon Eve, I'll teach you how to catch bees without them getting the ouch thing in you. Eve. Out. Oh sometimes humans are no fun.

Eve walked into Ellie's domain. This wasn't merely Ellie's room this room *was* Ellie. Ellie permeated the walls and infused the very air. Eve hadn't been in here much since... Well, now it was her room and she had to get used to that. Things were different now and she *is* Ellie. It felt strange becoming someone else. Evelyn Erikson had gradually taken the place of Eleanor. As long as Eve was Ellie, Ellie would never be dead.

Lowering herself into the swivel chair she took a deep, calming breath and Jake flopped down beside her. He sighed the sigh of a dog much older than his eight years and rolled his eyes to make his displeasure obvious. Five seconds later his heavy lids gave up the struggle to stay open and he fell asleep.

The computer's sensors had monitored Eve's approach and as she sat down it fired up. Eve envied the computer's ability to come alive within seconds of 'waking'. What the computer could achieve in thirty seconds, she aspired to only after a shower and three cups of strong coffee.

"Good morning Ellie." Said the computer-simulated voice.

"Good morning George," replied Eve. The new name was going to take some growing into.

"It is 8:54 am and the date is the 10th of June Two thousand and forty eight. What can I do for you this morning?" Asked the deep, though rather tinny, tones of the 'sex god in the box.' as they called him.

Eve slumped into the chair. The hairs on her arms began to rise and she was instantly transported back in her mind to another place, another time, another world where every morning an impersonal voice chanted the date and time at her. A place where she was a prisoner contained and controlled, unable even to think for herself. She wanted to run but her legs were leaden. She couldn't do this. She was mad to think that she could just sit here and continue where things had been left off. She raised her head and took some deep breaths. Jake alerted to the change in Eve's mood sat up, whined and cocked his head at his mistress in alarm. She *had* to do this; she owed it not only to herself but also to the only person in the world that she had ever loved. She would do this. She took one more deep inhalation just to check that she was calm and spoke in as reasonable a voice as possible to the computer."

"George, I will be coming in here at roughly this time every morning from now on. I only intend to say this once so I hope your receptors are focused to exactly what I am saying. I like your chirpy 'Good Morning' George, really I do. Sometimes yours will be the only voice apart from my own that I will hear in the course of the day. But, listen up my technological friend. If you ever tell me the date and time when I walk into the room again I will pull every single wire from your circuitry and stuff them so far down your memory hole that you will be choking on techno-spaghetti for a month. Do I make myself succinctly and unconditionally understood?"

The computerised voice was bristling with indignation when it replied "Well, there's no need to take that attitude I'm sure, I was only trying to be helpful," it then lowered its voice to a mumble "Succinctly and unconditionally understood. Huh anyone would think she's a writer."

Having done for the time being with whinging it raised its voice back to the default volume level "Will that be all for now Miss?"

"Oh George, drop the insulted affront or I'll pinch your emotion chip and use it for a solar token. Oh and remind me George to take a large sub-machine gun and shoot whoever it was who decided to give computers an emotion chip in the first place. It can be highly irritating. Right then George to business. I would like a squeaky clean, new document please. Today is the day I begin the new book."

"But Ellie you are only on chapter seven of 'Who Took The Morning Train' and if I might be so bold as to mention without endangering my delicate circuitry in your present mood, it is desperately in need of a decent edit."

Eve smiled despite herself. Sometimes it was hard to believe that blood and organs formed no part of the make-up of George. "New document please George and then that will be all thank-you."

"Very good Miss," said George in his finest simulation of the dutiful servant. "I'll just meld into the background then until the next time you feel the urgent desire to abuse me. Enjoy Ellie its good to be in service again." George brought up a new word processing document as requested and altered his status. The 'voice activation on stand by' icon appeared in the top right of the monitor screen.

"And George?" Said Eve bringing him back online.

"Yes?" he answered in a perfect long-suffering voice.

"I love you." Said Eve grinning, "Save every five minutes please, George."

"Will do Hun. Oh and you asked me to remind you to take a large sub-machine gun and shoot whoever it was that gave computers emotion chips." The screen momentarily went black and flashed with a huge red lips icon. The lips puckered and a large smacking sound crackled from the speakers they were replaced after five seconds with the document waiting to be written.

This time she laughed out loud "Bugger off George and let me work." The hardware that produced the voice of the computer seemed to know just when she needed cheering up, and she contemplated the white screen still smiling.

Eve took a great lungful of air and began by writing her pen name in the header. 'Eleanor Erikson'. The next five words produced the title. 'Better The Devil You Know.'

In the body of the document she began the first sentence of the novel that *had* to be written, that *needed* to be told.

She began with the words.

"Every novelist knows that it is the kiss of death to write about window gazing in their opening sentence…"

Chapter 2

Ellie was tired, her head swam and her feet ached. No she decided 'to swim' was far too energetic a verb, her brain floundered against a tide of incoming exhaustion and she was just plain knackered.

It had been one of those long hard days that everybody moans about on a Wednesday evening. Not close enough to the beginning of the week to be enlivened from the weekend, and too far away from Friday to feel a lie-in in sight. Really of course, in her line of work it didn't matter much what day it was, being entirely her own boss was both a blessing and a curse. Today though she hadn't been working on her latest book, today she had been going five rounds with hospital bureaucracy. She locked the car and wondered who had called, the gate was open slightly and it was her habit to always close it properly.

She was still pondering the identity of the caller as she opened the front door to see a small white envelope on the mat. She winced slightly as she bent to pick it up and then her pain was forgotten as all her attention focused on the unexpected letter and who it might be from. The first thing she noticed was the small neat handwriting, in a style not unlike her own. The other thing that drew her attention was the fact that the letter had no stamps, it had been hand delivered.

Inside was a single sheet of simple white notepaper folded once widthways. Centralised on the paper and in the same handwriting as the envelope, was a single sentence. It said.

Better the devil you know.

Jake whined from behind the kitchen door. He had been locked up since nine-thirty that morning and his plaintive whimper told of the utmost distress.

"Alright big fella, Mum's home. I'm coming to let you out," said Ellie in a half-distracted voice.

This only served to make Jake's plea sound even more urgent. She opened the door to be greeted enthusiastically by a six-stone furball, in the shape of a twelve-month old German shepherd dog. As she struggled to make her way to the back door with the dog leaping round her body and jumping up despite being constantly told that this was not a polite thing to do. Ellie crooned and spoke to him softly. If the dog noticed she seemed to have aged ten years since leaving the house that morning he was too well-mannered, in that respect at least, to let on. He just jumped and wagged and chuffed and preened, happy to know that he was a 'Good Boy'. Finally Ellie managed to turn the key in the lock with stiff fingers and the dog shot to freedom. He made straight to the lavender bush to shoot a few of those pesky late summer bees with a mighty fine blast of his own special fertiliser.

As she stood watching the dog the phone began to ring. She made her way through to the study where the nearest phone extension was located. The day had taken its toll and Ellie's footsteps were slow and laboured. She realised for the first time that over the coming months she would need telephone access in every room in the house. So far she had avoided the voice reactor telephones that worked through any building via the computer, but now it seemed she would have little choice but to move along with the newest technology. She picked up the phone on the eleventh ring and the receiver went dead in her hand. Three steps back towards the kitchen and it demanded her attention with its persistent command once more. This time she caught it on only its second ring.

"Hello?"

After a slight pause she could hear slow rhythmic breathing.

"Hello?" she repeated a little more urgently. Then once again the connection was aborted.

"Bloody hell," she swore aloud. "Wouldn't you think they'd have the manners to at least explain if it's a wrong number?"

While Ellie was making a cup of coffee, feeding the dog and fixing a sandwich for herself, Jake came in from the garden and dropped his rubber ring at her feet. He looked up at her expectantly wagging his tail, totally convinced that she was going to stop everything for an instant game of 'fetch'. Then he smelled his food and all thoughts of the ring game went out of his mind in an instant. The abandoned toy lay at Ellie's feet, perfectly positioned to trip her up had she not already seen it. Something else she was going to have to be more aware of in the future. Jake gave two single, curt barks clearly asking for his evening meal to be delivered to his feeding mat right this second. Ellie grinned at the mutt and complied. She patted him lovingly on his head as his nose dropped greedily into the dish.

So often these days Ellie couldn't be bothered to fix a proper meal for herself in the evenings. Tonight though she was so fatigued and mind-weary that she could barely be bothered to eat at all, even though her growling stomach had been reminding her for the last three hours that it hadn't been fed since breakfast some ten and a half hours earlier. The soaps would be starting after the early evening news, normally Ellie's routine meant that her day's work and household chores were finished for the evening by now and she and Jake would curl up together on the sofa while Ellie watched some television to unwind. Tonight the artificial lives of the soap stars held no interest for her. All she could concentrate on were the same three words, in the same order that kept circling round and round her mind in the same direction: Tay-Sachs Disease.

She had come to the conclusion that she deserved ten out of ten for originality, typical writer, always going for the dramatic angle. *'Oh'* she thought *'I couldn't have any old common or garden bout of terminal cancer, oh no, I have to go for Tay-bloody-Sachs disease that is not only extremely bloody rare but virtually bloody unheard of in adults. Nice one Eleanor girl, what do you do for an encore?'* If her thoughts had been audible the bitterness and anger would have singed the atmosphere leaving the acrid smell of burning fury in its wake. The test results today had only been for the purpose of formally crossing the T's and dotting the I's. The consultants, of whom it seemed she had many, were already almost certain of the diagnosis of her illness. Ellie had done all her crying in the three weeks previously. She had said her 'Why me's' and pouted at the unfairness of it. But although she had bitterly grieved the loss of her right to the menopause, senility and toothless old age dotage, she had *not* come to terms with her condition. And she had *not* accepted that she was going to die prematurely, and she had not run out of sodding swear words to fit her mood and she was most certainly *not* going to just roll over and play dead quietly.

As Ellie sat pondering, her mind took her past the loved ones she would leave behind. It went beyond the fact that she had between six months and ten years left to enjoy '*all being well.*' It skimmed over the treatments and alterations her life was going to have to welcome and endure. It took her to a place that she was more and more often scurrying to in an almost obsessive need to make sense of it all. Every time she thought of her illness she focused her thoughts on her writing. The formation of those recurring thoughts was so irrational that she laughed inwardly to herself as she analysed them once again. She felt tears stinging the back of her eyes as she thought of all the words that she wouldn't have time to write. To date she had six novels in rough synopsis in her mind. Scraps of jotted notes outlining the stories that wanted to be written, characters and plots, twists and one-liners. Six complete beginnings, middles and endings, which may never be read and may never be written. She worried about her final novel, the one that would be left incomplete. The only way to avoid that incomplete book would be to finish the current one while she was fit enough to do so and not begin another. How could she not write? Surely not writing was akin only to not breathing. As the thought that she might one day be too sick to write crept insidiously in amongst all those other thoughts, she shot it through the heart with an arrow and left it dying on the attic floor of her mind. She would *always* be able to write and if she couldn't then she hoped the end would come blessedly early.

Ellie concentrated on thoughts of her writing because to think of the bigger picture would hurt far too much. She couldn't let herself think of the day that she would leave Jake, or her long time boyfriend Matthew High or indeed her mother. Those were things that would hurt far too much to think about. So for now until her personal demons forced her to think those thoughts she would concentrate on how much the loss of her writing would mean. That was good. That was safe. That was very nearly bearable.

So unbearable had been the thought of her mother's anguish that Ellie hadn't been able to tell her about being ill. Her mother still lived in blissful ignorance of the situation. The greatest blight in Esther Erikson's life was the fact that her clematis was smothering the honeysuckle and that smokey bacon was up five pence at Asda. Esther was a law unto herself and lived in a world that Ellie didn't like to intrude on very often. Although Matt knew about the illness she hadn't been completely honest with him about the result date, she hadn't exactly lied to him, but when he mistakenly thought she was at the hospital the day after the date of her appointment, she never bothered to correct him. The guilt she was feeling was an extra weight to bear but Matt's anguish was at times smothering and this day was always going to be difficult enough to get through without having to cope with Matt's pain on top of her own.

The phone rang and as she was sitting right next to the lounge extension she picked it up before it had finished its first ring. Her thoughts must have been guilty of tweaking Matt's concern because lo and behold it was he on the other end of the connection.

"Hello gorgeous. How are you?"

His voice was deep and soft and like a big warm snuggle blanket. She ached anew with the thought of losing him. The joint in her right big toe had begun to throb too but that diminished in intensity compared to hearing Matt's voice and knowing how she was about to destroy his world. Matthew was the eternal optimist and truly believed that although the results were a foregone conclusion, something would come up at the eleventh hour to prove that Ellie just had bad wind or something.

"Hey Darling. I'm fine, a little tired but okay. What are you up to then?"

On hearing Ellie's contrived brightness Matt's voice instantly became heavy with concern.

"I can tell by your voice how tired you are. Do you want me to come over? After all I did as I promised and left you alone to work in peace today. And look what it's done to you, you sound exhausted."

"No, no not tonight Matt, remember what we agreed, Tuesdays and Thursdays we do our own thing, so tell me why you are here talking to me when you could be on your third pint with the lads?"

"Because you've got fantastic breasts and because the lads don't kiss me the way you do."

"So how do they kiss you then?"

"Too much tongue and bristle and not enough lipstick. Why, are you jealous?"

"Madly; I'm going to rip out their throats and play oesophagus guitar." They both enjoyed the lightweight moment and then Matt's voice became serious again.

"I love you Eleanor Erikson."

"I love you too sweetheart, I love you more than you can possibly know."

"Ellie? There's something wrong. What is it? What's the matter?"

'Damn him and his bloody intuition,' thought Ellie. She had wanted to delay the moment of destruction for just a few minutes more until she felt braver in herself. She knew well enough that she was a miserable coward for telling him on the phone and not face to face, but she just couldn't bear having to see his brick walls of conviction come tumbling town like paper streamers in a Christmas breeze.

"Matty, you're right love, I do have something to tell you." She paused not quite knowing how to go on, wanting to run away leaving the phone dangling on its flex. She wanted to flee to the comfort of her soft pillows and bury herself in Jake's fur until the madness that her world had become righted itself. She just wanted to sleep until a doctor came to say there'd been a terrible mistake, that her records had somehow been mistaken for another lady's with a similar name. But here was now, and now was here, and she had to tell Matt, the truth.

"I went to the hospital today."

Matt cut in on her before she could go any further.

"What is it? What's the matter? God I knew you'd over do it with that bloody book. I knew I shouldn't have listened to you, if I'd been there…"

"Matt, sshhh let me finish please." Matt fell silent but she could hear him breathing hard on the other end of the phone. She knew that he was gripping the receiver too tightly and that his knuckles were white with the pressure, she knew he was biting down hard on his bottom lip the way he always did when he was perplexed. She knew that the pressure point in his left temple was pulsing visibly and that if she could just kiss it gently he would let the tension go and relax with a great sigh of release. She wanted to spare him the next sentence, but couldn't.

"Matty love; I got the test results today."

"But that's not until tomorrow. I'm coming with you to the hospital. It's all a big mistake. Everything's going to be just fine and I'm booking a table at Clancy's to celebrate." His breath broke on the final word into a loud heartbreaking sob.

"Ellie if you'd just waited until tomorrow everything would have been all right. I know it would." The last sentence had risen in pitch and held a note of near hysteria to it.

"They came back positive."

Ellie's voice had lowered to almost a whisper as though by speaking the hateful sentence so quietly it would lessen its power, that somehow the string of events put into motion by the words would not be triggered.

"No. No. No." Each 'no' was drawn out longer than the last. The small word needed to be stretched to hold all the pain that was coming across the phone connection at her. He was sobbing loudly and could barely speak he was crying so hard.

"I'm on my way."

"NO!" Ellie almost screamed the word at him. "Matt, no. I'm sorry darling I know how much you are hurting and I wish I could hold you and take the pain away for you, but tonight, just this night, this one night. I need to think about me. Tonight Matt my needs have got to be greater than yours. I'm so tired and I desperately need to sleep. I'll see you tomorrow I promise and we'll talk. Book that table at Clancy's anyway I want to go out. You can buy me the most expensive meal on the menu. Hmmm Steak Dianne with the works. I love you baby."

Ellie knew that her words had cut into Matt deeply. She didn't mean to imply that he was selfish and that he put his own needs before Ellie's. He wasn't and he didn't. He just wanted to help and didn't know how. But she hadn't the energy to be any more tactful; she just wanted the conversation to end so that she could fall into bed. Despite the devastating news she thought she would sleep without any problems that night. Matt took a moment to recover and she heard his sobs quietening.

"Gold digger!" He managed with a false little laugh. "You only want me for my money, I know your type. All diamond necklace and deep pockets."

"Tell you what," she countered, "Take out some life insurance and then if you die before me I'll inherit. You'll have to be fast though."

"Not funny Ellie. Not funny." There was no sign of tears in his voice now just a heavy sadness that seemed to have knocked all the life out of his lungs.

"It's the only way I know how baby. I don't know what else to do but laugh at the bastard. The disease doesn't seem so scary when you laugh at it. I need to sleep love. I need to sleep so badly."

"You go to bed and sleep tight sweetheart. I love you Ellie."

"I love you too." Suddenly she couldn't bear the thought of him hanging up the phone. She didn't want to be alone. Every second they had together was precious now. Was this the start of the mood swings the doctor told her to expect? She didn't want to give in to the bone numbing tiredness and fall into a deep sleep in case she never woke up from it. She wouldn't give in to this evil disease that wanted to rob her of her life. All she wanted at that moment was to feel the strength of Matt's arms around her. She didn't want to go to sleep she wanted to make love. She was still alive so far dammit.

"Matty?" she said in a low murmur that he almost missed over the static of the phone.

“Yes love. God Ellie what can I do to help you.”

“Will you come Matty, I can’t bear it. Will you come now?”

In his haste to get out of the house Matty forgot to say goodbye, without another word the line buzzed its disconnection in her ear. Ellie couldn’t help but smile through her tears.

All thoughts of sleep banished from her mind as she went upstairs as fast as her aching body could carry her. While the bath filled she shaved her legs. She didn’t have a lot of time before Matt arrived and she wanted to be clean and fresh to seduce him. Only ten minutes earlier she had been totally enervated and the thought of doing *anything* was a thought too tiring, now she was filled with a desperate energy that was borne of fear. *Move or die, move or die, move or die.* She repeated to herself over and again.

His timing was perfect, she had just stepped out of the bath and was wrapping a large, white, fluffy towel around herself when she heard the door security scanning him for entry. She hastily squirted a light mist of perfume to her neck and wrists and feeling much better after her bath, she ran down the stairs to greet him.

Before he had the opportunity to say a word she wrapped her arms round his neck and kissed him. The passion that suddenly welled up from nowhere took both of them by surprise. What started as a sweet ‘Hello’ kiss, turned into a wanton need that left them breathless.

Ellie pushed Matt back against the front door. Her hands roamed freely over his body, her mouth ground hungrily on his and her tongue flicked over his top lip and into his warm, minty, mouth. His arms tightened around her slim waist and pulled her into his body. She felt his already stiffening penis drive into her thighs. She moaned into his mouth, not merely giving in to the need flooding through her, but drawing it savagely from her body and pushing it onto his. The heat from his hands on her back sent shivers of icy sensation prickling the length of her spine and she squirmed into a better position so that his hardness pushed directly into her.

He moaned into her ear in a voice heavy with passion and just a little disappointment. “Ellie we can’t darling, you’re not well enough. You’re tired…your illness?”

“Shhh,” she said her mouth covering his to still the words of illness that she didn’t want to hear. “I’m alive Matty and I want you so much. Make love to me now baby. Right now.”

His hands pressed firmly into her back circling ever lower, until he cupped her buttocks, she felt the pressure of his short nails indenting her flesh as their body’s ground into each other. Without hurting her, he bit on her lip, his teeth grazing the fullness of her mouth as her tongue again sought entry. He took his mouth from hers and dropped his head to take the supple flesh of her neck into his mouth. He sucked hard, stopping just short of bruising her before nuzzling into the cleft between her breasts. He was tormented at being just centimetres from reaching her erect nipple, from being able to feel it between his lips, without losing the pressure of his penis between her legs.

She could barely hear his words for the rasp of his harsh breath coming in gasps between each thrust of him against her. "Jesus Ellie. I want you so much. I need to make love to you too. Let's go up to bed."

"I can't wait that long babe." She backed her pelvis away from him and the towel dropped to her feet. He groaned at the momentary loss of her. This sudden sensual attack of his senses had been so unexpected that he came to full arousal far more quickly than ever before. After just two minutes of feeling her against him and sensing a need in her at least as great as his own he was already feeling the sensation of being close to coming. He knew Ellie's body almost as well as his own and her orgasm wasn't far from explosion either. Another minute and they would both have been exploding, and Matt was still fully clothed. He felt like a horny schoolboy. This was something that hadn't happened since the early days of their courtship when they tortured each other with long sessions of heavy petting weeks before they finally made love. Her hands clutched at his belt; her fingers clumsy in their haste to get it undone and release his erection to her. Within seconds his pants were round his ankles and his stiffened penis sprung free. A blast of heat rose from between his legs from the friction they had generated and the smell of him mixed with Lifebuoy soap made her salivate with the need of him.

She dropped to her knees and without the usual nuzzling took him straight into her mouth. He groaned loudly pushing his head back against the support of the door; the pleasure coursed from his groin to his brain and a feeling of sensational dizziness made his head spin. His scrotum contracted and he pulled himself from her before she had finished her first voyage down the length of him.

"No Ellie, I want to be inside you properly. I want to make love to you."

She tried to take him back into her mouth but he put his arms gently under hers and lifted her from the floor. He kissed her once quickly before she grabbed his hand and headed with him for the stairs. It took all Matt's concentration not to trip over his jeans that were still around his ankles and it was easy for Ellie to swivel him round and push him onto the stairs before he was fully aware of what was happening to him.

His penis jerked involuntarily He never grew tired of the sight of Ellie naked.

Lowering one hand to guide him into her she dropped onto him with a hard thrust. Her juices has been flowing fast since that first kiss and he slid inside her easily but with a force that made him gasp as his foreskin took a second to catch up with the rest of him.

Ellie tensed her pelvic muscles tightly and he felt himself being squeezed by the rippled walls of her vagina. She arched her back and began to ride him with more aggression and force than she had ever used on him before. The treads of the stairs dug into Matt's back and he made a bridge of his body, thrusting his pubic bone into Ellie's female arousal and feeling the extra half-inch of penetration that made her scream out in pleasure.

She was moving on him faster and harder with every energetic thrust. "Fuck me Matt, Fuck me."

Matt felt his passion waning slightly as the unfamiliar words issued from Ellie's lovely mouth. "Fuck me you horny bastard. Harder, harder come on make me scream baby." Sweat was pouring from her body and her breathing was ragged and rasping. "I'm alive and I'm well Matt and I'm going to be the best sex you've ever had."

He felt the last of his erection dwindling inside her. "Whoa Ellie, Ellie, ease up a minute love." She looked at him, her eyes clouded with confusion.

"What's the matter Matty don't you want me anymore?"

"Darlin' I want you more than I've ever wanted you before. The way you proved you still need me back there drove me crazy with a want for you. Ellie you *are* the best lover I've ever had, you know you are, but that's not because of your sexual prowess, not because of how hard and fast you can ride me, or how dirty you can talk. It's because of the way we feel about each other, it's because I love you Ellie. I don't want to fuck you; I want to make love to you the way we always have. And yes sometimes I like it a little bit rougher than normal, that's fun, that's keeping sex alive. But darling you don't have to prove to me that you are still the best even though you are ill, because even when lovemaking is difficult for us you will still be the best. More than that you will be the *only."*

He wiped the first tears from her cheeks and carried her upstairs. Kicking the door closed with his foot he laid Ellie down on the top of the bed. As she watched him, he took his clothes off and lay beside her. Keeping eye contact with her for as long as possible he stoked her soft body. She lay naked on the bed in front of him and finally he dropped his eyes to her neatly trimmed triangle of soft downy hair. Matt kissed her inner thighs at the very top of her legs, she parted them slightly and he kissed her softly teasing her back into the mood that had been broken. He didn't stay too long there; it was so sweet that very soon he wouldn't be able to stop himself from losing his gentle restraint and devouring between her legs until she writhed in ecstasy. It was important to Matt to re-gain a feeling of sensual lovemaking rather than rampant sex.

He came back to the head of the bed and saw that tears were still rolling down Ellie's cheeks, though her mouth was open and her breathing was hard and excited. He kissed each of the tears away tasting this second of Elle's fluids on his tongue, tasting her love for him. And then he kissed her parted mouth softly. At first she remained immobile the breath escaping through her lips, enjoying the feel of his mouth on hers. And then she responded, raising her hand to stroke his face and moulding her lips to his. Her hand was so soft and her lips so pliable that Matt felt a new love for her that was stronger than any he'd felt before. A small murmur of want escaped her lips the sound amplifying within his mouth. His hand brushed against her small breast, the nipple was hard and budded as it scraped across his palm. He cupped the breast and kneaded it slowly. It was more than he could stand, despite himself, his kiss became more demanding and this time Ellie took her lead from him. They soul kissed for a long time without any tongues and it felt wonderful for them both.

Matt's erection rubbed against Ellie's outer leg and he ached with the need to feel himself expanding inside her again. Ellie tried to resist him when he pulled her on top of him. She was embarrassed about earlier and wanted him to take the lead.

"You please, Ellie, I want to look at you while we make love, and that's the best view." He smiled at her cheekily and Ellie smiled back, her eyes still wet and shining but the tears stationary on her cheeks and no longer brimming over her lids.

This time they made love slowly, with long languid movements that delighted both of them. Ellie held back waiting for Matt to be ready. Normally she took her orgasms as they came having several to each of Matt's, but this time one was all she needed, She leaned forward and brushed her nipple across Matt's lip until he took it into his mouth. Her movements became shorter, tiny intense motions relying mainly on internal muscle contraction and when they came at the same moment the force of their love and mutual orgasm gave them both one of the most gratifying moments of their lives that neither one would ever forget.

Ellie sat up and one last tear fell from her eye to mingle with the perspiration on Matt's chest. She smiled almost shyly at him and her grey eyes shimmered with tears that were staying to moisturise her eyes. Matt saw in her a beauty that was something new, something more than the natural beauty that nature blessed her with.

Ellie was five foot six, with soft natural blonde hair, cut into a short bob, she was slender with small breasts that bloomed with perfection. His girlfriend was the most beautiful woman he had ever seen.

Afterwards Ellie lay in the crook of his arm and when she fell asleep within seconds he didn't have the heart to disturb her. What was a cramped arm compared to what Ellie was going through? He watched her sleeping for a long time and her dreams were pleasant. She never saw Matt crying silently long into the night.

Chapter 3

George interrupted Ellie's writing just as a vital clue was being uncovered.

"Somebody at the door Ellie."

Ellie tutted irritably, annoyed by being disturbed at such a crucial point in the plot. *'Oh no I bet that's Matt offering rich tea and sympathy along with a goodly dollop of his own self pity,'* she thought and then felt instantly contrite.

"Okay George, show me," she said, her voice heavy with resignation. The computer monitor went black for a moment and then the security screen came into focus showing a clear view of the front door, and of the fresh-faced young man standing upon the doorstep.

"Intercom please, George." The intercom system linked to the computer crackled.

"Hello. Can I help you?" Said Ellie, pleasantly masking any irritation she felt at being disrupted in her writing.

"Parcel for Miss Erikson."

"Okay love, just one moment please." Ellie got up from the swivel chair easing her aching muscles, she had been sitting in the same position for almost five hours and her lower back was killing her. *'It's time I took a break anyway'*, she thought wincing. Jake was instantly excited with his mistress's movements. Perhaps this activity at last meant that he might be in line for a walk.

She signed for the parcel, thanked the young delivery lad and brought it through to the study. She wasn't expecting anything, except for some manuscript edits from her publisher, and they would be in a large brown envelope displaying the company stamp. She tore off the outer brown paper packaging and inside was a fairly large, flat box with a lid. It had to be something from Matty to cheer her up, he often gave her an unexpected gift, it was just one of the little things that made him special. She smiled and lifted the lid from the box to be confronted with yards of bright red satin. *'Oh oh not my colour at all,'* she mused, as she lifted what she thought was a rather tarty negligee from the box.

What it turned out to be was a red satin cape. The rest of the box's contents consisted of a black cat suit, red tail, head dress complete with horns and a trident type three pronged fork, normally associated with the devil. *'What the...'* she thought, and then the penny dropped. Matthew must have arranged for them to go to a fancy dress party that night instead of going out to dinner. She pulled the invoice from the box. It seemed the costume was on hire from 'Fancy Pants' party shop and was due to be returned by four o'clock the following afternoon. Ellie was just a little put out by this arrangement. Matt was always dropping surprises on her like this; he had an intuition for knowing what would please her. Six months ago she would have been delighted at the prospect of a lively party *and* of his choice of costume for her. The black rubber cat suit looked very clingy and sexy, and could certainly lead to some post party fun, and her black stiletto boots with the five-inch heel would set the costume off to perfection. Ellie was disappointed at his lack of perception to her mood this time though. It seemed a little thoughtless of him to arrange a party for them when she had just been told she was dying. She thought back to their lovemaking the night before. Surely he must realise that she needed to relax and take things a little bit easier than she had been of late. She understood his need to cheer her up, and might be thinking that a return to normality would be the best way to do it. How many times lately had Ellie said that she just wanted to live whatever time she had left to the full? Tonight though, she didn't want to party, she just wanted to enjoy a quiet evening with her boyfriend and then, for them to come home to talk and make love. She thought he would have understood this. She would have to ring him to cancel.

Matthew said he was as baffled as she was by the mysterious parcel. There was no fancy dress party arranged and he had not ordered the costume for her. In fact the table at Clancy's was all booked for eight o'clock.

"You can keep the costume for when we get home if you like though, you little devil." There was genuine merriment chuckling in his voice.

Better the devil you know.

Five words fluttered into Ellie's consciousness.

She remembered the letter of the previous evening and told Matt about it.

"Someone's having a joke with you Ellie, it'll probably be Rob."

Rob Price was Ellie's close friend and agent. It would not be in the least alien to Rob's nature to play a practical joke on Ellie, he had caught her with some corkers in the past. After she had said her goodbyes to Matt, Ellie rang Rob.

"Okay wise guy, what's going on?" she said without any formal greeting after Shirley, Rob's personal assistant had put her through.

"Now then," began Rob. "Which of my literary starlets might this be? Maisy Dog author of *How to shag around and not become green and drippy.* Or Reginald Bott, writer of *The student's guide to recipes made with three-week-old milk?* Or then again maybe it's Ellie Erikson; pain in the arse, thorn in my side and general tormentor when I'm trying to work."

Ellie laughed, "So, getting back to the original question, what's with all the devil worshipping stuff?"

"Oh now this is getting more interesting by the second. Please tell me more, do we get to cover ourselves with goats blood and dance naked round an altar? You know Ellie I knew that one day you wouldn't be able to resist making improper propositions of a preposterous sexual purpose towards my personable personage, but hey; I didn't think you'd be *that* kinky."

Ellie explained through giggles about the letter and parcel.

Rob admitted somewhat reluctantly that he hadn't a clue what she was talking about and passed the buck back to Matt. Ellie explained that it wasn't Matt. And if it wasn't Matt and it wasn't Rob then who the hell did send the letter and costume?

"Wow! That's it now girl, you've made it bigger than big. Forget topping the best seller list, the true accolade to literary genius is having your very own, really truly, no shit, psycho-stalker."

Ellie laughed again and told Rob not to be so ridiculous, but a slight shiver travelled the length of her spine anyway. She made arrangements to meet Rob for lunch two days later on the Wednesday. Rob wasn't exactly keen on the idea. He said he had a hectic week ahead of him, but although Ellie agreed that it could wait if it had to, Rob was alerted to something in Ellie's voice that made him want to cancel previous engagements to be able to meet up with her. As she hung up, Ellie wished that Rob had been too busy for the arranged meeting. Putting off having to tell Rob of her illness would please Ellie no end, but as her agent and more importantly her friend, she knew that it had to be done and soon. Talking to Matt and Rob had put her in an unexpectedly buoyant mood, but she felt her balloon land with inelegance at the thought of telling her closest friends and relatives of her condition. Telling Matt the previous night had taken its toll both physically and mentally. One symptom of her condition was non-regenerative fatigue. A core-sapping weariness which went way beyond tiredness. One that a few hours decent sleep could neither help nor cure.

~*~

The bell jangled as she opened the door to the 'Fancy Pants' costume shop. The lady behind the counter looked up from the catalogue she was browsing and smiled in recognition. Ellie noticed she was chewing gum, and it struck her as odd for a woman of middle age. It was something that particularly annoyed Ellie when being served by young girls, but the constantly churning mouth of this lady seemed mildly amusing.

"Hello again lovey, didn't expect to see you back so soon. Is there a problem?"

Ellie was baffled and looked round to make sure that the lady was indeed talking to her. She was the only other person in the shop.

"I'm sorry I don't know what you mean, I've never been in here before.

I've just come to return this. It must have come to my address by mistake this morning." Ellie put the box on the counter.

The shopkeeper looked directly at Ellie, her eyes seemed somewhat accusing though her voice remained pleasant as she said. "But you ordered the costume this morning. I distinctly remember it was the red devil outfit."

Ellie didn't mind a joke in the least and was normally happy to play along and be a good sport. Maybe the news of the previous day had bearing on her next action. It was so completely out of character for her, or perhaps it was a symptom of the disease itself, but suddenly Ellie felt she was being made a fool of and she lost all control of her temper.

"Look! You stupid bitch. I don't know who has put you up to this, or why; but I have had to leave my work to return this sodding thing to you. I don't think that's very funny. Do you? It's taken me over half an hour to get here, and no doubt it'll take the same to get back, maybe I should bill you for my lost earnings. I never ordered the stupid costume. I don't want it, it's tawdry, and may I suggest that you might have a more prolific clientele if you didn't presume to make a fool of people as soon as they walk through the door. Now you can take your tacky little costume and shove it up that gorilla's arse for all I care. I don't want it. Do I make myself understood you frosty faced, cud chewing, old cow?"

With that Ellie flung the box in the general direction of an innard-less gorilla suit and flounced out of the shop leaving the dazed and confused assistant staring after her in bewilderment. The lady's mouth for the moment open and still, the chewing gum adhering to her tongue and defying gravity like a Ping-Pong ball to a paddle.

Pure adrenaline carried Ellie along the street and round the corner into the peace and quiet of a narrow back alley. A prowling tomcat eyed her with distrust. Perhaps he thought he would have some competition for the finest pickings of the alley bins, in the form of this intruder to his domain.

Ellie leaned heavily against the dirty wall. Her lungs repeatedly expanded with air that then beat her with vicious punches all the way from the inside out. Her eyes watered with temper and unshed tears of anger and humiliated self-pity. The blood pumped through the veins in her temple and she felt her heartbeat tattooing against the optic nerves, clouding her vision and making her head throb. Never in all her sedate adult years had Ellie lost her temper in public. It just wasn't her style to scream and shout like a common fishwife. Her cheeks burned with shame as she re-lived resorting to personal name-calling against the poor shopkeeper. She felt that she ought to go back and apologise, but sweat was clinging to her forehead and her upper lip and she had begun to feel quite ill. There was no way she could face the lady again. Maybe she would write her a letter later, at the moment Ellie was fighting two strong impulses one being to pass out, the other the urge to vomit copiously. Neither appealed to her, especially in this dingy back alley with the sinister eyes of a suspicious ginger tom watching her every move.

Jake's barking could be heard as soon as Ellie opened her car door, but that was the least of the noise confronting her. The dog was clearly upset, and there was something very wrong. She looked at the eye sensor for the security device to give her clearance but the front door swung open without the check being made. She always locked the door behind her, it was as much a habit as brushing her teeth in the morning, or washing the pots after tea. This time though, the door had been put 'on the snick' so that the locking mechanism wasn't connecting with the frame. Ellie was sure she had locked the door as normal when she left. The noise was deafening. Leaving the front door ajar, she rushed from room to room, two of the three downstairs plasma screens were on full blast, each tuned to a different channel. Only the one in the kitchen remained silent. The Carpenters screeched 'Only yesterday' from the lounge, and Jethro Tull's 'Too old to rock-n-roll' rose in combat from the computer's DVD in the study. Every single light blazed except those in the kitchen. As she rushed from room to room restoring silence and order while competing with the noise to soothe Jake she became aware of a constant hammering at the front door. This only became evident as she turned off the first two appliances.

"Coming," she yelled a little uncertainly as she pressed the last button to shut off the power to the lounge music centre. All was thankfully quiet except Jake grateful to be both let out and spared from the deafening noise, and the sounds of irritated nattering coming from the far side of the front door.

She regretted opening the door, and the smile died on her lips as she saw Mr Jackson her next-door neighbour standing on the step and going redder in the face by the second. Ellie had engaged in several altercations with Mr Jackson, usually caused by Jake when he was an even more loud and boisterous puppy than he was currently. Mr. Jackson didn't like dogs; in fact he didn't like anything much apart from complaining. Ellie had tried on many occasions to get on the good side of the cantankerous pensioner, but all to no avail. He was happy in his loneliness and misery and God help anyone who tried to deprive him of them. Ellie cringed inwardly.

"I'm so sorry Mister Ja..."

"Two hours! Two bloody hours I've had to put up with that. I knew you'd show your true colours eventually missy. Swearing at an old man like that. I served in the Falklands I'll have you know, and I've got rights. Well I'll tell you lady; I'm not standing for it. The police are on their way. Let's see you talk your way out of this one. And another thing, that dog of yours has been at my Pauline again God bless her. Can't the poor woman just be left to rest in peace?"

Ellie had to admit the Pauline situation was quite a problem. Mr Jackson had buried his late wife's ashes beneath her favourite honeysuckle bush. No matter how high Ellie extended the fence, Jake managed to clear it. When the neighbour wasn't complaining about the dog, he was complaining about the height of the garden fence and about the fact that it blocked the light from his kitchen window.

Jake loved to get into Mr Jackson's garden and his favourite place to dig just happened to be at the root of Pauline's Honeysuckle, he once managed to half uncover her urn and yapped excitedly to tell the world of his discovered treasure. Jake delighted in inciting Mr Jackson to go red and begin jumping up and down and shaking his fist. It was Jake's favourite game, even better than annoying the bees in the lavender bush. Mr Jackson was a wonderful toy to a happy puppy.

Now the irate neighbour was pointing at Jake who was grinning sheepishly and wagging his tail at the same time. Ellie put a hand to his collar, she knew it was only a matter of time before Jake wanted to take the game up a notch by jumping all over the angry Mr Jackson.

"You want to keep that bloody dog under control. If he comes onto my property again I'll take a garden spade to the back of his head. You foul-mouthed wench, the police will bring you down a peg or two, you see if they don't."

It seemed the rant would go on forever before Ellie could get a word in. Mr Jackson filled his lungs to continue and Ellie jumped into the space left by the ceasing of his torrent of words.

"I am so sorry about Jake, Mr Jackson and I will endeavour, as always to make sure it doesn't happen again." She raised her hand with an air of authority to halt her visitor's next outburst before it began.

"As to this morning's disturbance, I can only apologise for that as well, but you see someone has broken into my house and turned everything on while I've been out. It's all most distressing. Please if you saw anything at all, can you tell me, because I have no idea what's going on." Ellie got no further.

"Well I've heard it all now, you bloody, little liar. That's the line you're going to take with the police eh? So you deny gesturing to me rudely with your finger and profaning at me on your garden path this morning? I merely came out of my front door to see what all the noise was and there you were walking down your path and all that blaring music and stuff behind you. I know you only did it to terrorise me. Gives you pleasure does it, yelling at an old man like that? You with your butter-wouldn't-melt goody-goody image, Miss High and Mighty Author. I'll tell the police the truth; you won't get away with it this time. Harassment of an old man that's what it is harassment. And me a veteran of the Falklands too. You ought to be ashamed."

True to his word, as he stood yelling at Ellie on the doorstep, a police car rolled up outside her gate. Everything was taking on a nightmarish quality that didn't make any sense.

And things rapidly deteriorated. Her involvement with the irate neighbour and the two police officers became a fiasco. Ellie repeated her version of events several times; each re-telling caused Mr. Jackson to go a deeper shade of purple. He hopped and skipped and did a reasonable rendition of an Irish jig in his temper. It seemed his arthritic army wound had decided not to cause him any bother on this particular day. Harry Jackson was a right old pain in the nether regions, but even Ellie had to admit to herself he wasn't normally given to lying. Because he had *seen* Ellie after all the appliances had been turned on, and *spoken* to Ellie on the garden path the policeman said he had little option but to believe him.

The male police officer recognised Ellie from the sleeve of one of her books, and because she wrote under her own name he matched name with photo and came up with Ellie. However if she thought this would curry her any favour, then she was sadly mistaken. Eleanor Erikson wrote psychological-horror type mysteries and had quite a following in certain subversive cultures. The officer apparently thought that this made her a raving lunatic who may well be prone to psychotic episodes. Once he realised who she was he visibly retreated a step and changed his tone of voice to adopt the attitude one might take with an escaped convict, guilty of hacking up little old ladies in Asda. If the whole stupid experience hadn't been so humiliating, it would have been hilarious. Finally the ordeal was drawing to a close and Ellie was given an informal caution to 'keep the peace' and not irritate her law abiding and long suffering neighbour any further. As a side note he also requested she try her level best to keep her dog under control.

Suddenly Jake who had grown bored with the less than playful humans some time ago, realised that all attention was focused on him. That was odd he hadn't heard the Jake word.

Hmmm lots of people looking at Jake. How many? um two eyes. And um, yes, yes that's right four. Um four eyes. What's next, whine...oh, Jake Good Boy but Jake can't think numbers too good. Lots of eyes! That's it lots of eyes watching Jake. Must be time to play. Oh Jake likes playtime.

Suddenly, and without any warning at all, Jake took a flying leap at the policeman. In the process he bumped into the lady officer and almost knocked her flying. She stumbled backwards onto the lawn and trod squarely into one of the larger than average deposits that Jake had produced a few minutes earlier behind the police officer's backs, and much to Ellie's mortification. Meanwhile Jake had grabbed the sleeve of his new friend the policeman and was ragging it fiercely all the while wagging his tail at ninety miles an hour.

"See?" Said Mr Jackson, obviously delighted at this new turn of events. "That bloody dog's vicious. It's a killer, a killer I tell you. How can I set foot out of my front door when she could set that devil dog on me at any time? I live in fear of my life, and me a Falklands veteran as well. That animal should be taken away and destroyed."

Up to this point Ellie had been meekly taking the whole debacle on the chin and wearing it well. But the mere suggestion of someone destroying her beloved dog was just too much. For the second time that day her vision turned red and she let go with both barrels. She stopped trying ineffectually to drag Jake off the police officer, and turned to verbally rag out her neighbour, leaving the hapless policeman to his own devices. Ellie's face was just centimetres from her antagonists, her features distorted in a decal of pure rage.

"Well, you nasty, spiteful, venomous, withered old bastard." At this point she had to take a breath and re-stock on adjective missiles. Jackson took a step backwards, and Ellie took up the space with a step forward. Her finger came up between them to stab her point across and Jackson flinched as though she was going to strike him.

"That's right you feeble, twisted, pathetic little pariah of a man. You'd better be scared. You've pushed me too far this time."

While this barrage of words was taking place, both police officers were battling with the excited Jake. WPC Sally Woods was intermittently still wiping the side of her shoe on the edge of the grass as she hauled backwards on Jake's collar all to no avail. As she leant forwards over Jake's neck, her cap dislodged and fell to the path in front of the excited dog. Quick as an eagle on a mouse Jake dropped the policeman's arm and the policeman attached to it, picked up the cap, and was off across the lawn, dragging WPC Woods back through the already trodden-in dog-do.

"You think you're such a hero don't you? You're no hero; you're nothing more than a bloody joke in the village. Do you know something, Mr-Sanctimonious-Bloody-Jackson? Even your precious wife couldn't stand the sight of you. Many times she told me what a pain in the arse you are."

She watched as tears formed in Harry Jackson's eyes, and she realised she had gone too far. It was true Pauline used to chat to her about her husband's 'annoying little ways' but she always followed up by saying that it just made her love him and want to look after him all the more. In truth Ellie knew of few couples who were more devoted. It was only after Pauline had died that Harry shut himself away and turned his anger on the world that had taken his beloved Pauline. Ellie remembered when she had first moved into Cherry Tree Cottage, Harry would give her freshly picked strawberries despite the fact that she had her own strawberry patch. She felt ashamed and contrite.

At the same moment as her outburst spent itself and fizzled in the wake of its gasses, Ellie felt the firm grip of PC Ferguson on her upper arm. He threatened arrest if she didn't calm down, and she allowed herself to be led inside the house.

Jake stopped his game to watch his mistress being led inside and decided to follow, maybe there would be some food offered. *Biscuits perhaps, or chocolate. Jake liked chocolate best.*

Ellie listened patiently to the delivered lecture and stern warnings of the police. While Mr Jackson who had taken it upon himself to step into the house uninvited along with everyone else watched on smugly. Jake however was worried. All thoughts of food and play were chased from his mind as he wrangled with new input that needed sorting out. Jake put his nose to the floor in the kitchen, and followed a scent round the room. He traced it to the back door and whined. The smell was one that he could only describe to himself as a 'not Ellie' smell. It confused him, and he whined again. Nobody took any notice of him so he snuffled for a few more seconds at the back door and then went to his bed to flop down in a sulk. Jake didn't like being ignored, especially when he smelled a not Ellie smell in the kitchen.

After the police and her hero-of-the-moment neighbour had left, Ellie collapsed in a chair at the dining room table. Tears fell thick and continuously as she asked herself the same question over and over again.

Am I going mad?

She didn't feel mad. As far as she was aware there were no periods of time unaccounted for in her day, and yet two people were convinced they had seen her, when she hadn't been there. Nothing in her world or her understanding made sense anymore. Doctor Fielding, Ellie's consultant had assured her there should be no mental retardation, but because the disease wasn't common, this could not be guaranteed. And yet here she was just twenty-four hours post diagnosis, going crazy.

She laid her head on her arms at the table and sobbed, very shortly afterwards exhaustion took her to a place of tormented dreams.

~*~

That's how Matthew found her four hours later. She began to rouse herself, disturbed by Jake's excited greeting of Matty.

Matt normally made a huge fuss of Jake when he came in the house. Sometimes he even had doggie-chocks in his pocket or those little round biscuits that stopped Jake farting.

Jake is ashamed of farting. He would fart and then look at his rear end in horror and then run away from the smell. This made his humans laugh at him and that just made him more embarrassed.

Jake has not farted now. He smells his backside to make sure.

No; no fart. Matty is making that "Down Jake" noise. Matty doesn't like Jake today, but Jake's a good boy, he hasn't played 'chase' with Matty's hat. Matty hasn't got a hat so they can't tell Jake off for playing chase with it. Jake's going back to bed.

"Down Jake," Matt said again, more firmly this time, pushing Jake out of the way. Jake padded forlornly back to his basket as Matt rushed to Ellie's side in concern.

"Ellie? What's wrong? Are you alright love?"

Since the onset of her illness it took Ellie longer to wake up. She raised her head from her arms with eyes still puffy and red from sleep and crying, she squinted at Matt. Gradually the fugue of sleep left her. She looked at Matt and smiled before the events of the day seeped back into her mind, but come back they did, starting with a trickle and developing into a flood. Her eyes closed and she groaned at the recent memories.

"Hello Matty, nothing's wrong love. I'm fine. I've had a shitter of a day but I'm okay, honest."

"Are you sure you feel all right? You aren't bathed and ready to go out or anything?"

There was no accusation in his words just deep concern for her well-being. She remembered the dinner date and groaned inwardly again. Going out that evening was the last thing she felt like doing.

"I'm sorry love. I must have fallen asleep, give me half an hour and I'll be ready."

"You look shattered, listen Ellie. I know you were looking forward to it, but I really think we ought to cancel tonight. We can go out anytime. Let's get a Chinese and just relax here. What do you say?"

These words were a sweet soothing salve to Ellie's tattered nerves. God how she loved this thoughtful man.

"I think I'd like that very much, but only on one condition. For putting you out, tonight is my treat."

"No Ellie, I was going to take you out and now I'm going to treat you to a slap-up meal in. No arguments. Okay?"

The stranger who was becoming an all too frequent visitor, crept onto her shoulder and for the third time that day Ellie felt something snap within her.

"I am not a God-damned invalid. Don't you dare treat me like a crippled degenerate just because I'm dying. If I want to buy you a meal I will. All right? You come in here with your eyes spewing out pity, well you can take your pity and shove it as far up your good intentions as your moralistic finger will reach."

Ellie's voice broke on a desperate sob, and the tears began to pour down her face.

"I'm not going mad. I'm not going fucking mad. And I will not be treated like a broken doll. Do you hear me?" She only ran out of words when the snot at the back of her throat threatened to choke her and she was sobbing so hard that it took all the oxygen in her lungs, leaving no air to fuel her angry words.

Matt reeled in shock at her outburst. Never had she lost her temper with him in the entire two years they had known each other. She had rarely even raised her voice to him. Ellie was the most calm and placid person he had ever known and her gentle nature and goodness were what made him love her so much. As for swearing he had only ever seen that in her writing when a character called for it to be used. Apart from the night before when she seduced him, he had never once heard her use such language. He was shocked and upset.

"Oh Matty. I think I'm going insane. Hold me please." She whispered almost inaudibly.

He moved to take her in his arms warily. He didn't know where the notion came from that she was losing her mind, he had certainly never insinuated it as her accusation seemed to suggest, but this strange woman that he now held bore little resemblance to his sweet Ellie.

She moulded her body to his and cried herself out. He made soft placating noises in her ear and whispered gently to her as he felt all the anger and tension melt away from her body. Then as he felt her wilt with emotional exhaustion he led her through to the sofa. Gradually between the last residual sobs, she told him about the horrible day she had suffered. At least her irrational behaviour made some sense now, but he was still shocked by the vehemence of her anger. An hour later, Ellie announced that she was starving. Matt didn't dare offer to buy the meal, that was what had set her off earlier, so he sat quietly, his brow knitting into a jersey of worry lines as she went to get her purse. It was only a matter of seconds before the next drama of the day unfolded.

The back door was unlocked and Ellie's purse had been stolen.

Chapter 4

"Good Morning Ellie. It is 9:02 am and the date is 21st October, Twenty forty six."

"Thank-you George. I won't be writing this morning, I have to go to the bank. My purse was stolen from my handbag last night."

"Oh that's wonderful Ellie, I'm very pleased for you."

She grinned wryly and made a mental note to herself to download the latest update for her 'Personal humanicon organiser'. Sometimes George was so spot on with his responses that it was difficult to believe he didn't in fact have feelings, emotions and a wicked sense of humour. But just occasionally he would make the wrong choice out of his fifty thousand-word response database, and the results were often hilarious.

"Thank you George. That's very sweet of you," she said with a chuckle.

Ellie was on her second cup of coffee and just working her way through a morning cocktail of drugs when she heard Matt's key in the door.

"Come in if you're good looking and sexy." She yelled through to the hall.

"Hiya gorgeous. Hmmm breakfast, they smell good," he said sarcastically eyeing the handful of brightly coloured pills and capsules in Ellie's hand. "So have we calmed down any yet? Or are you still gunning for the whole national police force and anyone else who gets in your way?"

The previous evening when Ellie rang the police to report her stolen purse, she had been convinced that the police officer on the desk 'had a tone' to his voice. And although she was so tired that she'd run out of the ammunition necessary to give him a performance of her new-found temper, to say she had been frosty, would be like saying Antarctica was a bit chilly. She assured him that today she was placid and serene, and that the tantrums of the previous day must have been nothing more than a knee jerk reaction to her recent news. Matt sincerely hoped so, he didn't like the side to Ellie that he had never seen before the previous couple of nights.

The trip to the bank was blissfully uneventful, though Matt kept looking sideways at Ellie with concern. She looked tired and drawn and the skin on her cheekbones was starting to take on the appearance of having been stretched to fit. They listened to Mike Wogan and his pleasant banter, and Ellie made the decision to change the voice of George to that of Mr. Wogan's sexy Irish lilt.

She would do it when she downloaded the update, she decided. She smiled as she remembered family drives to the sea-side as a child, when her parents used to listen to Mike Wogan's father, he had been good too.

"Miss Erikson," Philip Hughes the bank manager, took her hand and shook it warmly, if a little wetly. He flashed her that large smile that didn't quite reach his eyes, and as always she found herself sub-consciously counting his teeth, surely he had too many in that insincere smile for one mouth. He ushered the couple into his office and invited them to sit down.

"I'm so glad you've come back. I hope you've had time to reconsider your decision of yesterday. And we of course are more than happy to welcome you back. Now if you step this way, I'm afraid there's going to be a little bit of paper work to sort everything out, but we'll soon have it done. And Mr High good to see you again too. So what's it like being linked with Cumbria's most eligible lady?" The manager laughed, it was a grating sound both high and shrill that contained all the sincerity of a fox in a hen hut, but without the strength cunning or wisdom of Reynard.

It had taken Ellie over thirty seconds to process the words prattling out of the stupid little man's mouth. Once she had made some kind of sense of them, her first thought was '*Oh God no, not again'*. She wasn't sure what was happening but she knew it wasn't going to be good. Rather rudely she interrupted Hughes as he launched further into his camaraderie spiel with Matt. Matt was more than happy to be rescued from the sickly man with the sweaty palms.

"Excuse me, Mr Hughes, I have no idea what you are talking about," began Ellie. "I have merely come to verify the report I made over the phone last night, that my purse containing all my credit cards has been stolen."

Hughes moved agitatedly from one foot to the other. He lived in an ordered little world, and this temperamental arty type had already disrupted his order once this week, to come back and do it a second time was nothing short of inconsiderate. He hated anything confrontational, and although the situation hadn't become difficult yet, it was fast becoming decidedly sticky.

"Purse…Stolen?" He repeated in a dry monotone. His mouth opened and closed a couple of times and he stared at Ellie and Matt as though they had walked into his bank naked. Ellie did a quick down-scan to make sure that she was indeed clothed, the crazy way things had been lately, meant that nothing much would surprise her anymore.

"Yes Mr Hughes." Ellie replied patiently, if with a patronising tone. "My purse, containing a lot of my personal details has been stolen. Bank books, credit cards, driving licence. The lot."

The voice that came from Philip Hughes was tiny, all the brash edge had gone out of it and he was becoming more uncomfortable by the second. "You left your bank books and credit cards here yesterday when you closed all your accounts." Despite his discomfort, the words once started had no intention of stopping. He didn't want her becoming difficult as she had the day before. He was on a roll now and there was no way he could stop. "And the thing is Miss Erikson, as we explained to you at length yesterday, it was most uncharacteristic of you to maximise the expenditure on your Goldcard like that yesterday lunch-time, and then to come in and close the accounts. Well, as you know we were most reluctant to acquiesce to this and give you clearance. It was only the fact that you have been with us so long and well to be honest you being who you are, that we acceded to your request, but we really do need to have those cards cleared within the month." He looked over at Matt hoping to find in the man an ally, Matt was emulating the open-mouthed 'fishing' of Hughes a few moments earlier. "We at Northwest National bank have always been impressed with the way you manage your accounts Miss Erikson, and quite frankly we were sorry to see you leave us. You have been one of our most valued customers. Ahem," he cleared his throat nervously. "If you are in any financial difficulty, I'm sure we can sort something out to help you. Our terms and conditions are very competitive."

The whole impact of his words finally made sense. *Cleared the accounts.* The words sounded hollow and didn't tally. Ellie *had* always been frugal, She lived a simple life in a reasonably modest house. Almost all her money was tied up in investments. Today she gave God-worshipping thanks to James Dawson her accountant. Due to his management, she kept only about one hundred, thousand Euros in the bank. The rest of her assets consisted of stocks and shares and a few private company deals, mainly aimed at helping the local community.

Hughes moved to sit behind his huge mahogany desk that contained three acres of Brazilian rain forest. Far from giving him stature and authority this only served to diminish his slight frame and make him look lost. He fidgeted constantly, unable to either meet their eyes, or sit still. He pen-twiddled and scribbled on his blotter, and he looked most uncomfortable.

Ellie made all of the now familiar protestations of innocence. She had no temper left in her after the events of the last couple of days and sounded worn and weary. She already knew what the outcome was going to be, and anything she could say was only going to be useless. When she told Hughes that she had an 'alibi' for the previous afternoon in the form of the local constabulary, it didn't aid her cause. Philip Hughes was instantly suspicious of anyone who had dealings with the police force. '*Maybe she smoked that mara-ju-ana stuff, all those arty types did these days,*' he thought, breaking up the word marijuana carefully in his mind. He'd heard about that stuff and the way it eats your brain cells. '*Yes*,' he decided, '*that must be it.*'

After another ten minutes of verbal tennis, the proof was displayed. Ellie and Matt were taken to the security office and the CCTV tape of the previous afternoon was shown. At two thirty three pm, just about the same time that Ellie had fallen asleep at her kitchen table, the video tape showed her walking into the bank and demanding to see the manager. She wore her green Adonis jacket that Matt bought her the previous Christmas, jeans and her Nova trainers. The video evidence showed her shaking hands with Philip Hughes and being led by a hand in the small of her back into his office. Thirty one minutes later the tape showed them coming out of the office with Hughes looking harassed and unhappy. Ellie left the bank, with her hair swaying and her poise jaunty.

There seemed little else to be said. Matt looked embarrassed and Ellie felt ashamed. They made an appointment to come back and re-open the accounts when Ellie felt a little less 'distraught' and left the bank with their heads low, relieved to be out in the bite of a rather chilly, late October breeze.

Ellie wanted to walk for a few minutes; she couldn't face sitting in the cramped interior of Matt's car. He had one of those awful vanilla air fresheners. It was cloying and overpowering at the best of times, Ellie felt sure that if she got back in the car then, she would vomit in technicolor all over his beige upholstery. She wanted to clear her head and to think for a while. They decided to wander down to the Windsor Café for a cup of coffee.

Matt realised for the first time; just how serious Ellie's condition was *now*. All he had considered to this point was her imminent death and how that would affect him; he hadn't really considered the ramifications of her condition pre-death. For the first time, he wondered if his love for her was going to be enough to see them through. He felt inadequate and the sickness suddenly seemed so much bigger than he was.

Ellie was numb. She wanted to think, but unless thought begets logic sometimes it's easier to just not bother with it. Ellie's world had a hole in the bottom and all the sense and normalcy had trickled out leaving a wake of shattered reason behind her. She had seen the evidence for herself. She wasn't going crazy at all. She was one hundred percent, spectacularly, totally, bloody insane. And now the only thing on her mind was whether to have a nice, strong, sensible cup of coffee or a decadent hot chocolate with lashings of whipped cream and chocolate sprinkles. By the time they came to order she had made up her mind. '*Sod it!*' She thought, *'what's the point of being a crazy dying woman if you can't take advantage of the fact.*' She opted for the chocolate *and* a large serving of raspberry pavlova with more whipped cream.

After leaving the café Matt wanted to nip into the newsagents for a paper. Ellie said she would walk on slowly until he caught her up. In retrospect the pavlova may have been a bit of a mistake, it lay heavily on her stomach and she felt encumbered by it. She wasn't paying attention to where she was going, and collided with a woman coming out of the fruit and veg shop.

"Oh I'm so sor…" Ellie never finished her apology. She looked up at the woman, to meet *her own* eyes, *her own* face, *her own* Adonis jacket.

"Boo!" Said the other woman.

Ellie grabbed the wall for support and wheezed in shock. After a couple of breaths to ease the sudden dizziness, she turned to look for her doppelganger, but the woman had vanished.

"Are you all right dear, you look a bit peaky?" A woman had taken her by the elbow and was looking into her eyes with concern. This woman bore no resemblance to Ellie; she was middle aged and slightly over-weight with warm brown eyes that seemed to care. It must have been this woman all along; Ellie could no longer trust what her senses showed her.

"You're not me are you? But you were a minute ago. Yes thank you I'm all right, but I've seen myself in the strangest places and now I'm other people sometimes too." It was perhaps the most ridiculous thing she had ever said. But before she had the chance to stop herself from talking more rubbish, and just as she was about to apologise for being nuts to the nice lady, the world went black. She never felt the pavement coming up to meet her as she wilted towards it.

Matt came out of the newsagents to see a crowd of people gathered a little further down the street. "Ellie!" he yelled. Instinctively he knew that whatever had drawn the crowd, it had something to do with Ellie. He set off at a run.

He pushed roughly through the tight wad of people and gave a little half scream when he saw Ellie lying on the floor, a small river of blood pooled on the pavement by her right temple. A lady had put her into the recovery position and was trying to bring her round. Sizing up the newcomer to the situation, the Good Samaritan explained that an ambulance had been called and was on its way.

Ellie regained consciousness to an abstract collage of writhing faces that came in, *"It's that author isn't it? Her wot writes?"* and went out, "*Yeah I've seen her with an Alsatian by the river*." of focus every few seconds. One face remained clear and un-blurred in the throng of fuzzy faces. *Her own face.*

"It's her." She said weakly. Matt, leaning forward to kiss her forehead, momentarily obscured her vision. She jerked away from him impatiently and the woman had once again vanished away from the crowd gathered round Ellie.

"It's okay sweetheart an ambulance is on its way," said Matt soothingly. "I'm here and everything's going to be all right."

"I don't want an ambulance," she said aggressively trying to get up and instantly regretting the sudden movement. She felt her stomach rebelling and seconds later she vomited all over the kind lady's knees. Ellie couldn't apologise enough, but she was suddenly so very, very tired. She heard the ambulance siren rounding the corner and summoned enough energy for a final protest.

"I told you, I don't want to go to hospital, you stupid bloody idiot." She yelled at Matt, and even though he wasn't the one who called the ambulance, it seemed he was the one to be singled out to bear the brunt of her anger. "On second thoughts, yes I bloody-well-do. I'm going to get that bastard Fielding, and rip his head off his shoulders. He said there would be no damage to my mind." This took the last of her determination, she closed her eyes and not so much lost consciousness, as embraced unconsciousness with relish.

She awoke once in the ambulance, vomited, told the ambulance man he had 'come to bed eyes' vomited again and then went back to sleep. Despite not being seen by the triage team, the ambulance men made the decision to give Ellie a mild sedative, her pulse was erratic and her respiration's not good. In sleep she gradually calmed and her breathing and heart rate returned to something - if not normal - then at least acceptable.

Matt explained everything in detail to Jeremy Fielding who had made himself instantly available to see Ellie. She was given an MRI scan and a CAT scan, seven vials of blood were taken from Ellie's precious supply for analysis and words were muttered quietly about lumbar punctures and other tests that sounded horrific to Matt.

After all the tests had been done and the immediate results analysed, Jeremy Fielding came to sit on the stretcher bed that Ellie had been allocated. He took her hand gently in his own. The man had hands the size of large baseball mitts, and yet they were soft and smelled of antiseptic soap and somehow when he stroked the back of her hand he made her feel calmer, as though he was in control and *would* make everything all right. She still wanted to kill the bastard for lying to her though.

Fielding explained that they had found no sign of brain damage and no indication of mental retardation whatsoever from the results.

"So what the hell is happening to me then?" She asked in a voice that was small and frightened but still managed to contradict itself with a hard-edged bitterness and anger that couldn't be contained.

"I'm sorry Ellie. I don't know. I just don't know."

The calm that he'd just instilled in her left through a side window and hitched a ride on an albatross flying south.

"Oh well, let's just have a party then; everything's just fine and dandy. You're supposed to be the bloody know-it-all, I'm the great I am, bloody doctor, and you haven't got the faintest bloody idea what's sodding well going on. I might as well go and ask the lady who cleans the public toilets what's wrong with me. She'd have a better idea than you, and she might just have the guts to tell me straight that I've just lost the plot and fallen into a sodding great slimy hole of insanity. And that's a damned sight more than you are telling me. You useless bloody tosser."

Fielding had to turn his face away from Ellie for a second to hide the smile that threatened to crack not only his face but also his professional demeanour.

Nurses, doctors, and the general public bowed and scraped constantly to him, fawning and cowing to his every word and whim. He was the Demi-God of St. Joseph's and nobody ever contradicted anything he said. To have this feisty little woman call him a tosser was like a stab of blinding sunshine breaking through the clouds on a grey and dismal day. It stung but with the initial sting came the pleasure of new experience.

"Ellie," He began hiding his smirk behind a small cough and trying to remain as head-consultant-ish as possible.

"You have to understand this is all new ground to us. There have been so few recorded cases of adult onset Tay-Sachs disease worldwide. There is no such thing as a textbook case, because there have never been enough cases to write a textbook. I said there probably wouldn't be any mental retardation, because we have no reason to suspect there would be. The effects in the previous cases pertaining to adult sufferers have been isolated physical symptoms rather than any mental impairment. Only in many classic TSD sufferers, which is of course the juvenile case scenario are there histories of violent mood swings and dementia. From what we have been able to read up on, the adult form is a completely different fish dish. Don't forget Ellie that TSD has been around a long time, and is traced back to East European Jewish fur traders way back in 70 AD, it's not a new yuppie condition you know. Although TSD in children is a rare disorder it is well documented and we have guidelines and procedures to follow. Adult onset TSD is much more obscure and difficult to A, diagnose and B, treat." Fielding finished his lecture as he saw Ellie's eyes beginning to glaze over with exhaustion, she had heard enough for one day.

"For Christ sake just stick me in a cage and call me Gus the guinea-pig." Ellie was pouting, she'd had enough and her normal good humour was at an all time low.

"Now young lady, what I suggest is this," Fielding's voice had taken on an air of knowledgeable authority. He knew what was going to happen next and he was back on familiar ground. Or at least he *thought* he knew what was going to happen next.

"I think you should stay in here for a couple of days to get your strength back, and we'll use that time constructively to run a few more..."

He got no further, and his familiar ground was about to be trodden underfoot by Ellie's steel toe-capped boots with soles of stubborn defiance.

"Oh no you don't. I'm not staying in here. There'll be plenty of time for that later when I've progressed to seeing flying elephants and hearing voices telling me to kill my consultant because he's the Anti Christ. I'm going home."

"Ellie I really think," began Jeremy Fielding. Ellie's face was grim, determined and set in an expression that would brook no argument.

"Oh sod it." He continued, for the first time in his life talking to a patient as he would an irritating but loveable teenage daughter.

"I can see I'm just completely wasting my breath. Go on, bugger off home. Try not to worry. I'll get back to you if I find anything new to report, and also to let you know when I get the blood test results. I'll give you a ring to get you in to see me at my clinic soon. And the only other thing I can say and I can't stress this strongly enough is … REST."

Matt half carried Ellie from the car to the front door. She leaned on him heavily, grateful for his support and strength, and she wasn't just thinking of the physical arm holding her up. They talked in the car about everything that happened over the last fourteen hours since leaving the house that morning, so long ago. It was almost midnight and Jake had been alone since nine thirty. He was whining forlornly as they tumbled from the chill of the night into the warmth of the solar panelled hall. Ellie's jacket hung on its usual hook behind the door, and it seemed to mock her. She thought again of the videotape plainly showing her coming out of the bank, when she had absolutely no recollection of being there that day. She shivered and Matt led her through to the lounge to sit down before he sorted Jake out and made them a hot drink.

On the table beside the settee, lay the 'stolen' purse. She must have left it there the previous day before she went to return the costume. That would explain why it had not been in her handbag when she returned to the house from talking to the police. She felt stupid and deeply ashamed. This was the last straw; she hung her head onto her arms and used the last of her energies in a good self-pitying bout of bawling.

What neither of them noticed that night was the matchbook on the second shelf of the bookcase. It bore a picture on its cover depicting a crude drawing of the devil's face and the name of the club it advertised, 'Demons' was printed in bold red and black font.

Chapter 5

Ellie counted to ten for easily the tenth time that morning. Matt was driving her further mad than she already felt. She wanted to write, she needed to write, and goddamit if she didn't get to write somebody was going to suffer.

"Would you like another cup of tea dear? Are you sure you are all right? Can I get you anything else? Oh my poor baby, you look worn out." Each of these was preceded by a timid knock on the study door and his pathetically concerned voice saying, "I'm sorry to disturb you again but…"

"George so help me, I'm going to train you to shoot to kill on sight, and Jake, look at you, lying there snoozing, shame on you dog. Can't you bite his ankles or something next time he sets foot in here?"

Although she had updated George's response database, and had given him the smooth talking Irish voice of the morning D.J., George's processing chip didn't seem able to come up with a suitable response to this one. The old George, pre-update would have said, "I believe there may be some very good software available for that. Shall I search the net for downloads Ellie?" New George just came off stand-by and said, "Awaiting instruction Ellie." Now he did say it ever so well, but it just didn't have quite the same giggle value as old George pre shiny new download.

Jake on the other hand, heard his name and knew exactly how to respond. He instantly jumped up and began prancing and whining for further attention. He didn't make much noise but it was enough to bring Matt scurrying back to the door. The same little knock, the same irritating voice.

"Is everything all right in there only I heard Jake? Are you all right my love?"

"No I'm bloody-well not all right," she muttered under her breath. "I can't get my filleting knife sharpened quickly enough." In as normal a voice as she could muster under the circumstances, she answered as pleasantly as possible, "Yes Pet, I'm fine thanks. Just as well in fact, as five minutes ago when you asked the same question."

"I'm sorry it's just that I'm worried about you." He sounded hurt, and she felt guilty for being a bitch with him. She was damned lucky, she told herself to have a man as caring as Matty.

"Tell you what? Why don't you take Jake for a run on the green and on the way back bring a couple of eclairs from the bakery, we'll have them with morning coffee. I've got to meet Rob at one, and I really need to finish editing this chapter before I go."

Reluctantly he agreed, mainly because Jake had heard the words *run* and *green.* Now these two words were pretty exciting as words go, by themselves, but together they were cause for great revelry to the happy dog. There was no way Jake was going to settle again now. Matt protested that he didn't want to leave her alone, but finally dog and boyfriend's retreat was heralded by the soft click of the front door, and Ellie felt sanity, at least for the moment being restored. However her peace and feeling of returned clarity were not to last long.

Ten minutes later the doorbell rang. Ellie groaned loudly.

"Show George, please." She waited for the security cam program to click open. There was the usual three seconds of black-screen and then, nothing.

"Show please, George." She said again, the irritation back in her voice.

"Security program open Ellie." He replied.

"Well it's not bloody working," she grumbled getting up and making her way to the front door.

She opened the door, with a 'who is it?' expression on her face, but there was no one there. Her feet knocked against the thing on the doorstep and she looked down. Lying at her feet was a circular wreath dressed with green ivy and white lilies. Alerted to a feeling of danger and of being watched she glanced up and saw the piece of black material thrown over the surveillance camera lens. Whoever had left this, did not want to be observed. Ellie was trembling all over as she bent to pick the wreath up. It struck her that life was becoming a cliché'd horror story. Rob's joking about a stalker seemed a little too close to home at the moment, but whoever it was scored no points for originality.

"Ellie we're back, baggsie the creamiest eclairs. Ellie? Ellie?"

Matt rushed into the living room, Ellie was sitting on the settee with the wreath on her knee, staring quietly at the card that she turned over and over between her fingers. Questions filled her brimming eyes as she looked to Matt for the answers he couldn't give.

"Why Matty? Why would anybody do this to me? I've never hurt anybody and I always put money in the Barnardo's envelopes. Why would somebody want to persecute me like this? I mean, if somebody wants me dead, it's not as though they are going to have to wait long is it?"

Matt didn't know what to say, so he sat down beside Ellie and pulled her body to him. Taking the card from her he read the words slowly, trying to make sense of what was happening but nothing gelled anymore. Their world had not only turned upside down but was spiralling towards some distant galaxy of which they had no understanding. He read the card for a second time, biting down hard on his bottom lip.

RIP: Eleanor Erikson.

Further to the hand-written inscription were the printed words 'In deepest sympathy' and the 'Send Some Flowers' company logo and telephone number.

"I don't know what's happening Ellie, but I'm going to find out." Matt's words were clipped and terse with a seething anger. "This is sick."

Although Ellie now had the voice activated telephone system installed, this could be over-ridden and the handset used in the normal way if privacy was preferred. Matt did not need to make the call in private but he did need to feel in control. Somehow he felt more able to channel his anger into a telephone handset, rather than just talking into air. The new system was still unfamiliar to him and he wanted to feel the comforting hardness of the plastic telephone receiver in his hand. He stabbed out the number aggressively, his right temple throbbing visibly above his eye. Ellie knew that he was furious.

After a couple of seconds the connection was made.

"Ah Yes, I wonder if you could help me please?" He spoke calmly and pleasantly but the underlying tension was clearly audible in his voice.

"We have just had a delivery from your shop and I wonder if you could check your records and tell us where it's come from please…? Yes it was a wreath with white lilies…What do you mean you have no record of such a delivery…? Yes of course I'm sure it was ordered through your shop. I have the card in front of me... I don't know who delivered it do I? They just left it on the doorstep... That is something to take up with your delivery person then isn't it…? Well I'm afraid he *did* just leave the delivery on the doorstep… I'm sorry but you had better just check your records again, my girlfriend has just taken delivery of a funeral wreath and is very upset. It's obviously someone's idea of a sick joke, and I'd like to know who that someone is please... Yes I'll hold.

Yes… Yes that's right Cherry Tree Cottage… Oh right…Personally collected…? Her Uncle George…? Cancer…? Yes that's okay… Yes. I do apologise…Thank you very much. So sorry to bother you, Yes, I'll be sure to do that…Thank-you. Goodbye."

He slammed the receiver back onto its carriage with enough force to send the phone crashing to the floor. Ellie winced.

"Well let's play twenty questions to guess who our sicko-freak is then, shall we?"

Ellie already knew what was coming. She shrank back into the cushions of the settee to get as far away as possible from the vehemence of his words. Never had she heard him so angry.

"You've just made a complete fool out of me Ellie. Funny is it? Playing these games, getting everybody jumping through hoops, mad with worry, only to find that it's you each and every time. You Ellie. You, you, you; Did you think I wouldn't recognise your handwriting? Well of course I damned well did, but I didn't want to believe it of you? What's happening to us Ellie? What the hell's going on?"

He lunged towards her, with each 'you' his finger became a foil of accusation, and she backed away even further from him. Matt was the most gentle, loving man she had ever known. She never had any reason to fear him, and yet now he was so angry that she hardly recognised him. The last few days had brought so many changes, changes in both of them. Ellie didn't know what to say.

"I don't know what the hell's happening to you Ellie, but I do know that I can't take much more."

With these words he deflated, the fury was compartmentalised and taken away, a box of misery of exactly the same dimensions was put in its place and where the fury had stung, the misery throbbed. Matthew felt wretched.

He walked over to stand by the bookcase and saw the 'Demons' nightclub matchbook. He didn't shout or bawl; he just picked it up and looked at it back and front. Then he opened the front flap and looked inside.

"What's that?" asked Ellie curiosity overcoming her newfound wariness of Matt.

"Oh, just a matchbook from some club called Demons that you've been frequenting."

He said this in a voice so matter-of-fact that it was more frightening than the yelling. Matt's temple was throbbing furiously and she could see the blood rushing through the bluish vein to his brain that was obviously working his heart too hard.

"I've never heard of a nightclub called Demons," Still a small voice, but this one was almost out of short pants as the indignation hit her.

"Course you haven't, that goes without saying doesn't it? *I've* heard of Demons Ellie. It's the new club that opened on Greengage Street in Barrow. I thought we might try it some time when you feel up to it, but you already have haven't you?" The last six words were spoken with a hard edge of bitterness.

"Honey I swear I've never been to the rotten club and I've never seen those matches before."

"Don't you honey me." He put the matchbook to his nose, "If you've never seen them before, why do they smell of your perfume. Eh Ellie? Answer that one."

She buried her face in a cushion and sobbed bitter tears.

"I just don't know you anymore Ellie." Matt sounded so sad and confused. I want to help you, but I just don't know how. This illness has changed you and it's becoming bigger than both of us and I just don't know what to do anymore.

He threw the matchbook at her and it landed open, on her knee, and she saw what was written neatly inside the cover.

Better the devil you know.

They argued again later that morning. Matt wanted her to cancel the meeting with Rob Price, but Ellie wouldn't hear of it, telling him that Rob had cancelled other engagements to meet with her. Ellie realised that they had fought more, in the last three days, than in the rest of their entire relationship put together. If she insisted in going ahead with the meeting, Matt said, then he wanted to be with her; that he'd only worry himself sick if he couldn't be there to keep an eye on her in her present… at this point, he became lost for words and floundered. Ellie finished it for him.

"While I'm as nutty as a fruitcake you mean." She couldn't help grinning at his pathetically guilty look.

She was ready to go and she was going alone. Dressed in tailored black trousers and a simple pale lemon blouse in the new Stymex material that rippled with a soft sheen when she moved, she felt almost good. The summer was fast becoming but a memory, and she hoped the yellow top would cheer her flagging spirits a bit. She brushed serum into her blonde hair until it shone a healthy natural flaxen, her elegant bob resting just below her ears. *'Might as well make the most of it before it all falls out,'* she observed wryly. One unpleasant symptom of her condition was that she would suffer unnatural hair loss and become bald. Matt had commented that bald people were sexy. *'Funny'* she thought now as she had one last look in the mirror, *'I've only heard of that as appertaining to men. Maybe I'll go the whole hog and develop a beer gut as well.'*

When she came back downstairs she could see Matt was still less than happy about her going out alone. Ellie promised not to dance naked on the restaurant table. She said she would at least wait until they were out in the street to indulge in any naked cavorting in case they wanted to use that restaurant again. Matt managed a weak smile.

"Watch out for frostbite, it's nippier than it looks out there today."

She wrapped her arms around him and they kissed softly, she half expected him to push her away, but he didn't. He needed the comfort that their kiss would give as much as she did. He felt impotent and small. Rationale told him that Ellie didn't mean to do any of the crazy stuff she had been doing, and that if he truly loved her then he had to try and help her through this weirdness, not be accusatory all the time. His anger was heat of the moment reaction. He found her recent behaviour embarrassing and shameful. He could only imagine how embarrassed and shamed Ellie was over it. Ellie told him to go home and get some rest. Neither of them had slept well in, it seemed like forever, but in reality it had only been three nights. Matt decided to stay and clean the house and make a nourishing evening meal as a surprise for Ellie, and as an apology for his temper and lack of understanding. The house would be warm, welcoming, and smelling of good cooking when she came home. Matt knew how her meetings with Rob could extend from one hour to four.

In the beginning he had been jealous of Ellie and Rob's special relationship, even though he knew that Rob was very happily married to Gail. Ellie and Rob had something that he and Ellie didn't. At first he had seen that as a threat, but as he became friends with Rob in his own right, and they double dated more and more as a foursome, he realised Rob was an asset to their relationship, not a threat. Any jealousy that he felt had long ago been replaced by a deep trust in both his girlfriend and his friend.

"I love you Ellie Erikson." He said as she disentangled herself and headed for the door.

She turned and smiled, and for the first time in days it was his familiar Ellie standing looking at him, "I love you too Matty, and don't you ever forget it."

~*~

The restaurant was crowded and bustled with lunchtime life as she was escorted to their table by the Maitre-d. Rob was already seated and stood to greet her out of courtesy when she arrived. Both Matt and Rob had lovely manners and she appreciated that in a man. Ellie remarked more than once that she wasn't one of those hard-edged, one-legged lesbians dressed in camouflaged Stymex, who wouldn't let a man open a door for her. Though she still considered herself to be every inch the feminist woman of the forties. The new millennia woman.

Rob helped her out of her coat and handed it to the Maitre-d, he then eased her chair into the table and she said thank you.

"Enjoy your meal." Said the waiter handing them each a menu. Ellie ordered an orange juice and the Maitre-d eyed the large mushroom that was standing on the table next to Rob's place setting suspiciously. Ellie remarked that he looked as though he was chewing on a dog turd as he walked away.

"I took the liberty of ordering you a vodka and coke," said Rob after leaning over and kissing her on the cheek.

"Oh Rob I'm driving, but I guess one won't hurt."

In all honesty Ellie could happily have guzzled down a bucket full of vodka and coke. She made no mention of the fact that she had been strongly advised against alcohol of any description with the strong medication she had been put on.

"Now I'm really worried, you always come to our meetings in a taxi. I'm sure a meeting with me is only an excuse for you to get totally blotto in the middle of the day."

As they ordered their food and talked, several waiters walked by, all eyeing the enormous mushroom as they passed. The couple continued making small talk for about five minutes, Ellie felt the vodka warm her stomach, and it felt damned good. They talked families and Matt, and touched on how the latest book was going. Neither one brought up the reason for the meeting and neither Rob nor Ellie had so far mentioned the upstanding mushroom that was currently leaking compost on the delicate pink table cloth. Finally Ellie could stand it no longer. She had resisted, truly she had, but now she was brimming over with curiosity.

"Okay wise guy. What's with your friend the mushroom?"

"Oh I'm sorry, do forgive my terrible manners. Ellie Fred, Fred Ellie." He motioned between the mushroom and Ellie as the 'introductions' were made.

"Hello Fred," said Ellie, "I am very pleased to meet you." She turned to Rob, "Not exactly a great conversationalist is he?" She said, grinning at her agent and enjoying the game.

"Well it's like this you see, I knew this meeting was going to be heavy, so I brought Fred the mushroom along because he's such a 'fungi' to be with.

Ellie stared at Rob in disbelief for a second and then she started to giggle. This was so like Rob, to go to so much trouble just to set up a totally pathetic punch line. The joke was never going to be worth the effort involved in executing it. Her giggle bubbled from the lowest point in her abdomen and turned into a chuckle, the chuckle became too big to contain and before she knew it she was laughing harder than she had laughed in weeks. She laughed, and laughed, and laughed unable to stop. Everybody in the restaurant turned to stare but there was no holding back. Every time the hilarity subsided and she thought she had control of herself, she'd look at the mushroom or at Rob who was also laughing hard, at her laughing, and off she'd go again for another bout. Her sides ached and her ribs were tortured. Tears streamed from her eyes and her jaw was tired with laughing, but she could not stop. The waiter brought their meals and eyed them and the silent Fred with obvious distaste, and off she went again. Her bladder was full and she had to jiggle in her seat to prevent an embarrassing flood, but still she couldn't get a grip. She was perfectly aware that she was making a spectacle of herself, and it felt wonderful. Finally she fell silent, but only because her body couldn't take any more.

Rob was still laughing at her and looked delighted by her response. "Well, it wasn't *that* funny," he said and off she went once more.

"Robin Price you have no idea the good you have just done me. Thank you." With that she burst into tears and had to go to the ladies both to relieve the pressure on her bladder and to tidy herself up and regain control of her emotions. Rob patted her hand as she left, his eyes full of concern. He had no idea what was happening with Ellie, but he knew his suspicion that it was serious had been confirmed. He was frightened of what Ellie was going to say.

"Well I've never been so humiliated in my entire life. How could you embarrass me like that in public?" said Rob as she returned to the table. Ellie might *just* have taken him seriously but for the twinkle in his eye and the fact that he had one of the restaurant's huge pink linen napkins tied under his chin like an old lady's headscarf from the last century. He looked ridiculous, and set them off giggling again.

They were both skirting round the news that Ellie had to impart. For Ellie's part, it was sheer cowardice, but for Rob it was as though he knew that once those words were spoken, nothing would ever be the same again. Rob never thought about it enough to realise until now, but he loved Ellie. He loved her in a completely different way to how he loved his wife. It was an innocent, sweet, pure and platonic love that was in no way harmful or wrong. Hell he was a modern man, he was even big enough to admit that he loved Matt, and if he was going the whole hog he'd have to say that he even loved that stupid great mutt of hers that dug his roses and crapped on his lawns. Rob was big enough to admit he was scared.

Ellie didn't do the excellent lobster royale and salad much justice. She picked at it for ten minutes as they tried to make small talk, but the *thing* between them had grown too big. For the first time ever, in the time Ellie had known him, Rob left food uneaten. As though on cue, they both laid their cutlery down and pushed their plates to one side.

"God I need a cig." Said Rob who hadn't had a cigarette since they became illegal in the twenties. "Just goes to show you gal, once an addict, always an addict." He twiddled with his napkin that was thankfully no longer still being used as a tribal headdress, as a waiter cleared the table. Then the waiter was gone, and with him had gone their excuse for not talking.

"So come on Darlin', give; what is it?"

"Oh God, Rob this is hard. And there is no way to say it that isn't going to hurt." She took a nervous sip of her second orange juice.

"I'm dying Rob."

"Well you kill me every time I see you."

Rob laughed a hollow empty laugh. As soon as she'd said the words he knew that it was true, that she wasn't joking, but it had to be a joke didn't it? They joked with each other all the time he and Ellie. It had to be a joke.

Ellie had gone on in a strange story-telling voice, distancing herself from the words that she was saying. They were words, just words. That's what she was good at, they were the tools of her trade. Only words and words can't kill you can they? Ellie knew that it took only three letters to kill you. Not even a proper word. T.S.D was all it took.

"I have this disease you see? Funny really I have this disease that doesn't affect adults, it only affects children. Well usually, I'm the exception to the rule as usual. Not only does it only appear in children, but it usually only affects

Jewish children, again I'm the exception to the rule. I think my guardian angel stamped Ashkenazi-Jew on my heaven records instead of Church-of-England. You can see how the two sound similar, after all they both have hyphens. He'll have been at the cheap cider again; he's already had two official written warnings about drinking on the job. You just can't get decent guardian angels these days. Hey, it's not all bad news though. I get to go bald, just think, no bad hair days. And I get to go blind, I won't see all the dust piling up. And you know the best bit of all; I only get to die the once. Not bad eh? Well, as nasty life-taking, killer-bastard diseases go."

"Shut up Ellie. Just shut up." Rob didn't shout at her but his words stung none the less. A tear that seemed way too fat to be an ordinary, every day tear hung on the tip of his nose and Ellie reached up to wipe it away.

"How long?"

There was no attempt at sarcastic wit this time as Ellie spoke.

"I don't know. It could be tomorrow, could be ten years. They reckon I've got between five and ten though."

"What is it?"

" It's called Tay-Sachs Disease. Very rare apparently."

And there's no hope whatsoever?"

"Officially no, but darling as long as I'm breathing, I'm hoping."

Rob stood up abruptly. Tears were streaming freely down his face now. He threw notes to the value of one thousand euros down on the table and grabbed her arm roughly.

"Come on let's get out of here. There's a park over the road. I need some air." His voice became gruff with concern as the enormity of what she had told him sunk in.

"Are you okay to walk? Will it be too cold for you?"

"Hey I'm not dead yet you know. 'Course I can, but I'm not sure I'll survive this death hold you've got on my wrist."

Rob looked down at Ellie's arm to see a deep red mark already forming.

"Oh my God. Ellie I'm so sorry. I had no idea I'd hurt you. I'm so sorry." He put his arm gently round her shoulders, grabbed her coat and prepared to lead her out of the restaurant. She shook his arm off none too gently.

"Hey, Rob, Don't. Don't do that to yourself. I'm still me you know? Still Ellie. Still here. Sure I get a bit stiff already, and I'm dropping things a lot, but I'm going to be a long time crippled later. Don't bring on my dependence sooner than need be eh?"

They started to walk out of the dining room and the Maitre-d called them back.

"I'm sorry, but you've left your, um … Fungus.

"Fungi! Fungi you fucking moron. You know fun guy to be with."

Rob could not believe his ears and stood rooted to the spot with his mouth open wide. He had never heard Ellie talk like that before. Ellie grabbed him and together they ran out of the restaurant giggling like a pair of teenagers.

For the next hour they walked in the park. Ate ice cream from a vending van, and Ellie spilled her heart to him about the other stuff, the worst part of the disease to date. She explained to Rob how she was going mad.

Chapter 6

Jake whined.

His nose was tight up against the bottom of the kitchen door and he was snuffling along the length of the gap between that and the floor. Jake was worried. Every so often he'd lift his head and sniff the air, but then, when he'd 'tasted' it properly, he'd drop back to scent the base again. He couldn't get very close to the smell but this is where *it* was closest to him.

It was the 'not Ellie' smell. Jake has the not Ellie smell in his nose a lot now. It doesn't go away for a long time even when he shakes his head; sometimes it makes Jake sneeze. He smells it in the garden, under bushes in the garden most, and even when he pees on the smell it doesn't go. The not Ellie smell, is just like the Ellie smell. The same as the Ellie smell but not Ellie. The Ellie smell is good and the not Ellie smell is bad. It isn't bad like 'white coat and needle' man, but bad that makes Jake's hackles rise. Jake isn't bad, Jake is a good boy.

Matt was enjoying himself. He had vacuumed right through downstairs and polished the lounge. He'd cleaned the kitchen until it gleamed and prepared a lasagne for the evening meal. On his way upstairs he put the palms of his hands together and bowed his head low to Aphrodite. She was a solid bronze statue of the Greek goddess that Ellie had fallen in love with in a very exclusive gift shop on Corfu. The celestial lady currently resided on the occasional table in the hall. Matt often paid homage to her on his way up the stairs.

He had his head in the bath and his bum in the air as he gave the bathroom a good freshen up. It baffled him why women made so much fuss about housework it was immensely satisfying. Then he remembered the festering pile of washing throwing out tentacles in the nether regions of his own bedroom, and amended his thought to the fact that *other people's* housework was immensely satisfying *sometimes*.

As he laboured, he sang an old song from the turn of the century, loudly, 'I like my men, like I like my coffee. Hot, strong and sweet like toffee.' After several self elected encores, he realised the window was open and he gave it up with a sheepish grin at himself in the mirror. He opted for 'A man's gotta' do what a man's gotta' do'. It didn't have much in the way of melody or tune, but it was a good manly song for a house-working bloke to be singing, Matt assured himself.

The bathroom finished, he gave it a final squirt of peach air freshener with a flourish and admired his handiwork. In reality the house looked very little different from when he'd started, Ellie had always kept it clean and tidy, but to him it was a masterpiece on virgin canvas. Matt was not often driven to have a go at things of a domestic nature, and he was truly proud of himself.

He was coming down stairs still singing happily, when he heard the security filter on the front door scanning. It could only be Ellie coming home, anyone else would have knocked. '*That's odd*,' he thought, '*she's only been gone a little over an hour. There must be something wrong.*'

Matt stopped on the third step from the bottom, lint duster flung across his shoulder and feather duster held out in front of him like a fencing foil. His other hand struggled with two spent toilet roll inners, and a can of Mr. Sheen. His surprise at Ellie being home stopped him calling out to her. Ellie home at this time, could only spell one thing …trouble.

The door opened and Ellie walked stealthily into the hall. She mimicked Matt's stance when she saw him on the stairs with his mouth open in surprise. She was the first one to close her mouth and she looked back towards the now closed door and briefly towards the kitchen, and then met his eyes and stood her ground.

The first thing Matt was aware of, was that Ellie was wearing different clothes to those she had gone out in. The other thing that hit him almost simultaneously was the fact that Ellie gave every impression of not wanting to be seen. She obviously didn't expect Matt to still be there, and the fact that he was displeased her. But more than that she seemed almost… it was ridiculous but Ellie seemed to be scared of him. So many things were flying through his brain and one of the split second thoughts took him back to the way he had yelled at her that morning. It was so out of character for Matt to lose his temper like that. The tension and anguish of the last couple of days had got to both of them tremendously.

"Just call me duster man." He said sheepishly brandishing his feather duster so that little particles of dust twinkled in the weak sunlight of the hall. "You're home early love, is everything all right?"

Ellie looked like a startled rabbit desperate for escape, but she recovered her composure and pulled her face into what was a forced smile. Matt had been with her long enough to know the real thing. When Ellie smiled the temperature rose with the warmth she shared, and the sun surrendered behind a cloud of defeat. This was no Ellie smile, just a weak imitation.

"Ellie, what's the matter? Talk to me love. What's happened?" He stopped himself just before adding 'now'.

Still looking unsure of herself, Ellie smiled again and moved a couple of steps towards him. He opened his arms to her and as she moved into his embrace he noticed that she was not wearing the eternity ring he bought for her after they had been together a year. He had been going to surprise her with an engagement ring, but when he had hinted at them getting engaged sometime soon, Ellie had said that she wasn't ready yet. The diamond and sapphire eternity ring had seemed like a good compromise. Ellie was delighted and said that the ring and its symbolism were all that she could ask for. Maybe Ellie simply realised that eternity was in fact a very small measurement of time and what had seemed so very far away for them was now approaching at a gallop. Matt was shocked to see that her ring was not on her finger. He tried hard to think of the moments just before she left, he felt *sure* that she had been wearing it when she left the house to meet Rob. And she felt different in his arms, unyielding, it was as though she didn't quite 'fit him' the way she normally did, and yet she had neither grown nor shrunk in the last hour and a half. *Why wasn't she saying anything?*

"Ellie, where's your ..."

Matt got no further; he felt a slight movement and moved back to look at Ellie. His mind registered two things. The first was the look of sheer hatred on Ellie's face, and the other thing he saw was the bronze Aphrodite statue they'd bought in Corfu, inches from his head.

Matt swerved to the left and the bronze came down with an almighty swing. In swaying out of the way he knocked Ellie off balance and the impact of the blow was deflected, had he not moved, he would almost certainly have been killed. As it was, Ellie's hatred of him was the last thing he was aware of as the lights, flickered, then dimmed, and then went out all together, taking with them the tremendous pain from the side of his head.

~*~

Matt opened his eyes and tried to raise his head. He was on the floor at the foot of the stairs. A fan of crimson speckling spread from the deeper ruby stain on the cream hall carpet. Ellie wouldn't be pleased about that. The carpet was ruined. Although Matt knew where he was, he had no idea how he got there. Ellie's bronze statue lay beside him, he must have knocked it over when he what? Fell? It was difficult to think with the pain in his head and his consciousness threatening to pack its bags and leave him again. Every time he attempted to move a wave of nausea slithered over him and left him feeling weak and drained. He must not throw up on Ellie's carpet she was already going to be pissed about the blood. He tried to call out to her but his mouth was dry and blood was trickling from the wound in his head down onto his lips some had already caked and it tasted like the back of a tarnished spoon. He remembered Ellie had gone to meet Rob. '*Something had bothered him about a ring. Her eternity ring. what was it...?*' He fingered the side of his head gently. The feeling of finger to raw nerve turned his digit into an electric cattle prod.

He licked his caked lips and grimaced as the disturbed blood came off in a congealing lump onto his tongue. He spat onto the carpet. '*Ellie would be mad.*'

His voice was small the sound not recognisable as his own. "Phone, George." He managed, but the effort of speech made him weak and dizzy. There were no sensors in the hall and the phone connection was not made. He slowly crawled the few steps to the study door and pushed it open. This time his voice was louder but the sound that came from his mouth was so alien to him that it was scary. "Phone, George ...number 999"

He almost cried with relief when the computer made the connection.

"Emergency services. Do you require...?"

The control room operator got no further.

"I've had an accident, need an ambulance."

The darkness was becoming more aggressive, wanting to take him back to the world of sleep. '*Must stay conscious, must stay conscious.*' He wouldn't give in to the darkness, was fighting it well, until his memory came in a rush with sticks and stones to beat him. He remembered Ellie's face full of hatred. He saw the bronze flying down to take his life, and he called the darkness back from its retreat and begged it to take him away.

"Sir? Sir? Are you there?"

~*~

Ellie nearly tripped over the can of Mr Sheen that was lying behind the front door. The hall table had been knocked over and Aphrodite lay on her side at the foot of the stairs. Ellie stared at the large red stain, her eyes followed its progress to the study. Three bloody fingerprints stained the door. There could be no mistaking them for what they were. A small groan began somewhere inside her and held the same note for a long time, she was unaware of the noise only of the blood drawing her to the study door. Gingerly she pushed the door further open, not knowing what she would find on the other side. Everything was as it should be and in order, she felt no relief, only a wild and crazy panic, her calm rationale was a herd of stampeding horses disturbed by an eagle's cry. The blood had no right to be in her home. She didn't invite it in. '*Think. Think. What to do. Think damn you. Ring Matt. Yes that's what she should do. No that's not right, need to... need to ... need to find out if the phones been used.*'

Instead of asking for Matt's number she instructed the computer to give her last number called.

"Emergency services. Which service do you require please?"

"Oh no. Nooo." Ellie broke down and told the operator between sobs that she thought there had been an accident. The cool efficient voice on the other end of the phone tried to calm her but to no avail. She checked the log and confirmed that a man had been taken from her address to St. Joseph's hospital that afternoon. She told Ellie that she had no further information and Ellie ended the call without remembering to thank the operator. She was already half way out of the house before the operator finished speaking. "Call end." she screamed back at the computer.

~*~

Ellie rushed into room 306, her face etched with worry and concern. Matt was sitting up in bed, the left side of his head covered in a huge white dressing, blood already beginning to seep through the gauze. A nurse offered him water to wash down the little white pills that were his licence for a pain free four hours.

"Oh Matt love, what happened to you?" she rushed to the side of his bed and flung her arms around his neck, being careful to avoid the bandage. Matt flinched away from her touch.

"Hello Darling." He said with a tight smile, "You came then?"

It seemed an odd thing for him to say, but she couldn't address it because the nurse was speaking to her.

"He's had a nasty knock on the head love and needs to rest. No more than five minutes please." She left the room in a bustle of starchy efficiency.

The smile left Matt's face and he pulled roughly away from Ellie, almost throwing her from him. His eyes were wide and he made no attempt to hide the look of revulsion on his face.

"Come to finish what you started have you?" his lip curled in contempt as he spat the words at her. "What the hell is wrong with you? You could have killed me. No let's be honest you tried to kill me. Didn't you? Didn't you?"

His voice had risen and although he was whispering the words so that they wouldn't be over heard he couldn't have instilled more bitterness or venom into his voice if he'd been screaming the accusations at her.

Ellie recoiled in shock. The anger that fuelled the words pelted her with force enough, but the meaning behind each one hit her with a second blow.

"Matt love, they said you have concussion. What are you saying? You think I did this to you? Don't be silly. You know that's not true. I love you more than anything in the world Matt."

Matt clapped his hands in a slow, exaggerated manner three times, and winced as a new pain shot through his head with the movement.

"Clever Ellie, very clever. An excellent performance as the dutiful girlfriend. What's the matter? Scared I've told them something? Don't worry your secret's safe with me. I don't know what I've done to make you hate me so much, all I've ever done is love you Ellie, but don't worry I get the message loud and clear. As long as I live, I will *never* forget the look on your face when you brought that statue down on my head." His voice lost its power as he whispered the last words he ever wanted to say to her. "Now piss off out of my sight. I never want to see you again."

"But Matt …"

He turned his face that was almost as white as the pillow he rested on, away from her and closed his eyes.

Ellie ran from the hospital crying.

~*~

Rob and his wife Gail dropped what they were doing to go to Ellie when she called them. Gail gathered Ellie into her arms and both women sobbed.

"I'm so sorry, I'm so sorry sweetheart." Gail kept repeating over and over again. "I can't take it all in, it's too much."

Ellie comforted the other woman, after all she'd had several weeks to come to terms with her illness, Gail and Rob had it thrust on them just that afternoon.

"How's Matt?" asked Rob.

"Not good, fractured skull and thirteen stitches. They are going to keep him in overnight for observation. They don't think there's any danger of damage to his brain. Just a precaution they said. But, oh Rob, he thinks I did it to him. How could he think that? I tried to tell him I was with you all afternoon but he didn't give me the chance."

"Shhh." Said Rob with an arm around both women. "It'll be all right we'll explain everything to him and when he's had a chance to sleep and get over the shock a bit, he'll be more of a mind to listen. Don't worry, we'll sort it out."

~*~

Matt rang Rob and asked to be picked up from the hospital the following morning. They had to wait an age in the waiting room until the consultant gave Matt the all clear and discharged him. Rob and Gail were the first ones to walk into the room. Matt's face broke into a relieved grin when he saw his friend. Rob shook Matt's hand warmly.

"Hey, how's it going mate?"

"Thanks for coming Rob, Gail, I can't wait to get out of…" his face set into a rictus of determination as he saw Ellie also crossing the room towards him.

She had what she hoped was a warm smile on her face.

"Get that crazy bitch away from me. She's a bloody lunatic." He ranted.

"Matt love," said Ellie a lot calmer than she felt. "We've come to take you home. Don't worry we can explain everything. It'll be all right now."

Matt refused to even look at Ellie, turning instead to Rob. "I am not going anywhere with her. I don't want to see her. Get her away from me."

"Matt mate the bump to the old noggin's addled your brain, Ellie didn't do this to you. I know she didn't because she was with me all afternoon yesterday. Come on, let's get the hell out of here and we can sort this out over a coffee at home."

"I've told you, I'm not going anywhere with her."

Ellie tried again to get through to him. She was crying openly now, and the patients in the other beds were all watching the scene playing out with interest.

"Matty. I love you. Come home and talk to me. I've got everything all ready for you."

"What? You honestly think I'm going to sleep with you after…" he checked himself. "After everything that's happened recently."

"Well, I'll make the guest room up for you then." Ellie spoke in a much softer voice, desperately trying to get a grip on her emotions and at the same time end the embarrassing scene.

Two nurses came onto the ward to see what all the commotion was about. Rob managed to smooth things over enough to get Matt out of the hospital and into the car by agreeing to take Matt back to their house instead of Ellie's. Having gleaned enough of what was going on to put two and two together, the nurses glared at Ellie on the way out. Matt had quickly become a favourite amongst the nurses during his brief stay.

Although Matt agreed to stay with Rob and Gail, he was still not happy about Ellie coming with them. The four-mile drive to their home was endured in terse silence. Gail tried several times to make small talk but the atmosphere swallowed her words before they had properly left her mouth. She cut her losses and gave up. Ellie sobbed quietly and felt that the few inches of space between her and Matt on the car's rear seat was an ocean that could never again be crossed. Not only had Matt accused her of terrible things, things that she was simply incapable of doing even if she'd had the opportunity or the desire, he seemed also to have completely forgotten her own illness.

Gail busied herself making coffee, and then sat beside Ellie on the settee, taking her hand and trying to comfort her friend. Matt had taken the armchair as far away from Ellie as possible and still refused to even look in her direction.

"That's it," he said sullenly. "You just sit there crying and gunning for the sympathy vote, never mind that you tried to murder me. You know something Ellie? You scare the pants off me. Can you imagine that? I'm scared shitless of my own girlfriend because I don't know when you're going to go off your head and do something crazy again. You're too much of a liability for me."

"Matt!" Said Gail sternly. "How could you, you know Ellie's..." She didn't want to hurt Ellie by saying the word but was so appalled by Matt's behaviour that she couldn't help herself. "Dying," She finished softly.

"Hah. Dying my arse. Who says she's dying? After all, we only have her word for that don't we? Did she tell you she lied to me about the result date so that I couldn't go? Bet she never told you about that did she? How do we know she's not making that up as well?"

Ellie couldn't believe what she was hearing. This was the man she had loved and cherished and wanted to share the rest of her life with.

"Listen mate," cut in Rob, "I don't know what the hell happened with you yesterday, but whatever it was you've made a big mistake you know. It had nothing to do with Ellie; she was with me the whole time that she was supposed to be at home caving your head in. What time did it happen?"

"I don't know." said Matt sullenly, "Sometime between half one and two I suppose."

"Well there you go then, at that time we were just tucking into an excellent dinner while a snotty waiter with a fancy title looked down his nose at us."

"Maybe she went to the loo or something." Matt was sounding more like a sulky schoolboy by the second. Ellie had tried to be reasonable, but now she'd just about had enough.

"Oh right, so I left the table, drove the eight miles home, tried to kill you for no apparent reason; though I could certainly come up with one or two corkers right now. And then drove back to the restaurant all in the space of time it takes to have a pee. That must be one helluva bladder I'm packing. I wouldn't get down hill of me, if I need a pee, you'll be washed away in the current."

"Right, but you forgot the bit about changing your clothes and taking off the ring I bought you. Which I see you have put back on now by the way. I don't know how the bloody hell you did it, do I? Or why for that matter? Especially why. I just know that you did." Matt looked at Ellie for the first time, and saw her glance down at her ring.

Rob spoke as though he was speaking to a small child. He enunciated each word, and was trying very hard to remain calm and keep the irritation out of his voice.

"Ellie was with me all afternoon. There was no time that she was away from the table for more than three minutes, and she did not hurt you Matt. You must have fallen down the stairs and are confused about what really happened."

Matt's eyes had opened wide. Finally he saw what he thought could be the only other explanation for what happened the previous afternoon.

"Of course. I'm such a bloody fool not to have seen it sooner. You're right

Rob, I was confused, but I'm not now. It all makes perfect sense. You're in it together. I know Ellie hit me over the head, because I was there and ***I saw her***. You say she was with you in the restaurant all afternoon. As it is impossible for her to be in two places at once, you must be covering for her. You are aren't you? You're both in it together to get rid of me."

Rob gave a mirthless laugh; he shook his head in disbelief. "Oh now you're just being bloody ridiculous."

"You're having an affair."

Rob looked furious. "Bullshit."

"Listen. It's the only thing that makes any logical sense. I hear what you are saying to me, but it's only words. What proof is there in a bunch of words? I ***know*** what I saw, I saw my girlfriend knocking me out and trying to kill me with an ornament. So she wasn't with you the whole afternoon. Therefore you must be lying to cover up for her, and why else would you do that other than because you are having an affair with her. I'm sorry Gail, I know it must be a shock for you, but it's the only explanation."

"Matt. I love Ellie. There you go I've said it." Rob gave a small rueful smile across the coffee table to Gail. "I'm probably a little bit *in love*, with Ellie too. Let's face it, what man wouldn't be, everything about her is gorgeous. But I've been with Gail seventeen happy years. I've invested my entire life in that woman sitting over there. I've loved my wife dearly through all the good and bad times we've had, probably in spite of some of them, and I'm telling you here and now mate, she's the only woman for me. I love her with everything that I am, and everything I aspire to be."

Rob and Gail looked at each other and the trust between them after what Rob had just said was like a wedding vow renewed. Rob had spoken with the open honesty that can only occur between two people who are truly secure in their love for each other.

Ellie raised her head. Her face was swollen with the tears she had shed, but she was done crying for the time being, now she was just plain red hot mad. Her grey eyes glinted like steel. She had tried to be reasonable; it was obvious that through whatever mis-guided reasoning, Matt truly did believe that Ellie had hurt him. The trust between Rob and Gail had touched her, and brought home the fact that she and Matt didn't have that level of trust to rely upon. If they had, then she would have been able to convince him of the truth, no matter what he thought he saw. She felt the now familiar knot of temper rising within her, she tried to swallow it down, but it was a force too strong to be beaten.

"Okay, Okay. You're right of course. Because you're always right aren't you Matty? Couldn't possibly be mistaken could you? So yes all right Rob and I are having an affair, and rather than just finish with you to be with him, it seemed to make so much more sense to kill you and leave you bleeding on my hall floor for the police to find. Lots of lovely forensic evidence, eh Matt. But it doesn't matter because Rob and I have a flight booked for Honna-bloody-lulu at three o clock," she glanced over at Gail too angry to hold back. "He's got his bags packed in the boot of the car ready for us to leave Gail. But hey, you won't have time to be upset about it because he's going to do you in too before we go. I mean, that's the logical thing to do isn't it. That's what we'd do if we're having an affair behind your backs." She looked back at Matt. "Well if that's what you want to believe, you go right ahead Matt. I hope you and your bloody theories and accusations will be very happy together. I'd just like to know which one of us it is that is crazy, because none of this makes any bloody sense to me."

Ellie was livid that Matt had put their friends in such an awkward situation. He had been jealous of her relationship with Rob when she and Matt first became partners, but she thought that had been well and truly put to bed a long time ago. It felt as though all the love they shared was dissolving into a simmering pool of bitterness and distrust, and it was looking as though there was no way back, no way to stop what was happening to them. She felt more alone than she had ever felt in her life before. There didn't seem to be any tears left to cry and she was exhausted and shamed.

"This is all getting way out of hand," Said Rob, trying to calm the situation and bring some order to bear. "Okay you only have our word for it that there's nothing improper going on between us. But Matt, everything else can be proven. You can go with Ellie to speak to her consultant about the illness. And we weren't the only people at that restaurant you know? Waiters will remember us; all you have to do is talk to them. We went for a walk in the park to talk after we'd made a pretence of eating. Neither of us was very hungry under the circumstances. We sat on a park bench in front of the snack kiosk. We drank several cups of horrendously strong coffee; the lady is bound to remember us. Don't take our word for it Matt. Ask. We can account for almost every minute of yesterday afternoon. We bought two ice creams with raspberry topping. Go and check it out, everything I'm telling you is the truth."

Matt dropped his head into his hands and tried to think. Rob was right everything they said could be proven, one way or the other, and if they had wanted an alibi then that wasn't going to be a very good one because Ellie couldn't have left for a long enough time without her absence being noted. Ellie had no reason for wanting to kill him, they had always been very happy and surely her illness couldn't account for her becoming a psychotic madwoman over night. Everything was so muddled in his head. His thoughts wouldn't clear because he kept coming back to the same thing. He actually *saw* Ellie hit him with that statue. It wasn't someone who looked like Ellie and wore the same perfume, it *was* Ellie. And yet it couldn't be, because Ellie had a restaurant full of people who were with her, somewhere else at the time. But he *saw her*, the national bank *saw her*, her next door neighbour *saw her*, the woman in the costume shop *saw her* and all of them saw her in places and at times when she wasn't there. He looked over at Ellie and she looked so tired, so miserable, so vulnerable, and he knew that no matter what, he still loved her and had to find a way to sort out the craziness.

The colour had drained from Ellie's face; it had all been too much for her. She said that she felt unwell and could she be taken home please.

Rob and Gail wouldn't hear of it. Gail helped Ellie up to the guest room to lie down.

~*~

It was dark when Ellie woke up. She must have slept for hours, the day had gone and the night was well and truly in. She had been partially undressed and covered with the quilt. The biggest surprise of all was the lean naked body lying beside her. Matt stirred and then came fully awake within a couple of seconds. He looked over and smiled tightening his grip, pulling her body into him, he put his finger to her lips to shush her, and then kissed her with all the love and gentleness that he felt for her.

"Oh Matt," she began "I'm so sorry about everything. I really didn't hit you, you know. Please say you understand that."

"Ssshhh baby, let's not talk about it any more. I don't know what's happening. I know that I think I saw you. Maybe the concussion has mixed everything up in my mind and I really did fall down the stairs and only imagined that I saw you. Maybe they sent an alien down to take your place. I don't know, but what I do know, is that I love you and somehow, some way, we'll sort this out and I'll be there for you for as long as you need me."

They cried and they hugged and then later, some time later, they made love.

Chapter 7

The next couple of days passed without incident. On Thursday Ellie insisted that Matt go back to his flat *and* back to work, he had been taking far too much time off lately. She felt stifled and they had talked round and round the happenings of the last week until they were dizzy. When rational suggestion didn't explain things satisfactorily their theories had gradually become more and more outlandish and bizarre. Although they laughed about it, Ellie was half convinced that she *had* been taken over by a crazed psychotic alien, or an evil spirit bent on destruction, or even that she was having out of body experiences and turning into a twisted, homicidal maniac during the episodes.

After Matt left, Ellie went for a long walk with Jake, first up Hoad Hill, and then round Ulverston market. All the time she had her eyes peeled for trouble, she constantly felt as though she was being watched but told herself that she was just being paranoid. She hadn't been able to settle to writing that morning, her hands were stiff and uncooperative, and her mind was restless and not willing to concentrate. After writing a mere couple of hundred words in half an hour, she gave up in disgust and felt the need for a cleansing wind to blow some of her anxiety away.

She came back feeling, if anything, more uptight than when she left. As she opened her garden gate, she very nearly turned away again; almost unable to face whatever horrors might be waiting for her on the other side of the front door, the same door that previously always seemed so safe and protective. On this occasion, she needn't have worried; everything seemed to be just as she'd left it.

On Thursday night the shadows in the lounge were long. Ellie and Jake snuggled on the settee together but Ellie was on edge, the room didn't feel cosy and warm tonight, it felt claustrophobic and in her face. The walls seemed to move in an inch every time she looked at them. Taking Jake out, the darkness closed in around her as the walls had done at home. The moon was high and the shadows were even longer and looked more oppressive outside than they were indoors. Twice she heard footsteps in the night behind her, within seconds her heart was thumping and she was in a state of panic. Jake picking up on her mood became nervous growling low and deep in his throat. Both times it was only people going about their business. Ellie felt that there was no escape from her paranoia, it clung tight and followed her even into sleep.

On both the Thursday and Friday nights, she slept with her bedroom light on; she hadn't done that since being a small child. Her sleep was fitful and troubled, and she woke feeling worn and irritable.

Saturday morning broke vivid and beautiful; it was one of those late October mornings reminiscent of the faded summer. One last rebellious splendour of autumn before it was bullied into retreat by the stronger more aggressive grip of winter. The sun shone bravely to melt the morning frost. And the world felt clean.

Ellie felt an awakening of hope. Nothing had happened for two days and three nights, maybe the nightmare that had taken hold of her life was passing. The illness she could do nothing about other than to keep fighting, but the awful ever-present feeling of danger and malice seemed to have passed. Ellie felt her hope for a short but content future returning.

Matt was coming by shortly. Although they had kept in phone contact the last two days she asked that he give her some space. Their relationship though still intact was fragile. They had been severely tested and both of them were left feeling bruised and delicate. She missed him and this realisation made her smile.

That evening they had decided they would meet providence with defiance. The night was to be part pleasure, part something else. It was decided, mainly by Ellie and against Matt's better judgement, to go to the night-club 'Demons' and see if there was any clue to explain how one of their matchbooks turned up in Ellie's lounge. It was also an excuse to live a normal Saturday night, a night of forgetting and forgiving and purely of loving and laughing. Ellie was looking forward to it; it seemed so long since she'd felt strong enough to go out clubbing, but this morning she wanted to conquer the world. Matt was calling briefly that morning to collect Jake and take him to his house; they would be staying in Barrow that night and Ellie was looking forward to seeing him and felt happy in her new confidence.

Matt didn't scan his identity when he arrived, he rang the doorbell. Ellie felt a second of sadness at this glaring sign that things were still not completely right between them. '*Never mind,*' she thought, '*tonight we will have plenty of opportunity to work on that.*' Jake got to the door before Ellie and stood whining and wagging his tail impatiently. She'd told him Matt was coming several times and the dog had been watching the door for him and waiting.

Instead of using George to open the door, she went to answer it the 'old fashioned way', her irritation at him not using his key had passed and it felt nice to be answering the door to her man in welcome. It had the feeling of being taken back to the early days of their courtship, when everything was new and exciting.

Jake's enthusiastic greeting almost battered the huge bunch of flowers he held in his hand. Ellie stood back smiling warmly, she knew she had no chance of getting a look in until Jake had been rough and enthusiastically petted and calmed. A blurring of anxiety clouded her sense of peace as she remembered the last floral delivery to her home, but she suppressed the feeling almost before it had insinuated its ugly self into her mind. Nothing was going to spoil today. Nothing.

"Hello sexy." She murmured softly, finally managing to separate man and dog. "They for me?" she gestured at the beautiful scented flowers.

"Nah, I bought them for Gertie down the fish shop, but she said they make her sneeze, so you might as well have them."

"Oh that Greasy Gertie has no class. They'll be far more appreciated by Jake and I."

Matt left after a light lunch that Ellie prepared while he showered. Their intense lovemaking had heightened the good mood that Ellie awakened in. And she sat in her dressing gown for a long time. For the first time in weeks she indulged in peaceful reflection. She would never be complacent about her illness or of the death sentence hanging above her, but she accepted it now. And whatever the knee jerk reactions had been that plagued her since she was given the results, they were now in the past, she *had* a future to look forward to and Ellie's future was all the sweeter for the fact that it had a shorter lease than most.

~*~

She was still sitting at the table when the doorbell rang. '*Damn,*' she thought. It was Saturday afternoon and she had clean forgotten that Jamie Matthews was due to arrive at one thirty. Jamie was a young lad from the town who came to help around the garden every Saturday for two hours. It was with mild embarrassment that Ellie used the computer to let him in.

"In here, Jamie." She shouted when she heard him taking his boots off in the hall. She usually made him a drink and they discussed what she wanted doing before he made a start. The only difference this week was that Ellie was sitting in only a short satin dressing gown and was painfully aware that she was unwashed since she had made love to Matt.

Jamie Matthew's seventeen-year-old eyes almost popped out of his head when he walked into the dining room and saw Ellie's attire. In his youthful ineptitude he couldn't disguise the 'body scan' he took of Ellie or the fact that his gaze rested just a split second too long on her exposed thighs. She pulled the dressing gown round her as firmly as she could and was furious with herself when she felt her cheeks beginning to burn. Jamie couldn't meet her eyes and shuffled from foot to foot as he examined his socks intently. He seemed fixated with the small hole through which his right big toe played peep-po. His face was crimson right into his hairline. Ellie daren't even begin to imagine what he was thinking, and prayed to the God of purity that he didn't think she was sitting like that for his benefit.

"Right Jamie," She adopted as normal a voice as possible under the humiliating circumstances. "You are going to have to sort yourself out with a drink this afternoon. I'm afraid I've had a bit of a headache all morning and stayed in bed." She forgave herself immediately for the outright lie. "I'm going for a shower, help yourself to something to drink and a biscuit and then see what you can find to do until I come out. Maybe you could begin by going over the lawns please. I know they were only done a fortnight ago, but we've had quite a bit of rain and they could possibly use a tidy up." *'And they aren't the only thing,'* she thought to herself, as she absently ran a hand through her tousled hair. This only caused her dressing gown to open revealing to Jamie who had apparently thought it safe to look up, the crescent of her left breast. Ellie beat a hasty retreat, knowing that the dressing gown only just covered her bottom and the very tops of her legs. *'Oh my God,'* she thought, *'the poor lad must be terrified.'*

In actual fact terror was not the uppermost thought in Jamie Matthew's mind at that moment. His thoughts were wholly to do with concealing the movement in the front of his boxer shorts.

Ellie felt her cheeks returning to their normal hue as the needles of warm water pounded into her naked body, her mind wandered to the young gardener as she soaped her body and stimulated her blood cells with vigorous lathering. They certainly didn't make young lads in the Jamie Matthew's mould when she was seventeen. Her male peers had all been pimply cretins with buck teeth and halitosis. There was no doubt about it, Jamie was a young hunk. Well past the six-foot average height. Lads were wearing their hair longer these days and Jamie's dark brown eyes always peered self-consciously from beneath a shaggy fringe that framed his sun-browned face. Ellie flushed again as she thought that Jamie probably had completely the wrong impression of her now. She just hoped that he didn't say anything to his mother about it. Or worse all the lads he hung about with in the local pub.

~*~

Jamie tried to concentrate on mowing the lawns. Ellie was a good boss and he was grateful for the extra Euros his Saturday job gave him. The new government paid all his tuition costs and living expenses at university but he still had to pay for his course materials. It was more than just job satisfaction though.

The truth of the matter was that it was an excuse to be near Ellie Erikson. They all fancied her. Pete Harvey even thought that she fancied *him* because she had asked him the time at the bus stop one day.

Jamie knew that Ellie was way out of his league, she being a famous writer and all that, and what with her fancy solicitor boyfriend, but he still had the hots for her in a big way. Jamie had yet to lose his virginity. Despite his good looks and confident demeanour in most things, he was shy and unsure of himself around females. They were a species he couldn't quite fathom, and Jamie was by nature wary of anything he didn't understand. Jamie had a good body, he knew that, and he had the rough unkempt looks that girls seemed to go for, but none of that was an automatic license to self-confidence. Jamie was clumsy around girls, but he had always been able to talk to Ellie, she was different.

The smaller front lawn was almost done. His balls ached and his dick throbbed despite turning his thoughts to the national failings of the English-only-new-government and its half-heartedly threatened, totalitarian regimes for social reform. He couldn't settle to his work after being taunted by his boss's naked tit almost flopping out in front of his face. Front lawn finished he carried the mower round to the back of the house.

He eyed the garden shed. It wouldn't be the first time he'd nipped in there for a quick wank. Risky though, he'd almost got caught last time. Well the alternative wasn't looking good either. She'd be out of the shower soon and coming to talk to him, he knew that unless he did something to ease his discomfort before then, that the second he saw her, his friendly mate would be swelling up to say hello. He moved the lawn mower to one side out of sight of what he assumed was Ellie's bedroom window and unbolted the shed and went inside.

He opened one of the garden seats and sat down. His penis was really throbbing now; he could feel a small, cold wet patch forming on the front of his pants where he'd already begun to leak. Lowering the front of his black sports pants slightly he freed his penis and gripped it in his hand. He looked through the shed window and into what he thought was Ellie's bedroom imagining what it would be like to be looking inside. His hand went straight into speed wank, not bothering to ease up the tempo gradually. Another minute and he would have been shooting the low shed ceiling, but his eyes came to rest on the set of ladders running the length of one wall of the shed.

Suddenly his voyeuristic fantasy took on a realism slant. He could have the ladder up against the ivy alongside the window within a couple of minutes, but what if she was already out of the shower and looking towards the window when he set the ladder up? Was that a chance he was willing to take? Damned right it was. He had gone from teenage masturbation fantasy to the decision to actually do it in a matter of seconds, yet he wasn't aware of actually making the transition. So engrossed was he in his plan, that the sexual urges that had driven him to action were for the moment forgotten. His penis lay neglected in his hand, still turgid but no longer on the point of release.

On his way around the path with the ladder, he wondered what he should do if he got caught, what would he say? What would *she* say? Maybe she'd *like* to think of him there looking at her and masturbating for her. His penis twitched once as he drew level with the rhododendron bush and his breathing accelerated again. The latter was partly due to the weight and exertion of carrying the now heavy ladder and partly through sexual excitement and a sense of danger.

Checking that the ladder was anchored securely in the flowerbed he began to climb. This was the moment if any at which he would be caught. Once he was safely up the ladder and in position, he could wait for her to come out of the bathroom and into the bedroom. Everything rested on the fact that she would not yet have come out of the bathroom, if she had then the slightest noise might alert her to activity outside her window.

He was sweating heavily as he reached the top and peered into the bedroom. He had one pang of '*what if I've got the wrong room'* before his hope and faith in the God of south facing sunlight was confirmed. It was her bedroom all right. He almost choked on the knot of excitement that rose from the pit of his groin to lodge somewhere in the region of his throat. Although his breath was leaving his body in loud rasps he didn't seem to be getting enough oxygen to his lungs. Never before had he done anything so bold. He felt daring and perverted and that only added to the excitement he felt. He almost wanted her to catch him there. Wanted to expose himself to her.

While he waited he peered into her bedroom with interest. The back garden was completely enclosed so there was no danger of him being seen by interested neighbours or anybody else. The not Jake proof fencing saw to that. Christ that room was girlie. A white duvet with delicate purple swirls on it dominated both the bed and the room. A black wrought iron headboard and loads of matching candlesticks gave the room a feminine but quite gothic feel. He imagined for a moment being tied with purple scarves to the headboard as Ellie performed various sex acts upon him, and his cock reacted so violently that he almost came in his boxers without even having to stroke himself. There was a dress laid out on the bed. A simple silver cotton dress with thin straps, it looked short and Jamie tried to imagine what Ellie would look like in it, but all his mind's eye could see was her sliding the dress over her head to expose her creamy-brown nakedness beneath.

The door was opening. '*Oh shit. This was it.'* Jamie pulled further back to ensure that he was fully concealed behind the overgrown ivy. His view of the far side of the room was slightly impaired but he could see the rest of the bedroom perfectly and would have a fine view of anything on show. '*Dear God, please don't let her close the curtains.'* Ellie walked into the room with just a short white towel covering her from just above the nipple to well above the knee and another towel on her hair.

She drew level with the bed and leaned over taking the towel from her head and rubbing at her hair vigorously. She was slightly in profile to Jamie's view and he was able to see all of her leg and just the merest hint of paler buttock beneath the other towel. His left hand slid down his trousers and his right tightened his grip on the ladder for support. He began to stroke his penis very slowly, he wanted to savour every moment of this and hoped it wouldn't be all over for him, and indeed all over him, too quickly.

Ellie straightened up and threw the damp towel on the bed being careful that it wouldn't land on her dress. She ran her hands several times through her hair, and then came the moment Jamie had been longing for. The moment he had fantasised about so many times was actually being played out before him for real. He felt his balls beginning to boil and had to take his hands off his dick and grab the ladder with both hands otherwise he would have come within another few seconds. He enjoyed the fact that he had left his dick hanging out of the front of his pants, and he pressed it lightly against one of the rungs of the ladder allowing a little pressure upon it.

Ellie removed the towel from around her body. She was magnificent. Jamie had never seen a live naked woman before, his fourteen-year-old sister didn't count and he'd only seen bits of her when he peered through the crack in her door. Here was Ellie standing stark naked in front of her mirror and in full view of him.

She began to rub her body with the towel and her tits jiggled up and down in time to the movement. Jamie moaned softly to himself, he couldn't take much more of this, the head of his dick couldn't throb any harder if it had been hit by a hammer. It took an almost super human effort on his part not to grab hold of it and wank himself silly for the last three seconds that he would hold out. He may never see this again and he so badly wanted it to last. It would have been nice if her tits had been a bit bigger, but apart from the size of them they were perfect. *She* was perfect. His eyes travelled down her body to her partially shaven pussy. He imagined her spread-eagled on the bed with his cock hammering into her all the way up the nine inches to his balls. This was without a doubt the best moment of his life to date. Better even than seeing Jane Prescott piss her knickers in fright when he had put a spider down her back in biology class last year. Better even than seeing 'Black Cyber' in concert.

Ellie was dry and Jamie was disappointed to see her reach for the silver dress. '*Wouldn't it have been amazing if she's frigged herself off in front of the mirror*?' He thought, imagining the moment when they would both have cum in unison. '*He'd better get a move on, if she was getting dressed she might be coming downstairs in a minute.*' He thought, grabbing his dick again and wanking a little bit faster now.

Ellie went to a drawer and took out a white thing that looked like a pair of panties but wasn't, it was a little triangle of white silky material with a couple of bits of elastic at the back. Jamie wished that he could feel it against his cock. He wondered how hard it would be to steal one at a later date. She slipped her legs into the garment and Jamie upped the speed of his wanking a notch. Her arse hung out of the fucking thing. It was the most awesome sight, like a fucking moon split in the middle. God her arse looked tight and smooth. When she turned round he could see the impression of the little bit of golden hair that showed through the white material. It was as sexy as hell. Jamie was close now, couldn't hold out much longer.

She slipped the dress over her head and studied herself in the mirror. Jamie studied her too. '*She didn't put a fucking bra on. Jeeezus fucking Christ.*' Her nipples stuck out visibly through the thin material of the dress. They were slightly upturned and there wasn't even the merest hint of sagging. She kept in good shape; Jamie worked out himself and liked to see it in a woman. Especially a good-looking woman like Ellie.

She seemed pleased with her dress and grabbed it from the bottom. In one fluid movement she dragged it from mid thigh to right over the top of her head. This was exactly the movement Jamie had fantasised about earlier. There was no stopping it this time, he wanked furiously, panting, he felt the spunk rising up his shaft ready to lubricate his blurring hand and a good portion of the dark green ivy. He bit down on his lip to stop himself from crying out as it jerked out of his cock in a three-spurt fountain. *'I'm coming Ellie, I'm coming.'* He whispered aloud imagining her watching him, even though he was well covered by the plants. *'Fucking awesome.*' he whispered again when he felt his penis diminishing in his sodden hand.

He realised he had better get a move on. He was taking a big chance on guessing that she would be drying her hair properly before she came downstairs, that would hopefully give him time to get rid of the ladder and clean himself up a bit. Jamie reckoned that he knew women folk pretty well, his mother and sister wouldn't dream of coming downstairs after bathing without drying their hair first. He was banking on Ellie being the same.

As he wiped his hands on his pants he watched again as Ellie took the pantie thing off and turned towards the drawers. She took out a 'normal' pair of panties and slipped them on. Downstairs Jake began to bark. '*Oh shit. Was someone coming? What if it was the boyfriend? Can I pretend to be cutting down the ivy? Will he buy that? Oh shit.'*

Ellie heard Jake and stopped half way through slipping into a pair of cut off jeans. She listened but heard nothing so continued putting the shorts on. Jake stopped barking and Jamie breathed a huge sigh of relief, it didn't look like there were any visitors, just that stupid fucking dog freaking out over nothing again.

Ellie was facing the window when she straightened to do up her zip. Jamie would have to wait until she turned round to be able to move. He needed her to be a hair dryer freak. He was going to be out of luck and out of work if she was a 'let it dry natural' girl. But hell it would be worth all the shit he'd get off his mother. Ellie was finished zipping up and Jamie was looking for escape when the wind was forced out of his lungs in shock by what he saw next. He couldn't believe his eyes. And there was nothing comic in the fact that he nearly fell off the ladder in shock and fear.

Jamie's eyes had widened into huge saucers of terror and his mouth hung open unable to scream out for a moment. He didn't know what to do next.

Ellie had walked into the bedroom. Her hand was raised above her head. The blade of a six inch kitchen knife glinted in the streaming afternoon sunlight but that couldn't be, Ellie was standing by the bed pulling on an orange halter-neck top with a bright yellow sunflower on the front.

Jamie's mind was processing what was unfolding in the room that he was peeping into. As a direct result of being a seventeen year old boy with the body of a man and the mental capacity of a trained chimp, as were most lads of that age, his first thought was for his own predicament. '*Here he was stuck up a freakin` ladder with his dick out, while his boss was about to be … murdered.*' As that last word seeped into his brain, it finally did its work and came up with a scenario. Jamie realised that a slap on his tired wrist for being a sick little pervert, which after all was perfectly acceptable in teenage lads, was not quite in the same league as being hacked to death by your evil twin. Funny you would have thought that she'd mention she had an identical twin, especially one that might suddenly pop up out of nowhere in her bedroom with a fucking big knife to kill her when a lad's indulging in innocent masturbation. Information was flashing rapidly through Jamie's mind in a manner that was making him quite sick. Less than two seconds had elapsed since the woman had come into the room and while Jamie had to think harder than pleased him, Ellie two had only taken three stealthy footsteps towards *his* Ellie. '*What if it was the other way round though? What if… The woman by the bed was not his boss and his boss was a fucking mad murdering …'* Two more steps and the woman with the knife would be within reach of Ellie. Oh shit *do something.*

Galvanised into sudden action Jamie hastily pulled the elasticised waistband of his pants up over his diminished boyhood.

He leaned out as far as he could on the ladder and hammered furiously on Ellie's bedroom window. He gestured for Ellie to look behind her and screamed out a warning.

"Ellie turn around, she's going to get you!"

The moment could well have been freeze-framed. For that one solitary, defined-from-all-the-rest, moment in time everything seemed to stop. Perhaps it was a mere blip of a second or maybe they all petrified for three weeks, it made no odds, time stopped.

Ellie looked up from dressing, she had her arms in the top, about to take it over her head, her tits jiggled again without the constraints of all encompassing material. Jamie didn't even notice. She saw him and dropped her hands to cover herself. Her eyes widened to ape those of Jamie and her mouth made an 'O' giving her the look for that tenth of a second of a blow up doll.

The other Ellie saw Jamie at the same time. She had almost come level with the bed and her arm was beginning to rise with the knife glinting in the sunlight. Her expression differed from that of Ellie, where as Ellie's mouth made an 'O' the other one's face seemed to close down. Only the eyes of all three players in the scene had the same wide startled look. Jamie noted that the eyes were the only true give away of fear.

The other Ellie was the first one to break the petrifying spell. She dropped the knife and turned to flee the room. At the same instant the Ellie that Jamie assumed was his boss heard the commotion and began to turn. She locked eyes with her 'twin' who still had the knife held out above Ellie's head, and drew air into her lungs to scream.

The kitchen knife made a thud louder than expected even in the silence as it hit the carpet, it bounced once as though in slow motion before lying still at Ellie's feet, a steel tongued serpent to hew her body into tattered layers. Ellie finished her breath and began to scream.

Jamie just stared.

The other woman clattered down the stairs.

Jake barked and threw his body against the kitchen door, desperate to get out. *The not Elllie smell was bad.*

Everything was sudden pandemonium. Barking dogs, screaming women, nosy neighbours coming in the front gate to see what all the noise was about this time. Jamie was scrambling down the ladder as fast as his feet would take him.

Ellie was scrambling into her top, as fast as she could wrestle with the material and neck fastenings.

And the other Ellie was flying out of the door and down the path, knocking Mr. Harry Jackson on his geriatric backside in the process.

Jamie was almost down the ladder when he missed the third rung from the bottom and landed heavily in a heap on the floor. He jumped up into a standing position and as soon as he put weight on his right ankle a bolt of white-hot pain shot through him. He didn't think anything was broken, but it hurt like hell, he had twisted his ankle when he fell. Ignoring the pain he gave chase across the garden and into the street, limping on the leg that didn't want to take any weight.

Ellie was the last to leave the house. She caught up with Jamie half way down the road. There was nobody in sight and a choice of several roads that the woman could have taken.

"Jake!" yelled Ellie. "Let Jake out."

Although she yelled at nobody in particular Harry Jackson was closest to the house, and the one in Ellie's eyeline when she yelled.

"Eh?" Said Harry rubbing his back and checking himself for injuries, seeing as nobody had bothered to stop and help him up. '*Two of them, two of them bloody blonde tarts from next door. No wonder I can't keep up with it all.'* He thought.

"Hey she knocked me over … I fought in the Falk…"

Jamie was limping badly now, the swelling already ballooning his ankle to twice its normal size, and the daft old sod from next door was going to be no help. Ellie turned and ran back to the house herself.

Jake had never been the most obedient of dogs, or for that matter a dog with a great deal of understanding. You said *sit* and he jumped, you said *lie down* and he licked while still following the former command of *sit* which translates to Jake as *Jump,* But the moment Ellie flung open the kitchen door and shouted, "*Jake find,"* he was off without hesitation. He understood danger as well as the humans did. In fact he understood it better because he could *smell it.* He tore off down the street in the direction the woman had taken.

Jake was gone about ten minutes while Ellie tried to follow but she lost him very quickly. Jake liked nothing better than to *escape*. He would run for miles until Ellie got the car out and went to track him down, sometimes he had been out for hours with no road sense and a personality too friendly for his own stupid good.

This time however he came home very quickly. Jake was miserable he slunk in the front door and rolled his soft brown eyes towards Ellie.

Jake was a bad dog, he had lost the thing that was not Ellie. He ran fast but the big red thing with lots of people and wheels ran faster. Jake was tired, and went back home to tell Ellie he was a bad dog.

Ellie was just putting coffee mugs on the table in front of Jamie and Harry when Jake came back in. She was trembling. She had called Matt and the police and was waiting for them to arrive. She made a huge fuss of Jake and told him what a big, brave boy he was.

The important fact was, the one thing that made the *world* crazy and not Ellie, was that this time, three of them had seen the other woman who looked just like Ellie. She felt terror at what had just happened but an over-riding feeling of relief that she was as sane, at least, as the miserable Mr. Jackson. Knife wielding look-alikes could be fought; madness had no form to battle with. Ellie was scared half to death, but at the same time felt strong in the knowledge that her mind had not deserted her.

Chapter 8

She stood in front of the cracked dressing table mirror brushing out her blonde hair. The brush swiped aggressively, her hair lacked lustre and appeared dull and motionless as the air swept through it. Her grey eyes stared back with a hard coldness that made them look steely and brutal.

"I'll get you; you bitch."

She yelled this aloud and it echoed slightly in the under-furnished bedroom that only had small squares of unmatched carpeting down on the floorboards for warmth.

"Oh yes, you might have escaped this time, but I'll get you, and your pathetic dog and your snotty bastard of a boyfriend too. I'll get you all and make you suffer. I'm going to make you die slowly for what you did to me. That was *my life, my life*," her voice rose to a crescendo on the last four words and then dropped to a sibilant whisper as she added menacingly, "And I'm going to take it back from you, just as you stole it from me. I hate you and I hate your face. Before you die I'm going to take your face away. You should never have claimed it for your own. I'm going to cut you Ellie Erikson. Cut you and slice you, and disfigure you and hurt you, hurt you, hurt you. YOU ARE NOT ME. You are not me, Ellie Erikson."

With that she took a step backwards and flung the hairbrush at the mirror with all the force that her hatred could summon. The already cracked and aged glass shattered and fell in a glittering shower at her bare feet, she seemed oblivious to the little shards coating the bare piece of floorboard and moved from one foot to the other ranting and swearing at her reflection in the broken mirror.

"Twenty seven years you stole from me. Twenty seven long years I watched you living your happy life, the life that was mine, and all the while I was imprisoned, denied everything but what I was fed of your life. Your life that was taken from me. You sit in your fancy house, with your fancy life, and your fancy boyfriend, how many times have you felt guilt over what you stole from me? I've read your books Ellie Erikson. *They* forced me to read them. *They* made me. That'd surprise you wouldn't it? Me reading your books, the words you wrote after you stole my life. Did you ever once think I might read your pathetic stinking books? Did you? Well they're a pile of shit, so there. I read your books, and I watched your life from a screen in the whitewashed room. And what did you ever do to get me out of there? …NOTHING."

Momentarily spent, she looked at the ruined mirror, and then her eyes dropped to the dressing table. She had bought a vanity set for one Euro at a second hand shop. In a pathetic attempt to make the hovel more homely she had laid out the items with care on the top of the dressing table. A brush with someone else's hair mingling with her own between the bristles. A hand mirror, comb and a matching powder puff. The items were old fashioned, someone else's junk, but they were doing her a turn for now, until she took back everything that was rightfully hers.

She looked at her most treasured possession; it took up all the rest of the space on the vanity unit. That had been an unbelievably lucky find. It was risky stealing it, but it was there, a gift from God, hers for the taking. Providence had led her to waste a couple of hours in the heritage museum. And fate had taken the curator out of the room to answer the phone. There had been two of them, one open, displayed for the visitors to gasp at. The other one had been at rest, lying beside the first, it's great mouth full of brutal teeth closed. She took it, and did her best to hide it underneath her jacket but the end stuck out and banged against her knees bruising them as she ran. The man in his office never even saw her leave. But she took flight anyway and didn't stop running until she was back in the safety of her squalid hole.

"I HATE YOU ELLIE ERIKSON"

Eve looked round the tawdry bed-sit, seemingly aware of her surroundings for the first time. The dirty cups left to go sour in the sink, the junk room furniture slung in haphazardly by an uncaring landlord. She could have afforded better with the money she had stolen, but this enabled her to melt into the lower class bed-sit-land culture of town. The only place where people didn't ask questions, where neighbours weren't neighbourly and the beauty of it was, that it was only four short miles away from the home of her nemesis.

She slumped down onto the bed with the stained mattress and dingy grey sheets formerly used by countless others and said once more in the small voice of a hurt little girl.

"I hate you Ellie Erikson."

Eve sat for a long time on the tattered and cigarette burned bed-spread, after a while, when her fury had completely left her, she began to rock. She crossed her legs as she rocked back and forth and very quietly began to sing.

Miss Polly had a dolly that was sick, sick, sick,
She called for the doctor to come quick, quick, quick,
The doctor came with his bag and his hat
And he knocked at the door with a rat-a-tat-tat.
He looked at the dolly and he shook his head

And he said to Miss Polly put her straight to bed
He held her down and gave her a pill, pill, pill
And forced her to follow his will, will, will.

She repeated the rhyme in a sing-song voice over and over until the moon shone brightly through the window and the shadows grew long in the corners of the room.

Chapter 9

The scene of crime team did their job thoroughly. Every surface was dusted for prints; every fluff-ball, fibre and follicle bagged and labelled as possible evidence, and everything in the bedroom had been photographed from every possible angle.

Ellie was still sitting at the dining room table gripping Matt's hand tightly and gazing out of the window as Chief Inspector Morgan fired the same question at her in a slightly different form for the umpteenth time.

Her mind had drifted in an unconscious effort to block out the attack; she focused instead on thoughts of Jamie and Harry Jackson who had been filtered off to the lounge and were currently sitting on *her* settee, drinking *her* tea and eating *her* chocolate biscuits.

'Huh!' She thought, *'One is a juvenile peeping tom and the other a cantankerous old bastard whose only pleasure in life is making himself and anyone else within a three mile radius of him utterly miserable.'*

However today, these two people were akin to glowing Demi-Gods in her eyes, and she could forgive them those and any other sins, because both of them had actually *seen her.*

'Punch and Judy' as Ellie thought of police constables Woods and Ferguson, were interrogating them now. Jackson had plenty to say and Ellie could hear his droning monotone drifting through to her as she watched a magpie pulling up worms from the freshly mown lawn. Jamie Matthews on the other hand was terrified. His first thought when he heard that the police, and even worse, Matt, were on their way, was one of flight. Sitting there, his cheeks frequently rosy with shame, was the last place he wanted to be. Various threats had been used to make him stay put for initial questioning. The relevant two being the old, *"We can do this here, or more formerly down at the station, which do you prefer?"* And, *"If you do not help us sir, we can, and will, place you under arrest on a public indecency charge."*

Jamie had little choice but to sit disgraced and sullen. He answered the less humiliating of their questions and squirmed awkwardly at the more intimate ones as he watched Harry Jackson munch his way through biscuit after biscuit until the plate on the coffee table was empty apart from a few scattered crumbs.

"Bloody disgusting!" The old man iterated at one point during the questioning.

He sprayed half-chewed chocolate digestive crumbs over the three other people in the room.

"In my day, you'd have been packed off to war laddie, no choice in the matter. You'd have had little time for playing with yourself then. Had to go to war we did."

This was not strictly true, as national conscription had ended nearly thirty years before Jackson's *day,* but it was the lead in Harry had been waiting for to boast about his service in the Falklands.

Ellie was rubbing her fingertips together, distractedly trying to remove the ugly staining from her hands. She and Matt had been fingerprinted so that their prints could be eliminated from the investigation. The Magpie had finished his juicy meal and her fingers offered her something else to focus on so that she wouldn't have to concentrate either on the probing, intelligent eyes of the Chief Inspector or on the words that he repeated over and over again. She wasn't thinking about the answers she gave to his questions now, he had asked and she had answered over and over, she had already told them all she knew and now her mind was ready to shut down. She didn't want to have to think and so she answered each question as it was asked without interest. Morgan may have been trying to trip her up, make her contradict herself on previous replies, or maybe he just wanted to try and squeeze out every retained memory of the attack while it was still fresh in her mind. Whatever his reasoning, Ellie answered each question quietly and truthfully, never once wavering from her first answer.

No, she did not know her attacker. Yes it would seem that she might be some long lost and unknown twin sister. No, she had not touched the knife. No, her mother had never spoken of another daughter, as far as she was aware she was, and always had been, an only child. No, of course she didn't have some sibling vendetta going with her sister. How could she? She had not been aware of her existence until all this started. Yes, she was aware that this is a very serious accusation. No, she didn't know where her attacker might be. Yes, she was quite sure that at no time did she touch the knife. And so the questions went on.

Morgan scanned back over the used pages of his notebook and made a show of looking puzzled. He was about to give her a hard time and had no idea why. His instinct told him that something wasn't right with this case. Chief Inspector Morgan had learned to listen to and trust his instinct over the years.

"Now then Miss Erikson, can we go back to an incident reported on Monday the 20th October please. Officers Woods and Ferguson attended a disturbance at this address. A Mr. Harold Jackson claimed that after complaining about loud music coming from this house you abused him verbally and aggressively made threats against his well-being. Would that be correct?"

"It is …but…"

“And that’s the same Mr. Jackson whose sitting in the other room is it?”

“Yes but you see…”

Morgan held up a hand to silence Ellie and she bit down on her lip feeling like a little girl standing before an irate headmaster.

He rubbed the tip of his pen across the side of his temple and again pondered his notes.

“It says here Miss Erikson, and I quote. *‘I don’t know what’s happening to me, nothing makes sense anymore. I am accused of doing things that I have no recollection of doing.’* Do you remember saying this Miss Erikson?”

“Yes … No …Look you’ve twisted that all out of context. I also added that at the time I was supposed to be raising hell at home, I was also talking to a shop assistant in the middle of town. So I couldn’t have been here could I? You see I’d just received some bad news, I have an illness and I put my odd behaviour down to that. But now it all makes sense it wasn’t me doing those things at all, it was her.”

Ellie listened to herself beginning to ramble, she sounded confused even to herself as she heard the jumbled words issuing from her mouth.

“…And I put my odd behaviour down to that.” Morgan repeated.

The silence that he let run on too long, said without him having to, that he was less than impressed with her story.

“This is the way I see it, Miss Erikson…”

“Bloody hell, Eleanor. My name’s Eleanor.”

“I put it to you Miss Erikson,” Said Morgan ignoring her remarks. “That you seem a little bored. I mean, stuck here in this house all day, with not much else to do but write your novels. I think that maybe you crave a little attention, want something to spice up your life a bit. Something to remind yourself that you are an important person. Perhaps if news of you being stalked by a crazed twin sister hit the papers, you’d sell a few more copies of your books eh? Boost the dwindling sales a bit? Now I wonder if that thought’s occurred to you too?”

Morgan glanced from Ellie to Matt as he goaded Ellie. He watched Matt’s temper rising.

“How dare…” began Ellie two points of furious colour rising to her cheeks. Matt cut her off and yelled at the Chief Inspector.

“Right inspector you have gone far enough. My …er Miss Erikson has been through quite enough, she is a sick woman, and is not strong enough to take this deplorable bullying. Can’t you see how tired she is? Some psychopath has just tried to kill her, now I suggest that instead of hounding Eleanor, you get out there and catch this woman.” He glared at the other man.

“And when you do inspector, you can also charge her with a serious attack on me. No in fact you can charge her with trying to *murder* me.” He stopped scowling defiantly at Morgan who met his gaze with cool reserve, as he looked pointedly at the healing wound on Matt's head.

"Let me understand you correctly Mr High. You are saying, are you not, that this woman also assaulted you?"

"It was more than that, she hit me over the head with a bronze statue and almost killed me, if I hadn't deflected most of the blow with my arm, I wouldn't be sitting here now. Now do you understand how serious this is?"

"Oh I never for one minute doubted the seriousness of the accusation, sir. I merely want to ascertain the facts and make sure I have everything down correctly. Now then, this blow to the head that almost killed you, did you report it to us?"

"No."

"I see. A woman tries to kill you with a brass ornament and you don't bother to report it?"

"Bronze, inspector, the ornament was bronze. A limited edition actually." Morgan coughed to hide a smirk at this unguarded show of snobbery, in retaliation to his intentional goading.

"Oh do forgive me Mr High my mistake. You didn't report being hit with a *bronze* statue to the police? Why?"

"Well…" Matt realised too late the trap he had laid for himself and his voice dropped to a low mumble.

"Well at the time I thought it was Ellie."

Ellie lowered her head into her hands and groaned inwardly.

Morgan raised his eyebrows and feigned shock as he looked from Matt to Ellie and back again.

" Pardon? Did you just say that you thought it was Miss Erikson who tried to kill you? Why was that sir?"

"Well I know now that it wasn't Ellie, it was this look-alike… um person."

"Miss Erikson's long lost twin sister?"

"Well whoever the woman is, yes."

"I see." Said Morgan.

"Look inspector," said Matt exasperated.

"There are two witnesses in the lounge who have also seen this woman. Why don't you go and talk to them if you don't believe us?"

"Oh I will Mr High, rest assured of that."

Morgan had everything he was going to get from these two. He had been in the force twenty five years and something didn't smell right about this case. His keen policeman's instinct told him there was more going on here than was being told. Something didn't add up, it was all too convenient, too 'made to fit'. He didn't like it. And yet despite himself he couldn't help but admire the gutsy little woman sitting at the table. There was something about the way she met his eyes. Her defiance impressed him. He had interviewed many hundreds of liars over the years, had a nose for them as a scent hound does for blood, and yet Eleanor Erikson didn't strike him as being anything but truthful … and yet!

"Just one last thing Miss Erikson, would you have any objection to us contacting your mother, just as a follow up to our enquiries you understand. Perhaps if you could just give me her address."

"Oh for goodness sake, is there really any need for that? I've told you everything you need to know." Morgan sat with pen poised waiting to write down Esther Erikson's address and Ellie had no choice but to go along with it.

After Morgan disappeared into the lounge to speak to Jamie and Mr Jackson, Matt helped Ellie into her bedroom to lie down. Any thoughts she may earlier have had of being the pleasant hostess in adversity had long since being driven out by sheer exhaustion.

"Matt," she said as he lay beside her on top of the bed stroking her hand. "Ring mum please, I want to go and see her."

"Okay love, we will tomorrow, but you need to get some rest now. I'll get rid of the circus downstairs and then bring you something to eat. You aren't leaving that bed until tomorrow morning at the earliest."

"But what about our night out?" She murmured drowsily.

"Er. I don't think so missy, do you?"

Ellie was asleep.

~*~

Ellie desperately needed answers. Did she have an identical twin sister out there somewhere? Had her mother packed off one half of the pair to an adoption agency and Ellie was the lucky bunny who got to stay in the happy homestead? Was Ellie the adopted half of the picture? That would make more sense when you considered her parents, being more specific, her mother. A large part of Ellie was scared of the imminent confrontation with Esther. Ellie pleaded with Matt to take the long route to Morecambe where her mother lived. Was she even her mother? Was there another woman out there with a hereditary right to the title that Mrs Erikson didn't have? Her head swam with unaccustomed thoughts and questions.

Driving from Ulverston, along the lakes road, gave her time to clear her thoughts, to work out how she would approach her mother, what she would say, the way she would play it. For the first half an hour of the journey she sat almost silent. Matt leaned forward and turned on the radio and Ellie asked that it be turned off, she wanted to be able to think clearly. Matt could feel the tension effusing from her like the heat from a lover on a scorching summer night. He gave her the silence she needed and concentrated on the twisting road ahead.

Ellie played out the scene, as it would unfold, almost the way she would run a new book synopsis in her head. Usually the lightest of conversations ended in full-scale war when the two women got together. Mrs Erikson had become a little *disturbed* since her husband had died. A mixture of offspring guilt for not doing more for her mother and genuine irritation always made things difficult when they came within yelling distance of each other. Esther Erikson lived in a world not inhabited by many people; her world was becoming, more and more, a re-lived time of the past. In her mind Esther replayed her time of *superstardom,* a time belonging only to her, when the entire world was before her and she made the supreme sacrifice to give it all up for marriage and Eleanor. In reality she had been a lap-dancer in a seedy club on the sea-front. And though when alive, Ellie's father had kept Esther grounded pretty much to reality, since his death she was dreaming again of greasepaint and sequins. She had even taken up tap dancing of late.

Backbarrow gave way to Newby Bridge and they left the serenity of the Lake District behind them, as Cumbria became Lancashire just south of Milnthorpe.

"Matty?"

"Yes love?"

"I'm not going to tell her about my illness today."

Matt's voice was calm and soothing as he spoke to her, he didn't want to interfere with her thoughts or force his opinions on her decisions, he only wanted to be a sounding board to help her to bring her thinking into tidy order.

"She needs to know doll, and the longer you leave it the harder it's going to be. You know what she's like?"

"Yes, I know, I know that, but it's too much, too much to cope with all at once. Too much for us as well as her, we need to find out who this woman is and that's enough on our plate for the time being. And yes I know exactly what mum's like. I also know that she's going to bring up the subject of her coming to live with me again. The problem is, well the way she's been losing it; there's no way she can stay there much longer. The neighbours are already up in arms about her. She's becoming more of a nuisance. Mrs Caldwell, who lives next door to her, rang the other day to say that Mother was tap dancing on the balcony in her underwear at night. Gave Mr Caldwell quite a turn apparently."

Matt had to smother a smile at the mental image of his future mother-in-law cavorting round half naked. Esther terrified him with her clothes *on!*

"Whatever's right for you love, is right for me." He grabbed her hand and squeezed it. "Don't worry I'll take my lead from you."

Matt turned right at the traffic lights at Bolton-le-Sands and within minutes they had their first glimpse of Morecambe promenade. This is where Ellie grew up and although the town had undergone many changes over the years, the sea remained unaltered for her. The tide was in and she wound down her window a little further and inhaled a lung-full of the fresh salty air. The water was reasonably calm, dark slate-grey, with a dangerous malevolence that had taken many a person unfamiliar with its anger over the years. But this wild sea was her friend. It knew her youthful secrets and had never told. It listened to her loneliness as she stood on the cliffs at Heysham and yearned for love. No matter how much she had come to love Ulverston and the calm of the Lakes, this was her home and the sea would always welcome her back.

She wanted to ask Matt to stop the car. They could walk along the prom, feeling the stiff breeze take their hair to sculpt it into a frenzy of medusa tendrils. She wanted to stop and stroke dogs, pass small-talk with their proud owners. She wanted the sea to protect her from what she was about to hear. Ellie felt cowardice rising within her, and she swallowed it down with a brave resolve that she had to grab by the throat and hold on to.

Esther Erikson lived alone since her husband died five years earlier. Her house was a beautiful detached limestone building on Sandylands, at the south end of Morecambe promenade. All the front facing windows opened directly onto the sea and the large back garden was secluded and surrounded on all sides by rambling rose bushes and fruit trees swollen with their autumnal bounty. As a child she had spent many hours sitting on the second floor balcony watching the trawlers casting their nets to the horizon, sometimes she'd wave at the fishermen on board, but they were always too far out to see her. She had liked the feeling of being so small; it was easy in those days to be overlooked, to go unnoticed.

Ellie cringed as they pulled up outside the house. Rings of neon fairy lights, thankfully muted by the morning sun, flashed on and off, as though in time to a beat from long ago. She could only imagine how gaudy the lights would look at night and Ellie glanced with a look, part shame and part pity, to the houses skirting her mother's. Two bushes, one either side of the door, had been draped with enormous pink feather boas, and a four foot plastic moulding of Robbie Williams in his black leathered hey-day stood with cheesy welcoming grin, to the left of the entrance. There could be no mistaking this as Esther Erikson's house. Ellie remembered the days when her father sat in the big front window looking out over the sea. It seemed her dad would always be there damping down her mother's exotic spirit. But now he was not.

She was not given long to contemplate her youth, almost before they got out of the car the front door was flung wide and Esther Erikson made her exit.

"Darlings!" she screeched like an upper class parrot.

"It's so lovely to see you. It's been too long. I've cancelled my bridge club this afternoon so that we can have a lovely time catching up. How lovely. Oh Matthew darling you look lovely. Eleanor you look peaky. Have you been eating five servings of fruit and vegetables a day? I've got a lovely casserole in the oven."

Ellie kissed the proffered leathery cheek; she resisted the desire to spit away the clog of loose powder that stuck to her lips and already the word *lovely* was grating on her nerves.

"Hello Mother. Yes I'm eating properly. Really, there was no need to give up your bridge club, we could have done this another time." The last was said to Ellie's shame with a tinge of petulance. *'Damn she was that never-quite-perfect-enough little girl again. To hell with my 'lovely' mother for having the ability to make me feel like that.'*

Once inside the front door, Esther waited while they took off their shoes and donned slippers from the rack by the coat stand. Ellie glared at her back, she had not failed to notice the way her mother's lips had held for a second too long as they brushed across Matt's cheek. Or that her fingers had sought the back of his neck, where she ran her scarlet talons across his skin. Esther continued to talk non-stop as she ushered them through to the lounge.

"Mrs Greystone thought your book was simply marvellous dear. I told her it was lovely that she thought so, I said that the ending was weak. She *said* she didn't find it so, but she was just being polite. Have you got rid of that awful animal yet? Dogs should be kept in a zoo dear, that's where they belong and where they feel happiest."

"So should mothers." Whispered Matt to Ellie.

"What was that Matthew?"

"Oh I was just remarking to Ell... er Eleanor how um lovely you look. So young, so vibrant."

"Silly boy. I'll turn fifty three next month."

Both Ellie and Matt were struggling hard not to laugh now. They both knew she was about to celebrate her sixty third birthday. When in her mother's company, Ellie spent half her time cringing, and the other half feeling wholly inadequate, but this was so typically 'Mother' that she felt a little of the tension lifting. She was determined that this wouldn't turn into a fight. She just needed answers. She had to know the truth.

Esther was a perfect mismatch of taste and tasteless, a contradiction of the upper-middle class widow, and the seedy one-time stripper. Once in the immaculately tasteful lounge that had barely, apart from one or two unavoidable additions, been touched since her father died, Ellie fell into her usual routine. She walked across the room with her head tilted towards the picturesque sea-view window and away from the ornate fireplace, where she stopped in front of the chair to the immediate left of the fire, and turned it a little to the right until it faced into the room. Then she dropped into it, sinking into a cream hole of feather-soft, under-sprung upholstery. Matt took the end seat on the sofa opposite and Ellie glared at him, lest his eyes dared to glance at the fire place wall.

Esther Erikson married at the turn of the century. Before meeting and marrying. very quickly, Eleanor's father, Esther had been a bar dancer in a seedy promenade night-club. Jerry Erikson hated any mention of his wife's former profession, allowing only small mention of the fact that Esther 'used to dance a bit'. Since his death, Esther had become liberated, she was free at last to brag about her time in the clubs. She had a small photograph digitally re-mastered and then transposed into oil of huge and glorious proportion, and now, her prized possession hung proudly above the fireplace. The picture would have been inappropriate in any lounge, but here amongst the restful cream décor it seemed an insult to the hard work Ellie's father had put into buying this beautiful home. She hated the picture and begged numerous times for her mother to at least move it into her bedroom if not to the tip, but Esther would not hear of it.

The gilt-framed portrait measured five by four feet. A very young Esther smiled provocatively through a glut of heavy make-up. Her slim body, naked, bar a tiny glittered G-string, posed shamelessly, her breasts slightly more pert and jutting than they had ever been in real life, depicted cleverly by one of the top artists in the country. Esther loved this reminder of her colourful youth. Ellie hated it with a vengeance and couldn't bear to look at it. Apart from the fact that its vulgarity clashed so noticeably with the prim perfection of the cream and eggshell room; it was an unpleasant reminder to Ellie of her childhood. One that she always tried so very hard to forget.

Esther finished making the tea and brought in on a golden hostess trolley an arrangement of silver and fine china. Both Ellie and Matt were far more comfortable with big chunky mugs. Ellie loved her *Dyllis Bear* mug that had a small chip on the rim but was still far too precious for her to throw away. Her mother would be as unlikely to use common mugs as to lose her ugly wig in favour of her own ageing hair.

Finally Esther was seated after making a large performance of 'pouring'. The tension in the room had risen Ellie sat as stiff as the chair would allow, twisting her eternity ring endlessly round her finger. It was time to speak and now she didn't know how to begin.

"Some things have been happening to me … to us, Mother."

"Oh yes dear, what kind of things?" Esther sounded disinterested her focus commanded by the stray Jake hair that had fallen from Ellie's sleeve onto the coffee table as she reached over for her cup and saucer.

"Somebody's trying to kill me Mum."

For a single moment the little girl desperate for her mother's security and love had shown through the years old mask. Esther bristled visibly by the common use of her maternal title.

"Really dear you do have the most extraordinary imagination. I'm not in the least bit surprised you became a writer. Don't be ridiculous. Who could possibly want to kill you?"

"My sister."

Ellie watched her mother intently as she made the blunt statement. There was no Royal Doulton crashing to the floor, no tremor of hands or sharp intakes of breath. Esther merely took a delicate sip of her Indian tea and stared in mild amusement at her daughter.

"Darling is this the plot for your latest book? What on earth are you talking about?"

If Esther was acting then it was a performance worthy of any awarded accolade. She did seem genuinely confused and still had the look of someone on the receiving end of a joke knowing that a punch line was about to be delivered.

"Darling what on earth are you talking about?" she repeated after a five second silence in which she hadn't heard her own voice. "You quite simply aren't making any sense. Did you put that silly policeman up to coming round this morning? All those ridiculous questions. I told him that ever since you were a small child you had the most extraordinary imagination. I told him you were always jealous of having such a famous mother and felt you had to make up your little fairy tales to feel important. Don't worry though dear, you aren't to be arrested, oh we did laugh over some of your more elaborate tales. He was quite dashing, and I think he had a twinkle in his eye for me you know."

" Tell me about my twin sister Mother." Despite her self-promised calm, Ellie felt her temper rising and the word 'Mother' was spat across the room.

"You know? The one you have never bothered to inform me about."

Esther's mouth had fallen slightly but elegantly open. Her eyes widened until she looked like a startled doe; her surprise was caused more by the venom behind her daughter's words than the actual words themselves.

"Eleanor. You are talking in riddles girl, and I'll thank you not to take that tone with me young lady."

"I am twenty seven years old for Christ sake. Yet you insist in treating me like an adolescent teenager. I want answers Mother and I want them now. Why didn't you tell me that I had an identical twin?"

"My darling, mis-informed daughter, it's very obvious that you are distraught. Now I don't know who has been feeding you these ridiculous stories but I can assure you, I have had one child and one child only, and that child is you. Now can I freshen up your tea for you?"

Matt spoke for the first time. "Esther."

"Yes sweetie. More tea?"

She raised the tea-pot and gave Matt her simpering sex kitten look, the one she had claimed numerous times 'that no man could possibly resist' Ellie thought the odds of her throwing up all over her mother's cream carpet were increasing by the second.

"Esther," Matt began again but with more temerity. "Ellie and I are in fear for our lives. We have both been under serious attack from a woman who is identical in every minute detail to Eleanor. The only conclusion that it is possible to draw is that she is a sister, possibly given up for adoption at birth. Or alternatively that Ellie herself is adopted."

Esther lowered the teapot and seemed to really take in what they were saying for the first time. Her face crumbled, the façade left leaving only the cast of its greasepaint behind, and the husk left sitting in front of them was that of a lonely, frightened and ageing woman trying to keep hold of the shadow of her youth the best way she knew how.

"But I only ever had you. I swear I did. Only you Eleanor, you were the prism in my otherwise colourless life."

In other circumstances Ellie would have laughed out loud at this remark. Esther Erikson's life had been many things, but colourless was never one of them.

"Did she have that little strawberry birth mark just below her waist?"

"Oh for goodness sake mother!" Snapped Ellie losing her patience again. Do you think she came lunging at me with a bloody great knife stark, pissing, naked?"

"Right that's it missy. I'm not having that. Don't you dare come in here, using your foul gutter-talk and flinging your promiscuous accusations around. I tell you if your dear Daddy was around he'd..."

Esther was slight and still had a reasonable figure despite her years. Now with legs elegantly crossed at the ankles she sat forward in her chair. She might, with a bit of change even be described as a still attractive woman but her hideously dyed and permed, pink wig flopped at the side of her head as she emphasised each word with a nod.

Her eyes, hooded with creased lids, had enough bright green eye shadow to cover an ocean liner. Pursed lips seemed to loom out of her face, in a barrage of crimson grease, despite the fact that her once supple upper lip had almost completely disappeared as age took the precious fullness from it. These days she applied a thick layer of the red lipstick up to the point where her lip used to be, only adding to the effect of a three-year old playing in mummy's bag. Now, as her under-padded bottom perched on the edge of her chair she had quite forgotten *what* Daddy would have said to Ellie, but as soon as she had decided Ellie was sure she would be ready to let fly.

"Mother. Just listen to me will you? Matty and I are in danger and you are terrified that your hallowed walls are about to come crumbling down on your head just because I said *piss*. We believe that you gave up a baby who was twinned with me. This woman, with a lifetime of bitterness and revenge, has come to find the family who abandoned her all those years ago. At the moment she is targeting me, but has it occurred to you *Mummy Dearest*, that the next name on her hit list might just be YOURS, the mother who didn't want her?"

Esther looked genuinely scared now. For once she wasn't flirting with Matt as she looked from Ellie to him and said in a tiny voice.

"Don't let anyone hurt me will you Matty. You know I'm no good without Eleanor's father here. I just can't do it on my own. Please don't let anyone hurt me."

Tears began to course down her cheeks, genuine tears borne from the loss of the man who looked after her, acted for her, and even thought for her, for over thirty years. Black mascara tracks left a ruined trench in the clotted make-up on her face. Ellie instantly forgave the fact that the woman considered only her plight in all of this and cared only, for her own skin.

Ellie went over to her mother and placed an arm round her bony shoulder. She felt Esther stiffen slightly, physical contact had always been uncomfortable between them.

"Mother, we will do everything we can to protect you, but for us to do that, you have to tell us the truth."

"I have told you the truth. I swear I have. There was you Ellie, only you. Jerry dear, I said after I had you, if you want another one of those baby things, you can hire yourself a breeding mare, I'm not putting on another two kilos for anyone. It was awful dear, I can strongly advise against you having children, nothing but a millstone round your neck."

Ellie winced at her mother's hurtful thoughtlessness.

"Thank you for that mother, I'll bear it in mind should the need arise."

Ellie and Matt looked at each other. The implications of Esther's statement whizzing through their minds.

"Esther." Matt spoke with the tone and authority that he would adopt towards a defendant in the courtroom, and Ellie couldn't help but smile.

"Are you quite sure you only gave birth to one daughter?"

"Matthew, darling, you are a man, and if I might say so, a very fine one at that. But you couldn't possibly have the slightest inkling of the pain, the mess, the humiliation. I can assure you that I am agonisingly aware of how many offspring I produced that day."

They discussed the ramifications of the problem for the next half-hour or so amidst more cups of insipidly weak tea, but it wasn't long before Ellie and her mother were fighting again.

"But why won't you buy the house next door dear, it would be so lovely. We could knock a door through the properties, and then we could do lots of lovely things together."

Ellie made not the slightest attempt to hide the look of revulsion that crossed her face at her mother's suggestion.

“Mother I can think of nothing worse than being at your beck and call all day every day. How would I ever write a word with you screeching for attention every minute? And anyway I already have a cantankerous elderly neighbour in residence and I don’t think he’d take kindly to me buying his house that isn’t even up for sale.”

Ellie realised she was being unnecessarily cruel and felt sorry as the hurt registered on her mother’s face.

“I’m sorry Mum, It just wouldn’t work, you know it wouldn’t.”

“But Ellie we could have a lovely time. I could take Jock out for lovely walks while you got lots of lovely writing done.”

“Jake Mother, his name’s Jake, and anyway you hate dogs, you’d have him sold off to the first tourist who stopped to stroke him.”

Matt looked at his watch and then with a rueful shake of his head, settled back into his chair until yet another mother-daughter war reached its usual conclusion of Ellie storming off in a huff and Esther slamming the front door pointedly behind them.

“You’ve never loved me.” ‘*Oh here came Esther’s old favourite,*’ thought Matt; it was never long before this one appeared.

“I gave up everything for you. I had a career that would have made me a star, but instead I gave all that up to look after you and your father. I gave my life up for you. And now, now that I’m not as young as I used to be, is it too much to expect a little of the love I lavished on you to be returned? I weep Eleanor, I weep into my pillow at night when I think of your ingratitude.”

“Oh here we go Mother.” retorted Ellie, echoing Matt’s thoughts.

“The ‘*I could have been a star*’ speech. Mother, you were a nude dancer in a seedy little club, your life was a sordid disgrace until dad found you contemplating suicide on the cliffs one night and pulled you from the gutter. The only stardom you came close to were the stars floating round the drunk’s heads as you rubbed your crotch into their faces. I never loved you? Well what about the love I deserved as a child, what about the love I craved, and yearned for, and needed. There was none of that was there Mum? No, because the whole world revolved round you. From the time when I was six years old, you always had to be the child, the delicate one, the one who needed looking after, needed attention. You were the one who dressed up in the evenings and gave ‘performances’ of your ‘talent’ singing and dancing in front of my father and his friends, always you mother. Whatever happened to *my* childhood?”

“Oh Eleanor, really, you always were jealous weren’t you? Such a jealous little girl. *Look at me daddy, look at me.* You used to say. You wanted to be just like me, but you never had the poise dear. You always tried to take your father away from me. But it didn’t work did it? It was me he loved. Always me. He used to watch me dance the ballet for him at our little soirees, and he was entranced.”

“Ladies please,” Began Matt, hoping to stem the inevitable before it got out of hand.

“Oh *do* be quiet Matthew.” Esther snapped.

“Yes shut up Matt this is between us and needs sorting out once and for all.” Said Ellie, perhaps agreeing with her mother for the first time in years.

“No Mother,” She continued. “He used to watch you lumbering round with a belly full of whisky in a ridiculous tutu and feel disgust and shame in front of his friends. Deep disgusting shame mother. Have you no idea of the misery you caused us, Daddy and I? Our whole lives were taken up with looking after you. Is it any wonder I broke away as soon as I could? Well never mind mother you have a new daughter now. And if she doesn’t murder you in your sleep, you and she can live happily ever after just as you would like. She can do your fetching and carrying. She can bow to your every whim. Just don’t leave any knives lying around the house mother, or you’ll find yourself wearing one sticking out of your head like a new fashion accessory.”

“Eleanor. How can you say those horrible things to me? Your father and I were devoted. Devoted, everybody says so.”

No Mummy, daddy was devoted to you. And you sucked him dry. He was tired, so very, very tired of it all, but still you whinged your pathetic demands upon him day after miserable day. And in the end Mother, I think his heart attack was a blessed means of escape.”

“Oh you wicked, evil girl. Get out. Get out of my house and don’t ever come back.”

“Oh really Ellie, that’s going too far.” Matt tried once again to have his say, but found himself ignored.

“Gladly mother. I can’t think of anything that’d please me more. But before I go, I have another little piece of news for you. Oh nothing as interesting as Yorkshire Street in Morecambe opening a new dress shop or anything like that, just the fact that I have a disease and I’m dying. When I go I’ll leave you to my evil twin as her inheritance. I’m sure you’ll both live in domestic bliss for many psychotic years together.”

Esther wasted no time in her retort. Not stopping for even a second to digest what her daughter had said.

“Lies, lies, lies. You are full of cheap attention stunts today aren’t you dear? People wanting to kill you, incurable diseases, Matthew darling, I think she needs to see a doctor.”

“She has been to several doctors Esther, and I’m afraid the diagnosis can’t be argued against. Your daughter is…” Matt’s voice was drowned out against the screaming females.

“I’ve seen my fill of them Mother. They all say the same thing, I have Tay-Sachs disease and it’s killing me.”

Still furious and not listening to a word Ellie had to say, Esther's parting shot was, "Well before you die off dear, close the door on your way out will you?"

And as Matt trailed after her still trying to make the women see reason, Ellie gave it a good resounding slam.

Chapter 10

Ellie fumed most of the way home, Esther always brought out the worst in her, and she ranted and cursed and cried a little bit too.

"Oh well," said Ellie, seemingly about to calm down either through loss of steam or lack of sufficient profanities in the English language. "Bugger her. I have enough on my plate to worry about without my mother's histrionics. I do have another theory though. What if I was conceived via invitro-fertilisation? That was very popular back then. If that was the case couldn't someone have stolen one of mother's embryos? They always harvest more than they need don't they? Damn I wish we'd thought to ask her about IVF back there, that could explain it couldn't it Matt? I'll ring to ask her when we get back."

In her temper Ellie hadn't even noticed Matt's silence, he had answered her when it became unavoidable and she couldn't be ignored because a direct question had been asked, but his answer had been an uncommitted monosyllabic grunt. In truth he had heard barely a word of what Ellie was saying to him. So lost in his own thoughts was he, that he noticed neither the fury of Ellie's storm nor the passage of miles. Matt was thinking hard and he didn't like what his reasoning was coming up with one little bit.

"I said, at least that solves the mystery Matt. Someone must have stolen one of the embryos and sold it on. Maybe Daddy was impotent and that's why they had to go down the route of IVF."

Matt's tone of voice was so deep and sinister in its timbre when he finally answered her that she was shocked into silence. It was so full of foreboding that she instantly became scared and the hairs on her forearm rose to dance to the tune of forthcoming danger.

"No Ellie."

"What do you mean *no Ellie?* Don't you believe mother's story?"

"Sadly I do, and that's the problem. Far from the mystery being solved it's only deepened and twisted further from all bloody logic and reason."

"I don't understand."

"Ellie we went to your mother's with a nice little egg box, and we took the pieces of information as they came about and slotted them neatly into position until the box was full and everything was explained. But Ellie, now the egg box lid won't shut, something is wrong and the information doesn't fit into its little slots all neat and tidy."

"What are you waffling on about? Explain."

"I'm trying to, just let me get the words out, I need to think."

She nodded her head; her eyes wide and filled with fear. Matt hadn't said anything to frighten her, but there was something in the numbness of his tone.

"Ellie, to produce an identical twin, having half DNA is not enough. To get two identical babies, they would need the necessary ingredients of both the same mother *and* father. Not only would they need the ovum from your mother, but also the sperm from your father."

"Well, maybe they stole some of that too."

" Okay, but I think we are getting into the realms of 'making things fit' again, you see sperm has a very short life once it's been cannoned into the big, wide world, so to speak."

"Yes but they had the eggs in one Petrie dish or whatever they use, and the sperm in a little test tube all ready. What's to stop them squirting some into one egg, that was later given back to my mother and one in to some other woman with a big, fat wallet?"

" Right. Now we get to the biggest mystery of all. Ellie," he continued, "I am neither geneticist, paediatrician, or midwife, but I think I'm correct in saying, that what you believe happened is impossible. Right, I'm not sure if this is correct, but I think it's near enough until I can check the facts. The moment of conception produces a single embryonic cell as a sperm embeds itself into the woman's ovum. That cell, I think it's called a 'stem cell', then begins to replicate itself. As the fission occurs at the first replication *that* is when an identical twin is produced. Then, and only then, you understand? Instead of the two new cells then dividing to become four, each of them begin to replicate independently, so producing two babies of the same cell. It's also at that point of first division that sometimes the cells don't divide properly and you end up with a con-joined pair of twins. So you see Ellie, even with your father's sperm and your mother's ovum, one of the other embryos could never be an identical twin to you. A twin yes, but not an identical match to you."

"Couldn't they separate the embryos at the point of fission when they separated into two babies instead of one?"

"No, Well I don't think so, I don't know, but why would they want to do that when they had a bowl of embryo's all ripe and ready that wouldn't involve an even more risky procedure? Don't forget, almost thirty years ago, IVF was still quite revolutionary. It wouldn't make any sense for them to split a forming twin sac when other eggs remained and would only be destroyed if the procedure was successful."

"True, but maybe the other woman isn't my identical twin, maybe she is from one of those other embryos and just looks like me. That can happen can't it? Look at my cousins Lesley and Patricia, they have two years separating them and still get mistaken for each other."

"Oh for god's sake Ellie." Matt's voice had risen in frustration.

"You've seen the woman, to all intents and purposes, she *is* you. She looks like you, walks like you, sounds like you, smells like you. Hell, her shadow even matches yours. This is no lookalike; she is the *perfect* double of you. Do you really think someone who bore a passing resemblance to you, could get close enough to me to almost bash my brains in? Bloody hell woman, have you forgotten all ready how convinced I was that it was you that day? Everything about her was the same as you, her manner, her essence, even the way she displaced the air around her. I was convinced beyond doubt that she was you. Ellie I would have made love to that woman believing she was you."

"Ellie screwed up her nose at his last remark, but this was too serious a time to come back at him with flippancy.

"So we come full circle to the original conclusion then. My mother's lying?"

Matt took a moment to consider this for the umpteenth time.

"No, I really don't think she is Ellie, I watched her closely, and your mother's just not that good an actress. I'm sorry Ellie love, but she's not that clever. Listen when we get in, I'll hit the net and do some digging round to see what I can find in parish records and such like. I'll check out all the information I can get on twinning too. Let's arm ourselves with as much knowledge as we can. And then we'll check out local fertility clinics and see what we can dig up there."

"Okay darling, but I'd still prefer to think of my mother as a scheming, conniving, two-faced, lying bitch."

This time she did manage a smile.

~*~

As Ellie walked Jake, played teas-maid, tidied up, and intermittently sat by his side adding her two pounds worth, Matt obtained birth certificates and parish record documentation concerning all children born to Esther and Jerry Erikson. There was no legal documentation that in any way indicated a second child born to the couple. He checked adoption records of the time. Closed files had been abandoned soon after the turn of the century and all adoption records were openly available in the public domain. Again he drew a complete blank. Several times he had to call Ellie in from the kitchen to identify herself in certain sites before documents could be obtained. This was done via retinal vein pattern recognition. She sat in front of the computer screen and a picture of her eyes was taken, this would then be matched up to her retinal print in the national hall of records. Via this method everybody could voyage the net feeling secure that they could not be impersonated.

The biggest piece of deflating information came from a news report dated March 2045. Apparently the Greendale fertility clinic in Keswick had been burned to the ground, Five people were killed in the fire and several others, including two firemen had been injured and needed hospital treatment. Further investigation informed Matt, that along with the Petrie dishes and turkey basters, all files and records had been destroyed when the clinic burned to the ground. The first thing that occurred to Matt was the coincidental fact that the burning of the clinic occurred within weeks of Esther's pregnancy.

Matt voiced his thought aloud; it was the first time he'd spoken since Ellie left the room earlier.

"Hmmm it all seems like too much of a coincidence."

He jumped slightly when the lilting voice of George broke the silence of the room. When she was writing, Ellie always turned the 'random chatter box' option off, so that George would only respond when spoken to directly, Matt had forgotten to do this. George had a database of several million words, phrases, and one liners to suit any occasion. While writing, if Ellie came up with anything she was particularly pleased with, she would often program that into the database too. When George spoke this time, it was a typical Ellie gem that came from the computer speakers.

"If it looks like a duck, and waddles like a duck, and quacks like a duck, it ain't gonna be wearing an elephant's tutu is it?"

"Eh?" said Matt momentarily confused.

"Matt dear," This was not only *Ellie speak*, but parroted in Ellie *tone*.

'If it appears to *be* too much of a coincidence, then it probably *is.*"

"Sometimes you are just too damned smart for a big hunk of plastic. Chatterbox off please George," said Matt, he was keen to get back to the job in hand *and* be able to give it his full concentration.

"I'm a hunk, a hunk of burning love." Said George as he flashed the screen twice just to be annoying and then turned himself to standby. The makers advertised these humanicons as the nearest thing to a human being - that isn't. The irritating jingle said, "It'll get under your skin and into your hair, it'll drive you insane but you won't care."

'Ain't that the truth,' thought Matt with a grin. Victor Khazana the inventor had become one of the world's ten richest men largely thanks to these computer programs.

~*~

The next few days passed quietly and without incident. Both Matt and Ellie were on their guard at all times. Ellie felt several times that she was being spied upon, but didn't mention it to Matt because she put it down to her paranoia playing hide and seek with her. Matt also felt that he was being watched he didn't say anything for exactly the same reason. Despite his heavy caseload, Matt continued with his investigations in between clients. He spoke on the phone to adoption agencies and fertility clinics; he met with council officials and doctors. And he tried every avenue that he could think of to gain information. It seemed everywhere he turned he drew a blank. The only option they had open to them now, was to wait for the next outburst of violence or mischief against them. They knew it was coming, and at least they could be ready. Surely soon she would slip up and give them a lead, otherwise ... Matt preferred not to think about *otherwise.*

Esther rang four times during the course of Sunday, the last time being at three thirty two in the morning. '*There was someone in the house.'* Not wanting to take any chances, they stayed on the line while Esther rang the police on her mobile. Sometime much later when the sun was risen and birds sang their morning songs; Matt and Ellie crawled gratefully back into bed. The police had searched the house and garden and found nothing out of the ordinary. Esther was on the phone again at twenty past eight. There was a strange noise coming from the kitchen. On investigation, it turned out to be the kettle switching itself off.

When Ellie asked Esther if she had been born as the result of IVF treatment there was a silence that lasted a half breath too long before her mother assured her that it wasn't the case.

"Don't be silly darling, I didn't even want to have a baby that much, and I can assure you your father had perfectly healthy sperm." Something in her mother's voice just didn't ring true and Ellie was left less than convinced but when she tried to question her mother further it only brought the usual arguments and she got nowhere fast.

The highlight of Monday was the fact that 'Let sleeping dogs lie' Ellie's latest book had made it onto the bestseller list. Rob phoned them early with the news. It was going to be a busy time for Rob and Ellie, once a book hit 'the list' a frenzy of publicity and PR began. Rob would be ringing magazines and talk shows to keep the momentum high. The book had gone straight in at number five; it was his job to see that it made the top-slot. Unfortunately four agents ahead of him and fifteen behind had exactly the same idea; it was a competitive game. Ellie would have a range of book signings and cocktail parties to attend. It would be an exciting 'however long it lasted', but also a tiring one. After the congratulatory phone call came to an end, Rob went off to begin splashing Ellie's name around the 'people in high places'.

~*~

Matt was just leaving for work on Wednesday morning when DCI Morgan called round with the results of the forensic evidence. Matt invited him in and explained that he was just about to leave. Morgan said that he would like Matt to hear what he had to say, and promised that he would only keep him a few moments.

Morgan refused a cup of coffee and said that he preferred to stand, his attitude was stiff and polite, but decidedly unfriendly.

"It took long enough to get the results Inspector." Began Ellie in an attempt to show that she wasn't about to be intimidated by his high handed attitude.

"Oh we've had them a couple of days Miss Erikson, but we wanted to take the opportunity to keep an eye on things for a little while before we got in touch. And *things* seem to have been quiet around here."

"By *things* inspector, I presume you mean that you wanted to keep an eye on us. Well yes, I'm very thankful to report, that apart from feeling as though we were being watched constantly, *things* have indeed been peaceful and quiet." Her voice was heavy with sarcasm, her chin upturned, her expression one of *challenge*.

Unabashed, Morgan decided it was time to get to the point, Matt looked discreetly at his watch every few seconds, and Morgan had a busy day lined up and wanted to move things along and close this case.

"Before we go any further, I'd just like to clarify one point from your earlier statement." He did the now familiar notebook-flipping thing.

"Ah yes, here we are. Are you quite sure that you never touched the knife at any time?"

"Quite sure Inspector."

"Okay. And can you perhaps remember if your…um, assailant, was wearing gloves or had any other form of covering over her hands?"

"No, she was not wearing gloves, her hands were free."

"It says here, quote; 'Everything happened so quickly, I turned round and she was standing behind me with a knife raised above my head. I panicked.' In those circumstances don't you think it might be possible that you wouldn't notice if she wore gloves or not?"

"Inspector, I'm sorry if this sounds pompous but, I'm a writer, a damned good one, and it is my job to observe, I notice things. I notice people. For instance I notice that you have changed your cologne since the last time we met and that this time you are wearing matching socks. And Inspector, I notice if knife-wielding murderers are wearing gloves or not. My attacker was not."

Morgan swallowed the urge to grin at this retort, he was flattered about her noticing his cologne and was embarrassed about his previous odd socks.

"And just so that I have this perfectly straight in my head. You did not touch the knife?" He knew he was pushing his luck with this astute and intelligent lady.

"Dammit Inspector, have I not told you time and again? I did not touch the bloody knife."

He knew she was lying, but despite himself, he had built up a grudging respect for this petite woman with the large attitude. She met him stare, for unwavering stare, and her grey eyes never gave an inch under his intimidating questioning. Morgan was about to close the case, and yet there were still loose ends sticking out of his neat solution. If there was one thing Morgan detested, it was a messy ending. '*Why would two independent witnesses who had nothing to gain by it, lie for her? For it was a certainty that they had. Why did she seem so bloody resolute and sure of her story? What was this woman's game?*'

"What if I told you I had evidence, that blew your story out of the water?"

"I would say that you were *lying* Inspector."

A shadow of doubt crossed her face, for the first time she was beginning to waver, but her chin rose to that defiant angle again none the less. She persistently demoted him to the lower rank of inspector, normally this would irritate him to hell, but he knew it was a deliberate attempt by her, to rattle his cage. She had been waiting for him to retaliate and Morgan had no intention of doing so. She was quick and bright and despite being under the line of fire she was holding her own remarkably well. Damn he liked this feisty woman. For possibly the first time in his career he was about to try and give someone an 'out'. His tone altered and he aimed for as much warmth as he could inflect into it. He didn't want to show Eleanor Erikson up to be a liar. It was important to him, for some God-only-knows reason that this lady's reputation should remain intact.

"Listen Ellie." It was the first time he had used her Christian name.

"By your own admission everything happened so quickly. Things become a little blurred round the edges sometimes when you are in a panic; you can forget little things that might seem unimportant at the time. Maybe when she dropped the knife you picked it up to give chase and then thought better of it and let it go again. That could be possible couldn't it?"

Ellie's tone was haughty as she replied without a moment's hesitation.

"I'm sure it could Inspector, but that wasn't the case. I am telling you once and for all. I never touched the knife."

Morgan sighed. He felt like a magician delivering the magic of a remarkable new illusion, but he derived no pleasure from what he was about to do. He took a piece of paper from the back of his notebook and unfolded it slowly.

"I have here the results of the forensic tests that we carried out. The knife showed several clearly defined finger prints."

Ellie and Matt both knew what was coming.

"All of them belonged to you."

"I never touched the knife"

Morgan asked them not to hesitate if anything untoward happened and they had need to call him, and then he bid them good day. As he walked away down the path, the statements of the two independent witnesses niggled at him like toothache. The evidence was clear, he had to close the case, but he didn't have to like it.

~*~

Rob phoned the next morning to say that arrangements had been made, and that Ellie, had a list of engagements pencilled in awaiting approval. The first of these was a party to be held at Killbriney Grange in Buckinghamshire for the following Monday evening. Lady Killburn, who, along with her husband, would be hosting the grand affair, was purportedly a huge fan of Ellie's. Several high-ranking members of the press and national media would attend and she would be shoulder to shoulder with quite a number of celebrities. It was to be a push the boat out charade, full of glitz and pretension. During the publicity for her first novel, Ellie had loved all the pomp and glamour involved in these impressive occasions. The food, the champagne, everything, was of the highest quality, and to find herself hob-nobbing with celebrities, made her dizzy with excitement. Now though, several books on, the insincerity and deceit had become wearing and the food and wine too rich. Now, these brash bashes were just one more element of 'work'. Of course it was still exciting to know that her book was doing so well, but the crystal chandeliers needed polishing.

Ellie was to be in London for a week initially and her time would be spent in a blur of interviews and functions, interspersed with daily signings at the larger bookstores.

Although he was expecting it, Matt was by no means happy about Ellie's imminent absence.

"Let me take the week off work and come with you. Expenses can run to an escort."

"Darling you have taken quite enough time off lately, you're needed here."

"What if you become ill, or that maniac shows up."

"Well if I have a funny turn there *are* hospitals in London too you know? And as to *her*, well I'm damned if I'm going to put my life and my career on hold on the off chance that she might show up in a blaze of mayhem and madness. And anyway Rob knows the score and will keep and eye on me, just think of the publicity if she did make an appearance, like that pompous git Morgan said, it wouldn't hurt my book sales would it?"

Ellie was being flippant and putting a brave face on things. In reality she did feel uneasy about leaving, she was worried about Matt. But this was the choice she made when she first put finger to keyboard and it was her duty to go. She was expected to attend these engagements being incessantly pleasant and shaking a lot of hands while smiling constantly. Writing the books was the easy bit of her job.

~*~

Saturday dawned and it was an anniversary of sorts. One whole week had sailed quietly passed without any sinister happenings. Although Ellie was to have a busy and tiring week ahead of her, she insisted that they have a good night out together before she left, they had all of the following day to be lazy and recover. Matt didn't want to go to 'Demons', he said it evoked too many memories of all the recent trouble, but Ellie was insistent. She was often fatigued and listless and they hadn't been out to a club for months. The times when she felt well and could summon up plenty of energy were becoming fewer and she had to grasp at these days and make the most of them. She was curious about the new club and wanted to give it a try since before the trouble started, but more than that, she felt that her double wanted her to go there. She knew that she was playing along, being led. As a writer she had a heightened sense of inquisitiveness that was an ingrained part of her psychological make-up, she was born to be curious. She had always been one to enquire into things, to want *to know*. Matt said that she was just plain nosey. Ellie instinctively knew that although things had been quiet for the last week, they were far from over. She didn't know a damned thing about the other woman, who she was, where she lived, why she was doing all of this, *but* she felt that she knew something about her *character*. There was no way her doppelganger was going to give up now. Some attackers may have backed off, been scared into defeat by such a near miss, seen it as a failure and dropped the idea altogether, but not this one, she wouldn't stop at anything. Ellie *felt* it. She may be lying low to re-fuel, but that's all she was doing.

That matchbook had been left in her lounge for two reasons. The first was *her* leaving a spoor, a mark that she'd been there, staked her territory. That she'd shown her prey that she could enter at will anytime she felt like it. But it was more than just that, it was also a taunt, an enticement, a blatant 'come and get me if you dare'. Ellie had no idea if anything would come of it, but she felt that she had to go to 'Demons' because she had been summoned and to not go, would be to admit cowardice and defeat. She had no idea when she was meant to be there, perhaps it was intended that she should go the night after the book had been left, but again instinct told her that the date didn't matter only that she rose to the bait. Ellie was all for rising, she wasn't dead yet.

Going through her wardrobe she tried several things on, she nearly decided on a pair of black trousers and glittery top, but in the end opted for the silver dress that she would have worn the week before if she hadn't almost been hacked to death in her own bedroom.

Matt wolf-whistled appreciatively, she looked stunning. He had a bad feeling about the evening, some instinct just as strong as Ellie's, told him that going to 'Demons' was a mistake, but he couldn't deny that he was looking forward to holding Ellie close and dancing with her. Ellie was probably right, a night of clubbing was long overdue and would do them both good. Apart from which, he knew this mood of Ellie's and the way she wore that defiant look when he protested, told him without her having to, that she would be likely to go with, or without him. Their life together for many reasons had become altogether too serious lately and they needed to let off a little steam. Ellie loved to dance and the look of sorrow in her eyes when she said that she would miss dancing, as she became more of a cripple had broken his heart. Tonight he just wanted to see his Ellie smile.

After depositing Jake in Matt's house at Barrow, they walked into town and wandered from pub to pub. They were both in excellent spirits and hadn't had such a good time in ages. Fielding told Ellie that if she wanted to drink more than a couple of glasses of wine, she could occasionally leave out two particularly aggressive tablets from her medication regime, for the first time she decided to give this a go. After several vodka and cokes she was feeling quite tipsy. They laughed a lot and enjoyed the sensation of holding hands and feeling all the love that used to be there but had been a little strained of late. Matt saw several men looking at Ellie and he felt overcome with pride and love for her. He was glad she'd persuaded him to come, they were having a fantastic time.

They arrived at 'Demons' a little after ten. The doormen barely glanced at Matt as they walked in, but they all smiled at Ellie.

"Hey," said a gorilla of a man with a laugh as he grabbed Ellie lightly by the arm. "No trouble from you tonight."

He let her go and they found themselves pushed forward from behind by the queue of people waiting to pay their entry fees. Ellie smiled at him weakly, and Matt just stared, but the opportunity to ask what he meant by that remark had passed and they were carried on a sea of people towards the stairs that led down into the basement club. The moment was lost to them, and they had to make do for now, with an exchanged look of confusion.

'Demons' was big on atmosphere. After leaving the brightly lit foyer it did feel as though you were walking into a demon's lair. The fact that the club itself was at basement level added to the impression of descending into a subterranean den. The décor was simple but garishly effective. Everything painted in red and black; the effect was sinister and exciting. A steady bass thumped up towards them and created the illusion that the music itself was pulling them further and further down, into whatever lay beyond. Matt squeezed Ellie's hand and she smiled up at him, loving every minute of it.

"Vodka and coke?" He asked.

"Hmmm yes please, love. Isn't this great?"

Just the look of happiness in her eyes was greatness enough for him. The club and all its glam faded into insignificance next to that. This was the first time for weeks that Ellie had seemed truly relaxed and happy.

It was the first time either of them had.

Matt ordered drinks and turned back towards her; just as a man dressed head to toe in black leather, walked past and grabbed Ellie's bottom hard. He took the whole of her left buttock into the palm of his large hand and squeezed. Ellie let out a shriek and turned round hand outstretched, palm upwards to hit the man, but he was gone. Lost in the sea of ever moving people.

"Hey." shouted Matt. He moved several steps in the direction the other bloke had taken but it was useless trying to give chase, he had melted into the people on the dance floor and all that could be seen was a mass of swaying torsos and flailing arms. He turned back to Ellie.

"Are you all right love?"

She managed a laugh, "Yes, fine thanks, cheeky bugger. Maybe he does that to all the girls." Ellie grinned cheekily at him.

"Huh well, if he tries it on with you again, he'll be sorry."

"Sshh he's not worth getting wound up about. Come on let's dance."

The music playing was a fast dance track heavy on bass and easy on synthesis. This was the new 'skull' beat, and although Matt had trouble co-ordinating his feet and his body, Ellie did great, and picked up the moves almost instantly. She was grinning like a loon, and flinging herself about all over the place and Matt felt a pang of worry as he knew she'd suffer for it over the next few days, and with the London trip looming, she'd be exhausted.

While they danced Ellie made eye contact with several people. They seemed to know her and nodded or raised their hands in acknowledgement. When Matt nodded a greeting, it seemed that they were weighing him up. One girl waved back with a look of uncertainty on her face but most of them just ignored him. The thing with the bouncer had been odd, but now it was clear that a large percentage of the people in this club thought that they knew Ellie.

This was proven all too clearly as they moved off the dance floor to find a seat.

Another man was making his way towards Ellie; he had a huge grin on his face.

"Eve. Evie honey. You look damned good."

Before she had a chance to stop him, and as Matt looked on with wide eyes, he grabbed Ellie and kissed her full on the mouth. Ellie pushed him off and he saw the look on Matt's face hardening.

"Hey man, check it. It's all right Eve and I are mates. So Evie you going to introduce me to your friend? Not your usual type at all is he? You going upmarket on me girl? Hey man, only joking, only joking. Any friend of Eve's and all that."

Ellie was still recovering from the stranger's rather full-on kiss; Matt was the first to get a handle on the situation. Realising that he must be mistaking Ellie for the other woman, he grabbed the man by the front of his shirt eagerly.

"Hey, hey you know her? You know the woman that looks like this?" He gestured towards Ellie.

Ellie jumped in on the conversation, her words coming fast, her breath harsh, this was the break they had been waiting for.

"I'm not who you think I am. I'm not this woman you call …Eve? Is that her name? Eve? Please, please, listen. This is important. You have to tell us everything you know about this woman. Who is she? Where does she live? Do you know where she lives?"

Ellie's voice had risen, partly to be heard over the loud music, but mainly through the exhilaration of finding this man. This man who knew Eve. Matt still had his hands on the man's shirt and Ellie gripped his forearm. The stranger took two steps back releasing their hold on him.

"Hey back off man." He raised his hands in a defensive 'don't touch me' attitude.

"Eve you want to slow down on those drugs my lady, they ain't doin` you no good." He started to walk away.

"Please don't go." Ellie screamed at his retreating back.

"Wait." Said Matt. But the man was already disappearing into the crowd shaking his head as he went.

They had attracted some glances in their direction. Sensing tension in the air a few people had stopped their dancing and talking, to watch the strange exchange. Matt used this as an opportunity. Meeting the curious stares of the people nearest to him he asked loudly.

"Does anyone here know this woman?" Ellie blushed but smiled at the blank faces in front of her.

One by one, all of the curious people turned away, Matt felt like a freak, he was impotent to do anything and was frustrated by the lack of response.

"Come on," Said Ellie, "Let's just mooch round a bit and see if anyone else says anything to us. But if they do for Christ sake let's just play it cool and not frighten them off." She began to laugh hard. "Oh Matty, you did sound freaky you know, like one of those old, street corner evangelists." She put on as deep a voice as she could manage and flung her arm out as she mocked Matt. "Does anyone know this woman, speak now or the fires of hell will burn around your soul for all of eternity." He put his arm around her and kissed her lightly to shut her up, but it wasn't the most romantic kiss ever as they were both laughing almost hysterically. So close, and yet all they had now, that they didn't have before was a name.

Eve. Ellie tried the name out in her mind. Suddenly the attacker had identity. It was a pretty name, not the sort of name you would associate with a crazed killer. It was sweet and earthy. Ellie wondered who had given it to her.

For the next half-hour they danced and mingled, although they felt eyes on their backs often, nobody spoke to them, and after scaring the last man off so brilliantly they were wary of making any approach themselves.

"I'm going to go to the ladies love. I need a wee anyway but not only that, you would not believe the conversations that unfold in ladies public toilets. When I come out we'll try the bar people and doormen. See if they can tell us anything."

"Okay, but don't be long or I'm coming in to get you, and then I'll be labelled as a pervert as well as an average common or garden weirdo." She smiled and moved off towards the toilets through the throng of tightly packed people.

~*~

She wasn't gone long. Matthew had only just sat down and got comfortable when she appeared beside the table.

"That was quick. Well?"

She looked confused, "Well what?"

"Duh, well did you enjoy urinating, did you find anything out about Eve silly?"

"Oh, er no. Tell you what I did find out though?"

"What's that then?"

"That I'm with *the* most fanciable bloke in the place."

"Oh really, and how did you deduce that Miss Holmes?"

"You would not *believe* what those horny women in there were saying about you. Made me want to take you home and show you how a real woman can handle you."

With that she leaned forward and kissed him. She wound her arms around his neck and when he tried to break the kiss she opened her mouth and ground her lips onto his softly and seductively. He pushed her off him gently.

"Hey 'Miss not in public' what's all this then. I think the vodka's gone right to your head. Come on woman show me some more of that fancy dancin' of yours."

He stood up and dragged her to her feet. Her body moulded into his side and he felt the warmth of her skin through the sheer material of the silver dress. Damn, if she didn't behave herself he would be walking onto the dance floor with an embarrassing prominence that he could do without.

"Hey, I've got a better idea, one I think you might just like Mister."

"What's that then?" He replied, enjoying her sultry voice.

"I've had enough of this place now, how's about we go home and do some dancing of our own."

“Oh yes and what about, having a word with the staff to see if they know anything about a certain crazy lady who wants to kill us.”

“Listen you. Either we go home this minute, or I’m going to start ripping clothes off, right here where we stand. Bugger the staff and everything else. I want to make love to you.”

“Lead on Lolita. A man can only resist for so long.”

As they left there was only one man on the door.

“Excuse me,” began Matt, but Ellie grabbed him by the arm and dragged him roughly into the stiff welcoming breeze of the late night street.

“Hey,” laughed the bouncer after them. “Be gentle with him Eve, don’t eat him all at once.”

Matt turned back, “Ellie, come on, let’s go and talk to him. Did you hear that? He knows Eve.”

She had already opened the door of one of the taxis lined up outside the club.

“Don’t worry Matt, he’ll still be there next time. Right now all I want to do is get home.”

Matt would much rather have stayed to question the doorman, but as usual, Ellie got her own way, he had little choice but to follow her into the back of the silver cab. It seemed that the alcohol had indeed hit her quite hard. She didn’t seem overly drunk but for her to become so abruptly disinterested in finding out about Eve it must have a lot to do with it. Usually when Ellie got something between her teeth she didn’t let go until she’d got to the bottom of it. *‘Still,’* thought Matt, *‘like she said there was always another time.’* It seemed Eve was a regular customer of ‘Demons’ nightclub.

In the taxi on the way back to Matt’s house Ellie was at her most beguiling. She teased Matt; kissing him softly, purring down his ear. He tried to tell her to behave herself until they got in the house and that the driver might hear or see something, but quite frankly she was exciting him to hell. He felt himself hardening by the second kiss and within seconds he was rock hard and ready for her.

“Saved by the bell.” whispered Matt, half-relived and half-devastated when his mobile phone began to ring ten minutes into the fifteen-minute drive. “Who the bloody hell could be ringing at this time of night?”

He reached into his jacket pocket for the phone, but Ellie pre-empted him and took it out of his hand. She smiled her sexiest smile, her eyes never leaving his for a second and she turned the phone off, and dropped it back into Matt’s pocket.

“Leave it,” she demanded as he went to reach for it, if only to see who had rung. “Whoever it is, they’ll ring back if it’s important, now Sir, I believe you were kissing me round about...here,” she whispered so softly in his ear that every hair along his forearms stood to attention. Whoever had been trying to get through to him was instantly forgotten.

Ellie's hand moved along his knee to his inner thigh. She stroked him gently, kissing the side of his neck, while poor Matt tried to keep his end of the weather conversation up with the driver. Her fingers were driving him crazy and when she ran her hand firmly over the front of his pants he almost let out a moan of pleasure. Thank God by this time they were nearly at the house. He placed Ellie's hand back on her own knee and searched in his pocket for money. Matt paid the driver and gave him a generous tip.

"Thanks mate, you have a good night now." The driver said with an exaggerated wink. Ellie thought it was hilarious that they hadn't fooled him for a second.

He was already moving away as he called out of his window. "See you mate, see you Eve, take care of yourselves."

Matt ran out in to the middle of the road, waving his arms and shouting for the driver to stop, but like most taxi drivers, once the fare has been paid, he was eager to be off to pick up the next punter, time being money.

"He knew her! He knew her too Ellie."

"Hey forget about it for tonight." she said slipping her arms round his neck and her tongue between his lips. "We've had a gut full of that woman and tonight I just want to enjoy my man. Lots of people know her. The net's closing in and we know how to locate her now. I'd say that was a good night's work, wouldn't you?" Ellie made sure that Matt was in no position to answer.

Once in the house Matt was eager to resume where things had left off only minutes ago. He pushed the taxi driver to the back of his mind. His erection had done nothing to diminish as he waited for the retinal prints to be established on the door pad. He remembered the last time they had fooled around with his back against a front door. And he wanted her so very, very much.

"Easy, Easy." She said as he kissed her hard on her mouth and neck. "Hey, hey, hey. Slow down I want this to be good. You fix us something nice to drink and put some good, soulful music on and I'll go and have a quick wash okay?"

Matt didn't want her to go and wash. She'd never come in and wanted to wash before. He wanted to make love to her with the smell of fresh perspiration about her body. He wanted to smell the club on her and taste the vodka she'd drunk, he wanted her just the way she was. But Ellie was already half way up the stairs. If that's how she wanted it to be, he could wait a few minutes. Matt went into the kitchen in search of a bottle of wine and a couple of glasses. But he was worried about the amount Ellie had already drunk, it wasn't a great deal, but with her illness he didn't want her to over do it and make herself sick. He was still deliberating over wine or coffee when he heard the bathroom door close and the bedroom door open. '*Well maybe he'd just take a bottle of cola, and join her up there,*' he thought.

~*~

She came out of the ladies toilets. Nobody had shown any interest in her while she was in there, despite her hanging round the mirror for longer than she normally would. She felt disappointed, but maybe the bar staff would be able to fill in a few blanks.

When she got back to the table, Matt was not there. The two drinks were still on the table, but Matt had gone. She sat and waited for a few minutes. Maybe he had also gone to the loo, and would be back soon. When he didn't return after a few minutes, Ellie started to panic. She searched the club looking for him. A deep sense of 'something' wrong was pounding in her head and it had nothing to do with an over abundance of Vodka. Everything seemed to be tightening in on her. The people felt tighter, the music deafening. No amount of 'excuse mes' seemed to be getting her anywhere very fast. The world had slowed down, and while she was walking in double four time, Matty could be in rapid-danger-time.

Finally she was up the steps and in the foyer. A fight had broken out between some men, and the doormen were in a huddle trying to keep them from doing each other damage. Ellie skirted neatly past them all and slipped through the door. Matt wasn't waiting for her out there. She didn't know what was wrong, but she knew that something wasn't right.

She reached in her bag for her mobile phone and rang Matt's number. *'Thank God,'* she thought, *'It's ringing.'* Three, four, five. Ellie counted the rings.

"Come on, Come on." she said aloud.

The phone cut off mid ring. A mechanised voice informed her that the person she was trying to contact is temporarily unavailable, but she could leave a message if she wished. Ellie knew that Matty would never switch his phone off. He was too responsible. The feeling of impending danger rose a couple of notches on the meter in her mind that instinctively warned of trouble. She jumped in the nearest taxi and gave them Matt's address. She begged the driver to hurry.

~*~

Jake was in an odd mood. He was snuffling at the interconnecting door and growling deep in his throat, a soft, low, grumble. He wouldn't leave the door and whined intermittently to be let out.

"Hey fella, come on now, you can't have her all to yourself, all the time you know. Come on; give a guy a break. We have some unfinished business to attend to and then you can come up and slobber all over my best bedding all night if you like, huh matey. Is that okay?" He put his hand down and stroked the dog's raised hackles. Jake raised his head for a second and licked the back of Matt's hand before dropping his nose once more to the bottom of the door.

"Come on get back out of the way now, you can come up soon I promise. Hey honey you all right up there? Coming up ready or not." Matt balanced two of his best champagne flutes and a bottle of cheap cola in his arms as he pushed Jake away from the door with his leg. It was no easy feat, Jake seemed determined to go and see his mistress.

As he drew level with the bottom of the stairs, he heard the front door click open. His mind did a double take, but there was only he and Ellie who had access to the door security, how the hell could anyone…

Ellie walked through the door and almost sobbed with relief when she saw Matt standing whole and healthy by the stairs.

Matt had been here before. The only difference was that this time Ellie was in the bedroom upstairs and needed protecting. He looked up towards the bedroom in a blind panic.

Ellie took in the scene; the two glasses, the bottle of pop, Matt in his stocking feet preparing to go up the stairs.

"Oh my God," she began.

Matt threw the first glass. In his panic his aim was high and it sailed above Ellie's head hitting the wall behind her with a tinkling crash. She moved rapidly to the side as the second glass hit her on the arm, it didn't break but fell to the floor to shatter in a thousand crystal shards.

"Matt, stop, you don't understand."

"Get away from me, you crazy bitch. Haven't you done enough damage? What do you want?" He was indecisive now, unsure of what to do next. Ellie took advantage of his pause.

She pushed past him and began taking the stairs two at a time. "It's me Matt, It's me love."

What convinced Matt, was the fact that Jake's manner had changed, the low growl had become excited yaps, he was scratching furiously at the door to get out. By the time Ellie reached the last step, Matt was only two stairs behind her.

The bathroom door was closed and Ellie flung it open as Matt ran to the bedroom door that already stood wide. "Be careful Ellie," he screamed at her as he burst through the bedroom door.

The bathroom was empty; the faint smell of Ellie's perfume permeated the air and the bathroom cabinet stood slightly ajar. A red lipstick had been used on the full-length mirror to scrawl the words *"Better the Devil you know"*

Everything had become silent. Matt hadn't said anything. Ellie was alerted to the sudden silence.

"Oh God," she murmured as she left the bathroom and ran full pelt into the bedroom. Matt was standing just inside the door, and Ellie rammed into his back almost knocking him over in her rush to 'save him'.

The window was standing wide open, the curtains blowing in the breeze. Eve had obviously made her escape from the window onto the garage roof, and from there down into the garden. She would have to be reasonably fit, but it wouldn't have been difficult, the drop from bedroom to garage was only about five feet and from garage to lawn only about eight. As long as she landed properly it would have been easy enough.

Further into the room two tall, black candles had been lit either side of the bed, their flames flickered slightly in the breeze but the window was far enough away not to be able to extinguish the little flames. Lying on the pillow was a black, silk rose, and a stuffed toy. The toy was similar to the 'snatch and grab' cuddlies in the machines at fairgrounds. It was a little red devil complete with horns and fork.

Matt's voice was quiet. "She had none of this stuff on her. She must have broken in earlier and laid them out. When she came in with me, all she had to do was light the candles."

"How did she get in Matt. Did you leave the door unlocked when you put Jake in?"

"No absolutely not, I checked it to make sure it was secure. The only people that could have got in were you and me. Nobody else is eye printed for my house, and there's no way Jake would have let her in the back, you should have heard him growling Ellie. I should have listened to him. I should have known. Oh God Ellie, why didn't I *know?"*

Matt sunk onto the bed and put his head in his hands as he remembered that woman's body all over his. He remembered her touch, her kiss, her fingers all over his dick for Christ sake.

"Oh God Ellie. Oh God." He moaned as he rocked backwards and forwards. I was going to make love to her."

Chapter 11

Things were progressing much as expected. The face searching the bathroom mirror for approval was not disappointed. Green eyes, spliced through with a core of psychotic intelligence, yet alive with excited joy stared back. The overall expression, was that of smugness, of being pleased with the day's work. Yes, it looked as though things were about to move up a notch or two. Time to sit back and watch the display of fire and ice explode in a volcano of flame and crystal spray. Such a lovely image to conjure, the cool of mercury to temper the heat of magma. One could feel the tension building, feel the emotions coming to the boil. The pawns were on the run, scared and scrambling for safety, yet still with a defiance admirable and demanded of a player in this game. If she had not been a worthy opponent of the black rook, then the white pawn would have been taken out at opening move. Desperate pawns were bound to take desperate measures, and events were becoming exciting.

The pawn was running scared, checking dark corners, jumping at shadows. But the rook, well the piece although performing pretty much as predicted was certainly playing a hard game. Cool one that, of course that was always apparent, cool on the top but with a gut full of bitterness and venom. The pawn would die soon; it was all coming to a head. The green eyes flashed and the cruel expression widened to a hard, cold smile. Yes, things were progressing nicely.

The eyes closed slowly, while The Creator enjoyed the mental images of pain and destruction. Hopefully the death of Eleanor Erikson wouldn't come too easily. It would be such a delight to be a part of her suffering.

Now all that was needed was to choose the perfect wine to accompany the grande finale.

Chapter 12

The goodbyes had all been said, the luggage packed right up to the roof of Rob's car, and Jake had been instructed to be a good boy and look after Matt. Jake liked the 'Good Boy' words, but Ellie was going away and leaving him, so he only managed a very small tail wag. Rob was driving down to London so that Ellie could rest, sleep had been a long time coming on the Saturday night and both Ellie and Matt had been nervous and jumpy since

Ellie slept solidly from the moment they left Ulverston until getting to Charnock Richards services on the M6. Rob had intended to stop for breakfast at Forton, but as Ellie was sleeping so soundly and snoring so sweet, he decided to leave her and carry on to the next services. By that time Ellie had a good couple of hours and Rob's stomach was growling in harmony with his passengers snores. He ordered food, while Ellie went to the ladies to freshen up a little bit. She hadn't felt hungry until she came back to the table and saw 'the works', full cooked breakfast, orange juice, a mountain of toast and fresh black coffee. She did the vastly overpriced, service station meal justice, and felt ready for anything afterwards.

The hotel was a five star dream. A bed that could accommodate a football team was only a minor feature of the 'suite'. In fact everything seemed to be of football team proportions. Ellie knew she would feel both decadent and horribly wasteful filling the enormous sunken bath just for herself. Every care had been taken to ensure that she enjoyed celebrity luxury. Expensive bathroom products overflowed a large wicker basket by the circular bath, champagne and fruit left on the dining table, chocolates by the bed, and fresh, exotic flowers in every corner. And yet the only luxury she yearned was to feel Matt's arms around her and Jake's wet nose begging attention. She missed them both already.

Rob had their itinerary mapped out in minute detail. First was a couple of hours rest, they had a long night ahead made worse by an early start in the morning. Then some light refreshment and a sandwich that they would take in her room, Rob's room being far less grand, leaving Ellie a couple of hours for a long hot bath and time to pamper herself in preparation for the party. A car was picking them up at nineteen hundred hours sharp. *'Oh the pretension,'* thought Ellie, *'what happened to good old seven o' clock?'*

She took her time getting ready, and was pleased with her efforts. If there was one thing Ellie detested, it was evening dress. Every woman the world round has some part of herself that she would like to improve on, for Ellie it was her height. She had a model's feature and figure, but a twelve-year-old's inches. She felt ridiculous in a full-length dress, she thought it looked as though someone had stolen her legs. But these occasions bore no respect for her stature and demanded that full evening dress be worn. Ellie's grumbles about her size were all born in her imagination, she looked good in whatever she chose to wear, and in some ways her petite size made her seem all the more elegant. The dress she had chosen for the evening could have been made with her in mind. It was simple, yet accentuated her figure to perfection. The colour had failed to stop at gold, but hadn't quite made it to bronze. The style was a shift that clung where it touched and floated where it didn't, and the hint of naughtiness lay in the cut away back that plunged almost to her bottom and showed off her gently tanned back. Ellie gave thanks that nature had been kind to her advancing years in the gravity department. Her underwear consisted of the most minimal thong she could acquire, and due to the clever and elegant design of the dress, it was not apparent from the front that she wore little underwear. The garment was classy without the merest hint of slut about it. Ellie felt good. Her legs were bare, her sun kissed colour the only coverage apart from the dress that they needed, and her shoes were elegantly cut stiletto heels, adding six precious inches to her height. Her almost shoulder length bob, had grown just enough to be put up. Ellie swept it off her face and neck and crafted it into a creation of random sophistication. Apart from one, final detail she was ready, all she had to do now was wait for Rob. Bang on cue there was a knock on the door.

"Come in if you're gorgeous." She called.

Rob walked in and gave a low wolf whistle as he shut the door behind him. Ellie twirled slowly to show Rob the full effect.

"Wow, you look fantastic. Poor Matt if only he could see you now. But you know something? There is definitely a vital element of that outfit missing."

"And what might that be?" She asked eyeing the black velvet box in his hand and knowing full well what was in it.

Rob opened the box and held it out towards her. Inside was a necklace encrusted with diamonds and amethysts. Rob took it out and motioned with his finger for her to turn round. He fastened the necklace at the back of her neck and it fell onto the front of her dress. The amethysts brought out the soft, grey of her eyes, and the diamonds sparkled in the light, Rob kissed the tip of her nose lightly.

"There, as your agent, and speaking purely on a professional level of course. You are going to be the loveliest thing in that room tonight. So wonderful, in fact, that were I not very happily married to my devastatingly beautiful wife, I'd give you one myself."

Used to Rob's banter, and knowing full well that he was only joking, Ellie, laughing, pushed him hard in the shoulder. She made a show of eyeing him up and down, lingering way too long on his crotch area; the tux did wonderful things for the man's generous physique.

"Well you don't look so bad yourself you know." She said getting her own back by moistening her lips and nodding suggestively towards his fly."

"Hussy," he retorted. "My wife warned me about girls like you. Now just remember that little trinket is on hire, for God's sake don't lose it."

Rob had been nagging her since her first book did well to buy some 'decent' jewellery, but diamonds and jewels weren't Ellie's style so they continued to hire her finery when the need arose.

"Come on Cinderella, we've got a party to go to." Said Rob offering his elbow and escorting her out of the suite.

The white chauffeur driven limousine took them through the city of London and then out into the open countryside of Buckinghamshire. It was a lovely drive and both of them enjoyed it. Ellie called home, using the impressive facilities built into the flash car. And was assured that everything was fine and that although Matt and Jake were missing her something terrible and were likely to wither from broken hearts if she didn't hurry home, they were actually coping quite well. Matt joked that he had mastered both the can opener and the microwave to produce at great extravagance a tin of soup. Ellie felt a pang of guilt as she thought of the fare that would be laid on for them that night. Matt laughed knowing he'd tickled her guilt button expertly, before admitting that he and Jake had eaten cordon-bleu pizza from the local take-away and had thoroughly enjoyed it.

Rob phoned Gail, and, after failing miserably to describe his client's dress in enough detail, ended up passing the phone over to Ellie. As the rolling fields sped past the two women giggled like a pair of teenagers. Ellie was happy. Perhaps this working holiday was just what she needed.

They joked along with the chauffeur, who turned out to be from Skipton in North Yorkshire, Ellie managed to worm the truth out of him about his clipped accent. Geoff finally, with much coaxing, admitted that he had practised for six weeks with a tape recorder to perfect the upper class accent and get the job. Far from being snooty he was fun and had a wonderful sense of humour.

Geoff indicated to turn left, and they drove through an enormous pair of open gates. The drive seemed to go on for miles, apparently, according to Geoff's philosophy, the richer you are, the longer your drive is. Even the way the gravel crunched beneath the tyres felt posh. They rounded the final bend and the house came into view before them.

"Reet lass," said Geoff who, just to please Ellie, had lapsed into his 'own' voice some minutes earlier "That theer is Killbriney Grange. Now, tha'll have to watch thee pees n cues in theer, or the old lass will have thee on tha hands and knees cleaning the kahzies out."

Ellie giggled delighted.

"Well divn't thee be worryin' lad, I'm telling thee now, I pee just the same colour pee as that lot in theer, and what's more, I can talk just the same amount of bullshite."

Geoff made a valiant effort to straighten his face as they drew up outside the great house. A man in starched uniform rushed forward to open the door for Ellie and she stepped out gracefully. Then she leaned back into the stretch limmo and said in her most refined accent. "Thank you taxi, I'll ring you about picking me up for the bingo next week."

The marble steps leading to the great entrance of Killbriney Grange were littered with strutting peacocks, not yet gone to roost.

They had expected it to be quiet when they arrived but in fact the party was already in full swing. The low hum of elegant conversation rose from several small groups of people stationed equally around the floor of the vast ballroom. The evening was warm for the time of year so they had no coats to give to the attendant who stepped forward to assist them. Another man in coat tails coughed politely beside them.

"If you would care to give me your names, Sir, Madam, I'll announce you now."

The master of ceremonies stepped up to a small dais and hammered twice to get everybody's attention. The conversation stopped instantly and everybody turned to welcome the latest guests.

" Ladies and Gentlemen, may I introduce to you this evening, Miss Eleanor Erikson and Mister Robert Price."

There were polite smiles all round and a couple of the people standing closest to them nodded their heads in acknowledgement.

A large lady in a black dress with plunging neckline walked towards them with arms outstretched. She took both of Ellie's hands in hers.

"Miss Erikson, oh how lovely it is to meet you. I've been so looking forward to it. I'm Cynthia Killburn dear; my husband is over there somewhere talking high finance to anyone who will listen to him. We'll but in, in a minutes and make him play host."

Ellie instantly liked the lady, despite the accent she didn't appear to be too 'up herself' at all, and Ellie saw instantly that her smile reached all the way up to her eyes and she seemed genuinely interested in meeting her. After Cynthia Killburn said a polite hello to Rob and shook his hand briefly, Ellie found her arm being linked with Lady Killburn's and she was whisked away to be introduced to a seemingly endless throng of people.

Rob was left in a wake of swishing dresses and clipping heels. He was used to being ignored at these functions it was the way they worked. In the early days Ellie had been so sweet, trying desperately to have him brought into any conversation she was a part of. Rob had to take her to one side on more than one occasion and explain to her that it didn't work like that. She looked crestfallen when he explained to her that she was a peacock, at these functions her role was to sell herself to the people. She had to be bright and vivacious, get herself noticed so that she would be remembered. It was all about splashing her name and her face around the people that mattered. Rob knew his role and he instantly recognised others in his place. Some of the other agents and managers of course he knew, he had dealings with them in the past, some were acquaintances and passed business between each other if a particular client wouldn't be suitable for one but slotted in well with another. But mainly they just had 'the look'. Rob would soon be in conversation with them, playing his part of the game. Selling his product. And although Ellie was there to impress the wallets and contracts, if any of them wanted to sign her for anything, it was Rob they would talk to. This had also driven Ellie insane at first. "Do I not have a brain? Am I not capable of knowing if I'm available to open a bloody charity gala on the fifteenth of next month? What the hell am I?" she had ranted at Rob. "A bloody Barbie doll with plastic for tonsils?"

As much as she hadn't liked it Ellie had learned the rules. She did her job sublimely and left Rob to do his. But although they may only meet for the odd few minuets here and there throughout the course of the evening, Rob would be keeping a watchful eye on her at all times. Looking for a sign that she needed rescuing from some amorous, drunken letch, or from the party bore. That was also his job but on this particular PR week, Rob would be keeping an extra close eye on Eleanor, partly because of all the trouble she had experienced, but also because of her illness. She seemed very relaxed and happy so far, and was enjoying herself, but it didn't stop him worrying about her, and he'd promised Matt that he would look after her.

"Ladies and Gentlemen," announced the Master of Ceremonies. "May I give you Mr…" The M.C. coughed uncomfortably, "Smartassed Jack and Miss Clarissa Croft."

Ellie looked dutifully towards the entrance. Smartassed Jack was a pop-star who had almost had his day, he was with the latest in a long line of models, whom he serially married and then dragged through the courts a couple of years later in an attempt to keep as much of his vast wealth as possible intact.He looked ridiculous in what could best be described as a black lace tuxedo. The garment was see-through and his most private of possessions were protected by a black garment similar to the underclothing Ellie herself wore.

Clarissa who could never be classed as a shrinking violet paled into insignificance in her flesh revealing white toga style evening dress. They made quite an entrance. Smartass, made a show of turning his head to listen to the classical music playing discreetly as a backdrop to conversation, and then began 'doing the monkey' across the floor. The monkey was last years 'thing' in the clubs. The whole youth culture had been centred round the jungle, clubbers talked jungle, danced jungle. Clothes reflected jungle, and a new range of tropical drinks had been launched to jump on the back of the craze. Nothing that hadn't been done before, but like most fads it was deemed worthy of another trot round the floor thirty years later.

"Ladies and Gentlemen. Mr Victor Khazana." He needed no other introduction, but typically of the shy Mr Khazana he seemed wary of any publicity or attention. He gave a curt nod to the room and drifted to the left as a hand shot out towards him with a cry of; "Victor Daaahling, come and tell me all your delicious news." Their hostess broke away from greeting the previous guests and moved over to welcome Mr Khazana.

Ellie was always glad to see Victor, he was such a kind gentleman. The son of a computer programmer he had come up from modest means and built his own empire. Khazana had become a household name over the last fifteen years. His early career had been in medicine. Born in Poland at the turn of the century he went into general medicine. Poland was still a mildly depressed country having never recovered from the Second World War. He had specialised in genetics and then something had gone terribly wrong. Through sheer hard work and determination he became one of the most respected men in his field world-wide. And in 2008, while still a young man, his research and endless nights of working through until dawn, paid off. He invented a drug that the world had been waiting for. The drug sailed through the trials; certain corners were cut to get it into the public domain as quickly as possible. He was assured that it was done all the time.

The day it went on sale women were queuing at health clinics across Poland hoping to be eligible for the treatment. But very quickly it all went very, very wrong for Victor and his patients. The scandal was kept as quiet as possible. The drug had not been released for sale outside Eastern Europe and so for the rest of the world it was small news. Some guy had invented another bad drug; it was like the Thalidomide disaster but this time the Ruskies got it. So what? Victor Khazana shamed in his own country moved to California and began working, as his father had done, in computers, only Victor was not a designer as his father had been, he got a lowly job in a factory working the conveyor belt on computer production.It was quite a story and Ellie admired his tenacity. Many men, guilt ridden and shamed would have taken their lot and lived with it, but Victor always lived with a dream of making life better for the people of his own country, the people he had hurt so terribly. Like his father he worked his way up into programming. And then he got to thinking about what the world really needed. He couldn't go into anything controversial. Medicine was a closed door for him professionally, but he had always been very interested in Psychology, as a young man it had been one of his majors. He thought about a revolutionary game. A game that everyone would want to play at least once in their lives. At night after working a twelve-hour shift at the factory he would, settle himself in his dingy apartment some miles from the famed Californian sea-views and he would work long into the night on his idea. In the early hours of one winter's morning the game of 'Psyche' was born.

Victor patented his idea, quit his job and set about the task of selling his product. At first he was laughed at. It was ridiculous, preposterous, board games had long had their day. He followed toy fairs and exhibitions, everybody ridiculed his idea. It was six months before he could persuade someone to at least sit and play the game and then they would see that it was so much more than just a board game. He was hungry and thin, if his rent arrears weren't paid he was going to be put out on the street. His landlord had been a patient man, but now he was money hungry.

At last someone took his idea seriously. One year later and he had a mansion and six cars. Five years later he had boosted the economy of his native Poland by several billion Euro and Khazana was made. From there he began working on several small computer programs. Psychology based games and teaching aids. Some years later he had an idea, just a little idea, to build an integrated program that would fit any computer. He had in mind the idea of inventing a sort of computer butler. A program that would sit in the background until needed and then prove to be invaluable. The 'Humanicon' was born. A program that five years later, no computer could function properly without and he became one of the richest men in the world.

Ellie liked Victor immensely but more than that she was very grateful to him. The man as an entrepreneur was always being asked to sponsor this venture or that. He never forgot his time in the factory or the months when nobody would take him seriously. If someone needed money to go into business, as long as they were hungry to succeed Victor would generally sponsor them, he was after all a businessman, he wanted his money to succeed so he would take an interest in the business and if it needed his name he would lend it to the owner until they could stand on their own two feet. He would then take his money out plus his cut and let the venture fly free.

That was how he'd come to be part of Steppingstone Journey Publications, the publishing house that finally gave Ellie her big break. He had taken a small but personal interest in Ellie's work, he saw in her someone like himself, someone who wanted to succeed. And they had become friends.

"Eleanor my darling, how are you?" Victor held her hands in his and kissed her warmly on both cheeks.

"Victor it's good to see you. I'm fine thank you." Ellie lied about her health, as she had become accustomed to doing. "How are you?"

"Oh I'm the same as always but a little bit worse." He joked. "Congratulations on yet another success my dear. I am very proud of you, you know?"

Ellie laughed she so admired and liked this big gentleman.

"Victor I wonder if you can help me, I'm doing some research. Do you know anything about Tay-Sachs disease?"

"Shop talk at this delightful soiree? Darling don't you ever come off duty?"

"Oh Victor I'm so sorry have I offended you?" Ellie was genuinely ashamed for having asked. Of course the last thing Victor wanted to do was talk about business. For Ellie the whole point of evenings like this was to conduct business but Victor was a made man and could talk about whatever he damn well chose.

He laughed heartily. "Sweetie I was teasing you, anyone else wanting to pick my brains at this time of night would bore me rigid, but you, my love, could talk about horse manure and I'd be hanging on your every word. Now then Tay-Sachs, yes I know a little about it, not a lot you understand it was never my field. What exactly did you want to know?"

"Well anything you can tell me about it really. Not tonight obviously as you so rightly point out, tonight is for laughter and merriment and getting sloshed, work and other boring stuff can be done when the stars aren't shining so brightly. Could we get together perhaps sometime soon?"

"Eleanor, I can think of no treat sweeter my love but unfortunately this month's out. Are you in any hurry? I've got seminars and boring business stuff to attend to for the next few weeks and then I'm flying out to The States for a conference that can't be delayed. I could e-mail whatever I can find to you in the meantime and then we'll get together for lunch when I get back.

Ellie almost didn't catch the arrangements. She was still trying not to laugh at the sentence. "Are you in a hurry?" Oh the sweet irony. It was only when Victor repeated her name that she came back to the present and she agreed to his suggestion.

"Khazana old man, here you can settle this argument. You don't mind do you my dear?" A man with a tuxedo screaming for mercy around his huge frame dragged Victor away, to argue about whatever it was men-of-a-certain-age argue about. And before Ellie knew it another cheek was proffered for the obligatory air-kiss and a woman with too much make-up and an insincere smile had cornered her.

Ellie was starving by the time the food was served. It was an elegant buffet that would feed a third world country for six months. The fare was rich everything of the highest standard, fresh caught, killed or sliced that morning.

And after eating there was plenty of opportunity to work off the calories when the dancing began. Ellie danced with many men, not least of whom was Smartassed Jack, much to his girlfriend's displeasure. Despite being larger than life, he was a very good dancer and Ellie enjoyed herself.

She was more than ready for home though by the time Rob tapped her on the shoulder.

"Excuse me Miss, don't I know you from somewhere?"

Ellie laughed and gave him a hug.

"Oh I don't think you missed me too much I saw you dancing with that Lady No drawers over there."

Rob grinned sheepishly. "Come on you Geoff's brought the car round and is waiting outside. Finish your goodbyes and let's get outta here."

Ellie pouted.

"Oh you're just a rotten old party pooper."

"Yes madam, and you just remember that when I'm banging on your door at six o'clock in the morning. Sleeping beauty will *not* want to get up after a bellyful of champagne, very little sleep and with a banging hangover and a case of alcohol induced vertigo, will she now?"

"Damn I hate you when you talk sense at me."

As much as Ellie's mind wanted to play, her body had indeed had enough. She sank into bed and was asleep within minutes.

Chapter 13

Ellie didn't realise just how bitter it was in a television studio at seven am on a chilly and frosty morning. She had to pat her arms to keep warm. Later when the lights-camera-action brigade got to work the place would be like a sauna, with huge overhead fans cutting in to stop the make-up turning to rivers on the show host's face-of-many-valleys. Ellie could see her breath in the air and her fingers felt stiff and uncooperative.

Surprisingly she had been up and at 'em with remarkable energy. She rose at six as Rob knocked on her door, not ten past or half past when Geoff would be waiting outside and Rob would be having a minor nervous breakdown worrying about being at the studio on time. Since getting away from her problems at home, or as she honed the thought down further, since putting distance between herself and Eve, she had a new feeling of joie de vivre. When the rolling hills of Cumbria had dissolved into the autumnal mist, and the M6 had been a heralding highway to take her a long way from Eve, she had been far more at peace. As each hour passed in London, so a little bit more of her eased up and let go of the tension. Oh, Mr Tay-Knacker-Sachs was still chewing away at her relentlessly, but the tension that had eaten into her bones was all but lifted. She still worried about Matt back at home but he was on his guard more than ever now. He had been badly upset by how much Eve had managed to fool him the previous Saturday and so they had devised a password to identify Ellie from Eve.

Ellie spent over an hour in make-up and came out with the same result that she could have achieved on her own in ten minutes, but then, that was show business. The expected hangover had not kicked in, Rob had insisted on a night-cap of fresh orange juice before she went to bed. She looked good and she felt confident. She had opted to wear a pair of camel coloured trousers, they were simple with a timeless cut and comfortable style. She wore black leather boots with an elegant heel, and a black roll-neck tunic set off by a thin gold chain belt. They had wanted to do 'something elegant' with her hair but Ellie insisted that she'd be more comfortable with it down and just brushed through well. The stylist came at her with serums and gels and various deposits of gunge in bright and gunky colours. Ellie declined and the poor man who *'had never heard the like'* moaned about his reputation being at stake *'oh the shame of letting her go on like that.'* In the end Ellie got her own way and the pouting man brushed her hair, that held no 'product' other than simple shampoo, he brushed it hard, until it shone under the harsh lights like golden filigree.

Talk shows had all but died out years earlier. They had their day and were tired and done, but recently a new husband and wife team had forced their way through to the limelight, and they had resurrected morning television talk shows. The 'Ben & Jerri' show followed the old format but was new and alive. This was Ellie's second appearance and the last time had been a riot, she had enjoyed their banter very much.

Ten minutes before she was due to go on, a fluttering of butterflies descended on her stomach. Rob had handed her a cup of coffee, but her fingers had left home. All sensation finished at the end of Ellie's wrists. Every nerve-end of feeling left her fingers, she had no control over them and no grip. The cup of coffee slipped right through her hand and splashed to the floor. Luckily, or not as the case may be for Rob, the coffee missed Ellie completely. Rob was thankful that he had been standing like a tit with two disposable coffee cups in his hands for ten minutes while the sound engineer fiffed and faffed round her. He was not hurt, but had he been any closer he might have been. He was though very soggy and Elllie told him he smelled all moist and exotically Brazilian.

The incident had knocked her confidence slightly and instead of doing a walk on, it was decided that the interview would begin from a sitting position. Rob would never have mentioned it to Ellie but the coffee incident and the fact that she had been seen by one of the runners, staggering into a wall on the way to make-up, sent a whisper round the studio that Miss Erikson had come in 'pissed'. Apparently she'd told Rob in the dressing room later that her medication was slow kicking in. She didn't normally start the day with so much activity and her meds could normally take their time, put their feet up for a while, read the morning paper, slip into the days work gently. Rob had almost insisted in calling the interview off but of course Ellie wouldn't hear of it and insisted she was perfectly all right.

"And now dear viewers, we are very excited, aren't we Jerri? Very excited indeed?"

"Well you are Darling, but don't worry just keep it covered with your hand and there'll be no litigation."

The camera crew tittered on mic obligingly.

"As I was saying, before my lovely fishwife butted in, we are very happy to be able to welcome back the best-selling novelist Miss Eleanor Erikson."

Jerri rose first and kissed Ellie on the cheek and then Ben followed suit. As scripted, Ben held the kiss too long, and then pushed Ellie back on the settee as he scrambled on top of her.

"Hose pipe." Yelled Jerri and a member of the crew rushed onto the set wearing a helmet and carrying an enormous fireman's hose.

Ben made a show of pulling a white handkerchief out of his pocket and waving it as a sign of surrender.

"Now sit down and shut up." Growled his wife.

"Yes," said Ellie playing along. "Sit down and behave or my sexy friend in uniform over there will see that you get it. Sucker."

The frivolities were over for the time being and Ben sat down to begin the interview proper.

"It's good to see you again Ellie and congratulations are in order. We hear you've done it again, made the best seller list that is. What's this third time? Fourth?"

"Third, and yes I'm very pleased. Thank-you."

"So how's life all the way up in the beautiful Lake District? What has been happening since last time you paid us a visit?"

The interview rambled along following the time worn tramlines. Ellie smiled politely and said that she would rather not comment on her love life and no, she would neither confirm nor deny that she was 'getting plenty'.

"But you are still with the same bloke as last time?" persisted Jerri.

Ellie laughed knowing that Matt would be taping the show to watch when he finished work that evening. "Yes I *am* with the same bloke and yes we *are* very happy. Now next subject please."

Uncharacteristically, Ben's face took on a sombre expression that for once didn't seem to be part of his comedy routine.

"Ellie, I know this may be difficult for you to talk about but you've had a nasty shock lately haven't you?"

Ellie stiffened. *'Oh God what did he know?'*

"Some health issues?"

Ellie glared over towards Rob who was standing watching the interview off set. He spread his hands and shrugged, miming that he had no idea how this had come about. Then he turned towards the research manager to find out where he had got his information.

Ellie's eyes were hard as she faced her interviewers. These people who two minutes before had felt like friends, now seemed to be prying scavengers, determined to prize out of her anything personal and intimate, anything that was private and belonged to her alone. Once again Ellie was reminded of the fact that *she* belonged to the public and was owned by the readers who paid for her book.

"Now then," she said. "Who's been filling your head full of rubbish?" She smiled widely for the camera but her eyes were like steel. They bore into her interviewer's face as though challenging him to continue with this line of questioning. "And anyway Benny, where did you get that tie? I hope you're going to sue."

Jerri, took over the role of interrogator. She smiled a sickening smile that was supposed to ooze feminine empathy. A smile that said *wherever you are today, I have been and I understand what you are going through, because I'm a woman too.'*

'Bullshit.' thought Ellie.

"Sweetie." She began in a voice seeping syrupy insincere words like puss from an abscess.

"One of our researchers was passing your dressing room and heard you and your agent talking about some illness you have. It sounded pretty serious. It might help if you talk about it you know. We are good listeners."

Ellie felt the old familiar temper rising. '*Good listeners? Help to talk? What to all three million and fifty seven of you?'* God how could she have liked this woman? She wore imitation sincerity as though it were a sable mink. Ellie had to swallow hard to send her temper back down.

"Yes I have some 'health issues' as you put it. I have a rare disease called Tay-Sachs. Some days are good, some days are bad, sometimes I drop things and I get tired easily. That's all there is to say about it really. Thank you for your concern." Ellie couldn't resist trying a sickly smile to put one of Jerri's to shame. Her voice was so heavy with sarcasm that she could barely lift it to say, "You're right it did help talking to you. I feel so much better now."

The effort was not wasted on a fuming Jerri. These two were renowned for making fools of their guests if they could get away with it but in typical celebrity fashion, weren't so keen if the tables were turned on them. Jerri bristled visibly and her face hardened into a tight knot that gave away the secret of every one of her fifty two and a half years and Ben was heard to mutter 'touché.' Whether the sensitive mic was meant to pick it up or not was known only to him, but the muttering and the smug grin that he flashed his wife, went out to several million viewers. Jerri glared at her husband. This was what made them so successful. Sometimes they bickered lightly between themselves and their guests but on a good day genuine, full-scale war broke out between the volatile couple and that was the stuff television was made of.

" Wanker!" retorted Jerri and the studio went into frenzy.

The producer yelled obscenities at Jerri down her earpiece and the camera crew cut to filming a blue glassed vase of flowers to deny the viewers coverage of the warring couple and the guest who despite her best efforts was smirking in amusement.

"Well, I think it's time to go to the phone-in." Said Jerri in a tight voice as she read the prompt.

"But, just before we do, I would like to apologise to the listeners for my unforgivable behaviour." She paused and then added, "again."

Ben turned to her, he wasn't about to lose this opportunity to wind her up.

With a grin he asked. “Sweetness what about me? Do I get an apology too, oh light of my life?”

Jerri wasn’t about to forgive him for appearing to side with Ellie over her. She was every inch the prima donna and an almost insanely jealous wife.

“Well you know what you can do don’t you? You can just f…”

The producer yelled so hard in her ear that her head jerked involuntarily to the side and she caught herself just in time.

“You.” She spat the word at him, “can just forgive me too. Dear.” she finished sweetly before launching into the phone-in.

“And on line one we have Michelle from Oxford. Good morning Michelle, do you have a question for Eleanor?”

Ellie noticed the fact that the more informal ‘Ellie’ had been dropped in favour of her Sunday name. She smiled, warm in the sensation of her victory. “Hello Michelle.” she said brightly.

“Hello Miss Erikson, I’m a big fan of yours.”

“Thank you Michelle, please call me Ellie. What do you want to know?” Ellie had made a good recovery and was back in control, she was now leading the interview and was ready for any trick that was thrown at her. They’d caught her off guard once but there was no way they’d get her a second time. She was enjoying herself again. This is what she liked about the PR game most, talking to people who loved reading her work. She enjoyed talking to her genuine, ordinary readers.

“I do a little bit of writing. I’m only just starting you understand, so I’m not very good. I’m writing my first novel and wondered if you could give me any tips about getting published.”

Ellie heard the hunger in the young girl’s voice. She knew how that felt. Being so convinced of your own talent, knowing that you can do it but needing that first small break to get you on the ladder. Of course Ellie, had no idea if this girl was any good or not but somewhere beneath the nerves of being on television, she could hear determination in her voice.

“Well the first thing you do is get your manuscript as good as it can possibly be. Go over it again and again and again. Then when you think it’s perfect give it another read through because no matter how good it is, it can always be better. A publisher or agent will not waste time on shoddy work. The next step is determination. If you believe in yourself don’t, even for one second, let anyone tell you that you can’t make it. Send your script out as many times as it takes to get it accepted. If you are going to roll over and die with the first rejection slip, you will never be a writer. I tell you Michelle, I have got a box full of ‘jeccy slips’ big enough to wallpaper Buckingham Palace. That’s the best advice I can give. Just believe in yourself and don’t give up.”

“That’s good advice, thank you. I’ll remember it when things get tough.

Thank you Ellie."

"Tell you what Michelle," Ellie flashed a look at Rob, she knew he wasn't going to like this. "Have you got a synopsis and the first three chapters done?"

Rob knew what was coming, he stood just off camera shaking his head wildly and making 'cut' motions by dragging his hand across his throat. Sometimes that woman was too much.

"Er, I haven't got a synopsis done yet but I have fifteen complete chapters." Michelle's voice had risen with excitement. Ellie purposefully ignored Rob.

"Right you put together a synopsis and send it off to me with the first three chapters, the researchers will give you an address if you stay online. Mark the envelope 'Ben and Jerri's Michelle, then I'll know it's from you. I'll have a look at it for you and I'll get my agent to read it too. No promises that you'll get anything more than a three chapter edit and some advice that you may or may not want to hear, but if it helps, we'd be happy to have a read of it."

"Oh Ellie would you. I can't believe this." Her voice had risen to a screech and Ellie grinned genuinely pleased to have made her so happy. "That is so good of you. Thank you so much."

Ben cut in. "There you go, Michelle what do you think of that eh?" without waiting for an answer he pushed on. "Well we have got Jennifer on line two. Good morning Jennifer and what would *you* like to ask Ellie?"

"Hello Ellie. I'd like to know where you get your inspiration from?" There was no preamble with this one, she sounded cool and got straight to the point.

"Hello Jennifer. Oh that's easy. I get inspiration from everywhere. There is drama in every situation and I get my characters from all walks of life. Sometimes I'll be sitting in a café, having a cuppa and I'll see somebody, or maybe even just a small part of somebody, the way they screw up their nose, or a certain speech pattern that strikes me as interesting. And so I take the person home with me. Not literally you understand, that would get me arrested, but as soon as I get home I scribble down whatever it is that struck me about them."

"That's a good answer, thank you, but what about your story lines, how do you come up with all the twists and turns. How do you channel your imagination?"

In the sound booth Ray Jefferies, chief sound engineer, gave all his attention to the recording monitor. Computers did everything these days and his only function was to make sure that all the levels on the huge graphic equaliser remained even. Every few seconds he gave a cursory glance at the screen to make sure the sound was being delivered to the subscription-paying public correctly. What he saw while Jennifer and Ellie were talking, made his head turn. He dropped his chocolate bar onto the side of the control desk and stared hard for a further few seconds to make sure that his eyes weren't deceiving him. Hey, Bill, come and look at this." He said excitedly, to the second sound tech.

As each person spoke, the sounds they made were transposed to a graph on the monitor. Ellie's line was green and the caller's line was red. Ray listened to the caller's voice closely, he had been in the job a long time and sound was his business.

"She's disguising her voice, listen, see there, how deep it is, you can tell from the timbre that it's not her natural voice, she's dropped it by an octave. See how she struggled on the word *from*?"

"Yeah, but why would she do that?" asked Bill.

"Anybody's guess mate, anybody's guess. But look at this. Have you ever seen that happen before?" he pointed to the two sound graphs. The red line aped the speech patterns of the green one perfectly. Both voices made identical waves on the screen.

"That woman's pitch, tone, inflection; everything, is exactly the same as the writer's. Even though she's trying to disguise the 'sound' of her voice, the pattern stays the same. You know Bill, if I hadn't seen it with my own eyes I wouldn't have believed that was possible. I think we'd better give Bernie a yell and tell him to look at this. I don't know what it means, maybe just a coincidence but I don't like it."

Bill left the sound booth in search of the program director.

"Thanks for the advice Ellie," Jennifer was saying. "It's been nice talking to you. Oh just before I go; I read in 'Spiral' magazine that you have a German Shepherd?"

"Yes, that's right, Jakey, he's my baby. I love him to bits. He's as daft as a clown in a joke shop and eats me out of house and home."

"That's lovely. I've got a shepherd too. A word of warning though." The callers voice remained light and never altered in its chatty friendliness. "You've got to watch those German Shepherds, little devils they are, you have to keep an eye on them, see they don't get into trouble. Mine's a right demon. You must miss yours when you are away from home. Will he be there to meet you when you get back? Give him a cuddle for me will you please? I bet he's a right little devil."

"Ben and Jerri looked at each other, '*what is this, bloody Cruft's?*' Thought Ben. Where had all this dog talk suddenly come from? He listened on his earpiece to see if they were lined up for the next caller.

Ellie sat for approximately three seconds, letting each separate word, each disjointed piece of information infiltrate her brain. In those three seconds, her natural colour beneath the stage make-up left her face like the last wave of the evening tide leaving the beach.

And then she was in motion.

She began ripping savagely at the microphone planted down her bra. She flung it onto the seat, a sob escaping her and being picked up by every viewer nation wide before white noise was all that transmitted from her discarded mic.

She set off across the studio at a run.

"Ellie ..." Shouted Ben after her. "Ellie are you alright?"

"Oh dear," Oozed Jerri, "I don't think she's very well. Puke bucket!" She yelled cruelly. Before adding even more heartlessly, especially after having just dragged details of her condition out of Ellie, "I don't think she's very well at all. Probably one too many complimentaries at the hotel bar last night."

Somewhere just to the right of set the producer cringed as he thought of yet another law-suit falling on to his desk over the next few days.

Ellie drew level with Rob.

"Ellie what is it? What the fuck's happening? Are you all right? Do you need a doctor?"

"Phone," screamed Ellie at the top of her voice. "Where's my mobile?"

She turned to run in the direction of her dressing room to find her bag, Rob caught her arm.

"Here." he said fishing his phone out of his breast pocket. "Use mine."

Ellie dialled furiously, not taking the time to thank Rob or look up her home number in his listings. He wouldn't be there anyway.

"Come on. Come on. For fuck's sake come on."

"Ellie calm down, Jesus, will you just tell me what's going on?"

No Signal.

"Shit."

She was off again, this time down the endless warren of corridors that would take her to the outside world and a phone signal.

Partly due to her illness but mainly due to the height of her heels she stumbled twice as she pushed her way through cameras and crew members. Without slowing her charge, she lifted first one leg then the other and pulled the elasticated ankle boots from her feet, dropping them as she ran.

Using every ounce of her energy she ran at full speed and then a little bit faster down the corridor. Unhampered by the high-heeled boots, she was able to lift her legs high, she pumped her arms to aid momentum and sprinted as she hadn't done since school–day athletics. Her bare feet slapped hard on the cold, tiled floor with each step. Ironically she took this moment to remember some snippet of an advert for hi-tech running shoes. '*What was it they had said? Ahhh yes. With each step something like the equivalent of half a ton of pressure was forced through the tarsal joints.*' That was a whole hell of a lot of pressure and Ellie was going to pay dearly for this tomorrow but she didn't care, she had to get a phone signal and fast.

Ellie burst through the swing door that would release her into the blustery day outside. She didn't wait to hold it open for Rob who was puffing and panting behind her as he tried to keep up.

It hit him in the chest knocking the air out of him. He managed to push through after Ellie and stood at the top of the steps doubled over with his hands on his knees waiting to see if his lungs were going to burst. They didn't. Maybe, just maybe he was going to survive this.

Ellie stabbed at the number pad on the phone. It rang three times.

"Good morning, Goldman, Graham and Smith solicitors how may…"

Ellie cut the receptionist off mid spiel.

"I need to speak to Mr. Price, don't give me any bullshit about him being in a meeting. I need to speak to him now, it's urgent."

Brenda recognised Ellie's voice, she had been instructed that if Ellie rang. Matt was to be found immediately for her. "I'm sorry Miss Erikson, but Mr High isn't in the office today. I believe he's working at home."

Ellie disconnected without courtesy or goodbye.

Damn he was at home after all.

The phone rang and Rob answered on the fourth ring.

"Where's Jake." Ellie screamed at him.

"Ellie what's the matter, I thought you were doing a show, I've got it taping to watch lat…" the hysteria in her voice finally sunk in and he got round to answering her question.

"Jake, he's just out in the garden, why? What's the matter?"

Matt had the back door open, he was just fixing himself an early lunch before getting back to the reams of paperwork he had to get through for his court appearances the following day. He had taken the opportunity of opening the back door to let Jake out into the garden to clean himself.

Suddenly the most sickening howl broke the peace of sleepy suburbia. The howl turned from one of surprise and shocked pain into a scream of terrifying agony.

Matt dropped the tomato he was slicing as he spoke to Ellie and ran for the garden.

Ellie clearly heard the sound of her dog screaming and she sobbed hysterically into Rob's shoulder.

Chapter 14

The woman remained motionless, her eyes glued to the television set long after the morning show guest had run off the set. The host said she was ill, but what did they know? She heard what the caller had said. She *heard* the caller.

Sitting in her rented flat, on her battered settee, in a dressing gown with one button missing and a cheap red wine stain on the left breast from some weeks earlier, she scrutinised what she had become. There were also at least two cigarette burns visible but she wasn't going to sit and worry about the possibility of burning herself to death in this festering hell, she had far greater things to think about than that.

She curled her stout legs underneath her, and let the thoughts in that were knocking on the door of her mind, begging to be brought in from the cold.

It *was* cold; she had been sitting there trembling for the last ten minutes. It had taken that long for the goose pimples to tell the nerve endings and the nerve endings to tell her brain stem and for her brain stem to tell her fat arse to get up and put the fire on. Her routine never altered; come down, flick the remote to activate the telly, ignite the fire and make a cup of coffee on a good day. A bad day had her hitting the red wine before the sun was properly risen. On those rare good days she'd go back up after an hour or so and wash, on the bad ones, she reasoned that there was no one there to smell her, so what was the point. This was the life she had to live for now. This was her hideout until she could emerge again into the light. This wasn't the way she wanted it but it needed to be so for now. She would emerge from this dingy flat a swan again when she didn't need the cover of anonymity. This way of living was only an interim a 'just for now' measure until she could once again take some control.

Today though her routine was broken, she came down, flicked the remote control to activate the television. Oh yes she still used phrases like 'activate the television' the cheap 'n' nasties hadn't turned all her brain cells to piccalilli yet. But then, after taking two steps towards the fire, she saw *her,* well no, not her, the other one, the writer.

"Is it too early for a drinkiepoo?" She asked herself aloud, she had taken to talking to herself more often as the days alone had lengthened into weeks. In reality, it hadn't been so many weeks but to her, it felt life a lifetime. It was their fault, bringing her to this, but it wouldn't be forever. In fact she'd be leaving

here and resuming life very soon if things went according to plan.

"Well, my dear," she answered herself. *"The jolly old cock is over the yardarm, so why not."* She giggled as her thoughts refused to align themselves sensibly. She was sure the saying had more to do with suns than cocks and that the old cock-a-doodle belonged to a different idiom altogether. Cocks related to mornings and may, or may not, have had something to do with worms, it was suns and yardarms that went together silly girl. That inevitably, set her mind off on a different train of thought all together. It was a long time since she'd had a nice bit of cock in the morning, or at any time of day come to that.

"Now then about that drink."

She was just about to heave herself up off the sofa, when the voice of reason put its oar in. Damn she hated the voice of reason. She didn't really have a drink problem, as she told herself she would stop it short the day she could leave this awful place.

"You can't have a drink. What are you going to do about the girl?"

'Why is it,' she thought, *'that voices of reason can never mind their own bloody business?'*

She wasn't old, only one generation older than Ellie Erikson herself and everyone knew that each generation spawned faster than the last, *'well hardly geriatric yet old lass,'* and yet she always thought of them, both of them, as girls, rather than women. She had known this moment of responsibility would come, hadn't she been waiting for it all these weeks. Waiting for a sign such as this, to show her that the girls needed her in their lives. *'Oh God, but that was funny. Life, life? This wasn't living, this was cornering. No let's be exact, this was being cornered and having nowhere to run. Well, not yet at least. But soon it would be very different.'*

She wondered, not for the first time, not even for the hundredth time, what had happened to her bungalow on 'The Heights'. Presumably by now someone would have discovered its lack of occupancy. Was anybody looking for her? There was certainly nobody to care about her disappearance, but police or social services or someone? Perhaps not eh? Packing a single rucksack (she had not dared be seen with a suitcase) and simply walking away from her home, her car, her possessions and everything she'd worked for all those years, had been the hardest thing she'd ever had to contemplate, never mind actually put into operation.

Was it divine retribution? God knew all right, God knew how wicked she'd been. She would tell the girls, she'd tell them with tears in her voice that she had wanted to stop it. She knew it was wrong but they, *he,* was too strong. That's what she'd say when she came together with them. All those years and now she was as trapped as the girl but she was trapped in a prison of her own making. She was incarcerated in a cell of waiting.

How much of it had been his doing and how much her own? This was a thought that sent a shiver down her spine when she mulled it over. Yes it had been exciting and she was a woman driven by need and excitement.

"So!" Said the bastard voice of reason, *"What are you going to do about it?"*

Her voice sounded weak and pathetic, whiney, like a reprimanded child.

"I could ring her."

"Oh bravo, yes you ring her, good idea, that's a sure way of flushing you out isn't it? How long after ringing her do you think it would be?"

"What?" she whimpered.

"Before the shit hits the fan."

Her voice came back a little stronger, thinking, thinking.

"Okay, so it's too dangerous to ring her, but I could ring *him*. Yes, that's it, if I'm very careful, I can ring the boyfriend. I can't risk giving too much away.

She got up from the settee with fresh determination. This was something positive, something concrete that she could do. It wouldn't atone, nothing could ever atone for what she had done this thought made her smile. Why would she want to do that?

Maria shuffled into her bedroom, and re-drew the curtains that she had drawn only half an hour earlier. Anyone entering the room might be surprised to see a crucifix standing on the dressing table. It was an ordinary crucifix nothing there to cause surprise, there were thousands of practising Catholics in the country even after Jesus had been proved to be nothing more than an urban legend. What might cause people to look twice at the crucifix was the fact that Jesus had been dressed like one of the scarecrows they used to use to protect the crops. Little tufts of straw stuck out of his neck and his floppy hat, and he wore tattered and torn farm hand clothes.

Maria grunted with exertion as she pulled her bed across the room and lifted the carpet back. Glancing around her to make sure she was still alone she pulled up the two loose floorboards and thrust her hand into the floor cavity. Eighteen piles of ten volumes. Her life's work. Twenty-seven years of human suffering and torment were contained within those benign ledgers These were hers, she'd earned them. These journals contained every foul deed Maria Kiltcher had ever done in her entire life.

Maria Kiltcher felt along the piles gauging which stack of ten would have the information she sought. Each collection was in its own storage box. Pretty lilac boxes bought from an expensive department store, boxes that belied the horrors contained within.

She located Eleanor Erikson's phone number quite quickly and checked on Matthew's name. She was edgy as long as the books were out. Unsafe, exposed a prime sitting duck just waiting for exposure.

Her hands trembled as the telephone rang, they were shaking so much that she expected the ring tone to warble. Four rings, five.

Hello, you're through to Ellie and Jake the wonder dog. Leave a message please and we'll be sure to get back to you just as soon as we can.

She hung up quickly.

"Damn!"

She rang half an hour later and then half an hour after that. On the fourth attempt she got a reply.

Chapter 15

One minute Matt was reassuring Ellie that everything was fine, the next the most God-awful scream of agony came from the garden. The dog's cry carried through the backdoor and into the kitchen on a wave of rising hysteria.

Matt dropped the knife he was using and began running as the first sound of Ellie's matching cry of anguish shot through the telephone exchange and into the kitchen to mix with Jake's.

Matt left the room at a sprint. Following the terrible noise to the rhododendron bush at the end of the garden, he skidded to a halt.

He took in the scene in a split second. Jake writhing, biting savagely at his hind leg without letting up on the maniacal scream for a second. Matt didn't know until that moment that dogs were able to scream. He could barely believe what his eyes were showing him. '*How could anybody be so bloody cruel?*' He thought. His first priority was to keep Jake still and try to stop him doing himself any more damage.

He flung his body at Jake's head and pinned him to the ground. Putting his knee firmly into the resisting flesh at the side of the big dog's neck, he struggled to hold him in position. All the time murmuring soothing words to him, trying to calm him with his gentle voice. Jake whirled on Matt trying to bite him, strong white teeth gnashing uselessly on empty space, hatred for all mankind in his eyes. Terrified and in such pain that he was beyond reason.

The merciless teeth of the poachers' snare had cut into Jake's left hind leg, tearing at the flesh and exposing the smooth white bone. Matt was sobbing in anger, frustration and pity for the dog as he tore the relentless jaws of the snare open. '*Where the hell had Eve got hold of this? These things were antiques. And how could she even consider using such a brutal and illegal death trap on an innocent animal?*' His thinking also told him that the crazy bitch would stop at nothing to bring destruction to their family. '*Because,*' he told himself, '*that's what Ellie and Jake and Goddammit even Esther too were to him, they were his family.*'

Once the snare was released from his leg Jake relaxed slightly, he was exhausted and shock was beginning to seep through his body like the chill from a snowdrift. His gums were white, all the blood retreating to feed his numbed brain. He continued to whimper, still in acute pain. But he realised now that

Matt was holding him and trying to help him. Jake loved Matt.

Jake didn't need to be punished. Jake was a good boy. Jake had looked after the house just like Ellie told him. It was the 'not Ellie' that punished Jake. He could smell it all around the bush. Jake wants to tell the 'not Ellie' that he's a good boy, then maybe 'not Ellie' will go away and not try to hurt them anymore.

Matt carried the bleeding dog into the house and gently laid him on the sofa. He continued to talk to him all the time, Jake had fallen silent. His eyes were heavy and he made no attempt to move as Matt put him down. His head lolled and he seemed listless, as though he had been sedated. He had to get him to a vet.

"Phone, George." Yelled Matt and then instructed George to dial the vet's number. He tried to remain calm as he spoke to the veterinary assistant but his voice cracked several times. He told the vet he was on his way with the hurt dog and for them to be ready when he got there. The vet said to apply a cold compress to the dog's leg and to keep him as warm and calm as possible.

Matt wrapped Jake in a travel blanket that they kept in the car and carried him out. He was worried about him damaging himself further by jumping around as he drove but he needn't have worried, Jake lay still and silent on the backseat. Not even bothering to try and lick at his wounded leg.

They worked on Jake for a long time. The nursing assistant suggested that Matt go home and they'd ring him but he couldn't forget the look of confusion in the dog's eyes. He knew he was a sentimental old fool and that he should go home in case Ellie rang there but he couldn't leave Jake. He felt that if he left, the dog would sense that he was alone. There would be time enough to go home when he knew Jake was going to be all right. He drank a cup of strong, bitter coffee that the receptionist pressed into his hands and barely tasted it.

He was ready for them when they asked what had happened to Jake. He said that he'd shot through his legs as he opened the front door that morning. He told the vet that Jake had run off and refused to be called back. It happened sometimes, Matt told them but he always comes back after he's had a nosy round. He made sure he got in mention of all the wood and farmland around the cottage in case later, connections were made to the type of injury Jake had sustained.

The vet reappeared from treatment room two with a reassuring smile on his face.

"Is he going to be all right?" Matt jumped to his feet his voice heavy with concern.

"Yes, yes he's going to be fine Mr High. It's a nasty wound mind, he's been lucky, just another inch and we'd have had to take his leg off. As it is there are no bones broken and I expect him to make a full recovery.

Now then, he's had a nasty old shock and still isn't feeling himself so we want to keep him in overnight, just to keep an eye on him. He's had some heavy sedation so he's going to pretty much sleep through. That's what his body needs right now, reduce the shock to his system. He'll be as right as rain in the morning and you can pick him up. And then I'll want him back in seven days to have another look and see that the stitches have dissolved properly."

Matt drove back to Ellie's in a daze. Every time he tried to think, his mind hit a roadblock of fury that he couldn't get passed. He tried for the umpteenth time to get through to Ellie but there was still no reply. He knew there was no way she'd have turned her phone off at a time like this, or gone on to her next engagement. That meant that wherever she was there was no signal. Matt knew Ellie as well as he knew his own mother. Sure as eggs were brown and came out of a hen's arse, Ellie was in a plane right this minute on her way home. Matt knew that she wouldn't wait for the car to get her back. *'Poor Rob,'* thought Matt; he'd be tearing his hair out. Matt decided to call at the supermarket on his way home to get something really nice in for their evening meal. Ellie may not feel like eating much, but after she heard that Jake was going to be okay, he knew she'd want something. It wasn't much but at least it was something positive that he could do. Matt felt guilty that this happened while he was looking after Jake.

He let himself into the house and there was a strange, eerie silence. This wasn't Cherry Tree Cottage, where was the bouncing dog yelping with excitement? Where was the warm soft kiss from Ellie? He went through to the kitchen with his shopping bags and stopped in disbelief.

The photo albums had been savaged. Each photograph of Jake had been cut into quarters. The pieces had been mixed up and every single surface, cupboard doors, worktops, the window, all of them were covered in glued pieces of Ellie's vast array of Jake pictures. Every single one of them ruined. The snare had been re-set and left triggered and ready on the floor. Matt didn't think this was a serious attempt to get either himself or Ellie, just a mockery, a bragging of her envisaged superior intelligence. *'How the hell was she getting in?'* Matt was sure he'd locked the door behind him. Nobody could access the eye scanner but himself and Ellie. He shook his head in disgust as he looked at the floor. A bottle of tomato ketchup had been abandoned on the worktop and scrawled across the floor in six inch high letters was the epitaph written in sauce; R.I.P. Jake. The viscous fluid had congealed and begun to stiffen. Matt was not surprised at Eve's lack of subtlety; this childishness seemed to be the level at which she remained.

'Well,' thought Matt, *'Little Miss Psychopath isn't as clever as she thinks she is.'* All this shows that Eve's assuming Jake is dead. *'Tough shit lady; Jake lives to tear your miserable throat out another day.'*

Matt was furiously cleaning the kitchen when Ellie rang to say she was on her way in a hire car from the airport and would be home within the hour. Matt reassured her over and over again that Jake was going to be just fine.

He'd no sooner finished talking to Ellie when the phone rang again.

"Answer please, George."

"Hello," For three seconds all Matt could hear was harsh, rapid breathing. Then the woman's voice cut in. She sounded anxious, scared, she began rambling not making sense.

"Is that Mr High, Matthew High?" Matt was about to confirm that he was but she gave him no opportunity to speak.

"Please listen to what I'm going to tell you. You have to listen to me, and God knows you have to trust what I'm saying, even though it sounds ridiculous." She took a deep audible breath, her voice sounded shaky her words tumbling over each other in a frantic attempt to get out and be understood. The lady sounded on the verge of hysteria.

"I know about Eve."

She knew that this was the single link that could get her back where she needed to be. She had given up everything because she had to lay low, to dissipate into anonymity. And here she was running the risk of bringing the whole asylum of lunatics crashing down on her. Delicious lunacy that kept the blood pumping.

"I know what she's up to and I know that Eleanor is in serious danger. But listen to me, it's far more than that. There's someone playing with all of you. He's tried to kill me. He thinks I'm dead and if he finds out I'm still alive, he'll hunt me down for sure and finish the job. He's pure evil, sick. Oh God there's so much more you should know but I've said too much already. I had to warn you. That's the least I owe Eve. But this is the most important part; you mustn't tell Ellie about me. You can't mention this conversation at all. I have to tell you; everything Eleanor sees, hears, or says goes straight back. Oh God please don't say anything to her, He'll Know! He'll Know!"

Matt interrupted the woman excitedly. This was the break they had been waiting for.

"Listen to me lady. You know Eve? You know about her? You have to tell me. Where is she? Who the hell is she? How is she connected to Ellie? Is she her twin sister? Why the hell is she doing all this to us? Please tell me what's going…."

The woman gave one loud sob and the phone clicked loudly as the connection was broken.

Matt was left reeling. The garbled message didn't make any sense at all. Who the hell was that? Eve's mother? She said that she owed something to Eve, and knew all about her. It must be her mother.

The woman on the dormant end of the broken connection smiled as she replaced the telephone back on its cradle. She took a last look at the hovel, picked up the Valencia suitcase and walked out of there for the last time. No trace, no trail, next roll of the dice.

"Last call search please, George."

"The number of the last caller was barred Matt."

"Okay George, standby."

It was pretty much as he'd expected but it was worth a try. Matt continued to go over the mysterious phone call as he finished cleaning the kitchen and prepared a meal. What did she mean; don't tell Ellie? And that everything goes straight back? Back to who? Or what? The woman's husband perhaps, Eve's father? What was he going to say to Ellie? Was the woman suggesting that somehow Ellie was relaying information back to this crazy somebody? Nothing ever made sense these days. Just three short weeks ago he'd have written the woman off as crazy but nothing was ever as it seemed any more. He had to take the warning seriously.

Ellie burst through the door with a very harassed looking Rob behind her.

"How is he? How's Jake?"

She dropped the small case she was carrying and Rob gratefully put down the other two huge suitcases and three bags in the hall. Matt rushed forward to greet them and pulled Ellie into his arms. He stroked her hair and kissed her cheek telling her again that Jake was going to be all right.

"I want to go and see him."

"Hey listen to me. He's been heavily sedated, he may not even be conscious. He's had a lot of treatment on his leg and he's exhausted. Even if he is awake all you can do by going there today is upset him. The second he sees you he's going to want to come home and all you will do is disrupt his healing. You look shattered darling. Let Jake rest today, you get some rest too and then in the morning we can go and pick him up. Okay."

"Okay but I want to ring the vets and talk to them. See that he's okay and that he's not pining for me."

Matt had been leading her through to the lounge as he spoke. The kitchen door off the lounge was open and Ellie caught sight of the snare on the kitchen worktop. Matt had been going to dispose of it, but he knew Ellie would want to see it and he had no idea if they were going to call the police or not. Ellie ran over to the worktop and picked up the snare. The ragged teeth still tipped with Jake's blood seemed to leer at her as she ran her finger over the cold steel.

"How could she?" Ellie asked in a small, quiet voice. "How could she do that to him?"

Matt drew her over to the settee and put his arm round her. Rob tactfully asked if he could use the study and set about ringing round to cancel the rest of Ellie's engagements.

"Ellie I'm so sorry. I am so damned sorry that this happened. If only I'd checked the garden before I let him out."

"Listen you," said Ellie sternly. "Don't you dare blame yourself for this. Don't you dare! This is her doing, that evil bitch. And when I get my hands on her I'm going to ram that snare down her throat sideways and clamp it securely to her bloody intestines. And then I'm going to hit her over the head and stab her with a knife. And then…" All the fight went out of her and she went limp in Matt's arms. "And then Matty, I'm just going to ask her why."

Rob joined them and told Ellie that everything was sorted and for her not to worry. Cancelling at such short notice was not going to help her career but that was the last thing on Ellie's mind. Rob had put the word out that Miss Erikson had suddenly been taken ill. A fact born out by what had happened on the Ben and Jerri show.

They talked long and hard about everything that had happened. Rob was all in favour of calling the police but Ellie wouldn't hear of it. She convinced the men that even if she could make *that prick of an inspector* believe her, there was nothing that could really be done about it. Matt told Ellie about the photographs and the re-setting of the trap. And Ellie cried as she sifted through the confetti images of Jake. Jake as a puppy, Jake with Matt, Jake with her, Jake in Scotland, all fragmented pieces of happier times.

"What's she going to do next?"

Matt had said it, but it's what they had all been thinking and worrying about.

"What if she comes back to finish what she started with Jake?" Ellie asked. "I don't feel safe, Matt. I don't want to be here alone any more."

Matt said that while Rob stayed with her, he would go home and pack some things. He was moving in until all this was finished and he wouldn't hear any arguments.

Ellie had none to give and that broke Matt's heart. Under any other circumstances he'd have been delighted to be moving in with Ellie but for her to give up her fierce independence without a word of protest was an indicator of just how frightened and worried she was.

"What about Jake?" She asked.

"Jake will be alright love, we'll be here to keep an eye on him. We'll just have to be more vigilant."

"I've got an idea," Said Rob. "Why don't I take Jake? Just until all this is sorted out. He'll be safe with me and you know we'll look after him well. Gail and I love him almost as much as you two do, but I warn you if he digs up my potatoes again, I'll do for the bugger myself."

"Oh would you Rob?" squealed Ellie. There was no thought, no hesitation.

'Another sign of the times,' thought Matt. For Ellie to be parted from Jake was an incredible wrench and a huge sacrifice in an attempt to put the dog's

best interests first.

"Yes. Rob. Please take him. Thank you so much. I know he'll be fine with you and Gail and you know how he loves to play in…"

Ellie had been about to say how Jake liked to play in Stanney Wood.

'Everything she sees, hears or says goes straight back.'

The sentence ran through Matt's mind and he interrupted loudly before Ellie could finish what she was saying.

"Well that's all sorted out then. Lets have another coffee should we?"

'Why had he done that?' It was ridiculous. What? Did he think the house was bugged or something? Instinct told him that they had to be careful what they said from now on. Maybe they would be better moving into his house, but he knew he'd have a devil of a job persuading Ellie.

Better the devil you know. Again the phrase drove through his mind. There were so many questions that they didn't have any answers to. Their time together was limited and precious and yet here was time that should have been spent living each moment to the full, this shouldn't have to be a time to hide away scared and insecure. He hated that he couldn't do more to protect Ellie but from now on, he would be with her round the clock to see that she was safe.

While Ellie went upstairs for a long soak in a hot bath, Matt took Rob into the garden, he told Rob in a hushed whisper about the strange phone call he had received. Rob had no better ideas about who the woman might be, other than perhaps an escaped lunatic. But they decided not to tell Ellie right away about the call. She had enough on her plate and didn't need another complication to the horrors frightening her.

~*~

Sometime later that evening Jake woke up as the veterinary assistant went into the hospitalisation pens for the last check of the night.

"Hey boy, you're back with us eh? I bet you'd like a nice cool drink of water wouldn't you?" She filled a bowl with water and lifted his head. Jake lapped at the cool drink and managed to dribble a lot and drink a little.

Jake's eyes don't want to open. Ooh round and round everything moving. Can't shake head. Head won't work. Oh dear head broken. This isn't kitchen, it isn't garden, it isn't get off the bed Jake. Hello lady whose not Ellie or Matt. Lady smells like white coat and needle man, but lady smells kind too. Lady's funny ooh Jake's laughing. Drink yes please, drink. Oh Oh Jake made a mess. Bad dog Jake. Jake laughing again. Head won't work, head broken, round and round. Funny. Where's Ellie. Jake must protect Ellie. Jake growl. Oh oh growl broken too. Jake so sleepy so very sl…

The assistant lowered the big dog's head and stroked him a couple of times. He began to snore rhythmically and loud almost immediately.

"Okay big lad, you sleep it off. I bet you've got quite a hangover. You are a beautiful fella."

Jake half opened one eye and chuffed. And then he snored some more.

~*~

The next morning news of Ellie's illness hit the nationals. It was only a relatively small column in each newspaper, some with a publicity shot of Ellie at her computer, but the word was out now that Ellie was terminally ill. They had all the facts, the name of the disease that was slowly killing her, some details about the condition, the fact that she might not complete the novel she was currently working on. Ellie felt unclean and tainted by media rape.

TOP NOVELIST STRIKEN BY KILLER DISEASE.

She felt that even her disease didn't belong to her anymore. She belonged to the media, the Press, the public. She would not be allowed the dignity of dying privately.

The phone rang as they sat down to breakfast

"Eleanor my darling." Esther was sobbing hysterically and it was difficult to make out what she was saying.

"Hello Mother."

"Oh Eleanor, how could you let me find out like that? Have you any idea the shock I've suffered? To read something so horrific in the News of the World. Please tell me it's a lie Eleanor. Tell me it's not true. What will I do without you? Why didn't you tell me Eleanor you wicked girl?"

"Yes Mother. I'm sorry you had to find out like that. But you know we did try to tell you."

"Oh Eleanor don't you dare try and blame me for all this."

"No Mother of course not." Ellie's voice remained flat.

"Well my darling child there's only one thing for it. I'm going to have to give up all that I hold dear and move in with you. Somebody's going to have to look after you. I'll put the house on the market this very morning."

"NO MOTHER." Ellie shrieked this down the phone making Matt spill coffee all over his toast and jam.

It took every ounce of Ellie's tact, diplomacy and persistent determination to stop Esther turning into a modern day Florence Nightingale. However her feelings were never going to be spared and the call ended in acrimony and hurt feelings. Matt looked over at Ellie with his face full of concern and pity.

"Bloody hell!" Said Ellie, "Can you imagine anything worse than having my mother moving in with us? Hell I'd rather invite Eve to be my nurse maid."

Her tone of voice was so serious and her face so straight, that Matt couldn't help laughing and soon they were both giggling like school kids and describing what life would be like living with Esther.

Jake was picked up amongst much hugging and 'good, brave boying. Nothing on earth would have stopped Ellie going with Matt to pick him up and take him to Rob and Gail's and Matt didn't even bother to try. If it lead to 'someone' knowing about Jake's whereabouts then they would just have to deal with the problem when it arose.

Ellie and Matt finally gave in to the bullying of their friends and decided on the spur of the moment to spend a couple of days with Rob and Gail themselves. Some normal conversation, good wine and pleasant company would do them both the world of good.

Matt went back home to pack some things for them.

Chapter 16

She hid at the bottom of the garden her face contorted with hatred; anyone seeing her would have been put in mind of a malignant pixie. She had forsaken her favoured hiding place behind what she now thought of as the snare bush, too risky, from now on she would have to make do with positioning herself at the back of the shed. They were bound to be more vigilant now that the dog was dead. From here she could be off over the perimeter wall as soon as the back door opened if need be without being seen.

Her plans were finally made; everything set in order, ready for her, ready for *them*. It was time to stop playing and get down to re-claiming what was rightfully hers. Everything so far, had been practise, little trial runs to prepare her for the big one. They were supposed to be confidence building but she had experienced her failures along the way. With the exception of the dog - he had to be got out of the picture because he posed too big a problem for her - she had not as yet tried to kill anyone. They were wrong about that. She was indignant that they should think that she had tried to kill them. She had more imagination than a tacky knock on the head and a stabbing. She had planned this long and hard; she had class, style. Did they really think that bitch was the only one with any finesse? Well it was finally about to come together nicely. No cock-ups this time, no slips. It had to be simply…. Perfect.

She felt bad about the dog. She liked animals. She'd never stroked one or known what it felt to hold something soft and furry and alive in her arms but she liked them. She knew that one day she would like to have something of her own. She would have taken over the dog, that would have been nice but he didn't like her. He was too taken in by the writing bitch. If only he could see that she was an impostor she wouldn't have had to kill him. She cried herself to sleep over that. She didn't want to do it, but she had to. It was regrettable but she had no choice.

She fingered the letter in her pocket. It had been hand delivered to her address that morning. It worried her. What was it? What did it mean? The single sheet of paper had been typed and read simply.

Password: Lilith

From a friend.

Well if Eve was sure of only one thing in this whole damned world, it was that she had no friends. Maybe they had tracked her down and were playing some games of their own. No matter, what they didn't understand was that *she* was calling the shots in this game. She had no need to pay the piper, she, Eve *is* the piper and when she said dance, they would all dance to her tune.

The letter had thrown her. She felt safe hidden in the anonymous bedsit; she blended and could come and go without being noticed. *Someone* knew where she lived, so she could never go back there but it didn't matter the game was drawing to a close anyway. Hastily she had thrown her few pathetic belongings into a rucksack before she left. She didn't have much and travelled light. The dress that she had bought with Ellie's money to emulate her, she no longer had any need of. So she burned it along with other stuff, some that she had taken from the house. Things that she felt grounded her to Ellie in a bizarre psychometry. She felt that if she held an item belonging to Ellie she could somehow psychically home in on her, feel her mood, her anxiety, her terror. Eve loved this feeling of ultimate power. The bitch knew she was hunted. She was trapped, trapped in Eve's web and she knew it. The slow, creeping smile on the distorted face bordered insanity. *Let the party proceed.*

As she passed the time behind the shed, she remained ever vigilant; she had a good view of the house and could see through most of the downstairs windows, she would know if anyone arrived. So far that morning everything was quiet. She would bide her time. It gave her freedom to think this through again, make sure that her plan was foolproof. Her thoughts drifted to the password **Lilith**. It had to be something to do with her impostor. It was clever all right. But what did it mean? Who was it from? The obvious answer was that it came from them, but that wasn't her dear sister's style. She wouldn't play cat and mouse. The fool would confront, like a fox confronting a tiger.

Lilith. Some of the more contemporary versions of the bible named Lilith as Eve's dark twin. The one who seduced and tempted Adam. Well as soon as the opportunity arose she was going to lead Adam by his prissy little tie right into her Garden of Eden.

She felt a thrill akin to sexual arousal course through her, though this was not sexual, it was *powerful.* Adrenaline flowed, dancing with the blood in her veins and she became restless. Her heart thumped to its own rock n roll beat and she was ready to run with the final showdown. *Bring on the clowns.*

Chapter 17

'Bloody Hell, which potions in this plethora of gunk products does Ellie absolutely ***need*** *to survive? Surely to God she doesn't splatter* ***all*** *this muck on her face every morning.'*

Matt read a few of the labels; toning cream, exfoliating cream, anti-ageing cream, skin tonic. '*What the hell was wrong with good old soap and water? Women! An alien breed'*.

He opened Ellie's largest vanity case and began throwing 'products' into it at random. Waxing strips, eye cream, avocado facemask, St John's wart; '*ugh, what's* ***that****, Ellie doesn't have warts!'* contraceptive pills; '*mustn't forget those,*' Royal jelly; '*kinky Ellie, Kinky.'*

The internal mysteries of Ellie's bathroom 'cave' became an education for Matt. He had lots of questions to ask her later. For instance '*What* ***do*** *you do with... oh never mind.'*

So engrossed in his labour was he, that at first he didn't hear George's voice informing him that he had a call. Perhaps this was partly due to the fact that in his indecision of which one to take, Matt had hung both Ellie's thick towelling dressing gown and her very sexy raw silk one, over the bathroom phone speaker. He removed them now and held them up with a frown. This was probably Ellie ringing and he could ask her which she wanted.

It was Ellie.

"Ellie my darling, never has a simple mission been so impossible and that Apollo lot thought they had it hard. Frumpy towelling or sexy silk my love?"

Ellie's voice was breathless with excitement.

" Eh? Oh, never mind that now. I've got some news."

"Oh yes what?"

He could hear her taking a deep breath as though she was steadying herself, to get the information across clearly.

"We've been doing some digging on the net, while you've been gone. Revenue records, things like that. And we've had a major breakthrough. We've found out where Eve used to work."

"Ellie that's fantastic."

"Well we assume it's her, we did an employment scan and came up with the name Evelyn Erikson. Sounds like her doesn't it?"

Matt felt a cold chill go through him. Erikson? He couldn't believe that the woman even used Ellie's surname. Again everything seemed to lead back to Esther. Matt was confused.

"But Ellie I did a thorough employment scan and came up with nothing. I don't understand."

Matt began to smell a rat. With the impact of the news he had forgotten to ask Ellie for their agreed password. His voice was guarded.

"Ellie?" he asked in an inquisitive tone. "What's the password?"

She laughed.

"Bit late in the day to be asking me that isn't it? Lilith of course."

Matt relaxed.

"Well come on, tell me what you've found out." Said Matt.

"Right, well it's not a lot really, and of course this woman may not be her, but she worked until two months ago at the Valleyside Institute and Research facility. Rob and I are going out there now. You follow us in your car eh?"

"Hang on, hang on. Ellie slow down and lets think this through first. At least wait until I get back and then we can all go together. You've waited this long what's another half hou..."

"No time Matty, We're leaving now, it's on the Bassenthwaite road, west of Keswick, just past Portinscale and it's a side road apparently that takes you down to the lakeside.

"Ellie just a minute..."

Matt was left talking to a dead connection. As much as he loved her, Ellie could be so irritating sometimes. Why the hell couldn't she have just waited for him too get back to her? It was a fair old drive to Keswick and it would have made much more sense to go together. Or better yet leave it until the next day, by the time they got there. It would be getting dark. That was so typical of her, bloody impulsive woman, flying off to God knows where without thinking things through properly.

He was still grumbling to himself as he headed his car towards the Lakes and set off to the melodramatic strains of the Milochov Symphony.

~*~

"Bugger" he swore quietly as yet another side road to the lake dwindled into a muddy dirt track barely big enough to get a vehicle down. Twigs were twanging onto the sides of the car and he thought worriedly about his metallic sapphire bodywork. He'd paid an extra ten thousand euros for the finish. Twice now he'd hit a dead end and had to reverse onto the darkening main road. It was only four thirty and yet already the night was drawing in, dusk was losing its battle to darkness and lengthening shadows were making visibility difficult. Not for the first time, he cursed his beloved girlfriend. '*Why the hell couldn't this have waited until morning?*' By the time he finally found the place, he feared that they would be closed for the night anyway.

Leaning forward he ran his finger over the power sensor on his car phone. He'd just have to ring her and get more precise directions for the bloody place. The phone was dead, the red power light didn't come on no matter how many times he touched the sensor. '*Damn, blast and bugger it*'. He'd only had the car eighteen months and twice during that time the phone had gone belly up. Leaning over to the passenger seat, he groped for his mobile in his jacket pocket. '*Bloody Japs have the right idea when it comes to making cars, small attention to detail, that's what they're good at. To hell with supporting home commodities in future. Oh for Christ sake.*' His pocket was empty and in his minds eye he had a clear picture of him putting his phone on the coffee table as he went in to Ellie's house, he couldn't remember picking it up again on the way out. *"Of all the bloody, stupid, empty-headed, dumb assed things to do,"* he admonished himself aloud. *"Fancy going into a situation like this without a damned phone."* He never forgot his phone, it was an extension of his pulse. It went everywhere he did. *'This is Ellie's fault,'* he decided, *'making him rush out of the house like that.'* Well he could only hope that she and Rob hadn't been as forgetful. Matt searched his pocket, but didn't notice the hole in the lining.

The fourth attempt to find the right, loosely described, road proved more fruitful. Half way down another rutted track, this, bearing so like countless others, was a small nondescript sign saying in discrete lettering, 'Valleyside Institute' underneath in much larger print were the words 'Private Property. Trespassers will be prosecuted.' '*Now why the hell couldn't they have this sign on the main road?*' Thought Matt. '*Bloody country yokels, not an active brain cell between them, how the hell is anyone supposed to find this place?*'

He bumped and lurched a little further down the track, before coming to a pair of large wrought iron gates, they stood open, a gatehouse to the left appeared to be empty. Matt felt the first fluttering of apprehension. Surely a place so protective of its privacy, would have locked gates and a manned gatehouse? He rounded a bend and what had once been a large country residence panned out before him. There was no sign yet of Rob and Ellie, Matt assumed they must be arriving in Ellie's car, Rob would have been here by now. Although the two men were good friends there was still a healthy rivalry between them. Matt grinned with the knowledge that they were probably touring endless dirt tracks in an effort to find the place.

The entire façade of the building was lost in thick molesting ivy. It made it look dark and forbidding. The original front door had been replaced by a more business like affair and on looking round him Matt noticed that the perimeter was skirted with high-electrified fencing, though he couldn't hear the warning buzz that indicated it was switched on. Not the friendliest of places, he noted.

Getting out of the car he crunched up the gravel drive to the door. The place looked deserted. No lights anywhere. Typical he knew that it would be closed. And yet it seemed more than just closed. It seemed lifeless, as though the building had not had human breath within it for some time. He leaned forward to read a brass plate on the door – he felt a blinding pain in the back of his head and that's when the world went black.

Chapter 18

"Where the bloody hell is he?"

Matt had been gone for over two hours and Ellie was beginning to worry.

"He's probably gone to his own place to pick up some stuff and got side-tracked. Don't worry he'll be here soon enough." Said Gail patting her friend's hand like a protective mother.

"Yeah you're probably right. Hell Gail I've never been the possessive Why-isn't-he-here-with-me type, you know that. It's just with all this Eve stuff going on, every time we're apart I start to worry. Come on lets get that veg done for dinner, and enjoy the fact that both our men are out, we've got plenty of time to gossip about them."

They were just about to go through to the kitchen when Ellie's mobile phone rang. Gail motioned to her friend that she'd go and make a start, but as she watched the colour siphoning from Ellie's face she sat down again.

"What is it Ellie? What's the matter?" she asked. Ellie didn't even hear her. All her focus was tuned to the voice on the other end of the phone.

"*Hey Ellie, guess who? And I'm telling you baby, it ain't Santa Claus. Oh before I go any further I was so sorry to hear about the dog, It must have been a terrible shock to you finding out he was dead."*

"What do you want?" Ellie's voice was cold, her hands gripped the mobile so tightly that the knuckles rose prominently from her fist, she began to tremble visibly.

"Oh, sister." Ellie winced as Eve drew out the word sister. "Don't be so unfriendly, it's not what I want that you should be asking. It's what I've got that you want. That's the question. You do want him I take it."

Ellie felt the hand of fear grip her as Eve's words sunk in, and fear's hand was ice-cold and unrelenting in its cruelty.

"Have you got Matt?"

"Hey you catch on quick, and I thought I was the sister with all the brains."

"How do I know you've got Matt, how can I believe you?" Gail gave a gasp as she realised what was going on, but Ellie was not aware of it.

"*Well Ellie, the dumb puss fell for it again, when I came for him he was asking me if you wanted your frumpy towelling or your sexy silk, isn't that just like a man eh honey? They have no idea."*

"If you've hurt him, I swear to you here and now, I'll kill you."

Tears were running silently down Ellie's cheeks, Gail moved to sit beside her and took her empty hand. Ellie squeezed down on it hard. Her finger nails digging into the soft flesh of Gail's palm. But all she was aware of was the hated voice on the other end of the phone and the fact that Eve had Matt.

Suddenly Eve's voice turned from tauntingly sweet to bitter and hard.

"Yeah, yeah, yeah, Save the dramatics for your books, bitch. It's time to listen up, and you'd better listen good, because play time is over and I'm not in the mood to be messed about. Right first rule you tell no one. No one you understand? If the police are informed, no doubt they'll get me, but sweetheart they'll get me hanging on to your man's dead body. You tell no one, got that?"

Ellie glanced at Gail; she put her finger to her lips and motioned for Gail to be quiet. Then she nodded into the phone.

"Yes I understand. What do I have to do? How much do you want?"

On the other end of the line, Eve began to laugh, she sounded genuinely amused, under very different circumstances, it would have been a pleasant laugh, but as it was it send rods of iced terror tram-lining down Ellie's spine. Insanity was not apparent in the laugh, but Ellie knew it was there.

"How much? You honestly think this is about money? Ellie I don't want your money. I want your life. The life you stole from me."

Eve's voice rose to a scream; it was tinged with fury. She went quiet and Ellie heard her taking deep breaths. Ellie recognised the effort Eve was making to get her temper under control. She had Matt and the last thing Ellie wanted to do was antagonise her further.

"Okay, Okay look I hear you, no police. I understand. Just stay calm and tell me what I have to do and I'll do it, I promise. What ever you say."

Gail pulled on Ellie's arm to get her attention. When Ellie said that she would not inform the police, Gail began shaking her head in horror. Ellie put up her hand to stop Gail from distracting her. She had to be able to concentrate on what Eve was saying. Matt's life depended on it.

Eve was back in control.

"Rob and his wife I'm guessing they're out. Right?"

So she didn't know that Gail had taken the day off work to stay with her. Thought Elie. She was thinking furiously, this could work to her advantage.

"Yes that's right." She lied.

"Okay, you go now, don't even think about leaving a note to tell them where you are. Get into your car and drive up to Keswick. Right listen carefully to these directions." Eve went on to give Ellie directions to the

research institute.

"And remember you tell so much as one living soul and your boyfriend's soul will find itself without a body. Don't doubt for one second that I will kill him Ellie. I await your arrival. You have one hour and then... I'll kill him anyway."

"I want to speak to Matt." Said Ellie. How do I even know you've really got him? Put him on the line." She didn't say please and tried to make her voice authoritative while staying calm so as not to antagonise Eve.

The other woman's voice was hard with fury again as she spoke to Ellie. "you are in no position to make your demands on me woman. You're right I might not have your precious boyfriend, but what if I do? What then?" The phone went dead.

Ellie sat staring into space for several seconds, tears were flowing freely down her face and she wiped them away irritably, she had no time to be crying. Either way there'd be plenty of time for tears later. The second thought that struck her was the one that told her that in fact she might never have another opportunity to cry. In trying to save Matt's life, they might both end up dead, but she had to do as Eve told her. She had no choice.

Suddenly she was moving. One hour. It was going to be difficult to get from Ulverston to Keswick in an hour. On a good day it would be hard, all she'd need was to get stuck behind a tractor on the twisty Lakes road and she'd had it. Surely Eve must realise that.

"Oh my God, I've only got an hour. I've got to go." She yelled at Gail.

"My God Ellie, You aren't seriously going to go along with that psycho. You can't."

Gail stood in Ellie's way and took hold of her arms

"Wait Ellie, lets talk this through, you have to go to the police. You have to let them deal with this."

"NO!" Ellie screamed this at Gail and shook herself out of her friend's grip. "No Gail, you heard what she said. If we ring the police she'll kill Matt. I don't know what the hell her plans are, but I know that I believe her on that one. It's me she wants. I'm sure that if she gets me, she'll let Mat go. I feel it Gail. No police, Listen when Rob gets in tell him what's happened, don't do ANYTHING at all for three hours and if I'm not back by then, well I suppose by then you can do whatever you like, because if I haven't come home, nothing will make any difference. Now I've got to go."

She bent down and patted Jake briefly, and then she was heading for the door with her keys and phone in one hand and her purse in the other.

"I can't let you go like this," wailed Gail who was herself, almost hysterical.

Ellie looked at her friend hard in the eyes and smiled.

"Gail love, you can't stop me."

With that Ellie left and thirty seconds later Gail heard her screech out of the drive and go roaring up the road towards the first meeting with her sister.

Chapter 19

Instinctively Ellie knew that she didn't want to wake up. Please God just let the blackness remain but wake up she did, despite her prayers. However what she had control over was whether or not she chose to open her eyes. Why the hell then did she opt to open the bloody things? Why not just remain in blissful ignorance of what was going on around her?

She did open her eyes. And it *did* hurt. God-sodding-almighty it hurt and that's swearing, something that Ellie Erikson rarely ever did. Just lately though, her placid vocabulary had been tested to the limits and she'd tried out all manner of delightful combinations of profanity. 'Fucking hell to twatting bastards' was the first phrase that rose unbidden to her brain. Not bad for a novice.

For all the accusations she flung at her mother regarding her childhood, Ellie had led a sheltered life and never in her twenty seven and a half years, had she ever experienced pain to equal that which drove like a jack hammer through her nervous system now. Whether due to the beating she had taken around and about her head, or simply due to the complete alienation of her circumstances, she couldn't at first work out why she was unable to move. She soon came to understand though that she was choking on a mouth full of blood that she couldn't spit out because of the tight gag that was rubbing cruelly on her broken mouth.

As she looked down, inviting the legions of hell's agony to burst torturing sunrays behind her eyes, the reason for her plight was plainly visible. She was tied at ankle and wrist to an uncomfortable chair. Because the seat was on castors and didn't have legs, her ankles had been tied together behind the central post of the seat. Her wrists had been similarly tied behind her. She tested her bonds and winced as a new, fresher pain bolted like the legions of the apocalypse through her trapped veins to the sites where the blood flow was restricted. In one rapid lesson she learned that it wasn't prudent to do that.

She smelled her before she saw her. Ellie recognised her own choice of perfume and yet it smelled subtly different on this other woman. *'Hah, maybe we're not so alike after all,'* she thought, *'she has no idea how to wear perfume.'* What was delicate and fresh on Ellie, smelled cloying and sickly on her nemesis. Maybe when she could talk, Ellie would explain to her the concept that a few drops was all it took, half a bottle only served to make a lady smell like a whore. But then again, she had Matt, so maybe she wouldn't share her beauty tips at all.

She came towards her and Ellie felt her body stiffen in the chair as she tried desperately to keep as much space between herself and the crazy woman as possible.

"Oh you're awake then? Thought you were going to sleep all night. In fact I thought I'd killed you at one point, now that would have saved me a job wouldn't it?"

Ellie tried to speak but the gag made it impossible. All that came from behind it was a muffled mumble and it hurt so much to try, but she had to know that Matt was all right. Now that she had come around properly the initial shock of the pain was subsiding. She still hurt all over but at least now it was a bearable hurt. She tried as best she could to look around her. Matt didn't appear to be lying unconscious- or God forbid worse anywhere in the room. This could be either a good or a bad thing. '*Oh where the hell is he. Dear God please just let him be all right.*' Strangely now that she was at the other woman's mercy, all fear for her own well being had seeped from her, her only concern was that Matt wasn't dead.

"Oh I see you're looking round my humble abode. Lovely isn't it? You see Ellie, this is where I lived for twenty seven years, while you were off having your piano lessons and riding your ponies. This was my life this one stinking room. Can you imagine that Ellie? Can you huh? Oh actually I'm not being totally honest, sometimes they had need to pig me out, clean my sty so to speak, so, you see that little door over there? Well they used, of all things, an electrified pole - a cattle prod Ellie, can you believe that? A cattle prod to usher me through that door and into another room, and you know what Ellie? Surprise, surprise, It was identical to this one."

Ellie was wincing under the bitterness of the other woman's words. Each word was spat towards her and stung as it hit home. Was she telling the truth? My God it didn't bare thinking about.

Ellie's eyes had finally come into focus and she could fully take in her surroundings. She gasped in shock and utter amazement as she looked eye to eye into her mirror image for the first time. Only it wasn't a mirror image because nothing was turned around the opposite way. Eve was identical in every minute detail to Ellie. Same height five foot five, same slim figure size ten, same blonde bob and blue eyes. It was no wonder Matt had been taken in by her.

Ellie tore her gaze away from Eve, she took no notice of the pain crashing through her temples, and looked round the room properly. It was a twelve foot square. With one door to the left of her and another much smaller door to the right. This was the door Eve had said led into an identical room.

There was no decoration and the room was sheer, brilliant white. Four walls, ceiling, and cold tiled floor. Into the wall in front of her were built two hatches, each two-foot square. When she craned her neck, she could just make out a single bed with plain white bedding along the back wall.

"See that bed?" Eve was talking again. "Well I once tried to hang myself with the sheets. They made me sleep without bedding for a month. Have you noticed something else Ellie? No toilet, can you imagine having to use a bucket your entire life? Could you live like that Ellie? Could you be someone's pet? They used to bring me a bowl to wash in twice a day and if I had a tantrum and threw it round my cell, oh I wasn't allowed to call it that by the way. This is my *unit*; if I threw my wash stuff round, or ate my soap to cause them grief I didn't get to wash for a month either. And that was messy, the time I ate the soap. For two days I was shitting and puking for victory and then I had to live in the filth for three more weeks and five more days. Not nice Ellie, not nice. We had a birthday during that month. I watched you blowing out your ten birthday candles. Daddy said, "My big girl's hit double figures," and I puked all over my floor again."

Ellie's eyes had grown wider as Eve talked. This couldn't be true. She shook her head at the other woman, trying to let her know that she couldn't imagine that kind of horror but the pain doubled in intensity if she moved her head too much. She tried to speak, but in all honesty she hadn't a clue what she was trying to say so even if she hadn't been gagged she wouldn't have made much sense at that point.

One part of what the other woman said was turning round and round in her mind. '*She watched me blow out my candles.*' Ellie remembered her tenth birthday. It had been a fun day, later on mother drank too much and daddy had to help her to bed, but that was later, after the party finished and all Ellie's friends had gone home. The party had been perfect. Every little girl's dream, with a hired clown and Punch and Judy, everything imaginable in the way of party food, and lots of guests. Yes, everything had been just perfect. Ellie felt tears pricking her eyes as she remembered the pride in her daddy's eyes that day. It had been such a happy birthday.

As if Eve knew what Ellie was thinking she began talking again.

"So there you were having your pretty parties in your pretty frocks, with your foreign holidays and your posh house, and here I was in this room, being fed your life along with their unpalatable food. Do you remember when daddy used to come home on a Friday night and you'd run to meet him? He'd open his briefcase and pull out…"

'A goodie bag,' Ellie thought the words at the same time that Eve spoke them. Such fond happy memories.

"A goodie bag. There was always a chocolate covered honeycomb bar. Do you remember Ellie?"

Ellie nodded. She remembered. Oh how she remembered. The physical agony she was suffering hadn't made her cry, but tears were flowing down her cheeks with the pain of the bittersweet memories of her father.

"And a lollypop on a stick. Sometimes there was one of those bags of sherbet to dip the lolly in. Half a dozen or more good things to eat. And a comic book. Do you remember those comic books Ellie? I used to sit on that bed over there and watch you curled up in the armchair by the fire reading your comic and sucking on your lolly. I'd never tasted sweets, but they looked so good my mouth used to water."

Ellie was scared now. These were *her* memories. How had this woman stolen her memories? There was no twin. No other child, just her and mother and daddy. They were *her* memories, but they seemed tainted and perverse spoken from another woman's mouth.

Ellie's mind was as clear as a June morning now. All remnants of fugue from the beating had left her. So many thoughts and questions were circling around in her mind that she became almost unaware of the pain still crashing upon her in waves of frothing torment. For the moment even Matt was pushed to the back of her mind as she tried to process the huge amount of information that was coming at her too fast to take in.

"You see Ellie, while you were living your clean little life, I was living it too. Every minute of every day, I saw everything you did, heard everything you said but I was just a two-dimensional understudy. From eight in the morning until eight at night I was forced to sit by and see your life passing away from me. I wasn't an interactive part of it, I couldn't make any of the decisions, feel any of the textures of it, all I could do was just sit and watch it all float by. And then after you were turned off, I had two hours before lights out to be me. But who was I? I was a none person. I didn't exist. So for those two hours I would live a little bit of somebody else's life again. I would read. I read fiction books, reference books, autobiographies. All I could do for myself was fill my head with knowledge, but even that wasn't of my own doing. They chose what I would read, when I would read, what I would learn. Always them and always you. Never me Ellie. There was never a me."

'When they turned me off?' Thought Ellie. *'What the hell is she talking about?'*

Ellie wanted to speak. So many questions, so much she wanted to ask. At least she now had an idea of *why* all this was happening to her. And yet how could she see Eve in the role of victim after all that she had done to torture them? She couldn't. Though at the same time as Eve spilled droplets of her non-life to her, Ellie could take no pleasure in the things she was hearing.

Her mind was filled with a horror so unimaginable, that she couldn't even begin to comprehend the enormity of what Eve was telling her. Had Eve really been locked in this awful place for her entire life? Why? She had told her so little, and yet she had told her so much. Images of what the other woman's life must have been like trapped in here flooded her mind. For wasn't she also trapped in this room that seeped twenty seven years of misery and yearning? Who had held her here? Why? And the old question that still didn't bear fruit, where had Eve come from?

Ellie studied her close up for the first time. She was amazing. Ellie had been to school with two sets of identical twins and although they were very much alike they were not completely the same, they could be told apart, especially when they were together. There was only one thing about this woman that was different from Ellie and that was the fury in her core. The anger in her shone through her eyes, everything about Eve was hard. Where Ellie had soft curves, Eve had steely hard muscles, the tendons of her forearms stood taught in the harsh fluorescent light. But it was the eyes that held Ellie as captive as the ropes that bound her to the chair. Eve's eyes were exactly the same hue as Ellie's own, but where Ellie's were a soft muted grey-blue, Eve's were as hard as galvanised steel. Mercury eyes without an iota of love anywhere about them. But apart form her hard essence, Eve *was* Ellie. It was uncanny, horrific, the stuff that nightmares are made of. A horror novelist's fantasy and Ellie's worst nightmare incarnate. Ellie closed her eyes to think.

"Hey bitch. Open your eyes don't you dare close your eyes when I'm talking to you. I'm calling the shots now you hear. I'll tell you what to do, what to say, and yes Goddamit even what to think. You got me? Because you need me to survive. See? See how the tables have turned Ellie? Miss 'little-oh-so-perfect' Eleanor Erikson, I'm now controlling your life the way you controlled mine for all those years."

Controlled her life, thought Ellie. Jesus I didn't even know she existed.

"I've got the upper hand now Ellie, because I know everything there is to know about you. Every single thing. I've watched you having sex. What do you think of that? I've watched you writhing on your bed, moaning and groaning and spewing out all your pathetic I love you's. Don't like the taste of him though, don't swallow do you Ellie? I would. I'd satisfy him in ways that you can only dream of. In fact I might just do that before I've finished with him. What do you think?"

Ellie felt disgusted. She shuddered, her most intimate, personal things, opened up and dissected by this...monster. Her home must be bugged, hidden microphones and cameras, yes that must be it.

Again it seemed that Eve was one step ahead of Ellie's thought patterns.

"And what about that other guy? What was his name? Oh yes I remember now. Tony, we liked him didn't we Ellie? What was it he used to say?" Eve put on a stupid voice.

"Oh Ellie, Ellie I'm going to come, I'm going to explode Ellie. Explode, explode, explode ahhh. Do you remember the first time with him? Up on Heysham cliffs, I bet you thought he'd scared all the sea-gulls away with his yelling. I tell ya Ellie that was funny. I nearly wet myself watching you that day. I didn't find much to laugh at in your pathetic life. You're not really a funny girl you know. You should have taken your role more seriously and entertained me properly. If I had to watch somebody else's life, why in hell, did it have to be yours? Sitting pounding away at that bloody computer for eight hours a day. Where's the fun in that Ellie? I ask you."

Ellie couldn't believe what she was hearing this was getting more bizarre by the minute. She felt ashamed, humiliated, raped. But every word that Eve said was true. That was exactly word for word what Tony used to say every time they had made love. At first Ellie had found it quite amusing, she'd almost laughed the first time, but after two or three times it became irritating, and after two or three weeks it became the biggest turn off ever. The relationship hadn't lasted long.

How did she know? That day on Heysham cliffs there had been no microphones, no cameras, just Tony and herself and the ocean. None of this had made any sense since the first day, but it seemed to be spiralling more and more in to the realms of The Twilight zone by the second.

"And Ellie you know that hot summer's day when you came off your bicycle, you know what I'm talking about don't you?"

Ellie knew what was coming but didn't want to hear, didn't want to be reminded. It was her biggest secret and until recently the worst thing that had ever happened to her.

"Yes Ellie that dirty old man who mopped up the blood. Took you to his allotment round the corner didn't he Ellie. Promised you some nice juicy strawberries didn't he? You were always so gullible, so bloody stupid. I saw it coming a mile off, me who hadn't ever seen a human being face to face; I knew what his game was. Didn't rape you though did he Ellie? Just a touch and a feel and a big sloppy kiss or two. How did his tongue feel Ellie? That big slimy tongue forcing it's way into your pretty little mouth."

Ellie felt sick. She would have put her hands over her ears to block out the sound, but they were tied tightly behind her back. She didn't want to hear anymore. Now she knew that Eve knew every little detail about her life. That was so private and she had never told a soul. She had never been able to find the words to tell Matt about that day in the summer of her childhood. Afterwards she had felt so dirty, so victimised, so lucky that it hadn't gone further than it did. Ellie knew she was lucky to get away from him that day.

He would have gone further if she hadn't started screaming at the top of her voice. She kicked him and ran still screaming until she reached the main road. All the other gardeners had turned to look, one reached out a hand to her, but she didn't stop. And then she was silent, hoping that none of the other men tending their allotments recognised her. Praying that it wouldn't get back to her parents. Ellie like many victims had blamed herself.

"You know what I was doing Ellie? I was sitting on my bed, yelling at him to rape you. Rape the bitch, you dirty old fucker, go on rape her."

Ellie felt the vomit rising in her throat. She panicked; the gag left no room for it to escape. She was salivating and her stomach began to convulse. She tried to keep swallowing, tried to calm her stomach, but the gorge rose and there was nothing she could do to stop it. She was panicking, her eyelids began to flicker. And then the world went mercifully dark and silent.

Eve watched Ellie with interest. She saw the other woman heaving and realised she was being sick. She revelled in the thought of Ellie having to swallow her own mess. Just the way she'd had to live in hers. But then it changed. Ellie's eyes disappeared into the back of her head and her whole body began to convulse. The chair overturned and Ellie crashed to the floor still tied to the chair. Eve watched as the ropes cut viciously into Ellie's wrists as the woman continued to fit across the room. Eve was scared. This was serious. And in that split second Eve knew that she didn't have it in her to kill. All this had been about making Ellie *know* what Eve had suffered. Making Ellie suffer herself, but she surprised herself in the knowledge that she didn't want to kill her. Up until that moment Ellie's death had been the whole point, the Grande Finale.

Eve didn't want to touch the woman who was having a seizure three feet in front of her. She didn't know what to do, and so she stood and watched, her eyes like saucers. What had happened to her control? Eve was supposed to be in control, but here was Ellie taking over again, taking back the control that belonged for this first time ever to Eve.

Ellie was making noises, inhuman noises, disgusting gagging, choking, moaning noises. Eve put her hands over her ears and began to rock. She didn't know what to do.

'Get a grip, get a grip.' Said a voice inside her head. She knew that Ellie was dying and that she was just standing by and watching her. It was horrible Eve didn't want this but there was no way she could run away, her legs wouldn't work and her brain kept her huddled there rocking backwards and forwards, out of control again.

"I don't want to hurt you. I don't want to hurt you." She moaned out loud into the sterile room. But Ellie didn't reply. "Oh God, you can't die. You are my sister, and if you die. I'll die too. Help me." Eve felt that she couldn't survive without Ellie's heartbeat. That somehow the two were connected. That if Ellie's heart stopped then Eve's part of the combined motor must stop too. She couldn't let Ellie die.

Eve shuffled on her bottom across the room to Ellie. She began struggling with the gag, but the more she tried to undo the tight knot the more her hands shook and the less she was able to untie it. Ellie was convulsing so violently that in the space of three seconds she had moved five feet across the floor and Eve had to shuffle again to keep up with her. The leg of the chair banged hard into Eve's leg and she cried out in pain. The gag came lose and dropped to the floor, the contents of Ellie's stomach followed it, and blood, such a lot of blood from the wound to her mouth. Ellie bounced through the vomit as she continued to vibrate and then suddenly, very suddenly she was still. Eve thought she was dead and began moaning. She didn't want to be a murderer. Not that, not a murderer.

But then Ellie gave a cough and stirred. Eve set to untying her captive. It was easier now that she was still, but the ropes at her wrists were slick with vomit and slipped through Eve's hands several times. She wiped her hands on her jeans and went back to work and soon Ellie was free of all restraint.

Eve heaved her over onto her side and wrestled her into the recovery position. She wiped Ellie's mouth to remove the last of the debris clinging inside it. After placing the pillow from the bed under Ellie's head and loosening her soiled clothing, Eve had done everything she could to make Ellie comfortable. And so she sat back against the wall to wait. Her heart was pounding and her anxiety once more gave way to hatred. She had the urge to go over and kick the recumbent form for causing her so much inconvenience - the dirty bitch had made them both stink - but she controlled her anger. Deep breathing would have helped, but the smell in the small room was overpowering. Ellie had urinated while she was fitting and the lesser smell of that mingled with the far stronger, sour smell of the vomit.

Ellie's eyes flickered and she began to slowly come round. She winced in pain as she tried to raise her head, but it was too much effort and so she lowered her head again on to the soft pillow, grateful for this small kindness. The rest of her senses kicked in and she wrinkled her nose and gave a small, ugh of disgust. Eve seemed to take this as an admission of guilt.

"Yes you dirty cow, you've made us both stink. Happy now?"

Ellie's blood supply was beginning an exploratory cycle of her body, to see where it now could and couldn't go. Her nerve endings screamed out in agony as the blood surged along the starved arteries and she began to flex her sore wrists to help the process along.

Her first attempt at speech only succeeded in releasing a meaningless croak. Her second try was better.

"Matt? Where's Matt?" She managed; her mouth tasted of vomit and blood.

A tear squeezed out of her tired eyes that she felt had seen too much, and she felt wretched. "I need to know if Matt's still alive." A little of her strength had returned to her voice and she was amazed at how strong she sounded with the last statement.

Eve's first thought was to tell her he was dead. To watch the gambit of emotions play out on Ellie's face to enjoy Ellie Erikson's suffering. But she realised for the second time in little over as many minutes that there had been enough suffering. She had no idea where things went from here, probably prison as far as she was concerned but she knew that it was all over. She had made her point and told a small part of her story. Maybe Ellie would let her tell more one day. Maybe not. She didn't care any more; she only knew that she didn't want to cause or feel any more pain. Revenge is a dish better served cold they say, well to Eve revenge had brought no feeling of relief. She was still angry, still bitter, still hating, but she realised the futility of going on. She thought she might commit suicide after Ellie and Matt had gone, hopefully before the police came, maybe she wouldn't but at least that choice was hers now. And if she stayed then this prison would be one of her own doing. All scenarios that Eve felt that she could live with. She had an answer to Ellie's question now.

"Yeah, he's still alive. I'll take you to him when you've got cleaned up."

Ellie saw the woman's shoulders slump in defeat; she had watched the inner conflict going on inside Eve as she fought with herself to answer Ellie. Ellie knew as well as Eve did that it was all over, she read it in her captor's eyes. She only hoped that Gail and Rob hadn't involved the police, Ellie didn't want that, she just wanted to be with Matt and to be free to go home.

She felt her first pang of genuine pity for Eve and she lowered her head and began to sob. She cried partly for herself, partly out of sheer relief and also surprisingly partly for the sister she never knew she had. She was too weak now to think about the future but maybe later when things calmed down, maybe...

"Please let me see Matt now," she sobbed. "I'll clean up later, please just take me to Matt."

"No."

Eve's voice was forceful and Ellie cringed away from her in fear. A little more softly Eve added.

"You stink. I'm going to get some stuff to clean you up. I've found where they kept all the things they used for me clothes and stuff." Ellie noticed that she didn't say 'my things.'

"I'll only be gone a few minutes. No funny stuff when I'm gone. Do you promise?"

Elllie nodded the bizarre irony of the situation not escaping her. The woman who had made her life a living hell for the last month was asking her for a promise of trust. And perhaps more crazy still she was giving it. Each woman taking the other at her word.

Eve could have let Ellie go to Matt then. Let them go, leave them to their own stinking mess and their own stinking lives but she didn't. It was important to her that Ellie should go to Matt as unharmed as possible. She had a nasty concussion and some cuts to the head and face, her wrists and ankles were a mess from the ropes cutting into her when she had the seizure. Eve could do nothing about any of that but what she could do was make sure that she went back clean and intact. Eve hadn't a clue why that was so important to her but she knew that it was. In her clumsy way, although she still hated Ellie for the life she had lived, Eve wanted to make amends, to show to Matt and Ellie that she hadn't really hurt them. Not much. Not really. Eve tried not to think about the dog. That was her biggest regret. She never wanted to hurt the dog.

Eve knew though that this was more than just wanting to make Ellie respectable to clear her conscience. This was because she wanted to spend just a little while longer with Ellie before it was all over. She hated the woman, that hadn't changed. There was no miracle bad-girl-turned-good story here. Eve couldn't think it through any further than her having a need to spend just a little more time with Ellie. Just that.

She left the room, carefully padlocking it after her, securing the two ends of the huge chain that she had bought in preparation weeks earlier. To the left was the room that contained Matt. To the right was a room that had been used as a utility room. She went into that one it was unlocked, had been unlocked since the day she left the institute for the first time. As far as she was aware, no one had been back since that day. The room was officious, stocked floor to ceiling with pine shelving, it had everything that a person needed for comfort and hygiene. At the end was a little annex that housed washer and dryer, sink unit and dishwasher. Eve busied herself with a bowl of water and flannels. She picked out a new tablet of soap and some clean clothes for both of them. She put hers to one side, after she had seen to Ellie she'd come back and clean up herself. Then she would take Ellie to see her beloved Matt for the fond reunion. She put everything on a two tiered trolley grabbed some clean towels and a couple of sheets to clean up the mess and then went back to Ellie.

As she let herself back into the cell, Eve was aware that Ellie could have been waiting behind the door to jump her, although she was prepared for that if it happened she knew that Ellie wouldn't do that. The women had made a pact, Eve was doing this nice thing for Ellie and Ellie in return had promised to behave. Each one trusting the other. Sisterhood in practise. Besides she had to be good to get to see Matt. Eve was smiling at this thought as she entered the room.

Ellie had righted the chair and she was sitting on it. Her clothes were in a heap at one side of the room and she was wrapped in a sheet off the bed. Another sign that she had taken Eve at her word.

Ellie's trust made her feel something that she had never felt in her entire life before. She felt good about herself, she felt her first pang of pride, knowing that out of all the harm, she had done something good. It felt nice but it also felt weak and Eve had felt weakness all her life. She stamped the feeling down and placed the trolley beside Ellie with an air of embarrassment. Neither woman spoke.

Ellie began to wash in silence, strangely feeling no embarrassment in front of the other woman. After all, apart from the extra muscle that Eve had they were identical in every way. Ellie tried her best to sort herself out, but she was weak and dizzy. After she had almost fainted for the second time. Eve walked over from the corner of the room and took the flannel from Ellie. She rinsed it in the bowl soaped it and began to wash Ellie's hands face and arms. Ellie was surprised that she was being incredibly gentle, so as not to hurt her. Ellie broke the silence for the first time since Eve came back into the room.

"Thank you." She said simply.

Eve didn't reply but Ellie noticed her cheeks redden. After she had dried her, Eve helped Ellie on with the clean clothes. Jeans, T-shirt and fleece. Simple clothing that Ellie would have chosen herself.

Ellie had so much that she wanted to ask, but she didn't dare ask anything. Although some common ground had been found between them, Ellie didn't trust Eve as far as she would trust Cleopatra's asp. The woman had shown herself over and over to be at best bloody dangerous and at worst, despite her protestations, a three times attempted murderer. She was a psychopath and was dangerous. Ellie held her tongue lest she set Eve off into another psychotic rage. Her thoughts were only with seeing Matt again. So she remained compliant and subservient under the other woman's manipulations.

"I'm sorry about the dog." said Eve. Her voice was thick with remorse and Ellie did not doubt that she was genuine. When Eve met Ellie's gaze her eyes were brimming with unshed tears. "I'm so sorry about the dog."

Now it was Ellie's turn to put Eve's mind at rest. She would never understand how Eve could hurt an innocent animal the way she had but she did understand a little more about Eve's circumstance and could see that Eve might not understand the love people have for their animals. That saddened her. When she smiled at Eve it was a genuine smile of not forgiveness or understanding but of love for her dog.

"It's okay. Jake's fine. He survived the..." Ellie was going to say snare but the word got caught in her throat. "...Accident, he's got a sore leg but other than that he's okay."

"So I never killed him?"

"No, he's really okay."

"Oh thank God." Said Eve and she smiled an awkward smile at Ellie. For the first time the metal had left her eyes and Ellie saw something akin to her own eyes smiling down on her.

"He's a nice dog." Said Eve as though her opinion would matter to Ellie.

"The best." Said Ellie wishing only that she could be with Matt and Jake right this minute.

Eve fastened Ellie's trainers for her and she was ready. She told Ellie that she would just get rid of the things she'd used and clean herself up a bit and then she promised that she would take Ellie to Matt and that they could go home.

Eve was only gone five minutes. When she came back she was dressed in a similar way to Ellie. The two women stood looking at each other. An uncomfortable silence hung in the air between them.

"Right then." Said Eve. "Are you strong enough to walk?" She seemed genuinely concerned for Ellie's well being. *'And so she bloody well should be,'* thought Ellie, *'this is all down to her.'*

"Come on then, I'll um, take you to Matt." Ellie thought for one second that Eve was going to apologise for everything she'd done but she didn't, she turned and walked towards the door.

"Wait." Said Ellie.

Eve turned.

Ellie couldn't believe what she was doing. *'Had she gone bloody nuts?'*

Here was Eve about to let her out of this nightmare and she had to go and stop her, risk upsetting her and having her kick off big style again. But she couldn't walk out of that room without Eve hearing the truth from her.

"Eve. I'm sorry for everything that happened to you, truly I am. I can't begin to imagine how much you've suffered. It's heinous and barbaric, but you have to know, you have to understand, and Christ, Eve you have to believe that I knew NOTHING about it. I didn't know anything about you until the day I got that first letter from you through my door."

"I know." Said Eve. "I knew that all along but it didn't make any difference. I still hate you."

"How can you say that Eve? How can you hold me responsible for something that not only did I have no control over, but something that I knew nothing about?" She knew she was pushing it but couldn't stop herself.

"I would *never* have left you in here had I known about you. I would have moved heaven and earth to get you out and to see that the people who did this to you were made to pay for what they did. Who was it Eve? Who held you prisoner here? Why?"

"I don't know Ellie. Sometimes I thought it was daddy. I thought that maybe he had too much to look after with you and mum, that I was just too much trouble so he kept me here."

Ellie's mind rebelled against this other person calling her parent's mother and daddy, but she held back her irritations.

"Eve my father was the sweetest, kindest man on earth. He would never have done that to you. Never."

"I know, I know that, I watched him every day until the day he died. But I saw you taunting me and it seemed as though you were all against me."

Ellie was confused.

"Taunting you? Eve how could I taunt you when I didn't even know you existed?"

"Remember Ellie? Don't you remember how you used to wish for a sister? You would sit on that balcony and when you saw a falling star, you always used to wish for a brother or sister to play with. Sometimes you'd look right at the screen when you said that. Your eyes would be flashing with laughter. I knew you were taking the piss."

Eve's voice had risen. Ellie knew she was dancing on very thin ice and that at any minute, the ground they'd made up would be shattered and then Eve might not let her out. But she had to make Eve understand.

"Eve that wish was genuine. If you watched my life then you must have seen how lonely I was. That tenth birthday party? Yes? You know? You said you saw it all? Well then, you must have seen the way the other kids were with me. They were there for the food and the party bags that mother made up. Every kid in the neighbourhood knew that my parents threw the best kid's parties. They all wanted to come, but they didn't like me. They didn't want to know me Eve. I had no friends. I know my life was nothing in comparison to the misery of yours but I grew up lonely and unhappy. Yes I had the pony, yes I had the holidays, but I had no one to share them with. All I ever wanted throughout my whole childhood was a sister. So you see Eve, what happened, didn't just happen to you, it happened to both of us. I don't know how you became separated from us, my mother, *our mother,* says she doesn't know anything about you either. But I do know that what happened to you should never have happened and I am so very, very sorry that it did for both of us."

She risked a look at Eve. She was giving nothing away, standing with her head hanging, looking like a confused child.

"Look Eve, I can't say that we can ever be friends or anything, but we do have things that we need to discuss. Can we talk? Please? Later sometime, when you feel better about things will you come and talk to me?"

Ellie cleverly put the onus of responsibility back on Eve. She felt that she needed to give her the power to choose, to feel that she was making the decisions. Also she was clearly saying to Eve that she wanted to see her again, without having to be bound and gagged to do it.

Eve nodded. Everything that could be said had been for the time being. Anymore would be overload for both of them. What they had already said to each other needed to sink in and be digested on both sides. Ellie just wanted to see Matt again.

Without another word, Eve turned to the door and Ellie followed her. Ellie knew that the interconnecting door was locked because she had tried it when Eve was out of the room. So that explained why they went through the external doors. The room to the right was chained with an identical padlock to the one with which Ellie had been locked in. Eve unlocked the door and pushed it open

Then she stood to let Ellie past.

Matt sat tied to a chair in the middle of the room, much as Ellie had been. The only difference with Matt being that his throat was cut so severely that his head was half decapitated.

Matt was dead.

Chapter 20

Ellie pushed passed Eve; the sob that was a half-scream wedged in her throat unable to be released. The truth was plain to see Matt was dead but Ellie couldn't believe that, she mustn't because that would make it real. She ran over to him. She didn't care what Eve was doing behind her. She didn't care about anything the crazy bitch did to her now. Nothing mattered any more.

Although tears were running freely down her face, the only sound that Ellie made was that of her raspy breathing. Her mind did one of those irrational flips that minds do in times of stress and trauma and Ellie was taken back to a thought she'd had just hours before. '*There'll be plenty of time for crying later.*' Ellie knew that had been false optimism. There was going to be no time for her to cry, because soon she was going to be dead too and she relished that moment. One thing she did know was that she wasn't going to play along with anymore of Eve's sick games. She had been so convincing and Ellie was kicking herself for being taken in.

Over the previous few weeks she had spent a lot of time coming to terms with the thought of the cloaked hag of death calling for her as she was forced to face her illness and now she was prepared to look her square in the eyes. Ellie was ready to die.

While all these thoughts had been going through her mind she had been working on Matt's bonds. She didn't care how her body would be found, if indeed it ever was, but Matt was going to have some final dignity. Once he was free of the bonds that were holding him up, Matt slumped sideways onto Ellie. She cradled him in her arms slumping to the floor partly carried down with the weight of his body and partly with the density of the grief that was flooding through her. Her only wish now was that there was something after death and that when she went over, Matt would be waiting for her. As she rocked Matt's body backwards and forwards she made little shushing noises, as a mother would calm a fractious child. Her fleece and T-shirt were saturated with Matt's still wet blood, and her tears fell from her face onto his head.

Ellie became aware of Eve saying something and lifted her head to look at Matt's murderer for the first time. If she had expected that smug gloating smile then she would have been surprised but Ellie expected nothing and had no shock or surprise left in her, only a churning wad of molten hatred.

Eve stood a few feet to the side of the closed door. Her eyes were opened wider than human eyes should ever be. She too was rocking slightly and her lips were moving, whispering the same thing over and over again.

"Hate her, hate her, hate her."

Ellie was getting just a little bit sick of hearing about her dear sister's hatred, and she had a few thoughts on that one of her own. She couldn't believe that something, that was obviously a second half of herself, could be so mindlessly evil. All those childhood dreams for a sister had apparently been answered but oh how she wished she had never had the faith in goodness to pray for them in the first place.

She laid Matt's head gently on the floor and stroked the side of his cooling cheek once. And then she was motion. She was up and flying across the room at Eve. Even without Ellie's wasting illness, Eve was probably twice the strength of her sister, but Ellie was fuelled and propelled by a hatred stronger than any love had ever been. Using her bodyweight as a battering ram she cannoned into Eve knocking her several feet backwards until she came up hard against the wall. In the same second that her body made full contact with Eve, Ellie grabbed her sister by the front of her fleece. She had two bunched handfuls of clothing and she heard a satisfying rip as she further aided the momentum by pushing backwards with her arms as well as her body.

When the wall was behind them and they could travel no further, Ellie began to bang Eve's head against it. The initial impact knocked the wind out of Eve's body with a forceful whoosh, but the other woman gave no indication of having been aware of it. Again and again her head bounced off the wall as Ellie shook her by the front of her clothing. Eve's eyes were still wide and glassy, her lips were moving in between gasps as her body ricocheted off the wall. She made no attempt to stop Ellie, didn't even try to fight back. And now Ellie could hear more plainly what Eve was saying, it wasn't *hate her.* What she was repeating over and over again in a hushed whisper was the single word; '*Creator.*'

There was no reason in this woman, Ellie knew she was insane but until now she thought it was a rational kind of insanity, if there could be such a thing. An insanity born of valid reason in Eve's eyes. Now Ellie knew that the woman was just plain round-the-bloody-twist-unhinged. Ellie hadn't the physical strength to keep lifting Eve's body away from the wall, to slam it back up against it. She was becoming fatigued, but she wasn't done yet. Although she couldn't keep ramming Eve physically, she could still batter her with her venom and anger. Ellie screamed obscenities at Eve still holding tightly onto her and shaking at her ineffectually.

One second Eve was limp and compliant under Ellie's grasp the next it was literally as though she had become charged with power. The glazed look left her eyes, and as though a lever had been pulled a keen intelligence flooded into them. She tensed her body and Ellie felt the limp rag that she had been throwing round become a solid force.

"We've got to get out." Eve screamed. Her body became animated and she jerked and squirmed as she tried to free herself from Ellie's grasp.

She brought her hands up and shook Ellie's fists away from her as though she were nothing more than a piece of fluff attached to her clothing. Aping Ellie's former hold, Eve now grabbed hold of Ellie, the tables were turned but Ellie was too far lost in her rage to back down she continued to scream at Eve beating at her chest with balled fists. One of her punches flew wild and connected with Eve's mouth. She winced as Eve's tooth sliced through the stretched skin of her knuckle. But Ellie was gratified to watch her enemy's lip split wide open and spill her blood in a free flowing rush down her chin.

"You psychotic, crazy, fucking cow. I believed you. I actually believed all your bullshit. You make me sick; you make me feel physically sick, you murderous, fucking bitch. Why? Why Matty? It's me you wanted. Well I'm here Eve, you've got me, and you know what, you miserable freak? There is nothing more you can do to hurt me. I know you're going to kill me too, you bastard. And you know what? You know what sicko? I can't fucking wait. I want to die. There that's taken the wind out of your sails hasn't it? Pissed on your chips good style eh? You can kill me Eve, but you can't hurt me anymore."

Ellie continued to scream into Eve's face splashing the other girl with acrid spittle. Eve slapped her hard across the cheek with an open palm. Ellie screamed as the sting burned through her face. She brought both hands up to her cheek and stared at Eve. Finally she was quiet; all the fight sapped out of her.

"We've got to get out of here." Eve repeated. "Listen to me Ellie. You've got to listen to me." Eve wiped some of the blood off her face with the back of her sleeve. Her voice held a breathless urgency.

"Listen to you. Why should I listen to a murdering bitch like you?" Ellie got no further though she was settling in for another tirade.

"Ellie for God's sake I haven't got long to convince you of this so you're going to have to believe me, and you're going to have to trust me."

Ellie opened her mouth to begin her fresh rant a second time, but she disgraced herself by shrinking away from Eve as the stronger woman raised her hand to hit Ellie again.

"Shut up Ellie. Just shut up and listen. I don't want to hurt you but if I have to knock you out I will. And if I have to leave you here I will." Eve's voice had risen but she wasn't ranting. Her voice sounded urgent, desperate.

"Ellie I didn't kill Matt." Eve's eyes kept darting warily towards the door behind them that still stood ajar.

"Oh right, of course, you didn't bring him here and…"

"Goddamit Ellie. Yes I kidnapped Matt but I didn't kill him. Please believe me. He's here. The man, who kept me here all those years, he's here and he's playing with both of us. Come on we've got to get out of here now. We haven't got a lot of time. He's probably on his way down here now."

Eve started to drag Ellie bodily towards the open door.

Ellie wasn't about to fall for another of Eve's twisted tricks. Not this time. And there was no way she was going to leave Matt either. If Eve was going to kill her, then she was just going to have to do it right here.

"I'm not going anywhere."

"Ellie come on. We've got to move now. We have to get out of here. If you don't come then I'm going to go without you."

Eve looked at Ellie waiting for an answer, Ellie met her gaze with a stubborn defiance and Eve shrugged her shoulders with an air of defeat and went to brush past Ellie.

Something snapped in Ellie. How dare this murderer just walk away from what she had done. She wasn't going to let her go. She was going to force her to stay here in this room and face the evil that she had committed. Matty was lying dead, his blood congealing on the floor beside him and Eve wanted to walk out, like the first one to leave a party. No way.

Eve was a foot away from the door.

Ellie grabbed Eve and spun her round hard. Just moments before she had been exhausted by her first attack on Eve but now she was fuelled anew with hatred and anger. Eve tried to pull away from her. Her eyes never leaving the door now only inches away. She screamed at Ellie to let her go but Ellie pulled her back with every ounce of her strength. Eve made a desperate lurch for the door and as her hand grasped for the handle…it slammed shut.

There was a loud click, as the door was locked from the outside.

Eve's eyes grew wide in terror. There was no mistaking the woman's fear.

"Nooo," she moaned. "Oh God no. Please help us." She leant against the wall staring towards Matt's body and began to cry.

Ellie clapped slowly three times, as she brought her hands together for the third time she remembered a time just a few short weeks earlier when Matt had lay in a hospital bed and had made the same sarcastic gesture towards her. She felt her eyes brimming with tears and glanced over at Matt. *'Soon my love, soon we'll be together again.'* She thought, but for now she had to deal with the snake in front of her. This was a game of wills now and Ellie was determined not to give Eve anymore sport.

"An Oscar winning performance Eve, any chance of some song and dance next, it's so very quiet in here." Ellie's voice was pulled down with bitterness and grief.

"So what's next Eve? What's happening? Are we just going to sit here until you decide it's time to go into the next round? Okay suits me. Bring it on."

Ellie went to sit beside Matt, but she made no effort to touch him this time. She knew that wherever Matt was, it was nowhere near his broken body, but still being close to it, gave Ellie some small glimmer of comfort. She pressed her back into the wall, it was aching now, red-hot needles of pain were pulsing through her and she needed her medication. She had her purse with her when she arrived, but there was no way she was going to beg Eve for anything. The pain was strong but it was bearable. She raised her bent legs and rested a hand on each knee. She lowered her head and closed her sore eyes to rest them. She tried to blank her mind. Happy images of Jake and Matt running in the woods were too much to bear but as much as she pushed the images away they returned. Hot tears washed over the burning handprint on her cheek.

"I didn't kill him." Eve had spoken, but Ellie made no sign of acknowledging what she was saying.

"He probably won't kill us you know? I think he'll keep us here for years and experiment on us. After just one month you'll wish that he had killed us."

Ellie raised her head and opened her eyes. There was no emotion in her voice as she spoke.

"Eve I already wish I was dead. There's nothing left for me now."

Eve sat against the opposite wall to Ellie in exactly the same position. They appeared to be a mirror image of the same person. Both covered in blood, both with tearstained eyes, both locked in their own world. Ellie's world was one of grief and misery, she could only guess at what was going through Eve's mind.

Eve began to cry quietly.

"I deserve this. I know I deserve this. I never wanted it to happen. I was going to let you both go. I was going to come to your house and talk to you. It was all going to be over. Not this, never this. We're stuck here now Ellie. You and me, sisters of hatred, we're going to be cooped up in this room for a long time. I know, you see, I know what The Creator is doing. I thought I was so clever, when he sent me the letter with the password. I knew the net was closing in but I never expected him to look for me here. I was going to disappear, not go back there, he'd never find me. But he has found me. Oh God he has."

Eve was on the verge of hysteria. Each word ending on a wail, each syllable tinged with terror. Ellie had to admit she sounded convincing. She was good.

"He sees everything you know? He's watching us now, listening to every word we say. Laughing at us, playing with us. He could have been here by now; he's here maybe only a room or two away. But he's biding his time, watching the soap opera unfold, making notes. The fire only damaged the outer labs; it never touched down here. Nobody knows about this area, it's shut off. We'll never be found. Even if they come looking for us here, they'll only search the top place. Nobody knows about this area it's shut off. Isolated."

'What was she talking about, fire?' Ellie tried to remember something

about fire burning something. *'Oh yes the fertility clinic,'* it seemed fire was often prevalent where Eve was concerned.

"So there was a fire here? Did you start it?" Ellie was actually being sarcastic but Eve took her seriously.

"No, but I think he did. The Creator, I've thought about it a lot and I think he wanted me to escape. I think he knew I'd come looking for you, seeking revenge and this is exactly what he wanted. I thought all the time that I was doing the calling, but now I see that I've been lead and manipulated just the way I've always been led and manipulated. Do you know that even my clothes were chosen for me every morning? I couldn't even make that decision for myself."

Ellie had heard enough of Eve's self pity, she might have fallen for it before, but she was wiser now. She knew the rules better now. Eve wanted to play the buddy-buddy act, get Ellie trusting her and then she'd pull her next psychotic stunt.

"So Eve, What's next then eh? Surely you're getting bored sitting there. I'm not buying it Eve, so you might as well just do what you're going to do. Come on. Get up. Come on and kill me." Ellie felt her hysteria rising, suddenly the room felt too hot. She felt the walls closing in on her, claustrophobia was gripping her in a fist of steel and squeezing the breath from her body. A line of perspiration appeared on her bottom lip and she gasped huge drafts of air in. Breathing hard, hyperventilating. She ran to the door there was no handle on the inside so she hammered on the door. She couldn't breath; the world was beginning to swim out of focus as the panic attack gripped her.

She couldn't breath.

She felt Eve's arms around her body, pulling her away from the door. She heard Eve sobbing, but still she hammered Bang, Bang, Bang, on the thick unyielding door.

"Come on Ellie, come on. That's not going to do any good. Come and sit down."

They both stopped dead and looked up towards the ceiling. Eve's face registered horror; she knew exactly what this was. Ellie's features registered confusion. Her mind forming a question that she never got to ask.

The noise that had brought the women to a halt was a loud static crackle. Two seconds later an automated voice echoed round the emptiness of the room.

"Good evening ladies. The date is the twenty second of October, Twenty forty six, and the time is two minutes to midnight. I trust that you are comfortable and that you have everything you need. I am so happy to have my two girls here together. It's good to have you both home. Good night my Eve and my Ellie." There was another click as the connection was broken and once more the room was undisturbed by any uninvited noise.

The effect on Eve was shocking and horrific for Ellie to watch.

As the first word of the mystery voice was spoken she pulled herself away from Ellie. She dropped to the floor in what was a half faint, half regression to infancy and shuffled on her bottom over to the furthest corner of the room. Pressing herself as tightly into the corner as she could get, she curled up and began to rock backwards and forwards. Her eyes were wide with terror and she was trembling violently despite the sudden heat. Her mouth began to move and the pathetically innocent words that came out chilled Ellie like nothing ever had before.

Miss Polly had a dolly who was sick, sick, sick.
She called for the doctor to come quick, quick, quick.

This time, there was no denying the tortured woman's torment. At that moment the lights went out and they were plunged into complete and utter blackness.

Eve stopped singing and said instead. "No. Not again, not again, not again." She was whining and Ellie could hear the sobs catching in her throat as she cried.

"Eve. Take it easy. I'm coming over okay? Keep talking, that's it sweetie keep talking and I'll find my way over to you."

Ellie wasn't even aware of having spoken the endearment, all she knew was that they were trapped at the hands of some monster and somehow the roles had flipped out again and she was for the moment being cast as the strong one. She had to calm Eve and bring her out of this near catatonic state she'd lapsed into. Eve had to be coherent to tell Ellie what the hell was going on. What was happening now? Ellie felt like Alice but all her white rabbits were murderers and her dormice were psychopaths.

Following the sounds of the distraught woman Ellie made her way over to Eve and cradled her head into her shoulder. Ellie neither resisted nor softened into Ellie's embrace. She was rigid, locked in her place of horror and Ellie knew that she had to bring her out of it and fast before Eve sunk too far into the protection of her catatonia to be reached.

"Come on Eve, let's get it together. Tell me about this man. Who is he? What does he want with us? Tell me what's going on and we'll figure out a way to fight it."

Somewhere far away Eve felt the determination flowing from the other woman's body and into hers. And against her wishes she felt herself being tugged back from the blessed oblivion. She felt Eve's arms around her, smelled her body and discovered for the first time in her life what it felt like to be held by another human being. A surge of emotions rose up inside her, and for those few seconds, they even overrode the terror she was feeling at being imprisoned again in the unit.The mixture of feelings was alien to her, warmth, compassion, suffocation, confusion and comfort, all these different feelings fought with each other for supremacy. Eve wasn't emotionally strong enough to deal with them so she pushed Ellie away. For the second time that night Ellie felt Eve's sanity return. This time she believed in what was happening and realised how little it would take for Eve to go scuttling back into that world where she didn't have to deal with the present. Ellie only hoped that if she left again she'd take her too.

For the second time the speakers began to crackle, this time Ellie knew what to expect. She felt Eve tense beside her. If Eve's singing had been chilling, this was nothing short of petrifying.

Miss Polly had a dolly who was sick, sick, sick.
She called for the doctor to come quick, quick, quick.

'Good night my sick little dollies. I'm going now. You'll be here all alone but don't fear the dark my darlings for tomorrow I'll be here again bright and early.'

After the voice stopped there was silence between them for a long time as each fought their own brand of monster.

Some minutes later Eve groped in the dark for Ellie and when she made contact she grabbed at Ellie's arm. She had to be touching her when she said it. This time Ellie had to know the truth.

"I didn't kill him Ellie."

Ellie took Eve's hand and although she didn't resist Ellie felt it go stiff in hers.

"I know you didn't. I know that now."

Eve was crying quietly again. "I know it was all my fault and that if I hadn't kidnapped him it would never have happened but I didn't kill him. I swear I didn't."

"I know, I know." Repeated Ellie softly. It was the truth, she hadn't a clue what was going on but she knew that Eve was not the monster who had killed Matt.

Ellie's mind was trying to grasp something; something important that was just out of reach. Something to do with Matt. As they sat together against the wall Ellie tugged at her mind trying to tease out whatever it was that might be helpful to them. It wasn't his phone, Ellie had noted earlier that he didn't have his outside jacket on and his phone was always kept in the inside left pocket of that. Ellie felt a pang of longing as she thought about the amount of times she had nagged at Matt for leaving his jacket with the mobile in it in the car. His wallet he might have that on him though. *'Well what good is that going to do,'* she asked herself, it's not as though we're in an open all hours is it? And then enlightenment struck. Attached to Matt's car keys was a pocket torch, only tiny but still quite powerful. Not as handy as a mobile phone she told herself but a small strike to the little people.

"Matt's got a torch in his pocket." she whispered. "I'm going over for it."

Eve grabbed her arm in sheer panic and dug her nails painfully into Ellie's flesh.

"Don't leave me. Please don't leave me." Eve sobbed. She couldn't bear the thought of being alone in the dark for even a second.

Ellie winced and prised Eve's hand off her arm. "It's okay. It's okay I'm only going over there. I'll keep talking to you all the time okay? And I'll be back in a second."

Eve let her go, but Ellie was concerned as she heard a low moaning coming from Eve.

"Stick with me Eve, come on baby, stay with me now. Don't you go looping off into some magical fantasy land and leave me in this hell on my own. We're in this together now."

Ellie felt a stab of rapid hatred, as it came back to her that it was Eve who had brought her to this and got Matt killed. She bit down on the feeling. If they stood even the slightest chance of getting through this then they were going to have to be allies, whether Ellie liked it or not.

"You know Eve. Although I had no idea you existed until recently, I always sensed you. I always felt as though there was a part of my life missing, as though someone wasn't there. The feeling grew less as I got older of course but deep down I think I always knew I was only half of something bigger."

Eve had stopped moaning to listen.

"You stay with me now. You still there?"

"Yes," answered Eve in a small, frightened voice.

Ellie had reached Matt. Her groping hand had found his foot. When Ellie had laid him down on his side, his feet were lying on top of each other. Now the one that she dislodged fell to the floor with a heavy thump. Ellie screamed and recoiled from her lover's body. It had begun to stiffen, and his leg had felt unnaturally heavy. Ellie didn't know whether she could touch him to search for his keys. This was the man she'd loved and would happily have given her life for, and now she couldn't bear to touch him. She began to cry again.

"Ellie? Are you all right?" The concern in Eve's voice touched Ellie and reminded her that she had to be strong to get Eve through too. Later their roles might be reversed again and then she'd have to rely on Eve. The torch might be a godsend when they didn't know what was coming at them in the dark. Resolutely she felt along Matt's body, guiding herself up him as she felt along his leg. She had to heave him over onto his side more to be able to get her hand in his pocket and the movement forced the stinking risen stomach gasses out of his mouth. Ellie gagged on the smell and hurriedly thrust her hand in the tight jeans pocket in search of the keys. She had them in her hand. *'Thank God he hadn't dropped them.'*

As she pulled her hand back out of the pocket, the back of her fingers glanced across his already stiffened penis. What had given Ellie so much intimate pleasure was now a dead thing of disgust. She couldn't stop herself from wiping her hand on her pants. She had been holding her breath so as not to breathe in Matt's dead gases and now she let it out with a rush. She was already scudding back across the floor before she had to inhale again.

The torch worked and as it illuminated quite a large space around them it felt like a small victory in a great war. Ellie wanted so much to leave it switched on but they had to conserve the torch's energy for when they really needed it. Eve began to cry again, and the women huddled together, hoping that the night would soon draw to a close but dreading what horrors the new day brought. Emotionally and physically exhausted, the women slept, ignoring the small bed against the southern wall they remained upright using the floor as a mattress and the wall for support.

So much was left unsaid but the gentle hand of nature had taken control and brought them both to healing sleep.

Chapter 21

For an hour and a half Gail sat and did nothing. The slightest noise made her look hopefully towards the door but Rob still hadn't come through it. Three times she'd asked for a call to be put through to the police and each time she had cancelled it before the computer dialled the number.

Normally she could ring Rob anytime but this meeting was with the publishing house Darley Bryant, one of the biggest in the country and Gail knew that it was an important meeting. Rob was hoping to sign on the lucrative line and score a huge contract for Shadine Williams. This year's hottest romance novelist. Shady wrote steamy historical romances despite being a confirmed lesbian with a long-standing partner of some twenty years plus. Gail knew that it would appear unprofessional to ring Rob with a domestic crisis that would cut short their deliberations. But surely they must have eaten and finished with the business side of things now. It was turned five thirty so they must be to the point of congratulatory brandies by now.

It was this last thought that finally made Gail put a call through to her husband. Rob had taken the car, so he wouldn't have anymore than one after lunch brandy to clinch the deal. It seemed that no matter how many signatures were put to how many pieces of paper, until a contract was sealed with alcohol it wasn't truly binding. During small client meetings Rob never exceeded his one drink limit but in important meetings such as the Darley Bryant contract he had been known to leave the car and take a taxi home. Time was getting on and it looked as though this might be the case today. '*Oh God,*' thought Gail, '*what if we have to drive to Keswick.*' Her mind was made up.

Rob answered after the third ring.

"Hello my little gilded Lily with no aged tarnishing. Are you all right sweetheart?"

"Yes Rob I'm fine." Gail worked hard to keep her voice light and cheery.

"No darling of course I'm not having an affair, that thing with the maid was all lies, I was merely helping to relieve her poison ivy rash."

Gail smiled despite the tension that was bubbling inside her. She could almost see Rob winking at his dinner guests. She knew from his joking manner that the meeting had gone well and as she knew he would tell her later, '*he had them eating out of his hand.*' She heard Rob excuse himself.

"Are you nearly done there, love?"

"Yes just having a drink here and then I'll be home love. Won't be long."

"Rob," Gail didn't want to give anything away in her voice but she just wanted him home quickly. By the time he had finished his drink and drove home it was going to be another half hour at the very least. "You aren't over the limit are you?"

"No love, I'm bringing the car home, why?"

"Oh no reason, listen sweetheart, just get home as soon as you can will you. I miss you."

After speaking to Rob, hearing his normal calm voice, knowing that he was oblivious to what was happening at home, she felt no better. Far from feeling reassured that Rob would soon be home, she felt even more helpless. When she heard his voice she wanted to hear that he was just pulling into the driveway, not that he was still sitting in the Canterbury enjoying fine brandy and the taste of success.

Jake knew something was wrong, he was restless and wouldn't settle. Whether it was down to some canine sixth sense of danger, or whether he was just picking up on Gail's anxiety she didn't know, but the dog was pacing the room. He'd lie down for a few minutes and then he'd be up again padding to the door and then back to Gail. Every few minutes he'd give a little whine just to show that he was worried too. Gail tried to calm him, but still he wouldn't settle. She remembered reading somewhere that dogs can hear the change in heartbeat of someone about to have a fit or heart attack. Not surprising then that he should be able to smell her fear, she could almost smell it herself.

~*~

Rob's face worked itself into an expression of concern as he pressed the disconnect button on his mobile. Gail often rang to check when he'd be home, it was a woman-nurturing thing. Women needed to know exactly what time they should put the lasagne in the oven, so that it would be cooked to perfection when they sat down to eat. It didn't matter how much the world had evolved in the last hundred years, how new woman had become, or how even newer man had, that was a fundamental essence of woman. She always had, and always would, need to know exactly when she should put the lasagne in the oven. So it was not unusual for Gail to ring, so what was niggling Rob? She had sounded perfectly normal, and yet…

He turned back to the three people he had just finished doing business with, who had become engrossed in a conversation about characterisation while Rob had taken the call. They hadn't yet noticed that his conversation had ended.

"Excuse me guys," he said including Shady in the 'guys' colloquial, I hope you don't mind but I'm going to have to shoot. Listen if there's anything you need to discuss, don't hesitate to call." Hastily he gathered up the strewn papers and stuffed them into his briefcase, and then he shook hands with them and kissed Shady on each cheek.

By the time Rob got the car out and had left the twisty country road behind, another twenty five minutes had past. He had a sudden sense of urgency to get home. Twice he tried to ring Gail but there was no signal on his phone. Too many damned trees he thought. Once he was on the open road he called again and this time was gratified to see the blue power bar of life shine from the mobile.

"Hey sweetheart I'm on my way, I'll be home soon love."

There was no mistaking the sound of relief in Gail's voice as she spoke to him.

"Okay Gail, come on cut the crap. What's wrong? I've known you too long darlin` not to be able to pick up on the fact that something's bothering you." Rob wasn't unduly worried. It would no doubt be an unwelcome bill that she wanted to discuss or some minor domestic incident. Gail was one of those people who would brood on something until she'd had a chance to talk it through and share whatever was worrying her with Rob and then she'd be fine.

Rob heard Gail begin to cry quietly and he was instantly worried sick. For all the fact that his wife was a bit of a worrier, she was not given to tears for no reason. In fact it was so rare that Gail cried over anything, that when she did, Rob was usually overcome with a huge need to protect her and make her smile again. Gail was probably the happiest person he had ever known.

"What is it Gail? For Christ sake tell me what's happened?"

"Oh Rob." Suddenly the floodgates were open and there was no holding back. She sobbed so hard that Rob could barely make out what she was saying. "Matt's been kidnapped and Ellie's gone after them. Eve rang demanding that Ellie meet her and Ellie's gone off on her own. She wouldn't let me call the police or anything. Oh Rob I'm so scared. I'm going to call the police now."

"What?" Rob Stormed. "When?" How long have they been gone?"

"She took Matt sometime this afternoon and Ellie got the call about half four I think."

"For God's sake Gail why the hell didn't you ring me?" Rob was yelling hard down the phone. "What the hell are you playing at?"

"Don't you yell at me. It's not my fault. You were in an important meeting but apart from that Ellie wouldn't let me do anything. Eve said that if anyone else got involved then she'd kill Matt straightaway. We believed her Rob. And now it looks as though she's got both of them."

Rob swore as he rounded a corner and came up behind a haulage truck. Although the road here was open and good time could be made if it was clear, he was still in relative Hicksville and there was no passing place for over three miles.

"I'm going to ring the police Rob. This has gone on long enough."

"No Gail. Don't do that. Ellie's right, Eve's a loose cannon waiting to go off. If the police, in riot gear go storming in, there's no telling what she might do. Let's hold off on calling the police just for now. Where is she; Ellie's place?"

"No. No she's at some research place near Keswick, told Ellie to meet her there alone. She only gave her one hour and then she was going to kill Matt. And now she's got both of them."

After speaking to Gail. Rob rang Ellie's mobile number, he realised that if Ellie was hiding out somewhere that the phone ringing might give her hiding place away but then he reasoned that in that situation Ellie wouldn't be stupid enough to leave her phone switched on. If the phone was off that was a good sign ...wasn't it?

The phone rang seven times and then there was a loud click as someone deliberately turned it off. All his instincts told Rob, that it wasn't Ellie on the other end of that phone and his shirt stuck to his back in patches of ice-cold sweat. At that moment Rob realised that should the need arise, he was a man capable of murder.

It was six forty-five when Rob finally got home. He stayed long enough to change into jogs and sweatshirt and give Gail a cuddle and then after confirming directions he was off again.

"Please let me come with you Rob. Don't leave me here alone."

"Gail I need you by the phone in case they ring. Don't call the police baby. Promise me on my life now that you won't call the police. I'll check out the situation when I get there and if it's looking bad I'll call them myself okay?"

After more reassurances that he'd be careful Rob was ready to leave, he got to the front door and then stopped. As an afterthought he turned back to the kitchen and picked up Jake's lead.

"C'mon big fella, let's go and rescue your folks eh?" Jake cocked his head on one side inquisitively but once he saw his lead being picked up he didn't need asking twice.

Rob was never quite sure why he took Jake along with him that night. After all a dog with a damaged leg was a liability. Maybe it was that he felt Jake had a right to ride along, or perhaps it was just that Rob yearned the contact of another living being and couldn't put Gail's life at risk.

~*~

It was eight twenty pm, when Rob finally found the place. He left the car just outside the large iron gate, by the sign that warned trespassers off. Giving

Jake a firm order to be quiet he locked him in the car and set off up the twisting drive. He kept into the side so that the bushes planted to either side would give him protection from being easily seen. The grass verge under his feet stopped him crunching up the gravel. He was more scared than he'd ever been in his entire life. As he rounded the last bend and the huge dark building became visible, a car gunned to life a hundred metres in front of him. Rob leapt back into the bushes and cursed the fact that he'd left the car in full view of anyone leaving. The headlights of the car never came on. And Rob resigned himself to the fact that when it drove down the drive, his cover would be blown. From this distance he couldn't make out any details of the car, but he doubted that the occupants were Matt and Ellie. It drove quickly towards him and moved in darkness to the head of the drive. When it was about thirty metres from Rob, it suddenly swerved to the left and ploughed through the dense bushes at the side of the drive. It disappeared from view but as it crashed through the foliage and its back end shot off into the night, Rob had a clear glimpse of the two teddies sitting on the parcel shelf. The car that had just been hidden from view belonged to Ellie.

Rob strained his ears and heard a car door slam. He listened intently but there were no more bangs to follow. '*Just one person then,*' he didn't know if this was a good thing or a bad one.

A few seconds later Rob heard a figure crashing through the undergrowth making no attempt to be quiet. Obviously Eve felt secure in the knowledge that Ellie hadn't been followed. Now that *was* a good thing. Reluctantly Rob pressed himself further into the bushes covering him. This meant that he didn't see the person who came out of the darkness, before turning back to run up the drive. Rob peeped out just in time to see her disappearing round the side of the house, bent over and taking long strides, covering the ground quickly.

Once the dark figure had disappeared, presumably into the institute, Rob cautiously made his way back down the drive. Jake whined as he opened the car door and jumped in. And Rob had to waste a precious minute stroking and calming him. He took the car and left it half a mile down the road, hidden from prying eyes down one of the many dirt tracks leading to the lake.

"Come on then fella, let's go. But, Jake mate, you have got to be quiet, you understand me man? Quiet."

Jake cocked his head.

Of course Jake understands the word quiet. Jake is a good boy. A clever dog. He knows when to be quiet. And he knows this is bad. This isn't walk-in-the-woods-chase-squirrels, this is something to do with Ellie, and not Ellie and it is bad. Jake will do what Rob tells him. Jake is a good boy. A clever dog.

Rob set off back towards the institute. Jake stopped to relive himself once but didn't bother with all that sniffing-at-everything thing that dogs do. His injured leg didn't look to be giving him any trouble, when he was moving quickly he just tucked it high into his stomach and limped along on three legs, he moved as rapidly as Rob could and seemed to understand that this wasn't an evening stroll. It was as if the dog knew the urgency. Rob had Jake's lead in his pocket but had not fixed it to his collar, the dog walked perfectly by his side. Stopping occasionally to listen to the sounds of the night, he heard nothing that concerned him and they would resume their mission. Rob was glad he brought the dog, not only was he an odd form of moral support, but he would alert Rob to any danger before he heard it himself.

Rob got as close to the house as he dared and then hunkered down to think and decide what he should do next. Somewhere in the distance he thought he could hear a mobile phone ringing but it might have been just a trick of the night.

Being very careful to keep as much as possible to the shadows, he made his way round the back of the building. There was a car parked outside a small door about half way along the rear of the main house. The thing that shocked Rob the most though was the fact that what couldn't be told from the front of the place, or at least under the cover of darkness it couldn't, was the fact that there had been a terrible fire here recently. Many of the windows had been blown out, the broken glass swept and loaded into an orange skip. At least there were plenty of places to gain entry. Rob hardly dared to risk tipping the balance of fate by thinking about the many places to escape too.

The car was an Audi GZ Titan, new, flash and fast. This puzzled him. Eve had stolen a considerable amount of money from Ellie but nothing like enough to buy something as flash as this. But then they didn't know Eve's background so perhaps she had funds of her own and stealing from Ellie had only been for the thrill of being able to do so. '*Sick Bastard,*' thought Rob not for the first time. Another thing niggled at the corner of his mind. There weren't many cars like this one around, solar panelled roof, 0 to 90 in four seconds. These babies were noticed. Why would Eve want to drive one of these when she was trying to keep a low profile? Or at least Rob assumed she was trying not to draw attention to herself, his mind wanted to remind him of the figure he'd seen running round the corner but Rob wanted to focus on a door twelve windows down from the one that the car was parked outside. Telling Jake to be quiet, he sidled up to it and gripped the handle. He pressed his ear up against the cold glass panel, one of the few that remained intact. Silence. So he tried the handle and swore softly when it wouldn't yield to him.

"Fuck, it's locked."

He was running back along the row of windows to try the other door. Bent low running at a crouch so that he couldn't be seen from the inside, when he heard the sound of a door shutting somewhere deep within the institute complex. Swiftly altering his course he ran to hide behind some trees at the rear of the skip. She probably wasn't coming this way but he could not afford to take chances.

Two minutes later the door opened, confirming that his instinct to hide had been a sound one. No light shone from behind the open door, whoever it was, they were used to the lay out, comfortable with travelling within the institute in the dark. Rob was assuming Eve was in this on her own, but he didn't know for sure and was taking nothing for granted. He knew that if he didn't keep his wits sharp and honed, then this night might well become his last. The moon barely gave off any light and all Rob could make out was a dark figure opening the driver's side door and climbing into the Audi. Jake growled low in his throat as the door opened and Rob put his hand on his head to quieten him. He felt the dogs hackles rise along the length of his back, his body taught, every muscle stretched and ready to pounce. Seconds later the engine gunned to life and two shafts of light illuminated the night breaking through the shadows and throwing beams out across the acres of grassland, that were purposefully kept just slightly too long to be called lawns. The sudden beams of light startled a family group of deer strolling just outside the woodland and they fled back into the safety of the woods in a matter of seconds.

If Rob had chosen to hide in front of the car rather than behind it, which he would surely have done if they'd got as far as the first door, which was level with the car, he would have been illuminated by the headlights for sure. Rob trembled with the realisation of the close call. He heard the car disappearing down the gravel drive and out into the night. Perhaps Eve was returning to her lair, maybe her work here is finished, thought Rob with a shudder. He couldn't let himself believe that, so comforted himself with the lesser evil thought, that Eve had just gone to get something and would be back shortly. Neither thought filled him with delight but this was by far the better of the two. He would not relax his guard.

Taking advantage of the lack of moonlight but keeping his body low to the ground, Rob ran to the door with Jake trotting along at his side. A quick listen to see that all was quiet and then he tried the door handle, as expected it was locked with a simple barrel lock. The retinal scanner was intact but inactive. Either the fire had blown all the electricity in the building, or the alarms and scanners had been turned off. That would explain why the electric fence was also lying dormant. What was someone else's misfortune, was one little black lead ounce of luck placed on his side of the scale plate. Rob could force the door easily, but he knew that would alert Eve, should she come back, to the fact that someone had broken in. He chose to take the less elegant option of struggling through one of the broken windows, he didn't know whether Jake would make it with his damaged leg, so he picked the big dog up and put him through the window first. Jake was scared and tried to scramble in Rob's arms, he didn't want to be dropped into this awful place of darkness, but once he landed on the other side he instantly got a whiff of something familiar. It was vague, indistinct, but unmistakably his beloved Ellie. He shook his head as he smelled *not Ellie*, too that didn't please him and he whined softly but he could smell Ellie and Matt and that made him very happy.

Rob warned Jake to keep quiet. Had he been stupid to bring the dog? He wondered again. Jake could blow everything if he became excited. Rob looked at Jake, as he landed none too gently on the floor beside him. It was as though the dog had a right to be there, as if he was owed at least that much. Rob motioned with his hand for Jake to come to heel and they began walking down the corridor.

Jake's nose instantly went to the floor and he began tracking the smell of Ellie. It was hard for him, there were so many bad smells here. The smell of fear and misery were easily the strongest. *Jake didn't know why Ellie and Matt would want to come here, it was a horrible place, Jake didn't like it, and hoped that they weren't going to start bringing him here on his walks.*

There were rooms off to either side of the long corridor. They could be inside any one of them. Rob was going to start searching them all but Jake seemed to know where he was going so Rob was happy to trust to his judgement. Any ideas Jake had, he was happy to go along with anything rather than have to think this through for himself, he was scared and the only idea he seemed to be coming up with was to go home have a long bath and a very large whisky.

Every half dozen doors or so, the corridor met an intersection where other corridors branched off the one they were travelling, this place was a rabbit warren. At the third junction Jake veered off to the left.

"Are you sure boy?" Rob whispered.

Jake looked at him and whined very quietly.

Am I sure? Am I sure? Huh why do they always think they know better? When it comes to itchy-scratchies and cold, cold, spray they probably know best but when it comes to noses Jake is the smell king. I'm coming to get you Ellie. Hang tight honey. Me and Bozo here are on our way. Whine bad smells, bad smells. Not fun here Ellie.

Half way down this corridor, Jake stopped at another junction. He seemed indecisive and padded on a few paces keeping to the same path. He snuffled the floor turning his body round in circles. He whined, even Rob could understand that it was a whine of frustration. He waited patiently not wanting to confuse the dog any further or rush him, even though he knew that Eve could appear in true Freddie Krugeresque fashion at any second. Jake made his mind up and took the new path, once back on the trail he set off with determination.

"Good boy." Said Rob.

"I know." implied the look that Jake shot back

He stopped half way down at a set of double push open doors. They were the kind of doors you get in hospitals with the rubber on the bottom, designed so that stretcher trolleys and wheelchairs can be pushed through with ease. This room must have had some through-traffic of heavy equipment.

Rob listened intently. Everything seemed to be quiet, so taking a deep breath he pushed the left hand side door just enough to let himself and Jake through. Even Rob had to screw his nose up in disgust as he walked into this little house of horrors. The room was some kind of lab, dominated by machinery and computer banks. It was enormous, the size of a warehouse, or the ballroom in a stately house. *'That's what this is,'* thought Rob, the old ballroom, once filled with satin and lace, now housing smoke damaged equipment and the dead bodies of so many suffocated animals. Rats, mice, dogs, pigs, monkeys, hundreds of tortured animals given the final blessing of death. *'Why the hell hadn't anyone been back here to clear this room out?'* It didn't make any sense. Rob knew that the things he saw in that lab were going to stay with him for a long, long time. *'The stuff that nightmares are made of.'* He closed his eyes and shook his head. At his side Jake was impatient to get away from this horrible place. Trying not to look too closely at what had happened to the creatures *before* the fire hit, Rob followed, his heart heavy. If someone could do this to innocent animals, what could they do to Ellie and Matt? The fact that Eve had worked here fitted his mental pattern of her perfectly.

Almost at the end of the lab, Jake began to whine at a small door set off in an alcove to the right hand side. Rob pushed the door, expecting it to be locked, but it swung open as he turned the handle.

"Nah, there's nothing here lad, this is just a store room."

Jake had other ideas and while Rob looked at the jars of formaldehyde that weren't even under lock and key, he had his nose back to the ground, following the scent to the back wall. He stopped at the wall but only because he had to, looking back at Rob he wagged his tail.

"What?" he said to the dog. "You want me to open the wall? Right. Uh it's a wall Jake, your nose is tripping out on you this time mate. Come on let's get out of here."

Rob turned to leave feeling rather stupid that he'd been happy to follow a dog whose only tracking experience to date was to sniff at the lavender heads in the garden and the food in his dish. *'Bloody dumb mutt.'* At the door Rob called Jake, no point in hanging around here, though at that moment formaldehyde cocktail with a cherry on the top and a slice of lemon seemed a pretty inviting prospect. *'But...'* thought Rob in his best mock camp, *'there's not a cherry to be had, what's a fella to do?'*

The dog gave one sharp yap but refused to move. Rob shushed him. Jake looked from the wall to Rob several times and then opened his mouth as though to bark but no sound came out. Rob had the feeling that Jake was threatening him, that, if he didn't look around for a way through the wall as requested, he would indeed start barking. Rob *knew* at this point that he was losing his mind. *'Being blackmailed by a German Shepherd, for Christ sake man, get a grip.'*

"Okay, okay if you insist." he whispered.

The wall was completely smooth with no levers or pulleys. Rob figured that the dog had become confused with the smell of all the dead animals. The room was small and stacked floor to ceiling with wooden shelving housing all manner of drugs and products in a seemingly haphazard mess. Sterile suture kits stacked next to a sack of rabbit pellets, water feeders next to IV drip paraphernalia. It seemed an odd way to conduct a medical establishment. Rob began to feel along the shelving nearest the wall, while Jake whined at him impatiently.

"All right, all right, I'm doing my best here okay? I'm new to this stuff."

His fingers ran over something on the underside of the top shelf. He bent his head to look and sure enough there was a little red button.

"Bingo!" he said as he pressed it. The wall slid back on itself revealing a long corridor with the seemingly obligatory doors off to each side.

Jake gave him an *'about time too'* look and padded through.

The scent must have been stronger now; Jake flew along the corridor without stopping to relocate any lost scents.

He stopped at a door three quarters of the way down and knew that his Ellie was on the other side of it. He forgot to be quiet and barked happily, his tail wagging furiously.

Ellie, Ellie, it's me Jake. I'm here. Come on Ellie let me in. Want to lick, want to lick. Whine.

Jake began to scratch wildly at the door. Rob had to run over to him and wrap his arms round his neck to try and keep him quiet.

Ellie woke reluctantly, her neck was stiff and her back was burning with a fire from hell. There was none of that awakening fugue, that blissful few seconds of not knowing where you are. Ellie knew exactly where she was. Eve's head had dropped into Ellie's lap. *'Oh well as long as one of us was comfortable eh?'* She thought sarcastically. She had been dreaming about Jake. The memory of her beautiful Jake brought instant tears to her eyes. Ellie peered through the darkness to where Matt's body lay and the tears spilled down her cheeks in a torrent of misery and pain.

Jake barked a second time and continued scratching at the door.

"Jake? Jake? Oh Jake, my beautiful, beautiful, fella."

Ellie fought to disentangle herself from a waking Eve and flew over to the door. She had to grope for it in the darkness but Jake's scratching guided her to him. Ellie hadn't thought as far as the fact that if Jake was on the other side of that door, then so was help. All she could think about was her joy that the dog was there. She was almost choking on her tears they were flowing so fast. Ellie doubted whether she would ever be able to stop crying.

Then she heard Rob's voice. *'Blessed, wonderful Rob. Thank God.'*

"Ellie, Ellie is that you? Are you all right?"

"Oh Rob," She could hardly speak because she was sobbing and trembling so much. "Yes Rob, I'm here and I'm all right, but listen." She broke down again and couldn't continue.

"Hey baby it's all right I'm going to get you two out of there. So you've been having yourselves a private party without inviting Uncle Rob eh?"

"Rob?" there was a long pause as Ellie gathered the last of her inner reserves. This was the first time she had to say it and just having the strength to spill those awful words was an effort greater than the effort of staying alive when Matt was not. "Rob, Matt's dead."

On the other side of the door, Rob sagged visibly. He rested his forehead against the cool panel of the door and breathed deeply. He heard the words plainly enough even through the thickness of the door but the meaning behind them was taking a while to catch up. He couldn't take in the fact that Matt was actually dead. He had no words of comfort for Ellie, nothing that came into his mind was big enough, all his simpering words were way too little to chip anything off the massive block of grief that her one sentence conveyed. But he knew that if he listened to Ellie's heartbreak any longer he'd give in to his own and be useless to them all. As Ellie herself had done, Rob took all the pain he was feeling and turned it into anger.

"Ellie I'm going to get you out of there and then, I'm going to track down that evil bitch and kill her. Do you hear me Ellie I'm going to kill the bastard."

Eve had shuffled up behind Ellie and put her arm around her, offering comfort Ellie assumed; though why she should think that she needed *her* support Ellie had no idea. At Rob's final words she felt Eve flinch and although she hated the woman more than she ever believed it was possible to hate another human being, she felt a slight stab of pity for her too. Eve was as trapped as Ellie and at least Ellie had Rob, what did Eve have? Nothing.

Rob had taken all his anger and turned it into physical aggression. To hell with the noise, he was past reason, past stealth he was angrier than he had ever been in his life before. He *wanted* the bitch to come down the corridor towards him. He would welcome her with clenched fists. He had never hit a woman in his life but, by God, he was relishing the prospect where Eve was concerned. Rob began charging the door with his shoulder. It did not give an inch. There was no way he was going to be able to break the door down with brute force and he was too consumed with anger to think, so he continued charging the door anyway, he'd worry about his bruised shoulder, when he'd finished worrying about their lives.

"Rob, listen there's something else I have to tell you, stop that and listen...Eve's trapped in here with me."

"What?"

"Rob stop shouting, I don't know how long we've got. I haven't got the time to go into it all with you now, there'll be time enough for that if we ever get out, but you have to believe me when I tell you that Eve did *not* kill Matt. Someone else did Rob and he's pure evil. He's still out there and he's dangerous so for God's sake watch your back."

Eve spoke for the first time.

"Rob, it's Eve."

Jake growled, his hackles rising.

Rob felt every hair on his arms rising as he heard no change from Ellie's voice and yet he knew that this wasn't Ellie speaking, he was consumed with anger and hatred for this woman.

"Rob? Are you there?"

"Yeah, I'm here and I warn you. If you've hurt her. If you've harmed her in anyway, shape or..."

Eve stiffened against the onslaught of sheer fury coming at her through the door and for a split second she was almost glad that it was locked, if the dog didn't tear her apart, the man would.

"Rob listen to me. You have every right to be angry but there's no time for anything destructive now. We have to work together to get out of here. The man ...He's called the Creator ... He'll be back and when he comes, he will not hesitate for one second if he needs to kill you. What he has planned for Ellie and I is anybody's guess. Every second is precious. Look, you won't be able to break the door down and it's protected by a combi-lock so you'll never bypass that. I've had a long time to think about getting out of here. Listen there's a skylight. It's high, about thirty feet above my head. It'll be a squeeze but I think we'll just about fit through. We need a long rope."

Rob's heart sank as he clearly remembered lending a neighbour his towrope a few months earlier, as often happens with loaned items it was never returned.

"I haven't got a towrope," he shouted back. "That would be ideal if we had one. I'll have to look round here and see if I can find something."

"I've got one." Ellie cut in. "Rob, I've got a towrope in the boot of my car. The driver's door should still be open; I left it unlocked in case I needed to leave in a rush. The car's out front by the fountain."

Rob knew otherwise, but didn't have time for small talk.

"Right Ellie I'm on my way to get it. I'll be as quick as I can. Try to keep calm. You're going to need all your strength to get out of there."

"Rob, we've got a torch so you'll know which skylight it is." Shouted Eve. "We'll give you five minutes and then start flashing it."

Rob had to admit that Eve's self control was going to be of benefit, Ellie was so immersed in her grief that she was going to have to be treated gently.

"Make it ten," shouted Rob it'll take me that long to get to the car and back, he dumped it in the woods at the side of the drive."

Rob could hear Ellie still sobbing, it took all the strength he had to turn and leave her alone with that madwoman, but he had no choice.

"Come on fella let's go," he said to Jake but Jake refused to move. There was no way he was going to leave Ellie with *Not Ellie* he could smell the danger. Jake knew this wasn't walk-in-woods-chase-squirrels and he wasn't going anywhere. Rob could see how miserable the dog was feeling he felt the same but they had to go and get that towrope. He clipped Jake's lead onto his collar and dragged the dog against his will along the corridor.

Rob had to drag Jake all the way through the building to the entrance but once he threw the dog back through the window, Jake seemed to realise that there was little point in trying to be difficult. He went along with Rob quietly but his ears were flat to his head and he was depressed. Every few yards he looked back to the horrible place where he had left Ellie crying. Jake couldn't understand why Rob wanted to leave her there.

Once in the open air, they set off at a sprint. He had no idea how many people there were involved in this but his gut instinct told him that there was only one lunatic running free that night wanting to kill them and possibly another one locked in a room with Ellie, he had to move fast. Eve seemed to be supportive but what if it was all an elaborate trick? Despite the cool evening breeze, droplets of sweat were rolling from Rob's forehead.

The dense greenery at the side of the drive had corrected itself remarkably well considering a ton of metal had recently crashed its way through. Rob wasted valuable minutes finding the place where the car had been taken through. He was within feet of Ellie's car when he heard the phone ringing. *'Ellie's phone? It might be important.'* He scrambled through trees and over rocks in an attempt to get to the car before the phone stopped ringing. He wrenched the door open and flung himself across the front seats before he realised that the ringing was not coming from Ellie's car.

He froze. Somebody was in the bushes, waiting for him, playing with him. Slowly he backed out of the car and stood at the side of the open door. Although it was dark he could just make out the silhouette of a dark shape a few yards from Ellie's white car in the woods. The phone was still ringing, surely most people would have given up by now, it must be relevant. It was him. It had to be.

Rob plunged headlong through the bushes to the other car, Matt's car. The door was unlocked and as he swung it open the ringing of the mobile phone intensified. Matt's jacket was on the passenger seat, he picked it up and groped in the inside pocket it wasn't there. He quickly searched all the pockets. They were empty and yet the sound of the ringing phone was coming from Matt's jacket. Again he thrust his hand into the inside pocket and found the hole in the lining. As he put his fingers through the hole … the phone stopped ringing.

"Shit." He said, his voice sounding unnaturally loud in the still of the darkness. He found the phone and transferred it from Matt's pocket to his own. He must remember to turn it off before setting off back to the institute.

Quickly he moved from Matt's car back to Ellie's and opened the boot. The way their luck had been recently he either expected to find several headless corpses in the boot, or at best the lack of a towrope, it seemed that this time at least, luck was on his side. He picked up the rope slung it over his shoulder and slammed the boot shut after him. He was just making his way back through the thicket when Matt's phone began to ring again.

His heart started thumping and now that he had hold of it, he couldn't decide whether it was going to be best to answer the phone or not. Finally he pressed on the little green 'yes' button and said hello.

"Oh thank-God." It was a woman, breathless, talking rapidly. *"I've been ringing all night. I can't live with this any longer, the guilt, it's too much you see. Too much."* She sounded drunk.

"She's not there is she? I can't say anymore if Ellie's there. It all goes back to him. The Creator knows everything."

As soon as he heard the word *Creator,* Rob straightened up. Until then he thought he was talking to one more nut in a world that suddenly seemed over-run by them. '*Huh maybe he still was.'*

"Who is this?" said Rob, tense, ready for the unexpected.

"It's Maria, Matt, you remember we talked last week. I need to talk to you, we need to meet."

Suddenly Rob came up to speed. Of course the phone call that Matt received from the mysterious woman.

"Maria, This is Rob a friend of Ellie and Matt's." he heard her gasp. "No please don't hang up. Listen you've got to help us." A note of hysteria had risen in his voice "Matt's dead. He's been murdered but not by Eve by someone else. Ellie and Eve have been locked in some room at the institute and I can't get them out. For God's sake if you know anything tell me now."

He could hear the shock in Maria's voice, it shook alarmingly with her next words.

"They are at the institute? You have got to get them out of there quickly. It's his lair. Don't you understand it's the place where he feeds? He'll be

back, he'll be back."

Maria started rambling. If he didn't keep her focused she was going to be useless to him.

"Maria the door code. Do you know the door code?"

Her voice lost all expression, she spoke as though she was in a trance.

"Dolly"

"What?"

"Dolly the code is dolly 36559."

At first Rob couldn't make any sense out of what she was saying but then he realised she meant that the numbers corresponded to letters, like on a phone. Maria continued to speak in the same dull monotone.

"I've got to go now. He's going to kill us all. I've already said too much. I have to go."

"Wait." Shouted Matt into the phone forgetting to whisper.

"No, I'm going now. I'll be in touch." With that the line went dead.

Rob's head was reeling as he ran back to the locked room. He still had the rope slung over one shoulder just in case. This time he had left Jake locked in Ellie's car. Rob knew that if Jake came face to face with Eve he'd tear her apart and Rob would have no desire to stop him.

Back at the room Rob shouted through the door.

"I've got the code. I've got the code." As he punched the numbers in with trembling fingers.

"How?" yelled Ellie.

"Never mind, tell you later. Let me get this bloody number in before I forget it."

36559 He waited for the click. Nothing happened. Maybe he'd entered it wrongly.

36559 nothing.

Grabbing for Matt's phone he lit his lighter and looked at the display.

D-O-L-L-Y 36559 Still the door refused to open.

"Fuck. It's not working."

"He must have changed the combination number after the fire." Shouted Eve.

Ellie began to cry again softly. For a second there she had the wonderful thought that they might be able to get out of there. More importantly that they could get Matt out of there, give him the dignity of a decent burial. But now she knew that she was trapped. That she and Matt were not going to leave this room.

All three of them were aware of time running out. Rob knew that their captor had been gone for over an hour now. They had no idea of where he'd gone or how long he'd be, but somehow they all knew that he wouldn't be away for long.

"The skylight." Shouted Eve. "I'll shine the torch."

"Okay." Shouted Rob. As he tore back along the warren of corridors he took a few seconds to feel irritated that suddenly Eve seemed to be running the show. '*Who the fuck died and made her the supreme ruler*?' And then he remembered Matt and felt a moment of deep shame that for a split second in his haste, he had forgotten that he had been killed. It didn't matter who the hell called the shots. Until they were away from here and safe they had to work as a team, putting aside their personal feelings. He just hoped that the bitch could be trusted.

Rob cursed the rich Steak Diane he had eaten with relish so few hours before when he was a man living a normal life, in a normal world. He puffed and struggled as he scrambled up wall and guttering to reach the top of the roof. '*Is this a good time to remember that I'm terrified of heights?*' He asked himself and smirked at the irony of the situation. He stood on the roof for a second with his eyes closed, trying to imagine how the Black Magic man would act in a time like this. He stood straighter, tottered slightly, despite there being nowhere to fall from this point, and then bent himself over again. Straight was not good, he was no hero. He was just an ordinary bloke who lived life a little too well and should never have been put in this guise of hero that didn't suit him. He tried to get his bearings. Everything seemed different from up here on the roof. He worked out where the corridors branched and then when he was semi-confident of the direction he should be taking, he set off at a crouch, keeping to the middle of the roof and trying desperately not to look down.

Ellie continued to cry, her heart was shattered and she was about ready to give up.

"Come on it's all right. It's only a minor hassle we'll just go back to plan B. As long as we've got just a little while longer, we'll soon be out of here."

"You might be but there's no escape for me. I'm stuck here."

"What do you mean? Rob's on his way, we'll be out of here and away in quarter of an hour. Just fifteen minutes more, hang in there and stick with it. Don't go jelly on me now Ellie, we need to stay focused until we're out of here."

"I'm not going anywhere."

"What? Are you crazy?"

"Eve I'm dying. I have Tay-Sachs, it's a muscle wasting disease and there is no way that I'm going to be able to climb a rope thirty feet and then climb through a tiny skylight onto a bloody roof. You'll have to get out when Rob comes and call the police."

Ellie saw the fear cross Eve's face at mention of the police and knew that she was doomed.

Eve pulled up her sleeves and in the glow from the torchlight she flexed muscles that would put most men to shame.

"Ellie while I was locked in here I had little to do with my time. I spent hours of every day meditating and working out. Look at me Ellie. I'm strong enough for both of us. I'll help you up the rope." Her face-hardened. "But don't think it's out of any form of misguided sisterly love. No police Ellie. Okay we can do this, but you have to promise me. No police. I know everything went wrong but last time we made a deal, I stuck to it. We need to make the same sort of pact of trust again. I can help you get out of here alive Ellie but you have to promise me that when it's over there will be no police."

Ellie looked at Eve, she had nothing to lose.

"Deal."

The next five minutes seemed endless but when they felt as though at least an hour had past, they heard Rob's feet coming cautiously along the roof towards them. Eve flashed the torch furiously up at the ceiling.

Rob tried several times to prise the skylight window open but it was stuck solid. There was no way that he could get it open even if he had had a crowbar to hand. This window had not opened in the last thirty years or so, there was no way it was going to open in the next few minutes.

"Stand back." he yelled. "I'm going to break the glass."

The twins moved over to the corner of the room, they crouched low and pulled the fleeces over their heads to protect them from flying glass. Ellie was sure that Rob would not be able to break the glass. One more set back in an endless night of torture.

Rob raised his foot forgetting his fear of falling and running now on pure adrenaline. He brought his heel down hard with all the strength he could muster but his foot just bounced off the glass.

The second time he took his leg even higher. All he needed was a little more momentum, when the heel of his trainer connected with the glass he was gratified with a tremendous crash. The window had shattered inwards coating the room below with merciless needles of broken glass. Despite knowing it was coming Ellie screamed but half way through the scream turned into a cheer.

Rob continued to kick at the skylight ensuring that all the jagged edges were removed from the frame. It was going to be a tight fit before, now the hole that the women had to climb through was four inches smaller. Rob had serious doubts that they were going to be able to get through. The hole was only really big enough for a small child to fit through.

Now he had to find something strong enough to fasten the rope to. He moved up and down the roof looking but there was nothing. Panic set in, to come this close and then fail was unthinkable. He had no choice but to use himself as an anchor. Rob was a big guy, six foot plus and eighteen stone. The girls weighed about nine stone each. He could do it. No problem he was twice as heavy as either of them. He tied the rope firmly round his waist and then dropped the loose end down through the skylight.

"Got it." Shouted Eve.

"I know, you nearly pulled me off the fucking roof and in there with you. Don't start climbing until I tell you okay?"

"Okay."

Rob walked over to the edge of the roof and lay flat, he held onto it with both hands, thankful that he had remembered to take his thick driving gloves out of the car. All he could do now was hope that both he and the knots were strong enough to hold on until the girls climbed out.

"Ready." He yelled. "Okay do it."

Eve's next words made his blood run cold.

"Right Ellie come on you're going to have to jump on my back. Don't hold on to my neck to tightly and for Christ sake don't fall off. We can do this."

'Of course, Ellie would never be able to climb the rope. How could he have been so thoughtless.' This was an even bigger ordeal for Ellie than he had imagined.

"Matt first." Said Ellie with determination. "Take Matt first, I'll wait until he's out."

"Are you crazy?" Eve screamed at her. "Ellie we can't take him. I won't have the strength to do this twice. We have to leave him behind."

"I'm not leaving without Matt." Said Ellie stubbornly in a small voice.

"Ellie," this time it was Rob who tried to talk some sense into her. "Ellie, I don't know if I can hold the two of you. I know I won't be able to take Eve's weight and Matt's at the same time. I'm sorry love but Eve's right, we have got to leave him behind. Matt would understand. Now come on. That maniac could come back at any minute and we're all sitting ducks here."

Rob breathed a sigh of relief as he heard the oomph of Ellie jumping onto Eve's back. '*Thank Christ for that.*' He was still worried about taking the strain of both the women at once. It was a weight roughly equal to his own and he only had the edge of the roof to hang on to.

Eve began to climb and Rob discovered what it was like to be a man tortured on the rack in medieval times. With each inch that Eve gained on the rope, Rob felt his body pulled further towards the skylight. He felt the edge of the roof cutting not only through the gloves, but into his fingers, he hung on and gritted his teeth against the pain. If he hadn't had the driving gloves he would not have been able to do this.

Eve was perspiring heavily, the tendons of her neck sticking out like electrical cables. For the first time she was beginning to doubt that they could make it.

Half way up the rope she felt Ellie's grip beginning to loosen.

"You okay?" She breathed.

"No I think I'm going to faint. I'm dizzy and I can't hold on much longer."

"Yes you can and you're not going to faint. One chance Ellie. We've only got this one chance and if this fails then we might as well just roll over and die." Talking was difficult but Eve knew that she had to be the strong one. Ellie was about to lose it both physically and mentally.

"Hey." She continued. "Remember that goofy song you used to sing when you were depressed? What was it now? Oh yes I know."

Eve was finding the going tough, just moving hand over hand up the rope was taking all her strength, but she knew that she had to do something to keep Ellie focused. Between ragged breaths she began to sing.

'Wherever you go, I'm gonna be there.'

"Come on Ellie help me out here. I can't sing this shit on my own you know."

Ellie's small voice joined in.

'What ever you do, I'm gonna be there.
Pure and simple, gonna be there.'

At last they reached the top and Eve was able to grab hold of the frame. That was the easy bit now came the real test of Eve's strength.

"Ellie one day those old songs are going to be the death of me."

Despite the situation, the tension, Matt's death and everything else the women laughed together for the first time.

"Right Ellie, you are going to have to summon up some strength from somewhere pet, because you are going to have to climb up me to get out. I would offer to help but as you can see, I've got my hands full."

The weight of Ellie's body was already dragging her down, she could feel the entire weight of the two of them centred on her eight fingertips. She was going to have to shut everything out and find somewhere quiet to retreat to in the hope of getting them through this.

"Rob, you're going to have to let go of the roof and come and help Ellie through."

"I can't, if you lose your grip you'll fall and pull both of us through with you."

"Okay. But just remember if we all end up crashing back down, I sleep on the left."

Ellie had gone horribly quiet she was losing it again.

"Quick Rob," Yelled Eve. "My fingers are slipping and I can't hold on much longer."

Rob grabbed Ellie by the shoulders.

"Right come on Ellie, use Eve's body to walk yourself up."

"I can't. Oh Rob I'm so scared, I can't move."

"I know you are honey, I know, we all are, but this is the only way out."

Rob began to pull hard under Ellie's arms.

Eve concentrated on slowing her breathing. She closed her eyes and imagined being by the sea. She had never felt the sensations of standing at the ocean but had lived it through Ellie many times. She used this method of meditation often. Her heart rate dropped from its elevated rate of one hundred and twenty through her normal rate of about sixty four. Steadily it continued to fall until it reached its lowest rate of forty beats a minute. Eve's heart rate had dropped eighty beats in little over thirty seconds, she had found again her quiet place where no one could hurt her.

Ellie's head was through the window and she was able to take part of her own weight by resting on her elbows. It had been a hell of a struggle getting her shoulders through but with a lot of shoving between the two of them they had got her top half through. Now Ellie was both exhausted and stuck.

"Come on Ellie, you can do this. Think about it. Your shoulders are your widest part, if you can get them through the rest will follow.

"I can't. I can't move."

"Come on love, put your arms around my neck and let me help you."

Rob centred his balance by placing his feet either side of the skylight and squatting. Ellie put her arms round Rob's neck reluctant to let go of the security of the hard wood against her arms. She buried her face in Rob's neck and smelled the cool citrus smell of his expensive French aftershave. It wasn't the same brand that Matt used but just smelling the closeness of a man near her reminded her of Matt, alone and dead on the floor of the sterile cell.

Rob began to straighten his legs. He had the whole weight of Ellie in his arms now and felt the strain in his lower back. He concentrated on lifting her through the hole. Remembering to lift with his leg muscles not his back, but he didn't seem strong enough, her slim hips were wedged in the tiny hole. He was about to relax and take a deep breath before trying again when Ellie suddenly shot through the hole with a plop. Rob flew backwards and almost *did* fall off the roof, but managed to regain his balance five feet from the edge. He lunged at Ellie and had grabbed her to him in a fierce bear hug. Ellie sobbed into his neck, Eve for the second forgotten.

Rob realised that Eve had not followed Ellie out of the window as expected and went to look over the roof. She was just hanging there and for a second Rob thought she had died in that position. He leaned in and touched her arm.

"Eve?"

She opened her eyes slowly as if waking from a long and restful sleep. She grinned up at Rob and put a hand out to him to help her out.

Rob wanted to take his fist and smash it deeply into the back of Eve's head *from the front.* Only the fact that she had seriously risked her own life to save

Ellie saved her, but Rob could not bring himself to take the woman's arm. He had seen the incredible strength of her and one pull and she could have him through the skylight and falling to the ground below. He looked upon her as a rabbit would upon a snake. He didn't trust her. He turned back to Ellie leaving Eve to get herself out.

As it was Eve had no difficulty at all, the two and a half minutes of transcendental meditation had revived her and she wriggled through the hole as though she were indeed an invertebrate. The image of Eve cast in Rob's mind as a serpent intensified. Rob shuddered violently and clung to Ellie in a mutual giving and taking of warmth and comfort. All Rob wanted to do now was ring Gail, she must be half out of her mind with worry. As soon as they were on the open road that was the first thing he was going to do. The second was have one of the black-market cigarettes that he had hidden in his glove box.

Getting back to Ellie's car hidden in the woods was no picnic but somehow they managed it. It was still dark but not pitch black, the moon had made a belated appearance and was very kindly lighting their way a little. Rob and Eve pretty much carried Ellie most of the way. The ordeal had taken its toll on her, she had been hours without her medication by this time and the Tay-Sachs was giving her one hell of a beating. Actually getting Ellie off the roof might have appeared, to anyone looking on, like a scene out of a badly scripted comedy. However none of the players were laughing, Ellie was rapidly reaching the end of her rope. Once again it was Eve who saved the day. Just as she had known exactly how to hurt Ellie when she was driven by her campaign of hatred, so she knew how to keep Ellie moving now. She reminded Ellie of Jake sitting in the car just a few hundred feet away waiting for her. It was just the push she needed and from somewhere she pulled just enough reserve of spirit to get her through. Rob hadn't thought of that and the smile he gave Eve over Ellie's head was part thanks and part grudging respect. Rob had to admit to himself that if it hadn't been for the combined efforts of both himself and Eve, there was no way that alone either of them could have found a way out of there.

Jake heard them coming long before they did. As soon as he saw his beloved mistress he was beside himself with joy and jumped all over the car in a bid for freedom. He also saw the one who'd been trying to hurt Ellie and he was a seething mass of confusion he was half joyous and half fury and didn't quite know how to behave. Ellie warned Rob to put Jake on his lead and keep tight hold so that he couldn't reach Eve and although Eve didn't need any telling she warned her to stay back out of his way.

While Rob was struggling in the car to get Jake's lead on. Eve stood beside Ellie with her hands loosely flopping at her sides in a gesture of not quite knowing what to do next.

"Right, I'll be off then." She said awkwardly, now that the drama was over at least for the moment she felt embarrassed. "I'm sorry about everything."

Before Ellie could say anything she turned and began to walk away.

"Er, where the hell do you think you're going? You aren't going anywhere."

Eve turned back round, her face had taken on that hard stony look again.

"Listen Ellie, you said no police, you gave me your word. I trusted you."

At that moment Jake came bounding out of the car with Rob struggling on the end of him. He ignored Eve completely and flew at Ellie in sheer wanton delight. She loved and crooned at the dog for a couple of minutes until he was calmer and then turned to talk to Eve. Jake seeing his enemy growled deeply, warning her that if she moved just one step closer to Ellie, he would have her.

"I know I did Eve, and I meant it." Said Ellie picking up the conversation as though they had never been interrupted. "There will be no police but if you think you can just walk away from this as if nothing's happened you must be out of your mind. My boyfriend has just been murdered and you want to just disappear into the night. I'm sorry but responsibility doesn't work like that."

"So what do you want me to do then? Surely you aren't suggesting that I come back with *you*? And I can't go back to my flat. Ellie we may be out of there but the danger is far from over. He's going to come looking for us and when he finds us, soon after, someone else will be finding us too, only difference is by then we'll be dead. Now I'm not going to just sit around and wait for that to happen. Are you?"

"So what are you going to do Eve? Where are you going to go? Are you just going to run away like a coward into the night leaving me to face it all on my own?"

"You've got it in one sister. That's exactly what I'm going to do. I'm going to start walking and as long as I live I'm never going to stop. Because he'll never give up looking."

"Don't you see Eve we have to stick together on this one. You owe me and yes, in some ways maybe, I owe you too. You've got at least some of the answers to this mess and together we might be able to find out the rest. Yes you brought all this on us but you also saved my life in there and for that I'm grateful."

Rob cut in on them speaking for the first time.

"Excuse me ladies I know you've got a lot of talking to do and Gawd knows I've got a lot of sleeping to do but there is a maniac out there trying to kill us remember. So can we just get home please and then if you so wish Eve I'll take you and drop you anywhere you want to be. Outer-bloody-Mongolia if that's what you want, but please let's just *move.*"

The next problem they had was sorting out the travel arrangements. There was no way Jake was going to let Eve in the same car as Ellie. They had three cars and the way Rob saw it one driver. Eve had never driven a car in her life before so she was out. Rob decided that they would just have to travel back in his car and try to keep Jake away from Eve as best as possible. But every time Eve moved the dog started snarling, so that wasn't going to work.

The only other solution was for Ellie to take her car with Jake, leaving Rob and Eve in Rob's car. Rob hated the idea but Ellie convinced him that after everything that had happened she needed some quiet time to herself. Rob worried about her taking ill at the wheel but Ellie assured him that just seeing Jake again and being free had returned a little of her strength and that she'd be fine. He had to admit that she did look better. Then he brought up the subject of them being followed. What if they met the mad man on the twisty, Lakes' road, if they were in one car they might stand a chance of out-driving him but in two they had had it. Ellie argued that the longer they stood there arguing, the more likely they would be of meeting their crazed jailer Ellie promised to wait at the end of the road for Rob to catch up and then Rob's car could tail her all the way home. This seemed the only solution and so finally he agreed.

Rob drove Ellie's car out of the woods for her and made sure that everything seemed to be in order with it. Luckily it had withstood the assault course well. Ellie got in and calmed Jake, within seconds he realised he was going for a ride. Jake loved only one thing more than walk-in-woods-chase-squirrels and that was going for a drive. So he assumed his usual position in the passenger seat and whined impatiently for Ellie to start the car.

She turned the key and heard the engine start up, there was a three-second gap in which the realisation of what was about to happen hit Ellie but before she could stop it the DVD player also began to operate. The tape that she had been listening to just the day before with Matt began to play. Ellie loved old music, stuff from years before, it was a particularly mellow album by Jewel and memories of Matt flooded the car as the music seeped through the speakers. She began to drive with tears obscuring her vision.

Once she made it to the road, she pulled into the side to wait for Rob. Paranoia struck her and she felt open and vulnerable as she waited for Rob's car to appear. When the lights finally did come round the corner she was hit by a bolt of panic so intense that she felt her body freezing. What if it wasn't Rob? What if it was *him* and she was just sitting there waiting to be picked off. The music of Jewel rang through her head and in those few seconds she could almost feel Matt's presence in the car with her, she could hear him in her mind, telling her to calm down and that Rob would protect her. Sure enough as the car drew close its lights began to flash and she felt herself relax.

The drive back to Rob's house was uneventful, and the ordeal was over, at least for the time being.

Chapter 22

You fool, you utter, utter fool. Big mistake. Big mistake, shouldn't have killed the boyfriend. Their fault. The dollies, they shouldn't have brought him onto the board. It was our game, ***ours,*** *nobody else's. He had no right to be there. No right. No right I tell you. Those silly dolly's they didn't think. Do they want to anger me? Anger the Creator? Do they think they can go against me and win? Do they?*

There'll be recriminations. There'll be consequences no less. Consequences I say. Who'll pay the price. Not I. Not I the Creator when the men in blue pound the doors Rat–a-tat-tat. Not my door. The dollies will pay, my broken dolls, my girls. They'll pay. Oh I'll make them dance on their tight strings until they can dance no more.

They shouldn't have let him come. And now they're crying crystal tears. Judas tears, that's all, Judas tears. They betrayed him, such a nice young man. A gentleman, regrettable indeed. They will not bring a white king onto my board, they will not THEY WILL NOT!

The man in the crimson smoking jacket punched the far wall. Though the dividing wall shook and the chandelier rattled he felt no pain, so far gone was he into his mania. It wouldn't pain him until later, when he would take to his boudoir to watch.

Temper temper! No need for it, no need I say. We do not display emotion do we? Indeed we do not. Cunning is the order of the day. Cunning, stealth and patience.

Things are hotting up sir. What is this bond striking up between the dollies? Well, well isn't that nice. We shall watch now. Watch for the fireworks and explosions. 'ello, 'ello, 'ello and they'll run. My poor broken dollies. Run for their lives. Run for their freedom. Run till their hearts pound and their breath rasps. Rat-a-tat-tat. Who made Matt smile so wide? Such a big smile in his smooth shorn throat. 'Not I sir' say the dollies but still he'll chase them.

Chase them, chase them, chase them. The men in blue will chase them. And then ***I'll*** *chase them longer with cunning and stealth and patience. Rat-a-tat-tat, Hello.*

He threw back his head in the near darkness and laughed.

Chapter 23

7th June 2018 (Twenty eight years earlier)

"Do you have to go out?" He was always moaning at her these days. If she'd known what it was going to be like she wouldn't have married him. "Why can't you stay in and we'll have a quiet night in front of the plasma?"

'Je-sus,' she thought, *'plasma, plasma, plasma, surely there must be more to life than this?'* She was thirty six years old and wanted to be out having fun. He could vegetate all he liked but not her; he wasn't going to pin her down to the dishwasher. He came up behind her and put his hands on her waist. *'God I hate it when he paws at me like that.'* She wriggled away and turned to face him, glaring.

"I told you yesterday that I'm going out and I'm going. Why do you have to be so bloody possessive? Since you made me give up work, we sit in night after bloody night, and what do we talk about eh? Nothing. Not a damned thing. When did you last take me out? On my birthday wasn't it? Nine months ago."

"Oh but you've got plenty to talk about with Jenny Bailey haven't you? Who she shagged on Tuesday night while Terry was doing the back-shift for instance. She's a tart and you told me when we got married that you were leaving all that behind you. Can't you see that I want us to have a decent life? I'm earning good money, we can build ourselves a future, start a family, be happy. For Christ sake woman I just want to make you happy."

She'd heard it all before, same old whinging, same old words. Nothing was going to spoil tonight for her, least of all that boring old fart.

She applied a third coat of lipstick. Lippy had died out over a decade ago. Pigment implants were available in the backroom of any pharmacy these days and cost little more than the price of a new top. But this season the fashions of the 1980's had made a come back and bright red lipstick was all the rage. She wore a black lace mini skirt with a sheer lace bat-winged blouse over a daring black bra. The neckline of her top plunged almost to her waist and the back mimicked the front, so that her torso was exposed in a V to her navel and, the back, to her hips. The deep leather belt was almost as wide as her skirt and the whole ensemble was finished off with black ankle boots with lethal looking stiletto heels. Her blonde hair was back-combed and teased until it stuck out from her head as though she'd stuck her finger in an electric eel. And though she thought it herself, she looked damned good as she turned in a slow circle in front of the full-length mirror. She loved the sluttiness of the old styles and her tiny figure showed them off perfectly.

He snorted in disgust and left the bedroom without another word, knowing that as usual he was beaten. She wouldn't be back now until the early hours of the next morning, coming in drunken and leery. It was a familiar story.

She met Jenny in 'The Crier', the place was heaving and the crowd in good spirits. From their working days in the local clubs they knew a lot of faces. With a bit of luck they wouldn't have to buy too many drinks for themselves tonight. From the 'Crier' they moved round town in a crowd, the women screeching like barn owls on the hunt and the men loud and bawdy in their beer-soaked aggression. When the pubs closed they moved on to the Carleton nightclub. The Carleton had been around forever and was still a favourite haunt of the clubbing fraternity of Keswick.

The women wasted no time in swirling onto the dance floor in a haze of cheap perfume and glitter dust. It was still early and the large dance floor was almost empty, they had plenty of opportunity to display themselves as they gyrated and moved their bodies to the beat of the thumping music. The women's dancing consisted of lots of stroking of their own bodies, their hands alternating between touching themselves in a suggestive tease and raising high in the air to better display their lithe, half naked figures. They never ceased moving, circling waists and flicking hips, seducing every man standing round the floor and at the bar.

"See that bloke over there?" Said Laura Jones pointing, "I think he's following us."

She'd noticed him too; he'd turned up in the last three pubs that they had been in shortly after they arrived. By this time she was drunk and barely aware of who *she* was, never mind anybody else, but she'd noticed him all right. Six foot odd, blonde and gorgeous. Any woman that pulled him tonight was one lucky girl.

He was looking right at her.

She held his eyes for three seconds, a long time in flirt language. And then with an expression of gross indifference, she flung her arms high into the air, stroking down her left arm with her right. She stretched her torso, so that it was long, she bent back slightly and moved in a slow, exaggerated, sensual wind. There was no mistaking the offer laid open on the dance floor. She was there for the taking.

The signals sent and received it was time to reel in the catch of the day. She left the rest of the girls dancing. Retrieving her bag from their table she walked elegantly towards the bar. She was drunk but as a seasoned pro, she knew how to walk the walk and talk the talk of the scene. He was standing at the edge of the dance floor, his attention re-positioned from watching all of the women, to focussing on just one. The tarty blonde, she was 'up for it' ripe for the taking. He was confident enough that she would be leaving with him before very much longer.

She passed within inches of him and flicked her hair so that as she moved past it would lightly graze his shoulder. Some of the hair spray had worn off with regular backcombing throughout the night, and that combined with a thin sheen of perspiration coating it from her moist neck meant that it would have at least some movement in it.

She stood at the bar ignoring the stares of lustful men. Her choice had been made and she had no interest in any of them now. She knew that if she'd read the game card correctly, he would follow her. She ordered a double Bacardi and coke and was making a show of scrambling in her bag for her purse when a deep voice beside her said.

"Please let me get that for you."

'Bingo!' She thought and smiled up at him.

'Bingo!' He thought, the money was in the bag.

Chapter 24

Aaron Quinn had been with the company for over two years now. He was a mover; he knew that in this organisation people were hand picked for the 'inner sanctum'. Most of the workforce lived their lives doing their mundane jobs and going home at the end of the day to their tired spouses and unbearable children. Everybody talked at one time or another about the restricted area. The gossip was rife about what went on in there. When a member of staff went beyond the restricted doors they were not seen in the labs or around the workplace ever again. The first anyone ever saw of them was when they were burned off at traffic lights in their brand new Subaru Stampede that had taken over the old Impreza a few years earlier. What they didn't know was that beyond the private part of the building perfectly innocent and routine scientific experimentation on innocent animals was carried out. Inspectors swarmed all over the place bi-annually and everything was strictly above board and legit.

Another thing they didn't know was that a private area, way beyond that private area, had been built. This most secret of secret places was currently being fitted out with the very latest equipment and gadgetry to set in motion the most controversial experiment ever conducted under the respectable heading of 'science'.

Quinn never would know about this, because he wasn't about to live long enough to find out.

He had been noticed though. He would be so proud if he knew that Griffin, the man in command of operations had not only spotted him but he'd been picked by *the* boss himself. Very few people in the company even knew that there was anybody higher than Mr Griffin. What had singled Quinn out for special treatment though was not his incredible drive and ambition. The thing that set Aaron apart was his sensational good looks. That and nothing else got him where he was going and his transport far from stampeding was going to be lead lined for comfort.

Ron Griffin was the 'white coat' that gave the place a clean bill of respectability. Ten years on, Griffin would be found hanging from company rafters when he discovers that his beloved institute is less than squeaky-clean. His suicide came at a most fortunate time for the one above even him. It saved hands being dirtied by the messy business of murder again and this man did so appreciate having spotlessly clean hands.

But that's still a long way down the road from the days of Aaron Quinn. He was going to be a key player in the whole experiment. He'd like to have known that, but never did.

Aaron had set himself apart from the white rats pouring over their microscopes and viewing tiny eviscerated pieces of other white rats. He knew that he was destined for greater things. He distanced himself from the canteen gossip choosing instead to spend his lunch breaks pouring over text books that he had little interest in. He didn't care what he had to learn to get into the restricted area. That was mere knowledge that had to go into his brain via his optical senses. He just knew that the big money to be had was earned behind that security restricted set of double doors and some big pound signs were waiting in there with his name on them.

Two months earlier Griffin had called him into his office and told him that he was to be offered the position of laboratory assistant in the all powerful and super wonderful restricted area. Well it wasn't the managing director's post but it was a damn fine start.

Quinn found the work distasteful, he spent most of his days elbow deep in monkey shit but the extra 600 Euros a week made it all worthwhile. He called it his conscience money and new luxury pillows helped to fend off the nightmares of tortured animals when they reached out to him in the night.

It was Friday night for fuck's sake. He didn't want to have to work tonight but old Griffin had put pressure on him to do it. The double pay was a nice little incentive but that's beside the point there was only one Friday night in every seven days and everybody knows that Friday night is party night. He was cleaning out the pens with a frown playing across his chiselled features. Hell, even if he managed to blow this place at a reasonable hour he'd have to go straight home because he stunk like simian.

Griffin was also not in the best of moods. Tonight there wasn't supposed to be any overtime on offer. He'd planned a curry and an early night. The memo had come through just that morning no less than demanding that he work the back-shift and keep a few people on to work with him. One of these people had to be the new bloke Quinn. Griffin knew better than to ask questions, in the past his livelihood had been put on the line more than once when he'd enquired too closely into things from above that he was told didn't concern him. He'd been with the company for five years for instance and yet he'd never once seen their mysterious benefactor and big-wig. He only ever liased with the totty that was his personal assistant if he had a problem. He felt he deserved more respect. But maybe his regularly accelerating salary was all the respect he needed. He had to make Quinn clean out the animals again just so that he had something to do. He'd already done them earlier and wasn't at all happy. What the hell could they possibly want with the lab-boy, and why hadn't they gone through him?

At seven thirty the top man's P.A. came into the labs and asked that Quinn go with her immediately. Griffin told the lad to wash up because he had an appointment with management.

This could only mean one thing, either he'd done well and was about to be promoted, or he'd fucked up big-style and was being given the boot. He weighed up the situation carefully as he followed the clicking heels of the lady down corridors that he'd never walked before. He couldn't help but note that she had a fine backside, anybody that sashayed along like that had to be approachable, didn't she?

"So darlin` am I going to celebrate or commiserate after this and where are you going to take me?" His charm always worked on these power hungry posh birds.

She stopped in mid stride so suddenly that he almost cannoned into the back of her, under any other circumstances he'd be happy to bump into her from behind but he didn't think this was either the time or the place.

"Steady love." He began but he stopped with his mouth still open as she wheeled round on one high heel and fixed him with an ice-cold stare.

"You will speak only when spoken to and then only to answer direct questions. You will not ask any questions and you will show the utmost respect. I will be addressed as Ma'am and the professor as Sir. Do you understand?" She barked these orders at him with such venom that had he not seen the cruel hardness in her eyes, he'd have thought she was playing the role of Nazi commandant for a laugh. As it was he figured she was taking on the role of Nazi commandant in deadly earnest.

"Yes Ma'am." he answered feeling very self-conscious.

She opened a door on the left hand side of a corridor and led him in to a plush anteroom. The burgundy carpeting was wall-to-wall luxury. The office-cum-waiting room had little in it but everything about the place screamed money. She walked to an inner door and knocked lightly.

"Come," Said a voice from within.

She ushered him into the room. "Quinn Sir." She said and left closing the door behind him.

He almost sat in one of the huge chairs this side of the enormous desk, but realised after a second that the man was staring at him and hadn't asked him to sit down, he hovered uncertainly.

Not sitting down had been a good move. The big man was smiling, showing a lot of teeth but his eyes were hard and cold as he appraised the lad in front of him.

"Turn around, turn around." He said making a twiddling gesture with his finger.

Aaron felt ridiculous, *'what the hell was going on?'* He pirouetted on the spot hoping to God that this was what was expected of him.

"Yes I think you'll do." Said the powerhouse, looking pleased with himself.

The man hadn't introduced himself. "Well sit down, sit down." He boomed and Aaron sat, feeling like a small child in the mammoth leather seat. He had to perch on the edge to enable his feet to touch the floor.

"I've been watching you lad." His voice was impassive and Aaron spent the next five seconds not thinking of something worthwhile to say but trying to decide if that was a good or a bad thing. He didn't feel it was in his best interests to ask. If there was one thing that could be said about Aaron Quinn it was that he learned fast. 'Catching on' on was a forte of his and he remembered the cold clear words of Old Gestapo Knickers. '*You will speak only when asked direct questions.'* Well he hadn't asked anything yet, so Aaron just spent his time squirming a bit in the big seat. His trouser leg rubbed slightly on the edge of the chair and made a farting noise. He felt himself colouring. The man-mountain didn't laugh and under these circumstances Aaron felt no urge to either.

"Are you trustworthy lad?" the man asked. *'Well for a presumably intelligent fella he asked some dumb-assed questions,'* thought Aaron, *'he was hardly going to say, no, I can't be trusted an inch sir, was he?'*

"Yes Sir." Said Aaron "I'm very trustworthy Sir and I won't let you..."

"All right, all right economise on the bleating. I only need to ask one more thing. Are you a risk taker Mr Quinn? Are you prepared to drive in the fast lane?"

Aaron gave passing thought to the Stampede with the Quinn registration plate that might be driving along his horizon this very evening.

"Yes sir." He said, "I am indeed." Suddenly he spoke with conviction. He had no idea what the hell was going on or why he had to prance around like a bloody ballerina, but if this bloke was willing to pay enough he'd dance Swan Lake in a pink tutu until the day he retired if need be. He obviously had something in mind for him.

"Well Quinn my boy, I think I might have a little job for you."

He leant down to a drawer in his desk and pulled something out. Aaron figured it might be a gun and he might be shot for gross misconduct with an experimental pig but he knew that he'd only ever scratched the pigs behind the ears before they went to torture, nothing else. The man pulled out a large white envelope with all the showmanship of an old fashioned magician. He put his hand inside, retracted a wad of money and spread it on the desk in front of him as though he was laying out a pack of cards.

Aaron's eyes bulged as he tried to mentally come up with an approximate sum total. As if reading his mind the employer stared him hard in the eyes. "There's ten-thousand Euros there lad." With a flourish he separated the money into two unequal amounts and pointed to the first. "That pile is approximately two grand. The job I have in mind is just a continuation of your overtime tonight. That pile of money is to be a little bonus on top of your wage payable to you when you leave this office. "Dramatically he pointed to the much larger pile of cash. "And this is my little gift to you for knowing how to keep your mouth shut, that you will receive on completion of the work. Do we understand each other Mr Quinn?"

"Yes sir, perfectly Sir. But what have I got to do. Is it illegal?" He was aware that he had spoken out of turn. The man looked annoyed.

"I thought you were a risk taker Quinn?" he boomed making Aaron jump.

"Oh I am Sir. I am." then he lowered his voice as though in shame and said quietly. "But I don't want anything to do with drugs Sir."

The man threw back his head and laughed.

"Drugs lad? Drugs? My what a vulgar word that is. I deal with pharmaceuticals lad, not drugs. No be at ease it's nothing like that. In fact I think you might rather enjoy what I have planned for you. I want you to pick me a nice lady Aaron." He used Aaron's Christian name for the first time. "Any young lady will do, your choice. And, if you serve me well boy, I may use you again for a little 'overtime' in the future."

For the next ten minutes the employer outlined to Aaron what he wanted him to do. The phrase 'dirty old pervert' ran through Aaron's mind several times and though he didn't like what was being asked of him, he certainly wasn't happy with it, only the thought of all that easy money motivated him to take on the job. Pocketing his approximate two grand he stood and shook the man's hand to seal their deal. Gestapo knickers then showed him along more corridors only these were richly carpeted with painted walls and hung works of art, mainly fat nudes, not his type of thing at all. He wondered if his current escort ever posed nude, now that's one picture he wouldn't mind appraising with an artist's critical eye.

She took him to a suite of rooms that any five star hotel would be proud of. He'd been told what he had to do, so was only mildly surprised when he was told to bathe and change his clothes. She said that he'd find everything he might need in the bathroom and to avail himself of anything he wanted.

Well he didn't need to be told twice. After she left he locked the door behind her and wandered through to the bathroom. He couldn't believe his eyes. Surely this was some weird dream or something. The bathroom was like none he'd ever seen before, not even on one of those ideal homes programs. A circular, sunken bath with voice activated controls and Jacuzzi dominated the room. It had solid gold taps and steps down into the tub. There were white towelling robes and towels. All manner of creams and gels for men, and soft sponges to wash with.

A shelf at the side of the bath had a selection of after-shaves and colognes all the top names nothing cheap or inexpensive. There were three open jewellery boxes, one with a dozen gold stella-links. These were the latest jewellery accessories for men. They worked as a replacement for buttons, fastening with invisible micro-grips to any garment. The second box contained a Psioden watch. Even he knew this was the genuine article. Psioden were the leading watchmakers in the world. The last box housed a tasteful gold ring. Nothing ostentatious or vulgar but a ring that spoke none-the-less with an upper-crust accent.

A gilt edged card rested beside the jewellery.

Dear Mr Quinn, I took the liberty of picking out a few trinkets and some suitable clothing for you. I trust they will all fit and that you find them to your liking. Please pick whatever you would like to wear for your evening out and consider both the clothes and the jewellery a small gift for you to keep.

There was no signature.

Well this guy certainly understood the finer points of bribery all right and Aaron was learning the rules mighty quickly. He looked at the small packet in his hand and for a split second the voice of his conscience tried to make itself heard but this was more than a dream come true this was fucking paradise unlimited and he'd be mad to pass it up. The guy had given his word that the girl would be released unharmed after he'd had his fun with her so where was the harm? He refused point blank to think about how the girl could be released after she'd seen both Aaron and presumably Pervy Percival too. 'Do not concern yourself,' he'd said. It sounded like damned fine advice under the circumstances.

The bathroom led off to a large dressing room with wall to wall mirrors. A rack of clothes all in the correct sizes had been left for him to chose from. There was everything from formal three pieces, to jeans and Jager shirts. He chose a pair of designer jeans and a deep purple shirt, a pair of black boots and a three-quarter-length leather coat.

The bath was the best he'd ever had and he was in no hurry to get out, as the man said as long as he delivered the goods the night was his. He'd even chucked in an extra ton to fund his evening's pleasures. Far from missing his Friday night out, this promised to be the best Friday night ever.

"Looking damn fine." He said to the good-looking man in the mirror and the gold ring with the tiny diamond shimmered in the overhead light.

Chapter 25

"Would you like some ice with that?"

She smiled up at him making sure that he saw the tip of her tongue flash out to moisten her lips before she spoke to him. "No thanks, the only thing you ever want to put with Bacardi and coke is, another Bacardi and coke." It was a rather fumbled take on an old joke and the original was far snappier but he smiled any way.

"Would you like to sit down?" He asked taking both their glasses and moving towards a vacant table before she had the chance to answer. He pulled out a chair for her and then pushed her gently into the table. He sat opposite and turned on the charm from dripping tap to full surging flow.

"I just knew when I saw you on that dance floor that I had to talk to you."

"And why might that be then?" she asked coyly, pushing her chest out towards him as she spoke. The gesture wasn't wasted on him and he only wished that he could have some fun with the girl himself before he had to deliver her to the boss but the man had been very clear in his instructions on that one. He said she 'was not to be tampered with' as though she was one of his official documents or something.

"So gorgeous, what's your name then? I could call you princess all night but I think it might get on your nerves after awhile."

"Esther, pleased to meet you. And you are?" She passed her slim hand over the table and when he kissed the back of it she ran her hand through his until her fingertip was pressed up against his lips. As was expected of him in this situation, he looked up to meet her eyes. Sure enough she was pouting, her body language telling him as plain as a wet pussy that she was as keen to get out of the place as he was, though for vastly different reasons. He knew that the longer he sat at that table with her, the more likely it was that her friends would be able to give a good description of him if anything untoward happened to her. It was all well and good Pervy Percy saying that everything was okay, but it wasn't him sitting at the table with her finger ramming itself half way down his throat.

He gave the finger a little suck to play along and then decided pleasurable though this might be in another time and place he ought to get down to business.

"Tell me about you." He said. Gazing devotedly into her eyes.

"But you haven't told me your name yet."

"Of course how bad mannered of me. I'm Pete Gardiner." Percy, as he now thought of him, hadn't told him to lie but that was a little precaution of his own. "Now tell me about the lovely Esther. Esther what? It must be something exotic to follow such a beautiful name."

"Esther Erikson actually, see ordinary as they come." She laughed, he was a bit of a ponce but with a body like that who cared. "And you might as well know so there's no misunderstanding, I'm married. I'm just a girl whose husband doesn't understand her." Esther was many things but one thing she hadn't learned yet was the art of lying. She lived in Esther-land, a place where only her needs mattered, so as she had little social or moral conscience, she saw no reason to lie.

She excused herself to go to the ladies. He was getting jumpy. He could see her friends talking to her and grinning; one was giving her the thumbs up sign. He wanted to be out of there but first he had to get more information and he had work to do. He took a drink of his soda water and gulped nervously.

Sitting back in what he hoped was a relaxed manner, he scanned the room for people close enough to be nosy. Everyone was too engrossed in their own nightly challenges to be bothered about him. Quickly he drew her glass towards him and dropped the small white tablet into it; he gave it a quick twirl and replaced it.

'I don't want anything to do with drugs.' He remembered what he'd said sitting in that overstuffed seat, talking to the overstuffed man. *'Well maybe for ten grand I do.'*

When she sat back down he pressed her drink into her hand. "Come on slow coach, drink up, the night is but an infant and we have a lifetime of ground to cover."

Esther didn't know if it was the drink or just the way this man had an uncanny knack of making her talk but within ten minutes she had told him virtually all there was to know about her. She was starting to get a bit bored of him. Suddenly she felt all tingly, the room was closing in on her and she needed to move while she still could.

"Hey d`ya wanna dance?" she slurred.

"I'd love to, but do you know what I'd really like? I'd like to take you out of here. What do you say?"

That was sounding like a helluva good idea. She felt most unwell and if she didn't move right this minute she knew that she was going to pass out right there at the table.

He helped her to her feet, the Rohypnol was taking effect quickly, too bloody quickly, if he didn't get her out fast she was going to be unconscious on him and cause attention that he could do without. Luckily her friends were all away from the table they must be dancing. The floor had filled up to become a heaving throng that was perfect, they probably wouldn't see them leaving. He had to support her and half carry her across the room.

The place was spinning and the sudden pain in her head that had only come on a minute ago dissolved into a black noise that rose to a crescendo. The last thing she was aware of before the world collapsed in on her was the glitter ball above her head, spinning on its axis, spinning her into blessed oblivion.

"Oh fuck, she's gone." He muttered aloud. At that moment he thought of dumping her and getting the hell out of there but that would only arouse more suspicion. He scooped her up into his arms, for a tiny woman the slapper was heavy when he had to carry her down two flights of stairs. He was gasping partly with exertion and partly with fear when he finally got to the exit. He glanced up at the doormen. "Some women just can't hold their ale, eh fellas?" he said with a small laugh. They opened the door for him to pass though and didn't bat an eyelid. They'd seen it all before.

His car was parked two streets away and he couldn't risk carrying her that far. Too noticeable and besides his heart wouldn't stand it, not to mention his screaming back. He ran as best he could with her to the alleyway at the back of the club. Half way along in almost total darkness was a door. He put her down there as gently as he could between two dustbins.

He wanted to run back to the car, he wanted to run like the wind, get in his car, drive and just keep driving as far away as he could get. His bottle was going. He wanted to run, but he forced himself to walk. All the way to the car he was wondering what would happen if she came to in the alley. Or worse what if she came to on the way back to the institute and realised that was more than a mere shot of Bacardi. He got into his car and drove sedately back to the alley. If his heart rate could have been measured by mile speed then he would certainly have broken the sound barrier by now.

She was still there. Only now she seemed twice as heavy as before. As a dead weight she was difficult to manhandle into the back of the car. He bumped her head hard on the top of the door and somehow it cut through her drugged state because she moaned. And then she was in and he was driving. If he'd stopped to look at her slumped motionless in the alley, maybe some premonition would have come to him but he didn't and it didn't. He was already mentally spending that great big wad of cash.

He drove as fast as he dared on a Friday night with police patrolling the place for drink drivers. And then he was out of town and heading along the Portinscale Road. He just wanted to get her dropped off and collect his money now. But he'd almost got away with it and some of his cock-sure attitude was slowly beginning to return.

He'd been instructed to drive round to an obscure little door at the back of the building. They were waiting for him and he didn't have to knock. Before he got out of the car two men, one of them the boss came hurtling through the door pushing a gurney in front of them. She was loaded onto it and taken into the building in a matter of seconds.

He swallowed and licked his lips. He didn't know what the hell Percy was up to but it didn't look like any sad bastard grope and fuck of an unconscious woman to him. Eight grand was a lot of silence money, and he didn't want to see anymore, he didn't want to know what was going on. He just wanted to get the hell out of there and turn up to collect the rest of his money as arranged the next morning.

The man in charge took the gurney and ran with it down the corridor, the other man stayed to deal with Quinn.

By the time Bernie Roberts had scrubbed up and entered the O.R. the boss, already in his greens, had stripped and prepared the 'host'. She was the second woman receiving this evening, the other a volunteer was in a side ward sipping a cup of tea and resting for the required five hours.

Esther Erikson had been given a light anaesthesia to ensure she remained still throughout the procedure. Her legs were fastened into stirrups and her private area washed in iodine. The embryo was taken with reverence by the boss and distributed in the womb of Mrs Erikson. Nature would do what was required of her. He had no doubt about that. He wanted only two infants so he planted only two embryos, one in each woman, not three or four in each as was usual in invitro-fertilisation. He was The New Creator and he had faith. If The Great Almighty God was with him on this one, he would bring each child to fruition. It would be his signal that all was well. He truly believed that he worked with God's blessing.

And so his scheme was hatched.

Chapter 26

A dog pissed against the wall, he sniffed at his produce, satisfied that yes it was still his, he moved on pleased with himself. He continued sniffing at everything in his path until he stopped at the bundle with every intention of peeing on that too but he didn't like what he smelled. He gave a little whine and trotted away from the nasty odour that followed him all the way out of the alley.

The body sat slumped against the wall, partly concealed by a rolled carpet casually thrown out for the dustbin people to collect. His eyes were wide and glassy, still looking in death at the last image he saw in life. Most of the lower half of his face had been blown away and from the position he assumed, part of a large exit wound was clearly visible at the back of his head. This was no opportunistic killing though because apart from having two thousand, one hundred and eighty-six pounds about his person, he died wearing expensive jewellery of the highest class.

The body in the summerhouse, beside the River Greta slouched in a similar position to the one barely a mile away. This one had a thin line of vomit drying on her chin, a larger amount darkening the material of her thin, inappropriate-for-the-weather, top. Unlike the other body though this one was just coming to. She woke as many hangover suffers do, timidly. And like many morning after drunks her first coherent thought after '*ouch,*' was '*where the hell am I?*'

She sat forward hands on knees, head in hands and let the events of the pervious night filter slowly through to her. '*A man, there was a man.*' She remembered everything now, everything until leaving the club. She was drunk, happy, but not drunk enough to suddenly pass out. Though her head pounded mercilessly she did a finger count of the number of drinks she'd had. She didn't run out of fingers so couldn't possibly have been that drunk. Esther was a regular social drinker; she had a tolerance to alcohol. It didn't make any sense.

She tried to stand and her hangover receded into the background as a new pain came to the fore, she was tender, very sore between her legs. She felt bruised. '*Oh Dear God no. What's happened to me? Went to the toilet, left him alone with drink. Shouldn't do that. Posters everywhere.* "Never leave your drink unattended." *Suddenly felt ill, very ill. Not drunk ill though different.*' It was starting to make sense. '*Oh God I've been out all night, Jerry'll go mad. He won't believe me. Oh what have I done?*'

A lady was walking towards the summerhouse. She stopped and looked over towards Esther.

'Oh don't stop, please don't come over, carry on walking. What must I look like?' The woman made her mind up and started walking over to the lady in obvious distress.

"Are you all right love? Can I help you in any way?"

Esther was the type of woman who needed to be looked after, she thrived on attention and sympathy focused in her direction was more than she could stand. She dissolved into sudden wracking sobs.

"Help me, please help me, I think I've been raped."

The woman was fantastic. She called a taxi to take Esther home and sat placating the distraught woman until it arrived. She believed Esther's story, she truly believed it. This nice, attractive lady didn't think Esther was a common trollop who had 'asked for it' she said the man was despicable and that it must be the way it happened. "Of course she wouldn't pass out on just a very few Bacardis' no one would. It was always nice people that it happened to," she said, vulnerable people like Esther. Esther gulped back the fresh onslaught of tears and agreed. "You're such a beautiful woman," she said. "Such a shame it should happen to someone as pretty as you," she said. The lady made Esther feel much better and soon the flood of tears had dried to a mere trickle.

"I'm not really pretty." Said Esther, turning doe eyes with attractively wet eyelashes up to the nice lady.

"Nonsense, That's rubbish, you obviously don't know just how attractive you are. You have a figure to die for. I'm not surprised the beast picked you out of all the other women in the place. Poor you having to pay such a dear price for just trying to keep yourself nice."

"Terrible, terrible," agreed Esther. She liked this woman and was almost disappointed when the taxi pulled up at the kerb. She'd much rather sit here and listen to this lady's compliments than go home to face a furious Jerry. She doubted he'd be so sympathetic. She felt her bottom lip beginning to wobble again.

"Well thank you so much. You've been ever so kind."

"Do you really think I'm going to let you get into that taxi on your own. You're far too upset to be alone. I insist on coming with you to see that you get home safely." Esther slumped heavily on the woman's arm, she really didn't think she could walk properly. In actual fact by now much of her strength had returned but Esther always did play the innocent victim so well. It was a role made for her.

She slumped heavily into the taxi it was all too much for her, too much. "Thank you Mary." She said to the nice lady.

“It’s Maria, love.” She reminded her. *‘Oh yes of course it was.’* Esther smiled at her apologetically. So upset was she that Esther had trouble remembering her own address, Maria stroked her arm reassuringly. And eventually they were on their way. Esther was genuinely worried about the reception she’d get when she got home. Jerry was going to be furious. She started to cry again, but this time quietly.

Maria leaned in towards her and whispered soothing words. As she did, her left hand slid quietly into Esther’s handbag, she groped round until she felt what she was looking for and then very slowly, very gently she pulled out Esther’s purse and tucked it quickly into her pocket.

When the taxi arrived outside Esther’s house, she groped for her bag but Maria already had money in her hand to pay the driver. She asked him to wait for her and went round to the other side of the car to help Esther out.

By this time Jerry was already striding down the path, looking very tight lipped and stern. He glared towards Esther before thanking the kind Samaritan for her help. Polite formalities were exchanged and Jerry insisted in reimbursing Maria for the taxi fare despite her protestations.

“Raped? Raped?” he shouted later when a tearful Esther had asked him to call the police. “Don’t be ridiculous woman. Why should anyone take by force something that’s offered on a plate? You disgust me you drunken whore.” That was the one and only time that Jerry ever truly lost his temper with her and lowered himself to name-calling. “It’s not the police you need Esther it’s a sound thrashing to knock some sense into you. You go to the police if you must, but I’m having no part in it, one look at you and they’ll laugh you out of the station. Let this be a lesson to you woman. And I’m telling you here and now this is the last time that anything of this nature is going to happen. Do you understand me?”

He really shouted and that was so out of character for the normally gentle man that Esther was genuinely ashamed of herself. Her shame would never last long, but that morning at twenty past nine by the kitchen clock Esther Erikson took a long, cold look at herself and for the first time in her life didn’t like what she saw. She pleaded with Jerry to be nice to her. She really had been through a terrible ordeal. All he’d done after all was sit up all night worrying about her. That couldn’t be half as bad as what she’d suffered, even though she couldn’t remember what it was she had suffered.

Eventually Jerry calmed. For all her faults he truly did love his wife and hated to see her so sorry for herself and miserable. He made her some toast with the crusts cut off, just the way she liked it and gave her a cuddle. “No more, Esther,” he said. “No more, things are going to change and I’m going to look after you.”

“Yes Jerry,” she said snuggling into his chest and falling asleep. “change.”

That evening just as the drama Global Warming was finishing, they had a visitor. Jerry answered the door and a minute later was ushering the lady who had helped his wife that morning into the lounge.

"Maria, how lovely to see you. Come in, come in." She had risen to take both of Maria's hands in hers.

"I just came to return this, you left it in the taxi this morning, it must have dropped out of your bag." She held out the purse to Esther. The lady of the house, quite back to her old self, ordered Jerry out of the room to make tea and she fussed around making their guest comfortable.

Esther was dressed in a long white mohair jumper and black trousers. She had fluffy blue mules on her feet and looked quite the grand housewife. A far cry from the last time that Maria had seen her.

"Actually I was glad of the excuse to come and see how you are. I was quite worried about you, you know."

The women sat and chatted while Jerry made his excuses and left them to it. Maria said she fully understood why they had decided not to go to the police. Terrible how the poor victim is treated like a common criminal she said, best to put the whole horrendous ordeal behind them and get on with their lives. It was over now, she said patting Esther's hand comfortingly.

One hour turned into two and Esther held Maria captivated with tales of her days working as a 'highly respected' dancer. Maria said she only held the position of doctor's receptionist in one of the Penrith surgeries, so she was suitably impressed.

"You are funny Esther," she said. "It must have been so glamorous, I wish I could be like you." The words almost stuck in her throat, she couldn't stand the sight of Esther let alone the voice of her, all that bragging and big mouthing but Maria had worked out within two minutes of meeting Esther that the woman thrived on praise and adoration. Maria was shrewd and had an intuitive feeling about the best way to insinuate herself into Esther Erikson's life. Flattery was the way to go, even though being in the vile woman's company for more than five minutes at a time was going to drive her nuts.

"Listen Esther," She said shyly as she stood up to leave. "I haven't been in the area long and haven't had the chance to make many friends. I don't suppose you'd like to go into town for a coffee and some shopping tomorrow would you?"

And so the two women became friends. It was Maria who was with Esther when she did the pregnancy test. She had been so strong and supportive. Esther wanted a termination but Jerry had been such an obstinate pig about the whole thing. He wouldn't hear of it.

"That could be my child you're carrying." He said. The word 'could' hung as though suspended from the ceiling by heavy chains that might snap at any moment. They both knew that as much as it could be his, there was a much greater chance that it might not be.

Esther was still set on termination, when Maria announced with a wide smile that she too was pregnant. That swayed Esther. It might be fun she decided being pregnant together just think of all those cute little outfits. A few weeks later the women hugged and laughed when they discovered that they were both due on the exact same date. Of course they didn't both deliver on the same day though. Little Eleanor was born whole and healthy but tragedy struck about a week later when Maria rang in tears to inform her that her baby boy had died in childbirth. Things cooled a bit after that, Esther was annoyed with Maria for losing her child, it spoiled all her plans for walking the babies in the park together. Maria still came down often always bringing a gift for Eleanor, but Esther threw them straight in the bin after she'd gone in case it was something that had been bought for Maria's dead baby. Esther really couldn't do with the other woman's misery around her all the time.

But Maria healed remarkably well and the two women remained friends, even after Jerry and Esther moved to Morecambe Maria would drive through once or twice a month to see them. Never the other way round, Esther was far too busy to make the journey.

Maria was such a good friend and she thought the world of Esther.

Chapter 27

Despite trying several times, Rob had no luck getting hold of Gail on the way home. He had an up to the minute micro-technology comminicom with fifty year old reliability. For Ellie's sake as much as Gail's he wanted to bring his wife up to speed on what had happened.

Gail ran out of the house as soon as she saw Rob arriving with Ellie. She stopped in her tracks though when she saw Ellie's car following with another Ellie in the driving seat. The dark twin must have followed them, surely they must know they'd led her right back to the house. Not knowing what to do, she reacted on impulse and ran behind Rob's car hoping to hold the enemy off. Three car doors opened simultaneously Rob was rushing towards her but she saw only the evil person who had caused so much damage.

"Get in the house with Ellie. Ring the police." She screamed. She was about to launch herself on the woman called Eve, when Eve launched on her with arms open and tears streaming down her face.

"Oh Gail, Matty's dead, Matty's dead. What the hell am I going to do?"

"Look," said Rob. "As far as we know it's safe here but we can't take any chances. Let's just get in the house and then we'll explain everything. Gail you help Ellie." Rob couldn't believe the bravery of his normally timid wife. After all these years of marriage there were times when she still had the power to surprise him and make him incredibly proud of her.

After making sure she had the right twin, Gail guided Ellie into the house and made her comfortable on the sofa. Ellie barely had the strength left to lift her legs so Gail lifted them for her and then got a quilt to cover her as she had begun to shake. Rob busied himself locking Jake away from Eve and then got Ellie's bag of medication. He might have been wiser locking his wife up and leaving Jake to reason with Eve because all hell had erupted when he walked back into the lounge. Since the day he met her, he had never once seen Gail lose her temper to the point of threatened violence.

"I said get out, get out before I knock your fucking head off your shoulders you evil bitch." She was screaming like a banshee and when her husband entered the room she turned on him. "Get her out of my house Rob. I will not have her here. Get rid of her."

Rob had to physically restrain his wife to stop her lamping the cuckoo in the nest there and then.

"She saved my life Gail." Said Ellie.

"Saved your life? Saved your life? She's been trying to do you in for weeks. It was only on the mention of murder that Gail finally processed what Ellie had said when she got out of the car just a couple of minutes before. She stopped her rant suddenly and turned almost in slow motion a look of absolute horror on her face.

"What did you say about Matt?"

The next few minutes were filled with tears, explanations, tantrums and questions. Reliving it again was almost as innervating as the nightmare had been first hand.

Eve tried twice to leave and Gail tried twice to help her, the second time was after she told Eve to choke on the hot chocolate that Rob made. The room was virtually crackling on raw emotion.

"So what have the police said?" asked Gail in one of her few calm moments. "I hope they aren't going to want to talk to us tonight."

"Well we haven't had the chance to call them yet love, there's things we need to discuss first," said Rob.

"What the hell do you mean you haven't called them? One of the sweetest blokes who ever walked the earth is lying dead in that house of horrors and you haven't bothered to call the police. What are you thinking about?"

"We were thinking about getting out of there before he killed the lot of us, that's what," said Eve.

"Shut your big fat mouth you before I shut it for you. Matt is dead, killed by some madman and **you.**" She spat the word across the room to Eve. "And now he might be on his way here to finish what he started. Sod talking I'm calling the police right now.

Gail stomped across the room and picked up the phone.

Until that moment Ellie had said very little. Everybody else was talking, screaming and yelling and she had sat quietly thinking about Matt and letting Rob and Eve tell it. Finally she spoke.

"No!" She didn't bellow, she didn't shout but the single word was said with such force that Rob who had opened his mouth to speak didn't. Gail with the telephone in her hand, stopped dialling after the first nine and Eve half way to the door again stopped mid stride.

"We can't ring the police."

"What? Ellie darling you aren't thinking straight. You're in shock; we need the police to help us. To help Matty."

"And tell me Gail love, what exactly are they going to do to help Matt now?" Ellie's voice dripped with sarcasm that froze before the words were fully out of her mouth with the ice that smothered them. She was instantly sorry. She dropped her voice the exhaustion and stress wringing out every word she said.

"We can't go to the police because I gave Eve my solemn promise."

"Ellie, can't you see it's because of her that Matthew's dead? She was as instrumental in his death as the man who did that terrible thing to him. You owe her nothing."

"I owe her my life," said Ellie in a voice devoid of all emotion. "And I owe her my trust because she gave me hers."

"Please listen to me." Eve had moved into the centre of the room and spoke in a calm and even voice. "Please Gail hear me out and then if you still want to call the police then please just give me five minutes to get away and then do as you must."

"Why should we give you even a second, it's more than you deserve." Rob put his arm round Gail's shoulders and shushed her.

"I know it's more than I deserve. I've done some terrible things, I know that now. But all I ask is two minutes and then I'll be on my way and you can do what you like. Like Ellie said there's nothing we can do to help Matt now."

"The police could get his body and give him a decent burial." Gail didn't want to be quiet, this was her home and needling the woman who'd brought all this about was her right to her space.

"Yes and we'll find a way to sort that out but we can't stay here. None of you understand this man. I don't understand this man; he's pure evil. He fed me a life of hated for twenty seven years. Now as long as we sit here he's going to find us. It's me and Ellie he wants. But as long as we are here under your roof, you'd better believe me when I say all four of us are just sitting here waiting to die. He knows things. He knows everything, sees everything."

"She's deranged," said Gail with a sneer.

"I know it sounds ridiculous but he has ways of finding out information. I don't know how, bugs maybe, cameras. He's probably got this place rigged and is listening to every word we say right now. If we want to live through this the only way is to get away, keep moving. If you'll let me, I'm going tonight, and if Ellie's got any sense she'll go somewhere safe too. Because you might think everything's hunky-dory here and it may well be but I promise you this. It won't be for long. He'll find us."

"So let's get the police in. They can take you both to safe places." She purposely didn't say 'somewhere safe' because she couldn't bear the thought of Ellie being in the same place as that woman any longer than she had to be.

"I'm afraid I agree with Gail," said Rob. "We need to call the police because this is too big for us. A man has been murdered, if we don't call them we are all accessories after the fact. And calling the police in is the only way we're going to get Matt out of there."

"Please, please don't call them." Eve began to cry. "I have been locked up with nothing I could call living for my entire life. If you call the police there'll be tests and evaluations. I'll be institutionalised and I can't bear to be locked up again. And what about Ellie, think about her. Can you imagine what the media will do to her if this story ever gets out? I was fed her life day and night since I was an infant, do you want the media prying into her life for the rest of it?" Eve realised the implications of what she'd just said and how short the rest of Ellie's life might be. Her hand flew to her mouth.

"Oh God Ellie, I'm so sorry. I didn't mean to imply…" Ellie smiled a wan smile and waved her worries away.

"She's right. I might not have long left and the last thing I want is to live in the media spotlight for the rest of my days."

"There's something else you haven't thought of too. I'm sorry Ellie but this man doesn't leave traces. I'd love to think that Matt's body could be brought out of there. I'm hoping it can, especially because I'm more than partly responsible for what happened to him but I'm pretty certain that by now he'll have wiped every scrap of evidence out of that place, including Matt's body. If there's no body, no evidence, no proof and only the testimony of a sick woman and her closest friends, where do you think the finger of suspicion is going to fall? They already think Ellie's tried to murder Matt once. Because I promise you if you call the police I'm going to do everything I can to get away before they come."

"I'll go back to the institute tonight and get Matt out." Said Rob with a voice full of bravery, which was exactly one voice full of bravery more than he felt. "He said he wasn't coming back until tomorrow didn't he?"

"He was lying." Said Eve in a dull voice. "Trust me he'd be back, the early hours of the morning are his favourite time. They are the hours when he inflicts his most terrifying tortures. Talking, talking, talking. Hours on end sometimes. He'll be there now and he'll be furious that we aren't."

Ellie remembered the horrible voice on the intercom and shuddered. She nodded her head in emphatic agreement.

Nobody said anything for a long time. They all had a lot to think about. Ellie sat on the sofa slowly shaking her head from side to side.

"I say we tie her up and take our chances with the police." Said Gail.

"No police." The voice though barely audible was emphatic. "She's right we've got to get away. First thing in the morning. I don't know where or for how long but I heard this man, you and Gail didn't Rob, I swear he's going to stop at nothing until he has us exactly where he wants us."

"There's one thing that we all seem to have overlooked." Said Rob. "If we don't report Matt missing, someone else will. What about when he doesn't turn up at work or get in touch with his friends and family? If Ellie doesn't make a report in the next day or two they are going to suspect her for sure."

They all let this sink in and tried to find a way out of the quagmire that just seemed to get deeper and deeper.

"I'll just report him missing then," said Ellie. "I'll ring the police now and say that he hasn't come home and that I'm worried about him."

"You can't Ellie, the police already suspect you of trying to kill Matt, they'll question you, for hours on end. Not tonight but eventually when he doesn't turn up. They'll know instantly that you're lying. You couldn't tell a convincing lie if you tried darling." Said Rob.

"Apart from that, there's no point ringing tonight. He's only been missing about fourteen hours," Said Eve. "It would look suspicious if she rang now. And she can't hang around here waiting for a suitable length of time to pass before reporting it because if we're going we've got to go at first light." Eve hadn't realised that she'd said 'we'.

"I could stall them," said Rob thinking aloud. "If you two take off in the morning, you'll probably have a few clear days before the police come sniffing round, possibly as much as a week or two. We'll think of somewhere for you to stay. When they come I'll just say that maybe the two of you took off for a few days to come to terms about your illness away from the glare of the media. I don't know what the hell we're going to do Ellie but at least that gives us breathing space to think things through more clearly. And Eve's right the further away you are from here the better."

"Oh no, no way mate, I'm going on my own. I'm sorry Ellie but I'm fighting for my life here just as much as you and I don't want to be hampered by a sick woman. It's going to be hard enough having a bloody famous face, without travelling as the other half of a set of identical twins. We'd stick out like King Harry's ears."

"But what if you travel as one person? We'll make reservations for one in a false name. Whether you like it or not, you two are in the same boat and need each other. Ellie's sick so you can help her cope and she can open doors with her credit and get things that an ordinary person can't. Think about it, it makes sense."

Gail had finally calmed down and all the spitting and clawing had left her. "But when they don't come back, Ellie's going to be under suspicion for sure. They'll arrest her for Matt's murder. She'll never stand that."

"But I could." They all turned to look at Eve. "It makes sense Ellie would never cope with the questions, she'd buckle in the first five minutes but if we get our story straight, I'll talk to the police and go through the interview process."

They argued and debated the ramifications back and forth, in the end they decided that making a run for it, and working the rest out later was the best option they had. The girls would leave at first light.

Chapter 28

By six in the morning, after just two and a half-hours restless sleep, the car was packed, only one of the travellers cuddled the dog though and the girls were ready to go. Their destination had literally been a 'pin in the map' job, if they had no advance notice of where they were headed, then neither would anyone else. Ellie visited Chester once on a book tour and it seemed as good a place as any to hole up for a few days and get some rest.

Rob got C2 his humanicon to bring up a list of hotels in the area and he set about ringing to make a reservation for one. The first two he tried at six in the morning got no answer at all. The third, a gentleman, obviously roused from sleep told him in no uncertain terms that if he rang between the working hours of nine and five then someone would be available to take his booking. As he was about to break the connection, Rob couldn't swear to it, but he was pretty convinced that he heard the man who was clearly not a morning person say 'wanker'. The fourth attempt was more successful.

After some discussion it was decided that a mix of truth and fiction was going to be the best way ahead. Ellie fell under the classification of 'D' list celebrity, which meant luckily for them that she was not quite 'dead famous'. But she had been asked to appear on the panel of several afternoon game shows. More often than not she could walk down the street without being mobbed but just as often she didn't go completely unnoticed. When Rob approached a Miss Wood, who was far more suited to early mornings than the previous gentleman, he asked to speak to the hotel manager as a matter of great urgency. He was expecting to be told again to ring back later but the nice Miss Wood located the manager within a few minutes of hold time. Rob explained to him that Miss Eleanor Erikson, the author, would like to stay at their hotel. However it was imperative that her identity must not be disclosed to any third person, be that his staff, his family or, God forbid, the Press. He said that Miss Erikson had recently had some tragic news about her health and since then had been literally mobbed by hoards of intrusive paparazzi. In a voice deep with sympathy for the ailing Miss Erikson he said that if news got out of where she was staying it would undoubtedly finish her. The manager didn't know how true that statement was.

"I can assure you Mr..." He forgot Rob's name. "I can assure you sir that

Miss Erikson's privacy will be respected and followed per instruction to the letter. We here at The Castle Mount pride ourselves on running a discreet hotel. And I personally will undertake to make sure that Miss Erikson is made as comfortable as possible," said the delighted man. In his three years at The Castle Mount they'd never had anyone famous, not even anyone a little bit famous like Eleanor Erikson so this was quite a feather in his cap.

"Good man," said Rob rather condescendingly. "I knew as soon as I heard your honest voice that you wouldn't let us down. No fuss though remember, Miss Erikson is still a little bit sensitive about her illness and needs lots of undisturbed rest."

Over latter years, Ellie had become accustomed to staying at the most extravagant of extravagant hotels. Only places with a five star rating and a world-renowned chef of volatile temperament were booked for her. The trouble with celebrity, even 'D' list celebrity is that you have a certain façade to live up to. Ellie kept her home life simple because when taken away with work, she had to live the glitz until it oppressed her. She didn't have a room in hotels, she always took a suite, usually right at the top of the bloody building with 'panoramic views' that were a pain in the arse to get to and she hated it.

Looking at 'The Old Ruins' as she instantly christened it, she knew she need not worry about the insincerity of opulence, there was none. The place had seen better days that's for sure. But although it was picked at random and not for its situation, it was secluded, in its own grounds and seemed little inhabited. This was no Estrelle Residence in Berlin, or indeed Caesar's Palace in Vegas, but it was for the time being home.

Eve knew what she was thinking, which she had a disconcerting knack of doing. "Not quite what you're used to eh Sis?" Her voice was laden with bitterness and sarcasm, the hostility, recently lacking, back again with knobs on. "Never mind, I'm sure you can slum it like a mere mortal for a few days." Ellie shot her a withering look.

They gave each other the once over for any flaws in their appearance and then while Ellie lay low in her seat with a magazine pressed up to her face, Eve took their single suitcase and walked into the hotel. Eve had to go in first, because not knowing how long they'd be 'on the road' they had to pack as many belongings as possible into the one case so as not to draw attention to themselves. Okay if she had been recognised, then a celebrity with a truck-load of baggage would be the most natural thing in the world but they were travelling as Mrs Janet Brown, 'Miss epitome of ordinary 2046'.

The short lady with mousy brown hair and large spectacles signed the register and was given directions to her room. "First floor fifth on the right. Got it. Thank you." She took herself up to her room and struggled only slightly with the heavy suitcase.

The receptionist had booked a double room on Rob's instruction. "So that she'll be more comfortable you understand?" A twin would have looked too suspicious. She queried the choice of a double room for a single person, saying that a single was ten Euros a night cheaper but Mrs Brown said in a faltering voice that if he could get away from the office, her husband would be joining her later.

"Of course madam." Said the receptionist knowingly, after three years in the business she could spot an extra-marital affair from half a mile away. This one looked strictly 'devoted home-bird' but it takes all sorts.

Forty minutes later Janet Brown walked into the hotel and passed reception. Elaine Wood, looked up from her VDU surprised. "Hello, I never saw you go out." She said in an almost accusatory manner. It was her job to be aware of all comings and goings in this hotel and she didn't like people going about their business without her knowing about it.

"Just went to the car for my glasses case," said Janet, holding the case aloft as though an exhibit for the defence, didn't want the woman thinking she'd just run out with the hotel's stainless steel.

As the woman went up the stairs, first door, fifth on the right, *thank God for a decent cell phone signal*, Woodsy smiled, she liked putting guests into types. This one was definitely married frump. Hardly anybody wore glasses these days, laser treatment took five minutes and lasted for years. *'I bet she loves cooking from scratch as well,'* she thought. *'Still the other fella must love her judging by the surprise he'd laid on.'*

Ellie launched herself on the bed as soon as she got in the room, within seconds she had an array of medication discarded around her. She was pale and the last few days had really taken their toll on her, Eve felt a huge pang of guilt.

"Can I get you anything? "Eve asked. "Cup of coffee?" She said holding a mug out. Ellie nodded and smiled gratefully. Eve still got a buzz out of boiling a kettle and making coffee. She was like a child with a tea set and measured a spoonful of coffee into each cup with care while other people would just spoon it in with practised lack of thought. This was the first time Eve had ever made a coffee for anyone else and she wanted to get it right.

"Not poisoned is it?" Said Ellie with a wry grin as Eve carefully put the steaming mug on her bedside table. Eve looked hurt and Ellie was immediately sorry, it seemed her siblings dark half had yet to develop a sense of humour.

"How do you feel?" asked Eve genuine concern in her voice.

"Safer," Said Ellie.

Eve was like a big kid. This was the first time she'd ever stayed in a hotel. She bounced on the bed, making Ellie's head rock, she opened and closed cupboards, turned the plasma box on and off and crammed one of the complimentary chocolate mints into her mouth.

“Can we call room service?” She asked excitedly with a mouthful of chocolate.

“No!” said Ellie, “Low profile remember?”

“Awww that’d be fun. Wonder what the bathroom’s like?” she went off to check.

Ellie was still smiling at Eve’s enthusiasm when five seconds later she backed out of the bathroom as though a venomous snake were coiling towards her poised and ready to strike.

She had a card in her hand and the look of horror on her face made Ellie’s stomach contract into a tight knot.

“We have to leave,” said Eve in a monotone.

With the opening of the bathroom door, the cloying sweetness of fresh flowers had already permeated the bedroom, Ellie pushed passed Eve and stopped short in the bathroom doorway. The bath, the shelves, even the toilet seat, and every spare inch of floor space was strewn with bouquets of exotic flowers. Lilies and orchids, lotus and artificially dyed blooms of such magnitude and beauty that any woman would be enraptured to receive such a token of love. Any women except these two. Ellie gagged on the perfume and thought for a moment she was going to be sick. She wheeled from the bathroom and slammed the door behind her.

Eve handed Ellie the florist’s card. Apart from the shop logo it was almost identical to the one Eve had sent just weeks earlier. The words printed in a neat hand read. ‘Better The Devil You Know. To my Darling Janet, Love always Matthew xxx.’

“The bastard, how dare he sicken Matt’s memory in this way. How dare he?” Ellie was furious. “We have to think Eve, how did he find us. It must be the hotel manager, he must have shouted my arrival from the bloody rooftops. I’m going down to have it out with him and to ring the florists to find out how the flowers were ordered, my guess is telephone.” She started walking towards the door.

Eve, in a blind panic, was throwing Ellie’s medication haphazardly back in to her medication bag. “No Ellie, he’s on his way to get us, I know he is. Come on we have to move. We’ve got to get out of here now.”

“But…” Eve cut her off.

“No time for buts Ellie, come on move, I was right last time wasn’t I? Now please, this time will you just trust me, I know him better than you. I know at least a little bit about how he works, how he *plays*. Come on move it.”

Five seconds later the girls were running down the stairs, not caring now about being seen.

When Janet Brown came into sight for a split second Elaine Wood smiled widely, ‘*she must be coming to enquire about the flowers.*’ The smile died on her face to be replaced by shock and confusion when not one but two Janet Browns ran straight passed reception and out of the front door. The last one with luggage in hand. *'She..they can't leave they haven't paid.'*

"Hey!" She shouted battling with the lock on the half door to get out from behind the desk. But the Janet Browns' were already climbing into their car, seconds later they were flying down the drive oblivious of the 20mph speed limit. She didn't even have time to get their registration number.

"Where to?" asked Ellie at the end of the drive.

"Just drive," said Eve, "left here."

"Then where?"

"Hell I don't know do I? There's a motorway sign there, it's four miles ahead, hit the motorway and then we'll have time to think."

"North or south?"

"Shit Ellie, whatever you think best."

"South then. London maybe, lots of people. Lots of places to hide. Plenty of places where you don't need bookings. We can just walk in off the street."

"Good plan."

Neither of them spoke for the next four miles. Once the congested A-roads gave way to the open plan of the motorway, it seemed to give permission for the thoughts they were thinking to pass from their congested minds into the open space of the car.

"On the other hand, Scotland might have been a good idea," said Eve. "You know, one of those little remote islands in the Hebrides or something."

"Eh?" said Ellie.

"Well we could have rented a cottage by the sea. He'd never find us there."

"Eve honey, you must have fallen asleep in your cell before those movies finished. The ones showing idyllic bliss on some remote island always, but always, turn bad. The bliss part comes just before the storm of all mother storms that cuts off the electricity and stops the ferry getting through. But the bad booger storm comes just after the wielding axe murderer lands on the island. I'll leave you to work the rest out for yourself."

"Hhmm," said Eve thoughtfully, "I told you London was a good plan."

Neither one of them wanted to bring up the subject of The Creator, but he was sitting there between them in the car, as though he was leaning forward from the back and pushing his face between the seats.

"How did he find us so quickly?" asked Eve in a very small voice. "Even if the hotel manager told all his staff, who then told every single person in a ten mile radius, it still had to get back to him. How could that be?"

What the girls didn't know was that the hotel manager did keep his word, "loyalty is one of the buzz words of the hotel," he later told police when days after they came enquiring about the disappearance of both Miss Erikson and her partner Mr Matthew High. Until that moment he hadn't mentioned a word to anyone about Miss Erikson's stay or her strange departure. He dealt with the police personally, Elaine Wood had a loose mouth and a penchant for gossip and he'd had to stamp down on her hard with threats of the possible loss of her employment if she leaked the story of the poor guest who left suddenly. Though he had never actually met her, Eleanor Erikson had, however briefly, stayed as an honoured guest in his hotel he felt somehow responsible for her. He felt affiliated with her and thought it his duty to protect her from the scheming sewer rats that called themselves the Press. He shut Woodsy up about the other Miss Erikson. '*Fancy her travelling with a body double it was just like the movies,'* he thought and all the lovely flowers seemed recompense enough for her very short stay. He made no mention of non-payment to the police and said that yes as far as he knew Miss Erikson had planned to meet Mr High there later because she had mentioned it. No he knew nothing of any disagreements between them. In fact they seemed very much in love because he sent hundreds of pounds worth of expensive flowers.

But the girls knew none of this and drove along fuming at the betrayal of the hotel manager. Or at least Ellie did, Eve had her own personal doubts that came a damned sight closer to home than hotel management.

"Ellie?" she had to pick her words carefully she knew damned well that she was on dangerous ground and needed to display tact and diplomacy, which she'd never really had an opportunity to learn. "Ellie, how well do you know Rob and Gail?"

"Very well, Why?" Ellie was negotiating traffic cones at yet another set of fifty-mile-an-hour road works. It took a couple of seconds for the accusation behind Eve's question to sink in. When it did she almost slammed her brakes on right there in the outside lane of the motorway. It was only the car behind furiously flashing his lights at her that made her catch up with the flow of traffic. She didn't say anything until she had come through the last cone and back into three-lane open road.

"No way. Forget it Ellie. Rob and Gail are my closest friends in all the world. No I will not even contemplate the thought that they might betray me. What possible motive would they have?"

"I don't know Ellie but the Creator knew where we were and someone must have told him. I don't see how it could have been the manager."

"Well the only other explanation is he must have tailed us to Rob's and followed, he could have ordered the flowers to be sent ahead, from his car while he was driving. I'm sure we aren't being followed now. I've been watching all the traffic behind us and the ones overtaking, nothing is with us for at least ten cars back that was with us when we set off." They reasoned that if they did have company, once they hit London there'd be plenty of opportunity to do some quick turning and lose any accompaniment.

They were still roughly two hours from the centre of London when Ellie began to take ill. "I'm going to have to stop and rest up Eve, I can't drive much further."

"No, we've got to keep moving, a moving target is harder to hit. I don't feel safe out here Ellie, as soon as we get to a hotel we can rest I promise. Come on let's sing, put the radio on."

Ellie pulled a face and turned on the radio, for a few minutes they sang along to whatever was on, but Ellie felt her eyes growing heavy, she began to shake violently and sweat was pouring from her forehead and stinging her eyes. The music had become too loud and irritating, she leaned over and switched it off. "I've got to pull over."

"Keep moving Ellie." Eve shouted it in the stillness of the car and there was no mistaking the threatening tone in her voice. "I'm trying to save our lives here. Please Ellie keep moving."

"Save our lives, you're going to kill not only us, but anyone whose fool enough to be near us when I crash this thing," said Ellie already pulling over towards the hard shoulder. She was retching before the car had completely come to a stop and just managed to open the door and lurch the top half of her body out of the car in time. She vomited violently several times. When she was finally able to fall against the support of the seat, her lips had taken on a deep blue tinge, her breathing was harsh and ragged and her face was as pale as a hospital sheet. She hadn't had a proper night's sleep since the whole nightmare began and the build up to the climax of the last few days had been too much for her. It would have been enough for anyone who wasn't suffering a terminal illness. Ellie had just about used up the final reserves of her strength.

"Okay. Okay, you've made your point," said Eve looking extremely worried. As soon as you can we'll make our way to the services I saw the sign a little while ago and it's only a few miles ahead. You can have one hour there, okay one hour? I'll keep watch and then we have to get moving again. Can you make it that far?"

Ellie nodded her head, "Deal," she murmured gratefully before adding, "Girl you're all heart."

Nothing eventful happened and they made London by late afternoon. It had been one hell of a day and Ellie was exhausted. At Eve's insistence they drove round London for a full hour to make damned sure that they were alone. She refused to let Ellie call Rob and begged that she just humour her on this one for a few days. Finally they found a small run-down hotel on Gower Street with parking to the rear. This was ideal because it was centrally situated and in a mixed race area where people minded their own business and didn't make eye contact. The Longland Hotel had vacancies without needing reservation and although the whole process of getting in as one person proved more difficult they were soon in the room. As before Ellie sank onto the bed and reached immediately for her medication. If it hadn't been for the different coloured bedspreads it could have been a re-play of their earlier experience. Eve went straight into the bathroom to ensure all was as it should be.

Ellie was too tired this time to even take coffee and as the first sounds of the steaming kettle filled the room, she was drifting into blessed sleep.

Chapter 29

Eve was still stirring her coffee and Ellie uttering her first soft snore when the telephone rang. Ellie's eyes opened wide on the first ring, instantly alert, a look of trepidation passing between her and Eve. Eve picked up the phone on the second ring.

"Hello?"

"'Ello ees this Mrs Chalker?" Asked the Spanish lady who had been manning the reception desk when Eve had signed in.

"Yes." Said Eve cautiously, answering to the new name they had used this time.

"I 'ave the message for you. The man said ee is Mr Matthew and ee says ee busy an has not the time to be put through right now, but ee be with you very, very soon. Important I say very, very soon. Thank-you." Eve was left staring at the phone in horror.

Eve ran round the room packing Ellie's drugs and picking up her purse for the second time in five hours. This time she stuffed Ellie's things into her own rucksack that she slung onto her back.

"Come on, pass me your suitcase we've got to go. He's found us." Eve still in a state of total panic relayed the exact wording of the phone conversation to Ellie. "I know what he's doing, he's keeping us moving. Not letting us rest or sleep. It's psychological warfare, pushing us to the limit knowing that you can't keep it up and will crack. He's waiting to see what will happen between us when you can't carry on any longer. But I'm telling you Ellie you have to carry on or you die."

"No way." Ellie was sitting on the edge of the bed now. I can't run again, and more to the point I'm not going to. It's a pity I didn't bring my best designer cocktail dresses we could have dressed up and gone out in style. Because I'm telling you Eve if he wants me tonight, he's going to have to come right in this room and get me, because I'm not running like a frightened rabbit again. Where the hell's it going to end? And how on earth has he found us again so quickly?"

Eve turned on Ellie the same thought occurring to her. "You stupid, stupid bitch." She spat at Ellie fury contorting her face into a mask of rage. "You rang him didn't you? You rang Rob when I signed us in. I told you it must be Rob. Do you believe me now? He's the only link from us to The Creator. I can't believe you did that Ellie. You promised me you wouldn't."

"I didn't Eve, I swear I didn't. And I'm telling you now Rob would no more betray me than betray his own mother. You are so, so wrong this time."

"Don't lie to me Ellie, you must have rung him, it's the only explanation, either he, Gail or both of them are in on this and you're too bloody prissy and trusting to even see it. Hell, for all we know Rob might actually **Be** the Creator. After all The Creator had left the building when Rob came to rescue us."

"Now you've completely lost the plot, don't be so damned ridiculous. I've only known Rob for eight years and yet you say the Creator has been holding you for as long as you can remember so how do you explain that one missy?"

"I don't know Ellie, I really don't know but somehow he knows where we are all the time, the only common denominator between us and him is Rob. So you tell me how he fits into the equation. Okay maybe he isn't the Creator, but he sodding well knows who is."

"Rubbish, if it hadn't been for Rob we'd still have been in that awful institute. He risked his life to save you, you ungrateful cow."

"Yes but did he? Apart from actually climbing up on the roof what risk did he actually take?"

"God Eve, the Creator could have come back at any time and caught Rob, then he'd have either been killed or ended up in there with us."

"In your tidy little mind where everything has a neat little compartment that's just the way it is isn't it Ellie? You take what you're told as the truth, will you just look at the facts? If you stop thinking about Rob as a friend for just one second and look at the cold hard facts, you can only come to one conclusion and that's the same one that I've already landed on."

"No there must be another explanation. We just have to think it through."

Ellie finally got Eve to sit and listen to her, they drank coffee, while the hunter came to take them. For over an hour they tossed things back and forth and Ellie tried to persuade Eve that she had not had any contact with Rob. They went round and round in circles both tired both irritable and neither one getting anywhere with the other.

"Well I tell you Ellie, you can sit here, be a target and think through whatever the hell you like, but as of right now I'm outta here. Eve turned to go and Ellie stood to stop her. Eve was just in time to catch Ellie as she fell to the ground. Ellie didn't answer when Eve called her name, she'd fainted. Eve had seen first-aid films, they were fed to her in the cell as part of her 'education' but watching a film and working on an unconscious woman were poles apart. Eve had to struggle for over a minute to get Ellie into the recovery position and see that her airway was free and open. She loosened the top two buttons of her shirt. Ellie came to gradually and sat up confused. Eve was sitting on the bed staring coldly at her.

“I was going to leave while you were out but it seemed cowardly.” She said, “And anyway you were breathing funny so I thought I’d better wait to see that you pulled through. If you hadn’t you wouldn’t have needed your purse and extra clothes so I could have used them.”

“Oh thanks Eve you’d make a wonderful nurse.” Said Ellie poking herself tenuously to see if she’d broken anything in her fall.

“You’re okay,” said Eve, “I caught you. Gave me a nasty crack on the elbow though if you want to check my bones out.”

Ellie grinned and held out a hand for Eve to help her up.

“Listen Ellie, you’re right you know, you’re sick and you can’t keep running. You should stay here and call the police now or something. I’m going to take my chances and get out of here. I stand more chance of getting away on my own and you’ll be better off with the protection of the law, hell if they lock you up in a loony bin for Matt’s murder, at least you’ll be safe from *Him*. But the truth is Ellie; I can’t keep carrying you. I’m not a nurse and I’m fighting for my life too. Ellie you’ve got a terminal illness, you’re going to die anyway.” Ellie looked at Eve shocked at the other woman’s bluntness. “I’m sorry but you are. I’ve only just been born in a way, so you see I can’t let you hold me back. Having to look after you we stand no chance, but on our own we might at least be able to find a way to make ourselves safe. Sorry Ellie but this is where we part company. Maybe one day another time, another place and all that.”

Ellie stared hard at Eve. “Are you quite finished?” before Eve had the chance to answer Ellie continued. “Well I think that’s a pretty selfish attitude but if you want to go then you’ll go there’s nothing I can do to stop you. And I’m sure as hell not going to lower myself to begging. But if you go alone now, you are going to run, and run, and run until he tracks you down and kills you like vermin. If we stick together we might run, but only until we get to the bottom of how he’s tracking us and find some answers. I know I’m holding you back Eve, I can’t help that but I can help us to think. Together we have to be stronger and harder to take out than alone as a single unit. I know there’s no love lost between us, we are together though circumstance not choice, but you have saved my life more than once, and I’d like to think I was instrumental in saving yours. We’ve supported each other through this so far. Let’s not lose our heads and make rash decisions now.”

“Nice little speech sis, but not worth getting myself killed for. Sorry doll but you’re on your own. Every second I stay here, is a second that he’s gained on me. I hope you getaway from this, I really do. I hope we both do. But I’ve made my mind up. Sorry.”

This time Eve made it through the door and didn’t bother to look back. Ellie heard her footsteps retreating down the hall. In a fit of sheer panic she knew that she couldn’t sit there alone and scared. She got up and followed Eve. Some of her strength had returned with the rush of fear and adrenaline, she ran down the hall and took the stairs two at a time catching up with Eve at the front door.

"Leave me alone Ellie. You can't stop me. Go back to the room and call the police." Ellie looked nervously round the foyer to see if anyone had heard what Eve said, but they were, for the moment, alone. Eve pushed the heavy door open, by the time she walked down the first two steps the night was suddenly filled with the scream of a persistent car alarm.

Ellie looked at Eve, they both instinctively knew that it had to be Ellie's car, though in the middle of London it could have been any vehicle in the area. Without a word they both started running to the car park. This was it. He had come.

The passenger side door of Ellie's car was standing wide open though the car park was deserted. Ellie screamed as she picked up the rag left on the seat. She was the first to recognise it for what it was ... the blood sodden T-shirt that Matt had been slain in.

Chapter 30

Ellie wanted to hold the T-shirt up to her face to inhale the sweet scent of Matty, but even that primal instinct was denied to her. The blood from the front had soaked through fusing back and front together and souring before it dried. Over the last twenty-four hours the shirt had starched as the blood dried to become stiff and brittle. There must have been a hundred thousand of these T-shirts printed but Ellie knew that this was Matty's shirt, with Matty's blood. She could feel him on it, not the smell of him because that had become foisty and metallic with the sheer amount of blood but the *essence* of him.

She was on the point of losing it, could feel the hot burning tears filling her up and rising to explode from her, pushed from behind by a force of anger more fierce than any emotion she had ever before felt. She instantly locked into her grief, not thinking, not caring. Without Matty what was the point of running anyway?

Eve saw Ellie knocked backwards by the discovery of the shirt. She saw her disappear in front of her eyes. Ellie was still standing there a look of sheer horror on her face but the spirit of Ellie was in some warped wonderland of the macabre. Eve could have run then, been away within seconds, Ellie wouldn't even have noticed but she couldn't leave her sister there to the mercy of the Creator. She was standing out in the open, maybe just feet from where he crouched in a bush, with no intention of fighting for her life.

Eve grabbed the shirt harshly from Ellie's hands and threw it into the shrubbery where hopefully it wouldn't be discovered for some time. For a split second she thought the distraught woman was going to follow it scrambling and snuffling in the under growth like a retriever until she came back out with the shirt.

"We've no time for this Ellie, later honey, later. Come on we've got to move." On hearing Eve's voice Ellie snapped out of her trance. She pushed down on the urge to weep, that would keep but the anger burning inside her was a thing of substance longing only for an outlet. She shot Eve a quick grateful grin. Grateful for pulling her back from the brink and more importantly grateful for not leaving her when she had the chance, they were in this together again.

"I'm okay." She said in a gritty snarl. The alarm was still blaring. It was amazing that no one had arrived on the scene to see what all the noise was about. But at seven o'clock in the evening maybe there was nothing at all unusual about a car alarm blaring in central London. Back in the real world Ellie ran round to immobilise the car and get the hell out of there.

"No!" screamed Eve at the top of her voice. "Don't touch the car, you don't know what he might have done to it. Come on we'll have to go on foot. Run, he's watching us and could grab us at any moment."

Eve pulled Ellie roughly by the hand and started dragging her out of the car park.

"What are we going to do?" Ellie grunted as her feet pounded the rough concrete. Adrenaline, fear and sheer outright panic had given her a new boost of fuel, but she knew damned well that she'd have to pay for it dearly later.

"I don't know, let's just wing it for now," Eve grinned ruefully at Ellie, "If we're still alive and free in ten minutes or so we might be able to come up with some sort of plan, but for now you just keep doing what you're doing `cos you're doing it well."

The side street they were on opened into Tottenham Court Road, a large gaudily painted tour bus, taking visitors round the London sights was coming towards them.

"The bus." yelled Ellie, "Let's get on the bus."

"It won't stop for us, there's no designated stopping place in sight."

"Oh yes it bloody well will," Said Ellie running into the middle of the road and waving her arms.

"Ellie!" screamed Eve.

"Hey," Said Ellie never taking her eye off the bus, "I'm dying remember, nothing to lose."

The bus screeched to a shuddering halt, far from the movies where the heroine's breath gets crushed by the mega-tonne vehicle and her nose leaves snot on the windscreen, this bus stopped with plenty of room to spare but the driver didn't look too pleased at his impromptu emergency stop. He opened his door and fired a torrent of angry words at the wild looking woman.

The second the door opened Ellie pulled Eve onto the bus giving the driver no opportunity to refuse them access. After making his displeasure noted, he reluctantly agreed to let them ride the bus, but not before he told them how low in his esteem crazy tourists rated. Ellie turned on her sweetest smile and blatantly gave the driver the eye. It cost them twenty-five euros each, they had to pay the price of the full excursion even though there was less than an hour to run.

They headed for an empty double seat towards the front of the bus and flopped gratefully into it. Ellie who had the window seat, scanned as much of the street as she could to see if they were being followed. It didn't look as though they were, certainly nobody had got on the bus. Eve was staring at Ellie open mouthed. "You flirted with him! I can't believe you just flirted with him to get us on the bus. Miss Erikson - pure as the driven snow just used her body to get her own way."

Ellie grinned, "Well it worked didn't it?"

They discussed in low voices what they should do next. It was decided they'd ditch the bus somewhere with lots of people. It was a green line get on-get off tour bus where you could lose one bus and grab another at any of the city attractions. They still weren't sure if they were being followed and had to make sure that they could lose anybody on their tail before they stopped anywhere for the night. This time they *would* find somewhere safe. After twenty minutes of discussion and argument it was decided that they'd spend the first hour 'melting' into the city, then they'd find somewhere to hire a car. No phone calls, no advance bookings, no chance of anyone getting a lead on them, just two more aliens in a city that didn't care.

They were still looking at the route map posted on the bus and trying to come to some sort of agreement when Ellie made a decision. "Next stop." She said decisively.

"Leicester Square," said Eve, "That's near Soho isn't it? We can lose ourselves there."

"No, I think I've got a better idea." The bus was slowing and Eve began to leave her seat, but Ellie held her back. "Wait, we'll jump off at the last minute in case he's watching for us to leave. It will give him less time to prepare."

The driver was just shutting the doors when Eve jumped up from her seat and cried, "Wait please. We're getting off here." They got off the bus leaving the irritated driver shaking his head and scowling at them.

They ran without looking back along the street to the walkway that led to Leicester Square proper. Along the bottom side of the gardens, opposite the Odeon cinema a line of street entertainers had attracted a large crowd. The girls pushed rudely into the centre of a mob watching an athletic fire-eater. People were looking at the bad mannered identical twins and they smiled their apologies so that the people would go back to watching the busker and not them. They heard one large lady comment to her partner that she reckoned the twins were part of the act. "Fire eating would be a doddle compared to this lark," whispered Ellie.

They watched for newcomers joining the crowd, anyone walking round with an air of looking for someone, or anyone who just looked suspicious. They seemed to be in the clear but were taking no chances. After ten minutes Ellie told Eve to keep close and follow her.

They only moved a hundred yards into the Odeon. It was as good a place as any to watch for company. They bought tickets but went straight into the ladies. Anyone following them would go into the cinema assuming they had gone in there. Or if unsure which film they were seeing they'd hang around the foyer.

Ellie needed to rest. The rest room was pleasant and had seating. It beat resting her bum on a cold toilet seat, but at that point Ellie would have been grateful to rest anywhere. Eve peeped out of the door three times before the foyer was completely empty apart from the lady manning the ticket sales and the people in the retail booths. She approached the lady and spoke to her quietly.

"Excuse me please, my sister has an illness and passed out in the ladies. Oh it's okay, she's fine now, but I was wondering if there's a back door or something we could leave by. She needs to get home and there's so many people out the front."

The lady was very helpful and showed the girls through the staff door. She remarked several times how pale Ellie looked and they had quite a job stopping her from calling an ambulance. Their escape was perfect. There wasn't a soul in sight until they rounded the corner into another bustling street. Ellie was tired, and they could have gone back to Leicester square and caught a bus from there, but it was too risky covering old ground. It wasn't a long walk from there to the Trafalgar tube, but to Ellie it seemed to take forever. To help her keep pace with Eve she chanted over and over again. *'A moving target is a hard target to hit. I am a desert lizard moving to stay alive. Move to live, move to live. I am a moving target.'* Eve felt vulnerable walking at half speed with Ellie but she never once said a word or cut in on her concentration. Twice when she stumbled Eve put a hand under Ellie's arm and gave it a squeeze. When Ellie had to stop at the bottom of the tube steps Eve said, "You did great, well done. You've got guts."

"Well maybe I'm not as ready to die as I thought I was earlier." She said. Her eyes were dull, her face was horribly pale and pain was written in a fine scroll of lines across her forehead. They made four tube changes. Twice just changing lines and twice leaving the station and walking to the next. Ellie had her destination in mind all along but didn't dare speak it even to Eve in case he was the person behind them in the carriage, listening in to their conversation for clues.

Finally they arrived at Euston station. Upstairs in the terminal they made their way to the hire car kiosk and rented a small run-a-round hatchback that was discreet and inconspicuous. They were both on edge until they were finally free of the city and cruising along the M1 at a steady seventy miles an hour. The traffic was light and after just less than an hour's driving Eve suggested they come off the motorway and head for the Pagoda roundabout, for no other reason than she liked the name of it. Once they had left the M1 behind and were driving along the darkly atmospheric A roads it was decided that they'd stop at the first hotel or bed and breakfast they came to. There wasn't another car in sight when they found the perfect place. The roadside sign said that the Palisades Motel was just five hundred yards on the left. They pulled into the car park and were delighted to see their journey's end. The motel had rows of chalet type accommodation, perfectly anonymous all with en suite, kettles and telephone. Perfect. The main office was brightly lit with neon sign and harsh fluorescent lighting. Eve signed them in under the name of Amanda Stephens and was out of the office, key in hand in less than three minutes.

Several of the chalets had lights glowing behind drawn curtains but other than that and the bored youth behind reception the place appeared deserted. They had a clear view of the road for hundreds of yards and there was not a vehicle in sight. Dispensing with the cloak and dagger stuff they walked together the short distance from the car to their chalet. Theirs was number forty-three and they counted off the numbers as they walked along the carefully tended path.

Eve put the key in the door and before it had even finished opening the phone began to ring. They tried to convince themselves that it was just the lad at reception ringing to tell Eve that she'd left her purse, or to wish her a good night and sweet dreams, or to ask for a date, but they both knew who it was. They knew the routine now.

Ellie picked up the phone but didn't speak. She could hear him breathing, waiting for her to say something first, revelling in their terror and exhaustion. Ellie counted off the seconds in her head. She only got to seven but it seemed like so very many more, an eternity of time ticked off in a mere seven seconds. She wasn't going to give the bastard the satisfaction of hearing her speak first.

"The date is twenty-third of October, twenty-forty-six. The time is eleven thirty seven. How are my dollies tonight? Still enjoying our little game? I have some news my children, it won't be long now. I tire of our toying. Shall we up the anti a little? How much are you prepared to stake on your lives?"

"Fuck off you Bastard." Ellie spat the words and slammed the phone into its cradle.

She looked over at Eve, they had been so careful. How had he found them? Eve wasn't madly stuffing things back in bags, for they hadn't had time to take anything out. She wasn't heading for the door, ushering Ellie into headlong flight. Eve finally realised that there was nowhere to go. Here in the Palisades Motel was as good a place to die as any and better than some. They hadn't known where they were going themselves, hadn't planned, hadn't told, hadn't even got through the door. But he knew. He would always know. There was no safe place on this earth, and they were going to die.

"He's a demon," said Ellie, "Possibly the devil himself."

"Huh tell me something I don't know, don't forget I've *lived* with this freak all my life."

"No I don't mean that. Don't you see Eve, this is something unnatural. He's tracking us with supernatural means. Telepathy or evil spirit guides or witchcraft or something. How can we fight the devil? Better the devil you know Eve, you said it yourself. Did you know all along what he is?"

"No Ellie, no I swear, that was just something intended to freak you out."

"Well Evie girl, let me tell you, I'm freaked. I'm freaked to little pink freaksicles and if there *is* a God out there I hope to hell it's not his night off, because I've a feeling that before we see sunlight again we are going to need him rooting for our side."

Neither woman had moved since the telephone call. They each sat on the side of a bed facing each other. Their faces had identical expressions, and the only difference between the two women was the obviously sick condition of Ellie. Knowing there was nowhere to run had taken all of the panic out of the situation though none of the fear. Their faces said they were done for, but not necessarily beaten.

They took the mattresses off the beds, then piled all the furniture up against the door. But he could still come through the window; hell, he might even be able to just float through the walls. When he wanted to come in, he had no need to knock and probably wouldn't be waiting for an invitation.

Eve made tea.

"What now?" asked Ellie.

"We might as well sleep, it's about the only constructive option left to us."

Ellie said she was too scared to sleep but she took a handful of medication and went out like a light two minutes later. Eve pulled her mattress against the wall just to the side of the barricaded door. She sat up to await their night caller but she too was soon banished to a world of troubled sleep.

Chapter 31

Ellie woke with surprise. That is, she was surprised to wake up at all. She came to instantly with none of the usual morning hanging fugue. She awoke with her eyes tight shut. She didn't want to open them, didn't know what she'd see and for a long time didn't dare look. She fully expected Eve to be lying on her mattress with her throat cut wide open. Or maybe she'd be hanging from a rope directly above her head. The chair would have been moved from against the door. It had such a pretty cushion. Despite the apathy of the pimply receptionist, the management wanted people to enjoy their stay here. It was a comfortable place to stay, but Ellie felt far from comfortable, she felt fear like she'd never known before. Taking her mind back to the picture she was imagining, Eve is dead either hanging or horribly slashed and the demon is sitting on the pretty chair, quietly watching her, biding his time, enjoying the anticipation of the final round of the game. He would be decaying and inhuman with red eyes, or yellow eyes, or no bloody eyes at all. Ellie tightened the grip on her closed eyes but risked a silent sniff at the air. She couldn't smell the decay, the pieces of rotting flesh that were falling off his long dead body, she couldn't smell the sharp metallic tinge of Eve's blood and that was a smell that she'd never, ever forget.

"Well it's about time you woke up. I've been sitting here for hours waiting for you."

It was Eve's voice, but it must be a trick, it was Eve's voice but it must be coming from *his* rotting mouth.

"Oi, come on stop pretending you're asleep, I know you're awake. I guess we live to see another day eh? Or at least some of it." *'Surely no demon could be as gobby as Eve, maybe she was still alive.'* Ellie's face broke into a huge grin when she finally risked checking out her roommate.

The girls got up and each one 'kept nix' while the other showered. While Ellie was dressing, Eve nipped out to the motel shop to buy hot croissants and sandwiches. Neither of them had eaten since five-thirty the previous morning and both were starving. Now that they knew the Creator was super-human an air of inevitability settled over them. It didn't matter where they went or what they did, when he was ready and at his convenience he'd come for them and zap them dead with killer rays from his eyes or something. With acceptance of this came a sort of eerie calm. They had survived the night because he chose to let them and now they would survive minute by minute until he came.

While they munched on cheese and pickle sandwiches Ellie sat cross-legged on the bed and opened her micro-pad. She had fourteen e-mails but only four were of interest. Three from Rob asking where the hell they were. Ellie felt sorry that she hadn't been in touch. Had she ever doubted him there for a second? Or had she stayed incommunicado just to prove to Eve that she was wrong about Rob and Gail? She would ring him in a while to bring him up to speed on their happenings.

The other mail was from Victor Khazana. She remembered asking him for information on TSD. It seemed funny that she was trying to find out about an illness that should be the cause of her death. Now if her body were ever found she would forever bear the title of 'murder victim'.

Victor said that since the headlines about her illness in the national press had been confirmed, he had been researching Tay-Sachs at every opportunity. His letter was full of well-meaning sympathy and not a little reproval for not coming straight to him. He said he was going to be away at an unavoidable conference in the States from the 23rd to the 28th but would like to meet up with her after that to discuss his findings. She wrote a brief note back thanking him for his concern, apologising for her deceit and saying that they'd arrange something as soon as he got back. It was an appointment that Ellie doubted she would ever make, let alone keep.

Just as she was about to close the hand-held micro a new message came through from Rob. They had agreed to only communicate by e-mail until the girls returned.

"Ellie ring me. Urgent, I have news."

Ellie read the message out to Eve, "What do you reckon it could be?"

"Your latest book's probably made number one in the charts," said Eve sarcastically. Ellie threw a pillow at her. The seconds it took to connect to Rob's phone seemed like an age. It was switched off. They weren't at home either so Ellie now alarmed rang the office to see if he was in a meeting at work. He hadn't been seen there all day so Ellie left a message that he call her on her mobile as soon as he got in. She left similar messages on his home phone and his personal and business mobiles. If anything was wrong they'd know soon enough either with a call, or by an ominous silence. Neither of them said what they were thinking but each knew what the other was mulling over. What if *he* had done something to Rob and Gail first?

Rested, fed and showered Ellie felt physically better than she had for days, it was as though the disease had finally decided to take a backseat for a while. Death didn't need to come at her from all angles, only the one would do. She sat in front of the vanity mirror and rubbed some moisturiser into her skin. She had dark circles under her eyes and felt as though she had aged ten years in two days.

She started to brush her hair. It was both the girls' practise to give their hair one hundred strokes morning and night. This was something taught to Ellie by Esther, forced upon Eve in the institute because she was ordered to emulate Ellie in every way possible, and carried on by both of them in adult life as a matter of habit.

Eve was slouched on the bed watching Ellie brush her hair.

Suddenly she sat bolt upright. Ellie alerted to the change in her attitude began to turn.

"Don't move," yelled Eve. "Don't move a muscle."

"What? What is it?" Ellie was terrified. She looked at Eve through the reflection in the mirror and then ignoring her instructions turned to face her.

Eve was kneeling up on the bed, her mouth was gaping and she opened and closed her eyes several times. Ellie began to speak but Eve held up a hand to silence her. She started looking wildly round the room. Her expression was not one of fright or panic. She seemed to be thinking something through.

"That's it," she screamed. "That's how he's tracking us. Oh my God Ellie it's horrible. I've been so bloody stupid. It's you! No probably both of us. He's seeing us through our eyes. Hearing us through our own ears. Ellie, somehow I don't know how, but somehow **we are fucking transmitters.**"

Ellie went to Eve and sat next to her on the bed. "What do you mean, I don't understand."

"Neither do I but somehow he's living through us just the way I lived through you for all those years. That's how he got the films of you. Listen, when you were brushing your hair in the mirror just now, I realised what's been staring me in the face all the time. The only time I ever saw you was in a mirror."

Ellie looked blank trying to take this new information in.

"I didn't see film of *you* Ellie, I saw film of what you were seeing. I was looking through your eyes the whole time. I should have realised before now, there were no camera angles, the scene wasn't coming from corners of the room, or from behind potted plants. They were coming from you. That's how he knows where we are every time. He's watching us right this second, listening to every word we say. And there's nothing we can do short of gouging out our eyes and perforating our eardrums to stop him."

"How?" said Ellie, "what does it mean? Is he inside us? Some malignant possession?"

"I don't know Ellie, but my guess is that it's scientific, not supernatural."

"Well that's good I suppose, no deadly eye rays."

"Eh?"

"Oh it doesn't matter just something I was thinking about when I woke up. So does this make our position better or worse?"

"I don't know." Said Eve, "I suppose that depends on *how* he's seeing what we see."

"Well let's assume it's not supernatural, for him to do that he'd have to have cameras wouldn't he?" She went on without waiting for an answer from Eve. "We must have tiny cameras and radio transmitters in our heads. Bloody hell Eve can you hear what we're saying? It all sounds incredible. Are you sure about this? Maybe you're mistaken."

"No mistake Ellie." Knowing fine well that he was listening in on every word, Eve began telling Ellie more about her life in the institute. They had talked a lot about it since escaping, every new detail made Ellie feel increasingly sorry for the suffering that Eve went though. Eve never had any toys. She lived Ellie's life, she learned through the books she was allowed and information projected on the walls in the breaks between Ellie's life, she ate, she washed and she slept. That was her existence for as long as she could remember. Apart from images on the screen she had never seen a human being. She had been shown films of her early life. In those days her food hatch was a work station, gloved hands came through the wall to attend the tiny baby who was deprived all human contact but the most basic essentials. She was fed, bathed and changed to a strict time schedule. She was never picked up when she cried and never comforted when she was upset.

When she was two years old the voice would issue commands. She learned to walk through starvation, if she wanted food then she had to walk for it. She was ordered to clean herself, if she didn't then she would be refused food until she did. She didn't speak her first word until she was five years old and that word was *Ellie.* The little girl hadn't been fed for two days. She didn't understand what the voice wanted, but she soon came to understand that if she didn't say "Ellie" then she wouldn't be fed. The voice was two people, a man and a lady, she preferred the lady, even though she never 'talked' to her only issued orders. Eve was raised without any stimulation other than the voice and the recordings. She was raised clinically and without love. She never had a cold or a virus. She never had happiness, but she knew that there was more to life than what she had because the real Eve was called Ellie and lived a full and normal life. Eve knew, as she grew older that her life was not normal. She toileted in a bucket for twenty seven years and she bathed from a bowl.

On her ninth birthday she watched Ellie's birthday party, as she had watched every other of Ellie's birthday parties. When it was over she received a present. The only present she was ever given in her life. It was a gift from Ellie the voice said. It wasn't wrapped in fancy paper like *her* presents were. It was passed through her food hatch without ceremony.

It was a doll, the voice said it was to be called Polly. It was a two-foot rag doll with a porcelain face. Eve knew what mockery was; she already hated

Ellie for her comfortable life. She tore the blue glass eyes from the doll; at least *she* wouldn't have to watch Ellie having fun. Eve hated Ellie and hated the doll as a symbol of Ellie. She used to punish the doll, but Polly didn't seem to mind and continued to smile her smug smile. Polly was her only friend.

Ellie was crying when Eve got up to make another cup of coffee. She was crying for Eve and she was crying for herself.

"Here let me do that," said Ellie.

"No please let me do it, I like it," said Eve. She hugged the coffee sachet protectively against her chest as if this small thing could be taken away from her too.

They were drinking their steaming coffees and talking some more when Ellie's mobile rang. They gave each other the 'Oh no not again' look and Ellie picked up the phone without giving the Creator the courtesy of hearing her voice. It was her small defiance against him.

"Ellie? Ellie are you all right?" It was Rob's voice tight with concern.

"Listen Ellie," he said when he had been brought briefly up to date. "In all the panic the other day I forgot to tell you about the strange woman." He told Ellie about the call from the woman who used to work at the institute and the call to Matt, telling him not to speak in front of Ellie because it all went back to the Creator.

Rob's voice rose in excitement when he told them that the woman had been in touch again through the local paper. Unfortunately she had left a date and time for the previous day. They had missed the appointment. The message read.

Eve. Thursday 23rd October. Macdonald's Portland Walk. WARNING! Don't tell Ellie anything, it all goes back. I'm taking a big risk sending this so please. Come alone.

They were devastated to have missed the appointment. This woman had answers and seemed keen to help them. But Rob reasoned that if she had tried to make contact once she would again. She had rung Matt's mobile when they were at the institute, so Rob was keeping it close to him all the time. He assured the girls that another meeting would be arranged. He'd place an ad in the same paper when they hung up. All three of them were all too aware that they might be setting up the perfect trap to catch themselves. This advert thing could all be another element of the Creator's game.

Ellie had been quiet for a few seconds. "Don't you see what this means Eve? You must be in the clear, it's just me with the head implants."

"Yes it looks that way, but for the moment we can't take anything for granted. Until we find this woman we don't know anything."

Ellie told Rob their theories about the cameras in their heads. They talked for ages before coming up with a plan.

It was going to be dangerous but Eve explained to Rob that he was as much on death row as they were. He knew too much, and what's more the Creator was aware of every single thing that Rob knew.

"He's going to kill you and Gail too, Rob. He won't let you live. He doesn't like loose ends."

Rob didn't want to do it, it was lunacy. Ellie and Eve didn't want him to do it, but it was the only chance they had to fight. At least it was *something* they could do to save themselves. They knew that the Creator was either listening to them planning, or he would have it on tape to listen to later. It was decided that Rob and Ellie would write down everything they knew about the Creator, all about the institute and Matt's death. As a small insurance policy, they would send the information in a sealed envelope to their solicitors with instruction that it was only to be opened if they hadn't made contact with the solicitor's office by Tuesday 28th November.

It wasn't much, and none of them really thought it would make much difference to a man as evil and sick as their enemy obviously was. But at least it was positive, aggressive action.

It was decided that the following night Rob would go back to the institute and if he made it, would locate and destroy all the transmission and recording equipment that enabled him to track them.

For the first time in his life, Rob truly understood the phrase 'Dead man walking.'

Chapter 32

'So tired, so weary, so bored. My toys have all become so dull, even my little boy dolly. Chase, chase, chase. The chase was fun for a while, but now I want action!

The sick bitch is dying anyway, that wasn't meant to happen. She wasn't meant to get sick, she's supposed to be perfect. I have no place in my game for broken dolls. Sick dollies become ugly dollies. I will not tolerate ugly dollies. Nasty ugly dollies.

It's no fun hunting something that's going to die anyway, not enough emotion, she played well for a time. I was optimistic about bringing her into the game, allowing the other one to escape, setting the fire, bringing my pretty toys together. My dollies should have been more sport. Snivelling weak dollies. They should be Amazon toys, my Amazon girls. Weak, sick, broken dollies. My girl let me down getting ill, that wasn't part of the deal. I let her be special, made her special and this is the way she repays me.

I roll a six Ellie dolly, you die.

The other one is still healthy but no fun for the game if she's alone. I need to make me some more dollies. Nice pretty new dollies. Perfect dollies.

I roll a six Eve dolly, you die, but not yet I have new plans for you first.

And my boy dolly had better shape up or I'll be rolling my dice for him.

From Adam's rib began Eve ... from Eve's rib begat lovely new dollies.'

Chapter 33

Rob was on his own. He seriously doubted that he would get out of this nightmare place alive, so he had left Jake at home rather than risk his already endangered life any more than it need be. Only now did he realise how much courage and moral support the dog had given him last time. Tonight he felt like a little boy finding his way to the bathroom in the dark.

He used the same window for entry as he had the last time. Every second inside that dark place of death and misery he waited for the spade falling over his head, or the chloroform rag pressing onto his nose and mouth.

He didn't know where to look for the freak's operations room. In cinemas the projectionist always has his little room at the top of the building, would that follow in this case? Good a place as any to begin looking. Listening diligently for the slightest sound he made his way along corridors and up any flight of stairs that he found. On every corridor wall and in each room he wrote his name and the date in large print with indelible black marker pen, in case the solicitor did indeed come to read the contents of his envelope. If this happened the police would be called and instructed to come straight to the institute, because if that envelope was ever opened then Rob was either already dead or in some serious trouble. The fire and smoke damage to the building was less severe up here and at first he was encouraged to find rows of smart offices. This all looked very hopeful. He searched one after the other, going through drawers and filing cabinets, wondering about the ones that were locked. Everything seemed very 'clean' and above board. He was no expert at deciphering scientific documents but there was no mention of their experimentation concerning caged and tortured little girls or murder. He felt safer using his torch up here, though anyone arriving from the drive would see it shining in the blown upper windows. Rob was confident that if the Creator was coming for him, he was already in his web flexing his mandibles and, waiting for his prey to come to *him*. Rob jotted down the names of one or two people that cropped up from the files, and stuffed a few pieces of paper in his pockets that looked interesting and might later prove to yield clues, but nothing seemed very hopeful.

After over an hour of searching he was no closer to finding the control room than he had been when he started. This place was a warren of connecting and inter-connecting rooms and corridors. The perfect place to hide, or to be pursued.

At least he had covered the top storey of the building, now he could methodically work his way down, room by room, cupboard by cupboard. He had a niggling feeling of worry that like the inner place where Eve had been kept; the control room might also be hidden.

Logic told him that if what he was looking for wasn't at the top of the building, then the best place to look is near to where the cell was, but he didn't want to waste time doubling back on himself if he was wrong. Also he didn't want to admit to himself that he was terrified of going back through the secret storeroom, into what lay beyond.

His search wasn't fruitful and finally he did come to the smokescreen in the guise of an innocent storeroom. Both on the corridor wall outside and in the storage space itself he wrote clear directions for the police of where to find the release catch for the false wall. He was sweating heavily, he could have been picked off at anytime not only tonight, but anytime over the last few weeks, but somehow he felt less safe here in this part of the building. It was as though the kosher façade of the institute outside the secret place provided some form of protection for him, just because of its clean image. Like Alice with the 'Eat Me' jar, he was about to walk into a land of otherworldliness.

As the wall closed to behind him Rob felt doomed. He hefted the eight-pound sledgehammer he had brought round to his front and held it like a shield, pretending to be ready for anything that came at him.

There were many rooms in this part of the building. A lot of them locked with eye scanning or combi-locks protecting them from intrusion. Anyone of them could be what Rob was looking for. When he got to the cell doors one of them stood open. It was the other one, not the one he rescued the girls from. He looked in half expecting the Creator to be waiting for him with the mad hatter and the dormouse. Alice would offer tea and the Cheshire cat would grin menacingly. The room was empty, only the overpowering smell of stale vomit gave away the secret of its recent occupation. He pressed on the interconnecting door between the cells, its lack of height further gave the impression of his whole Alice in Wonderland analogy. The door flew open and he gave a little girlie scream because he expected it to be locked. *'Dear God please don't let Matt be there with his throat all cut open.'* he begged silently.

The room was empty. This tiny room was where Eve had lived for twenty seven years, until the fire gave her sudden and unexpected means of escape. He felt a pang of pity for the poor little girl turned troubled woman. It was little wonder she felt the way she had about Ellie.

He shuddered, it may have been just a scared man's fancy but he felt as though malevolent and dangerous eyes were watching him. He turned and ran back the way he had come into the corridor. With every step taken he expected the door to slam shut in front of him the way it had done on the girls. Back in the corridor he felt a moment of relief, but he still had to do what he had come here to do and get out. He found the room where all Eve's clothes and toiletries were kept. As he went along he left huge notes on the wall. 'Cell where Eve was kept, storeroom containing Eve's things.' Gradually he worked his way methodically along the corridor moving left to right and checking every door he came to. The last door on the right was ajar? An invitation? A trap?

Rob pushed the door open without going in and hefted his hammer.

Bingo!

There was nobody in the room, but this was what he had been looking for.

The room was large and airy. Twin whirrings were audible once he crossed the threshold. Several black leather padded swivel chairs lined the central workstation. Three CCTV monitors stood in a row to the left-hand side, one of these was on, powered by a portable solar generator. The monitor was replaying a scene from ten minutes earlier. As Rob watched the screen transfixed, he saw a door opening into the second cell, a small scream preceded the hand that came through the door, followed by a terrified Rob. He stood in the centre of the cell visibly shaking as he remembered what they had been through.

Rob took the hammer to all three monitors and equipment and smashed them to smithereens. He didn't bother to turn off the power first and a loud bang was heard as the monitors blew that echoed through the silent building. Rob gave no thought now to being cut down where he stood he had a job to do. The note left in the middle of the desk just incited him to further ferocity as he took all his terror and frustration out on the projector and recording equipment. He paid particular attention to the black box on the floor that was presumably the computer at the heart of the operations. The thing that transposed what Ellie saw into film to be viewed by the sick monster hounding her. He smashed the lead crystal glass and the open, but loosely corked, bottle of champagne left by the note. He only stopped when his arms could not physically manage another swing of the hammer. He flopped exhausted by his exertions into the middle-padded chair, the one he sensed belonged to the backside of the Creator. He was wheezing and breathing heavily. But despite that he felt good at this minor victory.

He read the note again and then thrust it angrily into his coat pocket. Maybe this would prove to be a dire error by the Creator should the police ever be in a position to have a suspect and need a handwriting sample. Rob felt that he was becoming quite adept at all this fight for your life and live by your wits stuff. He thought about the note and wondered if perhaps it might be genuine. Maybe the great man genuinely couldn't be here tonight.

"So sorry not to make our little rendezvous my dear chap, have a drink on me, you've earned it. I would truly love to have been with you tonight but never fear, we will make up for lost time very soon."

He didn't sit for more than a few seconds. This could still turn nasty and he wasn't about to let his guard down. He turned for the door and jumped with another scream. Someone was by the door watching him.

The 'person' sitting in the chair by the door watching him turned out to be a doll. A horrible rag-doll, but she wasn't watching him because some sicko had taken her eyes out. The empty sockets of the horrendous doll mocked him as he ran for his life and didn't stop running until he was scrabbling with the handle of his car door.

As he drove away he couldn't help thinking that it had all been too easy. Getting back through the secret door had been easy, it wasn't locked never to open to him again, in fact on the inside there was a plainly visible handle that you turned to open the door.

'Why? Why had the Creator just let him walk away from this?'

Two miles down the road Rob swung his car into the opposite verge; he opened the door and vomited acid bile onto the grass. In his mind he imagined the Creator laughing.

The girls were delighted by Rob's victory. They whooped and hollered, high-fived and jumped on the beds like a pair of kids. They even hugged and kissed as though it was the most natural thing in the world. It was a ten point score to the little people. They were alive and the fact that he had *let* them score didn't matter. The gold, silver and bronze medals in this game were melted into a huge cast of life and this time at least they had come up tops.

Ellie's mobile rang with a withheld number. She answered it knowing beforehand who it was.

"Hello my dollies, quite a party you're having there, am I invited? I shouldn't wonder that you'll have a new bed to pay for with all this frivolity. I trust you'll be in later when I call to see you?"

Ellie hung up without saying a word. She wasn't going to gratify the bastard with a response. The room suddenly felt cold and all the joy had dissipated with the change in mood.

"It didn't work." Said Ellie simply. "We were so bloody stupid to think that he'd only have the one set of monitoring equipment. He says he's coming for us."

Ellie sat beside Eve and grabbed her hand. "We'll get though this."

"Will we?"

"No but it's something to say, maybe even something to cling on to," said Ellie. "The thing is, I know that any time now you're going to strike out on your own. You haven't got a head-implant telling him every time you take a crap. You might be able to get away. And there's nothing I can do to stop you." Ellie's eyes had filled with tears.

"We don't know that though do we? We are just going by the message in the paper. I could be just as bugged and buggered as you are."

"Don't you want to cut lose and see?"

"What's the point? I've got nowhere to go and he'd find me eventually anyway, he's not going to set me free. I've got no money. What can I do? I wouldn't stand a chance on my own anymore than I do here."

"I've got money, I could give you what you need to get away. You could use my passport, get out of the country. I'm dying Eve you could take over my life. Has-been writer's fade from the public eye very quickly. You could keep moving for a while and if you don't have an implant then he'd never find you. I can set you up, not for life, but long enough to build a life."

"Why would you do that, after all that I've done to you?"

Ellie sat quietly for a few seconds and Eve didn't think she was going to answer her. When she had collected her thoughts, Ellie said. "Because we've been through so much together in the last few days, because I don't want the bastard to win with a full hand. Because I care about you, most of all because I care about you."

Eve was crying. She felt weak and humiliated because of her tears. Nobody had ever said they cared about her before. Nobody ever had and Eve didn't know how to cope with her emotions.

"Well I don't care about you, so don't go getting any stupid ideas about us having some big, happy reunion. We're in this because we're in this, not because we like each other. As soon as this is sorted I'm off."

Ellie smiled.

"And what the hell do you think you're grinning at?" said Eve wiping her hand across her nose and leaving a trail of watery snot up her forearm.

"You do care Eve. I know you do because if you didn't, the second you knew you might not have an implant you'd have been off. Or if not then when we found the shirt in the car. Or now when I've offered to set you up. You're not staying with me because you have to. You're staying with me because I'm all you've got and because we need each other and because we *do* care."

"Oh fuck off," said Eve stomping off to the bathroom to compose herself.

They holed up at the motel for another two days. Waiting for his arrival, waiting for the hammer to fall. He never came. Everything was quiet and they rested, talked, and rested some more. Ellie was weak, the trauma had taken more out of her than she was prepared to admit, and Eve said she was a selfish bitch for getting sick, just when they could have become friends. Ellie laughed, sometimes Eve was like a stroppy little girl learning to cope with her emotions.

Knowing that their foe was listening to every word, Ellie used the telephone to set up meetings with her consultant, and her old friend Victor Khazana. Two weeks earlier the thought of two appointments in one day would have been too much for her to cope with, now it was like a gentle walk in the park.

There was no point to them staying there any longer. When the Creator chose to pick them off he would have no trouble doing so. Ellie wanted to get Jake and go home. Eve would have to keep her head down and behave herself. Old Jackson never missed a thing and his curtain twitched so often it was afflicted with a permanent tic.

"There's something we have to do first though," said Ellie. "We have to go and see my mother. It's time we got some answers."

"Won't that put her in danger?"

"No more than she already is," said Ellie, "no more than the butcher I go to on a Friday or the old lady I sit and talk to in the park. I've had this implant all my life, he already knows where everyone lives. Unless we find some way to stop him, everybody in my life is already in danger."

Esther's face when she saw the girls was a picture. She prodded Eve to see if she was real. Then she spent the next half-hour crying because Jerry must have had an affair with another woman to produce this woman who looked just like Ellie.

Ellie had trouble getting her to concentrate. Even when she told her about the institute and Matt's death, though she left certain parts out, all Esther could focus on was the fact that Jerry had been unfaithful to her. Esther could only perform for one trauma at a time and this was the only one that brought the focus of the conversation on to her and cast her in the role of the pitiful victim. A role that Eleanor's mother had always played to the hilt.

"Mum that's impossible," said Ellie "Look at us, we are identical in every way. Half sisters could never be identical as Eve and I are, we came from the same womb Mother, we must have done. Please tell us the truth, either Eve is your daughter as well, or I am not your daughter. It's one or the other."

Esther was having none of it. "Oh how could he do this to me? I thought your father was devoted to me. How could he hurt me so?" Soon the only word that Ellie heard was, 'me, me, me'. She began to get annoyed.

"Mother this isn't about you. Surprising, as it may seem it's about us. Eve and I."

Esther kept looking at Eve and shaking her head in disbelief. "Why did you have to come here and scare me like this? I don't understand. Ellie I'm scared. She's scaring me. Make her go away Eleanor."

"I'm sorry Moth…Mrs Erikson," said Eve I just want to know where I came from and how I ended up at the institute. I bear you no grudge, it's too late for that, I, we, just want to know the truth."

"I am telling the truth. I am, I am. Oh why won't you believe me you wicked girl?"

Ellie noticed that every time the institute was mentioned Esther shuddered.

"What do you know about the institute mother?" Ellie asked trying a different tack to stave off the next wave of Esther's self-pity."

"Nothing. Nothing. I don't know anything about any institute."

"But you did live in Keswick before I was born right?"

"Yes, yes right up until I was seven months pregnant. I remember because my back was hurting so much and my ankles were all swollen."

Ellie, looked at Eve, "Well that puts her in the right place at the right time."

"Oh don't you talk about me as though I'm some sort of criminal, I wasn't in any place I was pregnant." Esther was crying with indignation but her tears were beginning to wane. She went back to her favourite line of conversation.

"I bet it was that Maria, the dirty slut. She was never away from here at the time. She was pregnant too, and her with no husband. I bet it was all your father's doing, the dirty dog."

"Oh Mother for God's sake. Daddy didn't..."

Eve put a hand on Ellie's arm and stopped her from saying anymore.

"Go on Mrs Erikson. Who was Maria?"

"Oh just some woman who took me home when ...when... well something happened and Maria brought me home in a taxi, we became friends. But we fell out when she dropped Eleanor on her head. I didn't see her again after that, but if I could get hold of her now I'd..."

"What happened Mum? What happened? You must tell us."

"I can't, I can't it's too horrible." Esther saw the tables turning to bring her into full focus again. She buried her head in her hands and covered her face. Her shoulders heaved as she sobbed huge sobs. "Oh Ellie, don't make me tell you dear. Don't. I've protected you from it for so long. Oh well it was like this." Ellie and Eve exchanged glances over Esther's head, Ellie rolled her eyes and Eve smiled.

Once Esther began telling her version of events there was no stopping her.

"One evening Ellie, your father left me alone in a night club. Another man had been looking at me. He shouldn't have left me like that Ellie. He shouldn't have left me alone in that awful place. I was so young and so beautiful. I was an innocent Ellie, an innocent." Ellie patted her mother's arm reassuringly and risked a glance at the virtually naked portrait of the innocent Esther on the wall.

"Of course you were Mum, I know that."

"Well dear it was awful. The man you see, he came and sat down beside me. I tried asking him to go away. 'Oh Please,' I said, 'please leave me alone my husband will be back for me soon.' But he wouldn't listen the brute. Anyway Ellie you'll never believe what happened to me." The girls had to wait until the next flood of tears had passed before they found out. "He took me outside and raped me Ellie. I tried to be brave, I tried to fight him off, but he was too strong for me and I couldn't get him away from me. His awful breath was in my face and his weight on top of me almost crushed me. He smelled of beer and nasty male sweat Ellie and he raped me."

Eve busied herself making tea for them all while Ellie mopped up a soggy Esther.

"Oh no dear. No, that's no good at all. We have the lovely china cups, the ones with matching saucers. Tea always tastes better in Doulton I always say."

"I haven't been to Dalton yet," said Eve conversationally. Ellie smiled hoping that despite Eve and her mother, they could arrive at some useful answers. She bluntly brought the conversation back to the night Esther said she was raped.

"Where did he rape you Mum?"

"In Keswick of course, dear."

"Yes but where?"

"Well I don't know, somewhere."

"So you claim you were raped. Did you go to the hospital?"

"I was raped Eleanor, I don't claim anything, I was raped."

"Sorry mother, you *were* raped. Did you go to the hospital?"

"No dear, you see Maria came the next morning and took me home?"

"The next morning? Where were you all night?"

"I don't know. I don't remember."

Esther's tears seemed genuine now. Ellie lowered and softened her voice.

"Mother if you were raped, you must remember where you were and what happened?"

"Well I don't because he drugged me. It must have been something he put in my drink. I don't remember anything after I came back from the toilet."

"But what about his breath and the weight of his body?"

"Well that's how I *imagine* he felt."

"Oh Mother," Said Ellie exasperated.

"And then you see Maria came along and she was nice and kind and said I wasn't a tart, said it always happens to nice girls, girls like me. She took me home and then we became friends. She was pregnant too see? Even had exactly the same due date and everything."

Ellie and Eve looked at each other again. They knew they might be on to something here. If this was right it couldn't just be coincidence could it? If Ellie could just cut through the fantasy and get to the facts maybe they would have a clue to work on.

"So this Maria, she had a little girl too did she?"

"Oh no dear she had a little boy, he was born dead. It was such a shame you see we talked about how nice it would be if we both had girls. She even persuaded me to name you Eleanor dear. I wasn't keen at first but when she said she was going to call her little girl…" Esther's voice tailed off as she suddenly realised the enormity of what she was about to say, her voice became small and half incredulous and half frightened.

" She was going to call her little girl Evelyn."

This was no coincidence it was tangible stuff and both the girls knew it, they were going to have to find this Maria and fast.

Easter continued to talk in a small little-girl voice and the girls had to concentrate to catch up with the conversation again.

"We were friends for a little while and then when she dropped you on your head we fell out. You had a little mark just above your left eye. It's gone now, but oh it did give me a fright at the time." Both girls instantly came to attention.

"What do you mean she dropped me on my head Mother?"

"Well she didn't admit she'd dropped you on your head of course. She said you fell off the sofa and banged yourself on the corner of the unit. Said she took you to hospital too but they had no record of it. We had to take you back when the wound went septic but the hospital said they had nothing written down about you being in before. We decided then, your dad and I, that she wasn't to be trusted. Never seen her since."

"How can we contact this woman Mother? Do you have an address or phone number for her?"

"No silly. I told you she was no use to me after that so we didn't bother with her again. And I can see why now. I can't believe your father did that to me."

They talked for a little while longer but there was nothing more to be gained in the way of information that might be helpful. Soon it was time to go home and Ellie couldn't wait to get back to the place where she'd last been truly happy. The place that held all her fondest memories of Matt.

The homecoming greetings were ecstatic. Jake jumped, frolicked and 'talked' to Ellie for ages before Rob could get a look in to welcome her home. It was a further twenty-minutes of chaos, coffee making and keeping Jake apart from Eve while Ellie generally stamped herself back into her home before they could sit and talk.

Surprisingly the alarm hadn't gone up about Matt's disappearance yet, but they all knew his absence couldn't go unreported for much longer. Rob had been scanning the paper for replies to their advert but nothing had come through so far.

It was while they were talking over coffee that they had the next major breakthrough. They were discussing the woman and her messages to Matt and Rob when Eve had an idea. It was crazy but *what if?*

"Rob did the woman tell you her name?" She asked hardly daring to hope.

"No, No I'm pretty sure she didn't."

"Well think back over the conversation, think back about what Matt told you about her," she persisted not wanting to let the matter drop. Rob furrowed his brow and repeated as much as he could remember of the conversation, he had been wired, scared, in a state of wild panic, it was difficult to remember exactly what had been said. He became animated and waved his hands out in front of him. Not sure of the relevance but pleased that his mind had delivered the goods.

"Maria," He said jubilantly. "She said her name was Maria."

This was fantastic news; finally they felt as though they were getting somewhere.

Ellie had her medical appointments and a call to Victor arranged for the next day. Rob had a plan, he glanced at Ellie awkwardly and was thankful that *she* was the one who suggested she leave the room while he discussed it with Eve. Not even happy with that Rob insisted that he and Eve walk into the garden in case the house was bugged as well. By already discussing Maria between themselves they were all aware that they had opened her to danger. The fact that she had been able to call probably meant that she was in hiding, and presumably as yet the Creator had not found her. They had to get to her before he did for all their sakes. It was decided that the next day Rob would pick Eve up. He didn't trust either his home or office so arranged the use of a friend's house and computer for the day. They were taking a big risk on Eve not being tagged. Rob was loath to bring yet another innocent person into the web of horror that had befallen them all, but they had little choice. He arranged a chauffeur driven car to be available to Ellie for the day. The man would be armed and had been hired from a security firm that Rob sometimes used. While Ellie was as safe as she could ever be, he would be with Eve and they would spend the day going through births, deaths and marriages to find any Maria who might have lost a male child around about the time of Ellie's birth. It wasn't much but at least it was something.

After a bath with Jake sitting beside the door to alert them to any danger, Ellie came back downstairs looking much better. She stood in the kitchen archway watching as Eve and Rob worked in harmony on a huge omelette Eve had seen it done through Ellie's eyes but this was her fist ever attempt at cracking eggs. The results were hilarious and Eve and Rob laughed together unaware of Ellie standing in the doorway watching them.

"You know Eve," said Rob, "I can't stop myself from liking you. The real Eve is warm and friendly and funny just like Ellie but, honey don't take this the wrong way, I don't blame you for any of what's happened, I understand totally why you did what you did, but I can't help rueing the day you came into our lives. I want to say I'm glad I met you but if you had never escaped from that place." Rob's words were cut short as Ellie came into the kitchen she kissed them both on the cheek and Eve blushed furiously and pulled away from the arm that Ellie had draped round her shoulder.

"You still don't see it do you Rob?" Said Ellie, but her words were not unkind, "What happened was always going to happen anyway. I've got the tag, I've been monitored my whole life, he could have reeled me in anytime he liked. And with or without Eve being here, with or without the illness I firmly believe that one day he'd have come for me."

The conversation continued as they cooked and then moved to the table to eat. Eve finished a mouthful of omelette and looked up at the other two with a puzzled expression.

"There's something that I never understood before. When the institute caught fire, I should have been burned in my cell. And yet that day for the first time ever my door opened and I was able to just walk out. It was the middle of the night, it always puzzled me that someone unlocked the door, but until now it hadn't seemed strange that there were no people. No fire alarms, no emergency services, nothing. Just the smell of smoke, the sound of windows exploding far away and an easy escape route."

"What are you saying Eve?" said Rob.

"I'm not sure, but with everything that's happened what if it was the Creator who let me out to further his game. He must have known I'd come here at some point looking for you, and it wouldn't take a genius to work out that I'd have revenge on my mind."

It was a sobering thought and they munched on omelette and mulled over the ramifications of what Eve had just put forward. It made a lot of sense.

At eleven-thirty as Rob was finishing his last coffee before going home, there was a sharp, persistent rapping at the front door. Whoever this caller was, they were in a hurry to be acknowledged. They stared at each other, they weren't sure who their visitor was, but one thing was certain it wasn't the milkman calling for his money. The person or people expecting an answer were rapping harder and faster by the second. Jake's hackles had risen and he was barking furiously in the direction of the door. Whoever it was they didn't have a scent that Jake liked.

After eight seconds none of them had moved. Eight seconds can seem like a long time when someone is banging on the door as though the hounds of hell are on their tail. Ellie made to stand up; she was going into the study to get a door scan of the visitors. Rob put out his hand to stop her.

"I'll go," he said, sounding a lot more assured than he felt.

"Can I help you?" they heard him say, and then there was the sound of a scuffle. A woman appeared in the lounge doorway. She was middle aged, slightly overweight with long greying hair that hung in greasy tendrils across her face. She looked at the girls sitting huddled together on the sofa and nodded to herself. As she moved closer, from five feet away they smelled the alcohol on her breath. She wore black joggers and a sweater that was washed out and shapeless.

"Please forgive the intrusion, Miss Erikson. I am Maria."

She was confident that the mere mention of her name was her right of passage in the house, that once she spoke that one word she would not be thrown out on her ear. She was right.

"How did you find us?" asked Eve.

"Well, Miss Erikson is quite a local celebrity, I've known where she lives for sometime, but was fearful of intruding. When you didn't answer my advert in the paper I thought I might be too late. By then I knew that this was no time for manners and, well, please forgive the intrusion but here I am. I got this letter today you see and knew that I had to come and warn you." She handed over the rumpled piece of paper hastily drawn from her tatty handbag. It was a single line of print made up from letters cut from a newspaper and said simply.

"Found you! I'm coming ready or not."

"I'm so sorry to come here like this," continued Maria but he's on his way and when he catches up with me, he's going to kill me. Whatever happens my life is over, there's nothing left for me and I know I don't deserve it, but given the choice I'd like the dignity of ending my part in this evil in my own way. I have no right to ask anything of you, but please, please don't make me take this to my grave with me, hear what I have to say."

Eve made coffee and after pleasantries were passed they all sat round to hear Maria's story. There was little preamble Maria had come to get things off her chest and knew exactly how she wanted to say it.

"Please, time may be short. He could come any second, he watches us even now. Ellie this is going to be a shock, but I have to warn you. He can see and hear everything you do because you have a tiny transmitter in your head. It's harmless and can't hurt you, you've had it nearly all your life, but it allows him to see your every move."

Ellie said that they'd worked that much out. Maria hardly drew breath before she was talking again. "I have been a wicked, foolish woman. I know I can never atone for what I've done but I must tell you how sorry I am before my life is finished. If you could just let me start at the beginning and I will tell you what I know. My life is over. He will get me now. I'm ready to die one way or the other. But it might not be too late to save you and if I do nothing else before I die, then I'll know I've made some atonement for all the ill that I've done. I'm going to tell you everything I know and maybe you can find a way to use it against him.

I was seventeen when I met him. Young, fresh out of school with a head full of ideas, I wanted more than that poxy town could offer me, I wanted to be somebody. I was an idealistic fool."

"Who is he Maria? Please tell us the Creator's name." Said Eve leaning forward onto the edge of the sofa.

"I do not know his name, even after all these years I know so little about him. I only know him as Genesis that's what he liked to be called. He is a private man, he kills anyone who asks too many questions, you quickly learn to do as you are told and say nothing. I know that sounds ludicrous, but if anyone can believe that, then it's the three of you. But please let me tell it from the beginning, it is better that way, questions will be answered in order as they come along and it will make more sense to you, our time is limited and I've spent long hours thinking about what I would say to you all. Please. If I don't say this now, I probably never will." Her eyes moved from Ellie to Eve to Rob and pleaded with each one of them to let her do this her way.

"Go on Maria, we will listen," said Ellie in a voice that remained as calm as she could manage. They were all dying to pepper Maria with a million and one questions, but she was right, best to let her tell it as it happened from the beginning.

"I got my first job at the institute, I was only a runner, someone who set up equipment and cleaned up after the laboratory assistants. But you see I had this." She pointed to her face. "Oh not as it is now of course in those days I was pretty, very pretty and slim too. I thought I was really something when I was taken out of the labs one day by order of the boss. I met Genesis in his private office, he liked me, had been watching me. I was a foolish girl, this was my chance to shine and I took it. He fired his P.A. that day. He did that often when he got sick of someone, people knew to take the generous severance he offered and not make a fuss. I was given her position. I was hopeless; I couldn't make a decent cup of coffee never mind write shorthand and type. But I had other uses. I was eager to learn, I knew how I'd got the job, but I wanted to learn to do it properly and not just have a title and no work to go with it. True, Genesis and I became lovers, but I worked my way into competency. I was the brunt of office jokes, there was bitchiness and catcalling but who could blame the typing pool who worked hard for their living, when some moppit-up girl had over-ranked them all. I became a hard taskmistress and soon had them all towing the line. Genesis saw my potential and gave me increasingly more responsibility. He had pulled me out of the ranks to kneel between his legs, but I became worthy of my hire.

For some time I was his whore and his legitimate P.A. He primed me for his business and I groomed myself to go as far as I could. I was hungry for the money yes, but my real craving was for the power that I received working for Genesis. One day he took me to the inner sanctum. I served my time there, learned of the barely legal experimentation going on, horrifying work in genetics. Immoral experimentation that no government would ever give its name to even though it was government money that funded the projects. Anyone who left the inner sanctum for whatever reason was never seen again. But occasionally bodies would be discovered floating in the lakes."

They had become so engrossed in Maria's narrative that they hadn't tried to butt in with questions once. She took a drink of her coffee and continued.

"Genesis dressed me, he dined me and showed me off, he gave me responsibility and power. I made pay-offs, I smiled sweetly at politicians over dinner, I even slept with people he wanted sweetening. I learned my trade and I learned it well. After I had served a reasonable amount of time in the IS and proved myself to be a loyal and valuable servant to Genesis, He told me of an idea. It was vile, heinous but his eyes danced with the flames of a million naked fires and I was caught up in his mania. He told me his plans for the ultimate psychological experiment.

Two babies raised from birth, one raised in a normal family, loved and nurtured given everything needed to make the idiom of the so called 'normal' child. The other child raised in isolation, schooled, given only the reading material picked for her and fed on a daily basis the other girl's life.

It was wrong, evil but the social implications of such an experiment were immense. He spoke his plans with such surety and somehow convinced me that the experiment was a valid one for the good of humanity. We, the human race could learn much about social integration from such an experiment. I agreed to go along with his ideas, and then later when I wanted to pull out it was too late. When the maniac dream became a nightmare reality I begged him to let you go Eve, I said I'd take you, bring you up like a normal child and never utter a word of what had happened, but he was immovable. He had his girls, his dollies and nothing was going to stop him. You've got to believe me, I didn't want any of this, I begged him to let us go, Just you and me Eve. I wanted to make it all right. But he was too addicted to the power; he wouldn't free us. I tried my best to make your time in there as easy as possible. It was horrible, horrible.

But I'm moving forward. We made our babies Genesis and I. We had been lovers for five years by this point, but he wouldn't have it that I should conceive in the normal way. It had to be done through invitro-fertilisation. The experiment had to be clinical from the first stage through to the last. The eggs were harvested, now all we needed was a donor. A lad was taken from the labs, hired to pick up a woman in a club, drug her and then bring her to the institute. That woman was your mother Ellie.

The implanting of the eggs was done, one in her, one in me and then after several hours with our feet raised in stirrups. Esther Erikson was dumped still unconscious in the summerhouse by the river just after dawn. The Good Samaritan walking passed when she woke up confused and disorientated was the most natural thing in the world."

"You are my mother?" said Eve in horror. Maria only nodded in reply and tried to continue with her story.

"I…"

"Wait, Wait a minute, STOP." Shouted Ellie. "Are you saying you are *my* natural mother too?"

Again Maria nodded shamefaced. “Technically yes.”

“So that means that *Him,* Genesis, The Creator, is our father?” Ellie already knew the answer and didn’t wait for Maria’s timid affirmative.

“Oh my God, what the hell are we born of?” She was too shocked to care about the implied insult that included both Genesis *and* Maria.

Maria picked imaginary pieces of lint off her bobbly joggers and gave them a second to let the revelation sink in and then she continued as though nothing had happened.

“I befriended Esther. We discovered our pregnancies together, this formed a bond between us. Our babies were born, two little girls just as forecast. I told Esther mine, a little boy, had died at birth, but Eve you are my daughter.”

Eve didn’t respond in any way to the admission, she just sat back in the sofa with her arms locked round her legs rocking slowly backwards and forwards for all the world as though she was in a trance. Only the keen alertness in her eyes gave away the fact that she was listening intently to every word, trying like the others to glean answers from this crazy woman’s confession. Maria continued in a monotone, her eyes locked in the past, her mind tangled in evil.

“I visited you often Ellie, and when you were eight months old I managed to orchestrate an opportunity to have you to myself for a whole weekend. I took you to the institute and Genesis put a tiny implant into your brain, just behind your eye. This was a monitoring device that recorded both sound and vision. My job with you was done and I had no need to see you again. Your mother threw a tantrum when I gave you back to her with a tiny cut on your forehead and I used the argument to sever ties between us.

I’m sorry Ellie please don’t take offence at this but we were later disappointed with the random choice of surrogate. Esther wasn’t the care giver that we hoped she would be, but even so you were brought up well and worked for the good of the experiment.”

Ellie couldn’t believe that this monster with all the maternal instinct of a cement block had the cheek to criticise Esther’s parenting skills. She wanted to defend her mother, but no words would come. Maria continued to talk.

“He became obsessed, and although to the world he was still competent and still ran his institute as before, he was always a blind figurehead. He had total control but only the top of the institute management ever saw his face or knew of his Genesis identity. When the girls were born Genesis became the Creator and his cruelty and torture of Eve became increasingly elaborate and advanced.”

“He used to wake me in the night and not let me sleep,” said Eve in a small voice. “Sometimes he wouldn’t let me sleep for days and nights on end, until finally I dropped unconscious to the floor.”

“Yes Eve that was a human stamina exercise. As you know, if you have ever stayed awake all night, missing one night of sleep is not fatal. A person will generally be irritable during the next day and will either slow down or will be totally wired because of adrenaline. If a person misses two nights of sleep, it gets worse. Concentration is difficult and attention span falls by the wayside. Mistakes increase. After three days, they will start to hallucinate and clear thinking is impossible. With continued wakefulness they can lose grasp of reality. Your record Eve was a hundred and forty-six hours that's six days and nights without any sleep at all." Maria sounded proud of this fact. Most mothers were proud of their child's first steps or first picture. Maria bragged that her daughter was tortured for a hundred and forty-six hours and survived to suffer another twenty years of the same.

"How do you explain the times that he starved me, or left me without water for days on end, and the times when I had no light. I craved my screen, craved images of Ellie's life but all I had was my cell and the darkness that seemed to go on forever. I used to bite and scratch myself out of sheer frustration."

"It was the same thing Eve, stamina. You did fifteen days without food, water or light." Maria was proud of the statistics. Eve sat stony eyed rocking slightly on the sofa and Ellie was sobbing quietly. Rob was shaking, his fists tightly clenched in his lap.

He stood up. Rob had reached the point where he couldn't listen to another word. "You monster, you vile, evil, monster. Get out, get out of here and don't ever come back."

Ellie stood up and grabbed Rob. "No Rob we need to know how to find him, Maria's our only lead to this Genesis/Creator man. We have to keep her with us. He'll kill her if she leaves here now."

"Good I hope he does, now get out."

"I'm so sorry for what I did. I'd do anything I could to turn back time and make different choices, but if it wasn't me he'd have found someone else to run his obsessive experiment with him. At least I managed to set you free when I set fire to the institution when he went away on business and left me in charge."

"So it was you?" Said Eve.

Maria scribbled down a number on a piece of paper. "Here look, here's a number where you can reach me. If I can do anything at all to help you please ring at any time. If there's no answer then you know it's too late for me. I'd do anything to help, but all I can do is say how sorry I am."

"Get out," said Rob.

Ellie was about to speak again, Rob had screamed this last order and Jake stood up barking. Maria was the next to stand and Jake stopped barking but growled low in his throat and moved closer to Ellie.

"It's all right. I'm leaving. I'm sorry Ellie, Eve but there's nothing more to say. I could tell you more about the operations, more about life in that place, but you can get all that from Eve, there's nothing more I can say to help you find him. I know no more than you do." She made for the door and Ellie went to see her out, all the time trying to persuade her to stay.

"If you can't reach me on that number then draw your own conclusions. Goodbye Ellie and take good care." Maria moved forwards to embrace Ellie, but the younger woman stepped back out of reach. She could forgive Maria for being another pawn in the Creator's crazy games, but she didn't want to touch her. Maria left the house and shambled down the path.

They talked late into the night. Eve was withdrawn and quiet. Rob was seething with a white hot anger, and no amount of Ellie trying to persuade him that Maria was just another victim of the Creator would do any good.

That night Ellie dreamed a dream that she hadn't had since she was a small girl.

She was alone in a white room tied to a table and her mummy and daddy were a long way away.

"Don't struggle child it will be over soon." Said a cold woman's voice.

Ellie woke terrified and finally realised where her childhood monsters had come from.

Chapter 35

Ellie was troubled by the whole Maria drama of the night before. That morning they had rung their respective solicitors and asked that the sealed envelopes be held over for a further week without being opened. The fact that they were able to make the telephone call seemed a small victory in a bitter war.

The meeting with Mr Fielding the consultant was not a productive one. Recent events had taken a great toll on Ellie, and though of course Fielding didn't know the cause, he was surprised that her platelets showed such a marked deterioration of her condition. He wrote her prescriptions strengthening some of her medication, changing others and ensuring that the little time she had left to her would be comfortable. Tests were performed and recorded, bullshit about positive attitudes was spouted and the meeting ended on a firm handshake, but the damning result of the consultation was the fact that there was nothing more that medicine could do for Ellie now. The disease was very advanced. Ellie left the office knowing that it wouldn't be long before she saw her Matty again.

Victor Khazana was a big soppy form of concern and sympathy. He fussed and fretted and Ellie had never before seen this side of the hard businessman. He had always been kindness itself but never before had he shown the weaker side of himself. At first Ellie felt a bit awkward but Victor was so determined to find a way to save her that she couldn't help but relax into his presence as she always had.

He asked about Matt's well being and Ellie hated herself for lying to him as she said that he was away for a few days on business. Victor served excellent coffee and they sunk into the large leather sofas in his Lakeland offices.

Victor had never spoken to Ellie about his secretive past. She knew that he had been 'something in medicine' way back in Poland and had then made his millions in computing from nothing. Victor had worked hard to try to make amends to his native country for the harm he caused them. But he still had nightmares about how things had gone horribly wrong for him as a brilliant young scientist with the medical world at his feet.

Ellie went on to tell Victor about her consultation with Fielding, he was dismayed to hear that her platelet count was so low and that the disease had taken such rapid and savage toll on her. By the time she had finished her tale Ellie was sobbing quietly, the last few weeks had been too much for her and she longed to tell Victor chapter and verse about everything that had been happening. He placed a strong arm round her shoulders and gave her his silk handkerchief; Ellie would have preferred a cotton one to cope with the massive spillage she had produced. Victor continued to tell Ellie everything that he had learned about the disease, but there was nothing new, nothing that she hadn't heard and read a hundred times before. She had become quite an authority on the condition herself of recent months.

"If only..." Victor murmured into her hair, but his words tailed off. Picking up on a grain of hope in his tone Ellie lifted her head and sniffed in a most unladylike fashion.

"If only what?" she asked.

"Oh nothing my dear, I'm sorry I was thinking aloud. There is a treatment but it would be no good for you so I don't want to give you false hope."

"What treatment. What is it?" Ellie shrieked. "I'll try anything."

"Shhh Ellie, no I'm sorry I shouldn't even have brought it up, it wouldn't apply to you. In certain cases of paediatric Tay-Sachs where there are siblings with close DNA, some cells from the healthy child can be donated to the sufferer. The healthy cells reproduce and overtake the diseased ones. It's been very successful in other countries, but Ellie you are an only child so you wouldn't be eligible for the treatment. A donor with DNA that close to yours would never be found."

Ellie's heart was pounding like a runaway horse. "What about my mother? Couldn't we ask her to be a donor?" Ellie almost laughed at the thought of asking her mother to donate her precious life cells.

"No Ellie, I'm afraid that would be no good, this procedure only works with sibling DNA."

Well she had no choice it was time to face the situation.

"Well actually Victor I do have an identical twin sister." Ellie smiled shyly and shuffled awkwardly in her seat.

"You have what? Wow Ellie that's fantastic. You can't get any closer match than an identical twin. Wonderful."

Within minutes Victor was a whirlwind of activity and his phone must have been close to melt down under the intensity with which he used it. He rang this person and that arranging a clinic and theatre time and everything else needed to give the eleventh hour long-shot a go.

"But Victor I can't possibly do this now, things are happening, other stuff, It's impossible."

"Ellie you have no choice, if we leave it any longer you'll be too weak to undergo the treatment, the stronger you are at the time of transplant the more likelihood there is of this being a success. I've booked you in for nine o'clock this evening. Time is so important that every second gained is a second closer to beating this thing. We can't even afford to hold off until tomorrow to get you in and the preliminary tests done. You'll have to hurry it's a long drive to London, I've arranged transport for you and ..." His voice tailed off as he forgot Eve's name.

Ellie felt bamboozled, this was all happening far too quickly. She needed time to think this thing through, but Victor had been so good in arranging it all. But he had no idea of the danger he'd be putting himself in if this went ahead. Ellie felt she had no choice but to tell him everything that had happened.

She began slowly, the words cumbersome and difficult to enunciate because she knew that with every word she was pulling Victor more deeply into the web of destruction that the Creator had spun. But once she began the feeling of release was incredible. The words tumbled out so quickly that several times she forgot to breathe and had to stop to catch her breath. Victor sat quietly listening to what she had to say. Very occasionally he'd interrupt with a relevant question but for the most part he just left Ellie to tell it in her own words. When she got to the part about Matt's death Ellie's voice broke and Victor covered her hand with his own to give her comfort and to fortify her with his strength.

"So you see," she ended with a sob, "you are in danger too now. I'm so sorry Victor. He's listening to every word we say right this minute."

"Now don't you worry about me," said Victor patting the back of her hand as a grandfather would placate a troubled child. "I have some of the best security in the world and can soon bring in extra men. Ellie, I so wish you'd come to me with all this sooner. You see Ellie I don't know how much you know of my early life, but I worked for many years in the field of genetics. My work was involved with fertility. Although I no longer practise, I have kept myself up to date on any changes in that field. Trust me Ellie, I know of every big-wig geneticist and ground breaker going. From what you've said this guy knows his onions, and I know anyone who is a mover in this field. Don't you see Ellie I can blow this man out of hiding. The safest place in the world for you and Eve right now is in my friend's private Harley Street Clinic, where I can keep an eye on you both and see you don't get into any more mischief."

Ellie smiled he said it as though they'd been caught parking without a ticket.

"I'm going to find this man Ellie, and it's going to take all the efforts of all my top security men to stop me from killing him with my bare hands when I do. I'm going to get him for you Ellie and I'm going to hand him over to the proper authorities where he'll be put away for the rest of his life. I have some ideas of where to start looking, who to talk to. Believe me honey this guy's not so damned big and clever and I've got his card well and truly marked."

Ellie had always known Victor to be a powerful and influential businessman, but she had no idea he had these kinds of contacts. For the first time in weeks she felt calm and safe. Victor was more than a friend he was a father figure to her. With Victor going into battle alongside them and knowing how to fight the Creator, Ellie felt far more confidant that things might just come right after all.

Everything was sorted and Ellie was terrified at the thought of the procedure ahead of her. What if Eve wouldn't offer her DNA? What if it all went horribly wrong? Victor explained that as Eve was only a donor the danger to her was limited to the standard risk of anybody undergoing anaesthesia. Other than that it was perfectly safe. Victor wasn't so happy about Ellie's state of health, but she assured him that if she could come through the last few days alive and fighting then no little operation was going to get the better of her.

Victor insisted that as soon as the girls were fit enough to be moved, their post-operative care was to be undertaken at Victor's own London home. He said he had rooms that could very easily be turned into a comfortable recovery suite.

"Oh Victor, I couldn't hear of it, it's bad enough us disrupting your time this much without taking over your home as well. We'll be quite happy going into the general hospital to recover."

Darling I rattle round in that old mausoleum like a nit on a drum, I would barely know you're there, but I would be able to keep my eye on you and know that you are safe. I'd like to see this Creator fellow break through my security undetected. He'd be brought down in seconds. And there's a challenge for you old chap." He said looming in close and peering into Ellie's eyes, he finished by sticking out his tongue and waving two fingers in front of Ellie's eyes. They both laughed.

"Ellie," Victor said seriously. "I've rather tossed you along on my enthusiasm haven't I? Before we go any further with this I do need to point out to you that what I'm planning on doing is highly unethical. I am no longer a practitioner. I can do this procedure blindfold with one hand tied behind my back, it's child's play, but you must understand that I am playing God here because you mean so much to me. I've kept my hand in over the years with a few simple procedures and operations in my partner's private clinic, but I need you to understand that I was struck off the medical register a long, long time ago. So I'm afraid going into a local hospital for post-operative care was never going to be an option."

"Victor darling, I'd trust you with my life. I *am* trusting you with my life. Thank you Victor."

To lighten the sombre mood Victor finished by saying that he wouldn't trust her care to the town's hospital anyway.

"Pack of Philistines," he said, "Might as well entrust your care to a troop of trained orang-utans. After the Methicillin Resistant Streppilaccocus Aureus epidemic in the latter half of the first decade, I'd be loath to send a pet worm in there for treatment."

Victor referred to the super bug epidemic that wiped out half of the British population in 2008.

"Oh Victor," said Ellie, "you are funny why don't you just call it M.R.S.A. Much simpler all round don't you think?"

"My dear Eleanor," said Victor puffing himself out to immense proportions and sticking his ample nose high in the air. "Any name that damned big deserves to be enunciated with rounded vowel and in a tone of reverence and magnitude."

Ellie rang Eve and Rob to tell them the fabulous news. In typical Ellie fashion she didn't immediately mention the operation, only that Victor had offered them his help and protection and had vowed to beat the Creator and have him put away for the rest of his life. It was just the boost they needed. Rob and Eve had a fruitless search and came up with absolutely nothing, despite five hours pouring over old records and information. First thing that morning, Rob had tried ringing Maria on the telephone number she left. They got the dull ring of a disconnected line. Rob rang the service provider to find that the number in question had not been operational for some months and had previously been registered to a Mr John Smith. It seemed that Maria hadn't been as trusting of them as she had made out. Either she didn't want to leave a trail, or alternately, she was not all she seemed. Rob and Eve decided to revert to their original plan of finding out everything they could about her, after a full day's work that proved to be absolutely nothing.

Ellie said that she was on her way home and would meet them there in thirty minutes.

Her face was tense when she let herself into the house. She had beaten the others home and put the kettle on, busying herself with making sandwiches and coffee for their return. They were only a few minutes behind her and burst through the door full of excited chatter and questions. Ellie did her best to answer them all, but her voice was flat and listless. The operation was playing heavily on her mind and she dreaded having to ask Eve to help her. What if she said no? Then Ellie's one chance of survival would be shattered.

"Come on Elle," said Rob. "Something's bothering you what is it?"

For the second time that day Ellie didn't know what to say, but once she started talking the words fought over each other to get themselves out and heard. " …So I suppose, what I'm asking is, will you do it?" she finished, looking intently at Eve.

The other girl didn't hesitate in her reply and said that of course she would and everyone was hugging and shouting and fussing over each other. Jake leaped, frolicked, and even allowed Eve to stroke him though he gave her the benefit of the whites of his eyes. But his mistress was pleased by this new turn of events. Jake thought they were all jumping and laughing because he was in the room with them so he jumped and laughed too. *It was fun again and although he didn't completely trust the 'not Ellie' nothing was going to spoil this moment, only ice-cream cones could make it more perfect.*

The girls said their goodbyes to Rob and Jake, there seemed to have been a lot of goodbyes lately. Jake wanted to play and jump some more he didn't want Ellie to go away again. Especially not when she was leaving with 'not Ellie.' He lowered his ears and whined. The only good thing about the goodbye was that he got to go and stay with Gail and Gail loved him almost as much as Ellie did. So Jake was a good sport about it all.

The drive down to London seemed to take forever. Both girls were excited and frightened but Ellie trusted in Victor implicitly and knew that anything that could be done for her would be.

When they got to the Harley Street clinic they were shown straight away to their room and given gowns to change into. The next four hours passed in a blur of blood tests and examinations. If the DNA was a close enough match then they would be going down to theatre early the next morning. Victor personally sat in turn on each of their beds and put them at their ease answering any questions and giving as much information about the procedure as they needed to know.

It was Victor who came back four hours later with the results of the tests. The smile on his face told them before he got the chance to that the girls were a close enough match to enable the operation to take place.

Neither of them slept well that night. Eve's sleep was fitful and tormented by disturbing dreams; Ellie knew that being here was too close to institutionalisation for Eve to lie in comfort. Ellie for her part dozed a couple of times, but lay staring at the blackness for most of the night, knowing that this night might be the last she ever experienced. But it wasn't the first time that week that she had stared death in the eye only to meet the dawn breathing. Morning arrived and they were as ready as they would ever be.

They were wheeled down to the preparation room together and held hands on adjoining gurneys. Eve had never faced anaesthesia before and was terrified, convinced that once that needle went into her arm she would never wake up again. As the anaesthetist prepared their mix of drugs that would knock them into instant slumber he introduced himself as Bernard Roberts, and explained it was his clinic and that he was going to be assisting Mr Khazana with the procedure. Soon after they felt the cold fluid flowing through the canula and only seconds later the world went simultaneously black to them both.

Eve had only been given a very light anaesthestic, that and her healthy metabolism meant that she came round far more quickly than Eleanor. She was back in the pretty twin-bed room that had been allocated them. The first time she came round everything was a bit blurry she drank tea brought by Ellie's friend with the big hands. Her hand shook and she spilled some on the pristine sheet pulled up to her chin. She asked the man not to fuss, but he insisted on bringing a fresh one and faffing around getting it perfect. Such a deep voice, something about it made her shiver, '*sleep,*' she thought, '*must go back to sleep.*' Eve was so tired and just wanted to be allowed to go back to sleep, nothing else mattered at that moment except the need to sleep. Round a mouthful of what must have been feathers and duck-down she asked after Ellie's well being but was asleep before the man whose name she could not remember finished speaking.

The next time she came round might have been five minutes or an hour later, she had no idea, but this time she was instantly alert.

'*Ellie! Must find out if Ellie made it through the operation.*'

She turned her head to the left expecting it to hurt but there was no pain at all, just a peculiar heaviness filing her head with stuffing. Ellie was lying in the other bed, her face white against the white pillow. Eve figured she must be all right to be back in the room. She watched her counting the seconds off in her head.

'*Ellie wasn't breathing.*'

Eve flung the blanket back her heart pounding in terror and her eyes instantly filling with tears. Later when she had time to analyse the situation, Eve would know that it was at that precise second that she knew that she loved Ellie, though Ellie would have said that she knew it much earlier. Without stopping to think about her own condition Eve jumped out of bed and landed in an ungainly heap on the floor, her legs didn't belong to her, and the jelly-legs she had on loan didn't seem to have any bones in them.

Grabbing the bed for support she stood up gingerly, this time having far more respect for the borrowed legs. Once upright she began to shake and her legs which formerly consisted of gelatine and water had now set firm in a mould of lead. She had been fed the footage of the first moon-walk and this seemed to be her 'small step for woman'. She thanked God for the chair placed in between the two beds and sank gratefully into it. The world was spinning now and it took several seconds of deep breathing to make it stop, her whole body was trembling and all she could think about was Ellie lying dead beside her.

She leaned over Ellie's bed and took her hand. It was cold, horribly, unnaturally cold, but Ellie's eyelashes fluttered, giving the only indication that she was still alive. Eve sobbed with relief. Her sister's breathing was so shallow that it didn't raise even the smallest mound in the smooth sheet. Eve pulled Ellie's blanket up from the bottom of her bed to keep her warm.

Eve was cold too and it was another great effort to pull the blanket off her own bed to cover herself with. And that's how Mr Roberts found them when he looked in a few minutes later.

"All right?" he asked with a smile. He assured Eve that Ellie had come through the operation well and early indications showed that everything had been a huge success. Eve thought it was strange that there were no nurses fussing around, she had expected pretty nurses in stiff white uniforms, but this was an illegal operation so maybe they had all been given the day off. Seemed unlikely but Eve reasoned that she knew too little about hospital procedures to know. That's something she could find out about when they were both fully recovered and Ellie had her new long life to look forward to. They could sit watching all the hospital dramas on the plasma together and Ellie would tell her how unrealistic they are.

Ellie didn't wake for some time.

"Hey you," said Eve. "Welcome back sleepy head."

Ellie managed only one word, 'Matty' before she drifted off to sleep again.

Some time later Eve was given another cup of tea, and Roberts hovered over Ellie, feeding a syringe of medication into her canula. Eve had a raging thirst that she hadn't noticed until he came in with the tea, she drank it gratefully.

Ten minutes later she began to feel odd. Her limbs at fist became heavy and then refused to move at all. A tiredness unlike any other came over her and she couldn't resist it. She knew she had been drugged, she heard noises in her head, muted voices but couldn't make out what they were saying. A woman's voice, '*so there were pretty nurses after-all'*. It couldn't be familiar; she didn't know any pretty nurses. And then she was gone.

Chapter 36

The next time Eve woke she heard a man's voice. He was sitting, presumably in a chair, across the other side of the room. His voice was soothing, lulling Eve back to sleep, but although the words were coming at her down a long tunnel, she knew them well, they were disturbing words. Wrong words. Words that had no right being here.

The man was singing:

"Miss Polly had a dolly who was sick, sick, sick.
So she phoned for the doctor to be quick, quick, quick.
The doctor came with his bag and hat,
And knocked at the door with a rat a tat tat.
He looked at the dolly and shook his head,
And said, "Miss Polly put her straight to bed."
He wrote on a pad for a pill, pill, pill.
I'll be back in the morning with my bill, bill, bill."

'*Ellie, must see Ellie*,' thought Eve turning her head to the left but Ellie's bed had gone.

"No, no, no" she murmured trying to fight the lethargy that was trying to send her back into the world of oblivion. If she went there, she felt sure that she'd never come back. She turned her head to the right and there was Ellie's bed, '*See, silly, she's still here, just on the right this time.*' Everything was so very confusing and her mind refused to work.

Ellie was holding something in the crook of her arm nearest to Eve. It took a minute for Eve to work out what it was. Empty eye sockets staring at her.

"No," said Eve again.

Ellie was holding Eve's doll. Polly's empty eye sockets seemed to be mocking Eve. She gave into the sleep that rat-a-tat-tatted at her brain, gratefully, blissfully desperately.

The next time Eve awoke was the last time. She knew she wasn't at the Harley Street clinic anymore, was this Victor's house? She remembered his name now. The window was in a different place but what a window it was. The outside wall was almost *all* window it was a huge stained glass arch depicting the Madonna and child. It must have cost a fortune, these days even cathedrals had double glazing. The late afternoon sunlight was casting prisms of light across the room and Eve was transfixed with the pretty effect. She could hear lots of street sounds and figured that she was still in the city of London. There was heavy traffic and people shouting to each other and clip clopping as they walked down the street outside. She also got the feeling of height she felt she was several floors above street level. The bustle outside for some reason reminded Eve of Christmas. She lay thinking about a Christmas with her sister, she had never had a Christmas before and they were pleasant thoughts. She wondered what gift she would buy Ellie, for some reason a doll came to mind, a pretty porcelain doll.

And then her nightmare came back to her and she screamed fearing that she was once more back at the institute alone.

Victor rushed into the room less than a minute after Eve screamed. He assured her that she'd had a horrible dream earlier and patted the back of her hand like a concerned uncle. She looked over at Ellie, the bed was still on the right, but there was no eyeless doll bringing death into the pretty recovery room. She had even lost the drip that, while aiding her recovery, had made her look even more poorly. Ellie was beginning to stir and Victor went to attend to her. She was doing just fine. He said Ellie was going to make a full recovery and he had a big surprise for them later when she was conscious and sitting up. He stayed for quite a while talking in his deep soothing voice, convincing her that everything was going to be all right and that both her anaesthesia induced nightmare and her waking nightmare was finally over.

"Why did you drug me, when we were brought here from the clinic?" she asked Victor.

"You weren't drugged my dear, what a fanciful thing to say. True you slept deeply throughout the transfer, it must have been the after effects of the anaesthesia."

Before he left the room he helped Eve out of bed at her insistence so that she could sit with Ellie. She wanted to be beside her when she woke up so that she wouldn't be frightened. Victor wouldn't leave until he made sure that both women were warm and comfortable.

Ellie woke as Eve had done, fitfully, coming to several times before the fugue of the anaesthetic evaporated into proper wakefulness. They had snippets of conversation, Ellie woke drunk and giggled when Eve told her that they were dressed in matching nighties and had twin towelling dressing gowns and slippers. "Like two peas in a plonk," said Ellie and giggled herself back to sleep.

Victor had kindly left juice and tea-making facilities in the room and Eve shakily set about making a brew for them both. She had her back to Ellie and didn't realise that she had woken up.

"You're obsessed with making tea," She said in a voice that sounded weak.

If ever a voice could also sound 'thirsty' then Ellie's certainly did.

"Just what the doctor ordered," said Ellie as Eve handed her a cup of not too full tea. She helped her hold the cup for the first few sips so that she wouldn't spill as Eve herself had done. Eve told Ellie that Victor had been in and said that the operation had been a huge success and that she was expected to make a full recovery. Ellie was ecstatic and Eve didn't think she could ever have been so happy for another human being. Eve wanted Ellie to sleep, but they were both far too excited. They talked a bit about the Creator, but since Victor had taken control of everything, he suddenly didn't seem to be such a threat.

"There's just one thing that's been playing on my mind a bit," said Ellie.

"What's that then?" said Eve with a grin.

"When I told Victor I had a twin sister, he never once asked how that had come about. Doesn't that seem strange to you?"

"But you said that you had told him everything."

"Yes I did, but that was much later, when I first told him about you, he didn't bat an eyelid. It was almost as if…" Ellie stumbled on her words. "Almost as if…"

"Almost as if I already knew?" Victor breezed into the room with a huge smile on his face. They looked at what he had brought them.

And in that moment … they knew.

Chapter 37

Victor held the eyeless doll out to the girls.

"So my dollies are both awake and my don't you just look the picture of health. Look who I've brought to see you." He threw the doll towards Eve and she recoiled from it as though it was a cobra spitting venom. It landed on Ellie's bed; she was weak but managed to find the strength to throw the doll from her. It landed on the floor with a thump.

For a few seconds neither of them said anything, the shock was too immense. Victor didn't speak either. He just stood there with his arms spread wide an enormous smile on his face and insanity in his eyes.

Ellie was the first to speak. "Victor it can't be you, it can't be. You are my friend."

"I know," he said chuckling. "It's all worked out beautifully hasn't it, you came to me like a child to a paedophile with sweeties. You really are too trusting you know Eleanor, you made it far too easy for us, we do so like a tougher game. I'm disappointed in you."

"It's been you all along, you whose been trying to kill us all this time?" Ellie knew what was in front of her, but her mind wasn't coming to terms with it.

"Of course it was, you silly Goose, why do you think I set you up and backed you when you became an author? Surely you don't honestly believe that your writing is any good. You've been so gullible right from the beginning. Now Eve, my lovely, lovely Eve, she's my spitfire doll. They say an apple never falls far from the tree don't they? But Ellie my darling you play a tiresomely easy game, always have."

"You're my father?" Ellie almost choked on the words. The fusion of Genesis and Victor finally complete in her head.

"Good God, no." The smile left his face and his voice rose in anger. "I am nobody's father. I didn't merely conceive you; any insipid man could have done that. I *created* you. Don't you see how unique you are? You are my creation. Now please dollies don't anger me, not today of all days. Today is a special day because we are all together for the first time. I went to such a lot of trouble getting the use of the clinic again after all this time. That silly little man thought I'd thrown all that money at him to set up out of the goodness of my heart. Nothing comes free in this life my darlings. I'm quite hurt that he couldn't get us out of there fast enough. Now let's just enjoy our time together shall we? Did Eve tell you Ellie that I have a big surprise for you both?" He laughed; it was high-pitched and out of synch with his baritone vocal chords and his immense frame. It was the laugh of a megalomaniac high on victory.

Eve had moved closer to Ellie's bed they had their arms around each other and stared at Victor with wide frightened eyes.

"Oh come now, come, humour me just a little. You want to know what your surprise is don't you? Of course you do."

His eyes danced with merriment as he stared at his captives.

"Well seeing as you've been such well behaved little dollies I'm going to tell you. "Ellie, by the end of the week," he clapped his hands together in glee. "You will be dead. And do you know whose going to kill you? Oh no, not I my dear, no not I." He pointed his finger accusingly at Eve. "She is."

Eve spoke for the first time. "I'll never do it, never. You're going to kill us anyway, so we will not play your games. You think it will be good sport to make me kill Ellie. Well I'm not going to. So stick that up your arse and smoke it till the sun don't shine," she finished lamely mixing metaphors in her anger.

"Oh such sisterly love, such devotion, but never say never my precious little freak, because you already have killed her."

He threw his head back and laughed his insane laugh. This time he laughed so hard that tears rolled down his cheeks, and he grabbed at his stomach and bent over.

Eve made to move towards him while he was distracted but Ellie put out a hand to stop her.

"No Eve, he's too strong for us. What do you mean, she's already killed me Victor?"

He straightened up and his laughter died as quickly as it had begun. He spat out his next words in a fury and the girls shrank back against the end of the bed in terror. "Don't call me that. Don't you dare call me that. I am the Creator. The Creator do you hear?" With each of the last four words he had taken a step towards them, his face red with temper. They nodded mutely in an effort to pacify him. He was out of breath from his outburst and took a few seconds to re-gain his composure. The next time he spoke his voice was calm and soothing, the voice of a benevolent doctor talking to his patient.

"You see Ellie when I explained this morning's procedure to you, I only told a half truth. It's true that Eve's DNA will kill off all the diseased cells, but what I didn't tell you is that it will also kill all the healthy ones. You are currently dying at the rate of a million cells a minute and your dear; lovely sister is the one who's killed you."

Eve dropped her head into her hands and began to cry. "I'm sorry Ellie, I'm so damned sorry."

"Sshhh," Ellie comforted her. "You didn't do any of this Eve, he did. Listen to me." She pulled Eve's head up to look at her. "When I'm gone, don't you ever regret what you did. I was dying anyway remember, all you did was learn how to love. I love you too Eve, and don't you dare ever feel sorry for that."

Victor clapped his hands, "Very touching girls, I'll remember this poignant moment forever, but you've made one big mistake Ellie, you said 'when you're gone' assuming that Eve will still be around. She won't be dear. Don't worry you aren't the only one about to die, but Eve has a very important job to do first. Let me tell you the best bit."

"This won't work you know," said Eve. "You've left too many loose ends this time. Rob knows where we are. He'll come looking for us."

"Details my dear, small irrelevant details that are going to be dealt with, but I said LET ME TELL YOU THE BEST BIT." Victor lost control again and screamed at the girls. Ellie squeezed hard on Eve's hand in a silent warning not to rile him. They needed time to think and the longer he ranted the more chance they had of finding a way out of this.

"Don't interrupt me again dollies. This is the moment I've been waiting for for such a long time. You see I haven't told you the reason why Eve's cells are going to kill you Ellie. When I said Eve was a close match, I lied. She was a perfect match, as I knew all along that she would be. Perfect, can you see what I'm saying? No? Well let me spell it out for you. You cannot return function cells into the brain of the original host. It's an impossible procedure, one I made up. It can't be done. Now do you see? It's obvious you don't, you really are a pair of dim dollies aren't you?"

He paced up and down letting what he had already said sink in. He had a new role now, that of the college professor imparting knowledge into dullard students. He tapped on his bottom lip as he paced, until he was ready to continue his lecture.

"Think of your mother Eve. Who is your mother?" Eve stared at him too horrified and scared to open her mouth.

"Answer me Eve who is your mother?" Ellie answered for her, trying to placate him and keep his temper at bay.

"Maria?" She said in a small but clear voice.

"Wrong!" He lurched towards the end of Ellie's bed and loomed forward at her, plonking both of his hands either side of her feet. Ellie winced and both girls cowered away from him.

" Daughter, murderer. Murderer, daughter, one and the same thing. YOU ARE EVE'S MOTHER, ELLIE. You are. You were never twins at all."

"But that's lunacy, it doesn't make sense."

"Ah but it does my dear Ellie. You see you were my first ovum but you were just like any other in-vitro embryo. But here's where my genius comes in, from

Ellie begat Eve. Eve is my true *first woman.* She was born of you Ellie, not a twin at all but a clone. Before they had time to fully take in what he had just said he was talking again.

"And Eve my wonderful first ever clone Eve, do you really think you had it so hard? You didn't you know because it was an experiment of five parts. Two of them didn't fare well and died very quickly. But first there was Ellie." He raised one finger, "she was to be brought up with a charmed life, or if not charmed then certainly normal. You my dear were the middle ranker." He raised a second finger, "you were brought up and fed an existence of your alpha clone's life. But then there was Erika." He raised a third finger and waggled it excitedly at the girls. "My poor baby clone Erika. She led a similar life to you Eve; she lived in an identical cell not a hundred yards from yours. But she lived void of all stimulation. If your room hadn't been soundproofed you would have heard her screaming in the night."

Both the girls gasped and felt so much sorrow for the other little girl who suffered at the hands of this monster. "She never walked or talked and enjoyed playing in her own filth. Erika never heard another human voice, nor saw anything other than the white walls of her cell. We couldn't let her loose on the world so when we set the fire she had the blessed release of being burned to death. It was a spectacular execution."

"How could you do that? What kind of man are you?" asked Ellie horrified. They couldn't take in the enormity of what he was telling them about themselves, never mind come to terms with the fact that there was another one just like them.

"I'm a genius my dear. Oh how I wanted to show my beautiful girls to the world, but the world isn't yet ready to deal with a man such as I. It is still backward and retarded. But you see we've grown tired of you now. If you hadn't been sick Ellie the game might well have gone on longer, but you are no fun any more. Our possibilities have run dry and it's time to part company with you both. But first, first you have to know the very best bit of all.

We are going to make a brand new batch of dollies tonight. As you came from Ellie, Eve, so they will come from you. The room is all ready for us to begin. Are you excited my very special dolly?"

"What new dollies? What are you talking about?" asked Eve. "You keep saying we? We? Whose we? By this point nothing seemed unrealistic and if he said that he had come from Mars on a camel it wouldn't have seemed out of place in this conversation.

"Eve, Eve, Eve, don't be even more stupid than you've already shown yourself to be, you are going to be the donor for our brand new clones.

Victor opened his mouth to speak some more but his words were suddenly drowned out by a crackle of static.

"The date is twenty ninth, October twenty forty-six. The time is twenty fifty one."

The voice was distorted by the tannoy and unrecognisable.

"It's good to see you again so soon my frightened little rabbits. Don't look so puzzled, have you forgotten me already?" The voice became babyish and mocking. "Oh I'm so sorry, please forgive me before I die. I love you so much." The cruel laughter that was piped into the room was all the more sinister from the distortion.

It didn't take long for them to realise that the female voice belonged to Maria, but the tone was so different from the last time they'd heard her. This Maria had a voice as hard as a bucket full of iron and as assured as a queen. Eve also recognised this as the female voice that she heard for all those years in the cell. It was a voice devoid of all inflection or accent. But although it was the same voice it was more harsh and severe than she'd ever known it to be before. This was a woman incapable of human emotions.

It was Victor's reaction that was most surprising. The hard man of moments before went from smug bully to a smarmy little boy in the space of a second. His eyes shone bright and his face was one part fear to two parts rapt attention and wheedling subservience.

"Did I do well Mother. Did I? Are you going to beat me Mother Genesis? Oh please say you aren't going to beat me too much." In any other circumstance this bizarre turnabout would have been hilarious but in this time and place it just made the whole scenario more sinister and depraved.

"Mummy is *so* proud of you my little boy. I couldn't ask for a better little boy doll. What a good boy you are. No, you have served me well and I will not beat you too harshly. Now take my middle dolly to the cell and let the re-cloning commence."

Eve eyed the door. At the same moment Ellie squeezed her hand once and then let go of it so that when Eve moved Ellie wouldn't hamper her for even a split second. This was probably the only chance they were going to get and both of them knew there was no time for goodbyes.

Despite his bulk, Victor was surprisingly quick on his feet. Neither of them had expected the sheer speed or brutality of the man. They might have expected him to try and block Eve's way, she was ready to side swerve him to escape. But they never even saw the massive fist cut through the air. He was like lightning and was obviously no stranger to the boxing ring. His fist crashed into Eve's face with a sickening crush of breaking bone. Her head whip-lashed back and a spurt of blood splattered the wall nearest Eve's head. She was already out cold when she hit the floor.

"Tsk tsk silly girl," said Victor calmly. "I'll have to get the decorators in again."

Ellie was sickened by the unnecessary violence of the man she had always called a friend. She turned her face towards the blank wall she didn't care anymore what was going to happen to her. But if she thought she'd seen enough of this world's horror before she died, she couldn't have been more wrong. Victor had one more ace up his sleeve.

He walked over to the wall that Ellie was facing and removed a small square of moulding that she hadn't noticed before. He pressed a couple of buttons. And the wall before her eyes came to life. Ellie, wanted to turn away but couldn't. This, the greatest horror of them all and it was morbidly fascinating. The screen showed a little girl, maybe seven or eight sitting on a bed clutching an eyeless doll into her chest. She was rocking backwards and forwards slightly and murmuring to herself. The words were not clear enough to be heard, but the tone of the child's voice was menacing and threatening. She was herself watching a projection on a similar wall of another little girl enjoying a day at the circus with her parents.

Ellie wasn't even aware that she was crying.

"Now then my dearest Eleanor," Said Victor. "I trust you will not be bored with the in-house entertainment, I may be gone for some while. I know you're weak dear, but I'm sure you'll understand my precaution of locking the door on my way out. Wouldn't want you getting any silly ideas now would we? We'll be in the dungeon should you need us dear. It's a pity you became so dull Ellie, it's been a long and special relationship, I'll be sorry to see you go." His words were sickly sweet and Ellie thought that he actually sounded genuine. She wanted to shoot back at him with something venomous and nasty, but all the fight had been forced out of her. She never moved a muscle as she heard Victor pick Eve up off the floor and carry her out of the room. Ellie knew that she'd never see the woman she'd come to love again and that, on top of the loss of Matt, caused her heart to break again. She heard the locking mechanism click and felt nothing at all. Eleanor Erikson had accepted her death and was ready to shake it by the hand. The only thing she wanted in the world now was that somehow, Eve would find a way to survive this nightmare. They had already agreed that if Eve survived after Ellie's death then Eve would walk into the life that was all set up for her.

Ellie smiled once at the tragic little girl on the screen and a plan began to form in her mind. She closed her eyes to pray for the strength to see it through.

Chapter 38

Rob had been trying to get hold of Victor all morning. They had been scheduled for the operation at eight a.m. and it was now after twelve. He trusted in Victor and the girls' safety in his care implicitly, but something wasn't right. Rob couldn't help but wonder if Victor's security wasn't quite as secure as he thought it to be. God forbid what if the Creator had managed to break through the defences. Rob couldn't concentrate on work. He cancelled meetings for the rest of the day and decided to drive to London to find out for himself what was going on.

It was nearly six o'clock when he got out of the taxi at Victor Khazana's town house. He'd left his car on the outskirts of town; it was far easier to travel the city via the good old London cab.

The house was an impressive five-storey limestone, on a busy Knightsbridge street, its focal point being the enormous stained glass window on the upper floor. Rob knocked for five minutes but got no reply, there were no lights burning anywhere in the front of the house. Only a strange flickering glow came from the stained window. He tried shouting but his voice was lost in the noises of traffic. He needed time to think and somewhere quiet to try telephoning Victor again. Somehow he hadn't thought through what would happen if he got there and there was no one home. The girls should be there by now lying in bed, drinking hot sweet tea and recovering after their ordeal. Maybe something had gone wrong and they were still at the clinic. Whatever was happening, Rob could only think that it wasn't good. There was a small coffee shop across the street. The waitresses were clearing tables and there didn't seem to be many people still partaking of the fayre. It looked as though they were hoping to close. Rob decided to try and get a coffee there while he thought his predicament through.

The girl behind the counter eyed him balefully as he walked through the door. Bang went her extra half-hour to get ready for her date. She sighed in defeat and asked him in a bored monotone what he'd like.

Rob ordered coffee, and sat at the furthest table from the smattering of other customers. He had a view of the house from here and would see if anyone came home while he was in the shop. He thumbed in Victor's number; he'd rung it so many times that day that he had learned it by heart. Even in the café, the noise from the street was a disturbance. Rob had to turn his body away from the window and cover his ear with one hand.

It didn't stop him hearing the screaming of car breaks though, or seconds later the far worse screaming of terrified people.

He turned round in his seat to see people running towards something white lying in a heap on the pavement. A rainbow of small pieces of the shattered stained glass window littered down from the top floor onto the street. The last rays of the setting sun causing prisms of colour to light the muted scene. Rob glanced up and saw the jagged remains of the broken Madonna in the desecrated window frame. Five seconds later a deep crowd had formed obscuring the bundle from view. Rob was motion. His knees caught under the table as he stood sending the whole thing and all its contents flying. The vinegar bottle bounced three times, by the third bounce Rob was out of the café and running down the street with his jacket flying out behind him He pushed through the throng, manners forgotten. He already knew what that thing was lying on the cold pavement of a Knightsbridge street but he had to see it for himself to believe it.

Rob didn't know that one person could leave such a big pool of blood. It was glutinous and flowing in a thick stream off the pavement and into the gutter. Little pieces of the broken glass partially covered her like a pretty blanket. She was lying more on her back than anything else but he could still see the mess that used to be the back of her head. Her eyes were wide and staring. And someone was still screaming, a woman, a large woman over the other side of the street. She couldn't even see the carnage that he could see but she wouldn't stop screaming damn her.

He didn't know which one it was.

"Who are you?" he said aloud. "Dear God which one are you? Don't let it be Ellie. Oh God please don't let it be Ellie."

She was clutching a doll, a doll with no eyes. The same doll that had mocked him at the institute. Sirens were rounding the corner. Ambulance? Police? There would be both. *Lots of police?* What Rob needed more than anything in the world at that moment was a truckload of SAS teams in full riot gear. But the one patrol car was at least a start. Rob had a story to tell and somehow he had to convince the two officers that Victor Khazana was a megalomaniac murderer. And if one of the girls had thrown herself out of a top floor window to her death what must the other be going through? What Rob needed most was manpower. Manpower with fucking big guns.

Chapter 39

Eve came round without that moment of blessed amnesia when you first wake up. Instantly she was aware of a mouthful of blood and a head full of agony. She tried to put her hand to her head but she was shackled hands and feet to a table.

She looked down and saw that her feet were fastened with leather bands into stirrups, but this was no operating table. She was in some sort of dungeon. There were ropes and pulleys attached to the ceiling above the central contraption that she was firmly bound into. The walls were hung with strange apparatus, something that looked like a medieval rack, used for stretching people. Clamps, chains and whips hung all around the room. There were suits of leather and chain clothing. Boots with impossibly high heels stood beside leather pants with a huge black phallus attached to the front. Rubber head gear and strange masks grinned menacingly beside paddles and bizarre sex aids. It didn't even seem out of place to Eve that this was the place where she was to be abused under the false guise of medicine.

Victor had been waiting for her to regain consciousness. He wanted to do the procedure with Eve wide-awake and fully aware of what was happening to her. He began to explain what was going to happen once more in character as the pleasant professor conducting a lecture.

"We are very excited about our new batch of super-dollies Eve. You are very lucky to be chosen to enter this first phase of stage two with us. You should be honoured and humbled to be following in the footsteps of Mummy Genesis. She had done you many great services, she bore you remember. In fact it's so fitting that you're here because she bore you in this very room. Up there." He pointed to eight large meat hooks suspended on chains and springs from the ceiling that would hold a person supported in mid air. Can you imagine the exquisite pain she endured having you? And she never uttered a word nor screamed out in pain once. Her moans were that of sheer ecstasy. She still bears the scars from the hooks and sometimes when I've been very good she lets me open them with razor blades and I lick at her wounds of creation in reverence." Eve turned her face away in disgust.

"You could never tolerate the kind of pain that the great woman did, so we will use more conventional means for you. Mere bonds to hold you fast, unless, of course, you are a naughty girl and then we will see if you have any of the stamina of your surrogate mother." The threat was enough to still Eve's struggling against her binds.

"We have already harvested the DNA. In fact we have enough of your DNA to make a thousand babies, but today Eve you are going to have the supreme honour of being impregnated with five babies that are both mother and fatherless. These babies are purely you. We took cells you see, we watched them day and night and at the exact moment when the stem cells were about to turn into function cells we separated them. So that for every one stem cell we had two. And then both of the cells would continue to multiply until they metamorphosed into function cells, they would then replicate and divide in the normal way. This process of fusion is greatly simplified of course so that you can understand it. But you see the momentous piece of history you are making here Eve? For the second time you are being cloned. Five new people who are not merely *like* you, but are in fact simply *you*. By the way dear, feel free to scream all you like this room is completely soundproof so we are nice and private though we are of course making a film for prosperity. It shouldn't hurt too much."

He brought a trolley of instruments up to the table and began putting gloves and gown on. The mad scientist in his mad chamber of horrors, Mary Shelly would have been impressed. Eve prayed in earnest that she would die soon.

"The door flew open and Maria walked in. "Mistress, Mistress." Said Victor in delight. "It's Mother Genesis. Eve give praise for Mother Genesis dear."

This was Maria all right, but she looked far different from the last time Eve had seen her. Her greying hair had been dyed raven black, her eyes glinted cold and hard, there was no weakness no mercy in them just an ice-mania that Eve instinctively knew would brook no pleading. Maria wore heels and a beautifully cut grey business suit. She had worn false padding for her role as scared and downtrodden Maria because now she was forty pounds or more lighter. She wore nothing at all under the man's suit that had been tailored to her own measurement and hung perfectly. Her nipples were clearly visible under the lapels and her waist was trim, her legs long and her attitude powerful. This was a far cry from the downtrodden woman driven to drink of the night before.

Finally, after twenty-seven years, Eve came face to face with the real 'Creator' the force behind the nightmare, the true face of evil that had brought the madness about. Victor Khazana was the knowledge and the money, but Maria Kiltcher was the real force and the mania. It was her dream, they were her dollies and it was her madness that Eve was a part of.

"Let the cloning begin." Said Maria, from a mouth made up with perfectly applied crimson lipstick. "Begin phase two."

The Police and ambulance arrived at the scene simultaneously. He pushed through more people to get to the marked police car and in his distress he ran into the road before the car had even come to a stop. He planted his hands on the bonnet and ran backwards as the car finished its parking. He was shouting at the two officers inside to hurry up. Rob knew he was behaving like a madman, they might not believe him, but could they take the risk that he was just a delusional madman? What if there *was* another girl up there at this moment fighting for her life in the home of a crazed psychopath? Were they prepared to do nothing and be later held accountable? He had to make them understand.

"Thank God you're here," he yelled before they were even out of the car or had seen the body. "We have got to get in there. Please hurry for God's sake hurry, there's another one, another girl, her twin. Please just get in the house and stop him before he kills her too. It's the Creator. He's insane. It's all a crazy game to him." Rob was sobbing. And the policeman nearest to him put his hand on Rob's shoulder in an attempt to calm him. The other went to join the paramedics with the dead woman.

"Take it easy sir, you aren't making any sense. Let's just start at the beginning and see what's going on eh? Now do you know the lady who has fallen?" The policeman had led Rob through the crowd so that he could get a good look at the body. *'Lovers tiff,'* he thought, *'bloody messy suicide.'*

"She hasn't fallen officer, she's been murdered. Victor Khazana has murdered her." Khazana was a household name; this could be the biggest thing the young officer had ever had to deal with.

"That's a very serious accusation sir. Before we bandy things like that about I think we'd better get some facts." Rob interrupted him mid lecture.

"There's no time for facts. If we don't get up there and stop him right now, Khazana is going to kill her twin sister. It may already be too late. It's the doll you see, the doll, as soon as I saw it I knew it was him. Please officer, please do something and for the love of God, do it quickly."

Officer Gaskell hadn't a clue what this nutter was on about. He'd heard about people accusing celebrities of all kinds of things and the next thing you knew the celebrity went out and got a bullet in his head. Look at John Lennon wasn't that just what happened to him? Gaskell didn't like it at all.

"Please sir will you come and sit in the car for a few minutes and I'll radio my superior to come and talk to you."

"No I will not sit in the bloody car, aren't you listening to me? There's another girl, identical to this one up in that room and if that crazy bastard hasn't already killed her, then he's just about to. Are you prepared to take the responsibility of another girls death officer?" Gaskell felt out of his depth and needed back up to deal with this. *'What if there was another girl up there about to drop from the window like a dying swan? What then?'*

"Listen sir let me put it another way. I'm not asking you, I'm telling you to just sit in the car while I get some back-up here and then we can do something. If you don't comply to my request quietly I'm going to have to arrest you and you'll be taken straight to the station. So the best way of helping this other, er, your friend is to do as you're told." Rob had little choice but to get in the back of the car. At least the little twerp was going to get some more police down here.

Gaskell walked round to the back of his car and thumbed the phonacom. "Ma'am I think you'd better get down here. We've got one woman dead and some nutcase saying there's another one in the house about to be murdered. Get this though Ma'am; he says Victor Khazana is the murderer. Looks like suicide to me Ma'am but I don't like the look of this fella, requesting back-up."

The ambulance was taking the dead twin away. Rob ran from the police car to be with her. He kissed the back of her hand in his heart of hearts he knew it was Ellie. His goodbye was brief. He knew that Ellie would want him to do everything he could to save Eve, and with every ounce of his will power he was wishing desperately that he was wrong in his guess and it was Eve lying broken in the back of the ambulance and not Ellie.

Five minutes later another six officers arrived at the scene. A woman in street clothes went to talk to the two PC's and then came over to Rob. Seven precious minutes had passed while Rob sat useless and impotent in the back of the car. The other officers stood round the van doing absolutely nothing.

"Hello Sir, I'm Chief Inspector Woodburn, my officer tells me you think there's a hostage situation in the house. Now if you could just tell me your name please?" Rob couldn't believe she was wasting time taking his personal details.

"Listen love, I don't think anything. I *know* he's holding her hostage. She's probably already dead, please, please just get in there and stop the bastard or let me in and I'll do it for you."

"Try to keep calm sir, I know this is very distressing for you, but there's a certain way of doing these things. I understand that it must seem very long-winded to you but you have to understand that I can't send my men in there until we have a clear picture of what's going on. Now then you say there are two women? Twins I think you said."

Rob took a deep breath, he realised that he was only going to hold things up further by getting annoyed and shouting. For the second time, though this time more calmly and slowly he told his story. He explained that the novelist was either already dead and on her way to the morgue, or in grave danger at the hands of the entrepreneur Mr Victor Khazana. Nine minutes. Briefly he explained about Eve and the institute and Matt's death. Tears were coursing down his face, more through sheer frustration that nothing was being done than grief over the dead woman.

"And you never reported this murder?"

"No."

And so it went on fifteen minutes since Rob had been forced into the back of the police car. Finally C.I. Woodburn had enough information to take some action. She left Rob in the car and began assembling her officers. Rob had sat there doing nothing long enough and went over to the van.

When the police had been briefed and given their orders Chief Inspector Woodburn tried to stop Rob going in. Rob argued that they'd need him. He knew everything that was happening. DCI Woodburn knew that if this bloke was speaking even ten percent of the truth then they were walking into the biggest case of her career. She didn't want to go in completely blind. She agreed that he go with them, but ordered him to stay in the background. They stormed what appeared to be a completely empty building. One officer was sent to guard each entrance in case anyone made a run for it. Two more were dispatched to search the house from the ground floor up and DCI Woodburn, Rob and another officer made straight for the top floor bedroom.

Following their training to the letter, the search officers scoured every room of the house systematically. Every officer had his or her handgun drawn and all wore bullet-proof clothing and face shields. DCI Woodburn had donned trousers and a Teflon vest and shield, she threw a vest to Rob as they pounded up the stairs ordering him to put it on. The two original officers were left outside to clear the street and get the traffic flowing again. Rob was impatient, he wanted to get to the room where the woman had fallen from. Although they moved up each flight quickly, their approach was cautious and Rob was getting fed up of their damned training procedures. He nearly got himself thrown out of the house, and was barked at firmly to stay back and do as he was told or he was OUT.

Finally they got to the top floor room and the officer behind Woodburn kicked the door open. The room was empty. Two unmade beds stood side by side. The right hand bed had a drip frame standing near it in the corner of the room. By the side of the bed written on the wall in blood was the single word 'dungeon'. But it was the remains of the window that drew Rob's gaze. The jagged shards of glass cast dappled shadows onto the wall, leading his eye to an even greater horror.

A projector was playing onto the same wall. A little girl rocked on a bed and watched an identical girl playing from another recording.

It seemed that the unlikely rambles of this man were true. DCI Woodburn ordered more scene-of-crime teams to be on stand-by outside the house to collate the evidence for conviction. Rob couldn't tear his eyes from the pitiful scene being played out on the wall in front of him.

"Jesus Christ," said Woodburn watching the disturbed little girl staring at the screen and talking to the hideous doll with no eyes.

"She gouged the eyes out herself so that Polly, that's the doll, wouldn't have to watch Ellie's life too," said Rob. There was so much he needed to tell this woman to make her understand and yet he was talking about a doll. "Oh dear God where is she? Where's Ellie?"

"So you think it's Miss Eve Erikson who came through the window? You couldn't be sure which one it was before."

"Still not sure," said Rob, "Just hoping that's all, just hoping. Isn't that unforgivable Inspector wanting one woman's life to be saved even at the slaying of another's?" Rob shook his head sadly and wanted to move somewhere, do something, find Khazana, but he just stood looking at the young Eve, his heart breaking for her.

Woodburn's phonacom crackled into life. "Woodburn," she barked into it exchanging a look with Rob.

"Think you'd better come and see this Ma'am," said the officer. "Now," he shouted more urgently.

"Oh God no, this is it, she's dead isn't she?" said Rob. Woodburn didn't answer him she was already out of the door and running along the corridor to the stairs.

"What we got Josh?" she asked the officer who met them at the bottom of the stairs.

"I couldn't begin to tell you Ma'am," he said. "This you've got to see for yourself." He led them into a small room next door to the lounge.

"This is identical to the operations room at the institute." Said Rob quickly scanning all the equipment in the room; he was going to tell them more but the words never left his lips as he saw the unbelievable nightmare being recorded from another place.

A camera was relaying all the action in the dungeon room and playing it live through the plasma screen. Victor and Maria stood beside the leather contraption that Eve was strapped to. The officers piled into the control room and gathered round the screen.

"She's alive," sobbed Rob bursting into tears again. "Oh thank you God she's alive and I swear at this moment I don't care which of them it is. I'm just so glad that she's not dead too." He sank weakly into one the chairs. "Please stop him before he kills her. You've got to get in there." This time he spoke to the officers crowded into the small room. He put his head in his hands crying bitterly.

While Rob was talking the policemen behind Woodburn managed to see what was on the screen.

"Fucking hell, look at the size of the dick in those rubber pants. This is fucking mental."

Woodburn glared at the officer she indicated Rob with her head warning the officer to conduct himself properly while a member of the public was present.

“Carney watch your filthy mouth or you’ll find yourself on report.” She barked at him.

He hung his head and blushed, “Sorry Ma’am, just got carried away, sorry sir.” Rob didn’t even look up.

While the police summed up the situation in the dungeon, Rob pulled himself together.

“Who’s the other woman?” asked one of the police.

Rob noticed her for the first time. “My God he’s got Maria too. She looks different, but that’s her all right. That’s the woman I was telling you about who worked with him and helped him with the experiment. He’s been threatening to kill her, she’s been on the run. He’s got her too.”

The surviving twin’s voice cut clearly into the room pleading for her life. “Please just let us go, you’ve done all you can do to us. This crazy scheme is madness; you’ll never get away with it. Can’t you see that? Just let us go.”

Woodburn saw a microphone on the workstation. She flung her head round to the officers. “How the hell do you work this thing, get it working for me and get on the com for the negotiator.” One officer turned the mic on and explained how to use it, while the other called to ask for the hostage negotiator to be sent. Woodburn was about to speak into the microphone when Rob grabbed it off her.

“Please, let me, I know this guy, I know what makes him tick.”

Woodburn still had her hand on the mike and they tussled with it. “Listen, I didn’t even want you in here. I’m in charge of this investigation. I warned you at the beginning to stay back. We’re trained to deal with this kind of situation so please just let us get on with our job eh sir?”

Rob put his other hand over the top of the mike to stop her taking it from him. “This might be your case Inspector, but I know this man, I can rattle him, he’ll talk to me, he’ll want to gloat. Think about it, if he doesn’t know you’re here I can buy you some time. While I keep him talking and keep his filthy hands off her you can find a way in there to stop the murdering bastard.” Woodburn hesitated, her mind furiously trying to decide the best way forward.

“Okay, but listen don’t rile him, one wrong word and we could be dealing with two dead bodies not one. Our negotiator is a highly trained psychologist and he’ll be here any minute just keep him talking until then. And if I say cut, you stop immediately. Understand? Remember she’s relying on you.”

“Do you think I don’t know that?”

Woodburn was just about to relinquish the mike to Rob when the officer called Carney interrupted. “Ma’am, if they get panicked they might escape before we can get to them.”

Woodburn’s brow furrowed in thought.

“Good point,” she said, smiling her approval at the junior officer. “Right you and Todd, go and round up Watson and Jones and find the door to that place, we'll be standing by here. Do not, repeat do not try to enter until I give the word. Understood?"

"Ma'am," said the two men in unison.

While Woodburn and Rob listened in to what was unfolding in the dungeon without being able to do anything about it, Carney and Dave Todd went in search of the dungeon entrance. They found the other two men and they separated to search the house again in finer detail. More back up and the negotiator arrived. Paul Shannon was given directions to the control room and the rest of the squad joined in the search. They scoured the cellar wall by wall bit by bit, and disappointingly it turned out to be just a cellar made up of the predictable couple of storage rooms and a very impressive wine cellar. They decided to go back to the lounge and search drawers and cupboards for any clues

More than five minutes had passed and they were no nearer to finding the entrance to the dungeon. They came to the conclusion that maybe it wasn't part of this house at all and the recording was being delivered from somewhere else. They had to find an address for that dungeon and fast. They began ransacking the lounge. There was nothing to be found. Mike Watson leaned on the wall to catch his breath and right in front of his colleague's eyes, he disappeared.

"Mike? Where are you? What the Hell?" They ran to the wall where Watson vanished and felt for the place where they could just walk through the wall. Just like the images of the little girl projected on the wall upstairs, this was a clever projection. There was an area about as wide as a door that was a projection in thin air of a continuation of the wall. It was high tech stuff. They were in a short corridor with a metal door at the end. If ever the projector malfunctioned all any visitors would see was the corridor. It was the perfect camouflage for the dungeon entrance.

"This is a fucking fun house," said one of the new policemen.

"Man you don't know the half of it," replied Carney who hadn't had the chance to prepare them properly for what lay behind the metal door.

They called it in to Woodburn.

"Be careful," she warned Rob as he took hold of the microphone. He took three deep breaths to compose himself. Thankfully all that had happened in the almost ten minutes the men were searching was Victor preparing instruments on a trolley and rearranging the height and position of the twin on the table thing. Maria had stood silently assisting; it was as though Victor was psyching himself up to do something important. The girl had continued pleading for her life for about a minute before she fell silent and limp on the table. Rob didn't like it one little bit. The air in the dungeon was similar to that in a church just before a funeral. He took hold of the microphone and kept his voice as level as possible.

"The date is twenty ninth October twenty-forty six. The time is nineteen-ten. The game's up Khazana and you're busted. There's no escape now man, so do the sensible thing and let the women go."

When the unexpected voice broke into the reverent pre-ceremony in the dungeon, Victor was so shocked that he dropped a tray of surgical implements on the floor. The stainless steel scalpels and speculum clattered onto the floor and the echoes reverberated round the room for ten seconds. Victor stared up at the camera mounted on the far wall, his face contorted into an expression of surprise and shock.

The woman tied to the bed began to scream. And after a moment of registered surprise Maria flung back her head and began to laugh.

"The game's up?" questioned Victor recovering his composure, "my dear sir, you are very much mistaken. Phase two of the game has only just begun. Do you think any punitive efforts to stop me could effect us in any way? You think we're going to stop now just because the almighty literary agent says so? Sit down take a ringside seat and watch history being made for a second time. But of course you still don't know do you? These women, these marvellous, wonderful women are not merely twins. They are history. Little Eve here is the first human being to ever be successfully cloned. And right here, this very night, it's going to be done for the second time. We are about to make a new batch of clones using our Evelyn donor. I'm sorry you won't be able to watch her die because we are using her as both host and succubus and will have to keep her for the full gestation period. But never mind she can watch your death instead." He was about to go on but Maria held up her hand and speaking for the first time, she rocked Rob's perception again.

"Shut up little man and know your place. This is not your moment. It's mine, mine you understand. How dare you flaunt my law because you have an audience, you know the rules you speak only when you are spoken to. Do I make myself clear?" Although she was well out of Victor's range she raised her hand again as though to beat him. Victor hung his head and was instantly silent.

"So," said Maria turning to face the camera. "You have found us." She raised her hands and gave Rob a round of applause. "Very clever Mr Price, in fact cleverer than we thought. But no matter, all you've done is saved us the trouble of coming to get you. It does spoil the surprise for you though. You see we have several pieces of DNA evidence that ties you neatly to the murder of Mr Matthew High, a blood soaked shirt for instance. But that's not all my new plaything, because we have things that will look so pretty at the back of your closet or under the stairs, things belonging to Miss Ellie and Miss Eve. Things that are going to tell the police force, oh so clearly, that you have also killed both of them and then wracked with guilt and mania killed yourself too. It's all going to be quite a scandal. We will be keeping hold of Eve for the next nine months or so, she has a very important job to do for us, so her body won't be discovered for quite some time. But then there's your mousy little wife. Gail isn't it? Well of course if you do give us any trouble we have a back up plan all ready to set into motion. We can set *her* up for the multiple murders instead. Consumed with jealousy over your affair with the Miss Eriksons isn't she? Revenge of the woman scorned; worm turning and all that. An old story but a good one don't you think? And so easy to set into motion."

"You'll never get away with it," said Rob. "You've been just a bit too clever for your own good this time." Rob still couldn't believe that the previously scared shitless, drink sodden, Maria was in this mess up to her neck along with Victor Khazana. '*What the hell is their story?*' thought Rob, '*this is all getting crazier by the second.*'

"And why wouldn't we get away with it Mr Price? We have up to now haven't we? Almost thirty years and we haven't been caught yet so why should things change just because the Great Robert Price has walked into our little home? Oh wait, let me guess. You aren't silly enough to think that you've come to rescue them are you?"

Shannon the negotiator had arrived in the room and was being briefed by Woodburn while Maria ranted on tape. They had all the evidence they needed; now it was time for action. They had to get the three people out of the dungeon, preferably alive and unharmed.

Rob was reluctant to hand over the microphone to Shannon.

"You hang in there," Ellie he said. "We're going to get you out."

Shannon thumbed the mike. "This is the police, we have the building surrounded, there *is* no escape. We would like you to move away from the table and walk calmly out of the room with your hands raised where we can see them."

Victor and Maria hadn't been expecting any other company and for the second time in the last few minutes they stood still, shock painted on their faces as perfectly as Maria's lipstick. Eve was the first to speak.

"Help me, Dear God please help me."

Neither Victor nor Maria was armed. Victor held a surgical scalpel out in front of him but it was a half hearted gesture, like all bullies he was cut down to size when out numbered.

At first Maria screamed and spat and shouted obscenities at Shannon. Then she tried to reason with him, flirted with him coyly, told him he could be in on the 'biggest breakthrough in medical history'. She implied that what they'd done to Ellie couldn't be construed as murder because she was dying anyway. She sneered when she bragged that Ellie would be dead within the week. Hadn't they done the poor cripple a favour? Hadn't they spared her weeks or even months of undue suffering? This way Maria assured them she would drift into a painless and peaceful sleep when the time came. She had the gall to call it euthanasia.

“Oh I can assure you that Miss Erikson’s death was neither peaceful nor painless. She threw herself out of the top story window almost an hour ago to blow your cover and to try and save her…” he didn’t quite know what the correct colloquial for a pair of clones was, “sister,” he finished lamely. “Quite a heroic way to scupper your plans wouldn’t you say?”

Eve felt her heart twist in pain. Maybe they were bluffing; perhaps it was just a ruse, some plan they had for rescuing her. Since Rob had mistaken her for Ellie, Eve’s mind had been working furiously. She could use this to her advantage.

Her first attempt at laughter caught in her throat and sounded more like a cough. She wanted to break down and sob for Ellie, but her instinct for self-preservation had to come first for now. Her second attempt was more successful. Victor was shaking visibly and even Maria’s calm composure was ruffled by the advent of the police force en-mass.

“What are you laughing at?” she spat at Eve. “Nothing changes, nothing do you hear me. They are out there, but we have you. I’d call that a pretty tight stalemate wouldn’t you. Before they could get that door open we’d have split your pretty little throat wide open.”

“Give me the knife and I’ll do it myself right here right now,” said Eve slowly in a strong voice and with a serene smile on her face. “You see you talk about how clever you are and pat yourself so heartily on the back and you haven’t even the brains to know when you’ve been outwitted.” Eve had to be careful, to make them believe her she had to under play her hand.

“What are you talking about? Tell me, tell me?” Maria was outraged. This little slut wasn’t going to make a fool of her in front of others. Why was she not cowering away? What the hell was she smiling at? Maria brought her hand up and slapped Eve hard across her face with the back of it. Eve’s lip split, she was already sore from her earlier beating from Victor and she thought that she was about to pass out. The blow had knocked her head backwards into the leather of the table. Ignoring the threatening blackness she lifted it again still smiling.

In the control room Rob mouthed obscenities and turned his face away he couldn’t bear to see her being hurt.

“ Come on,” said Victor who had been silent up until now. “We’ve got to use the girl as a shield to get out of here.”

“You go if you like,” answered Maria, “You always have been gutless. Go on go, but she stays here with me. I’m not giving up now.”

“Well,” said Eve, “I agree with you, you know. It’s about time we got to know each other. Let’s see what you’re really made of shall we. Get rid of *him* and let’s play for real, one to one. Just you and me. My sister has had you all to herself up till now, but I think I can outwit you because I’m the one with the brains. In fact I’ve already won, if you did but know it. Come on let the procedure commence, as you are so fond of saying.”

The negotiator was repeating that they should leave the room with their hands raised above their heads, Victor was watching the altercation between the two women and Maria and Eve had locked eyes and neither one was prepared to give way in the battle of wills. Shannon was ignored and his constant monotone was but background noise to the melodrama unfolding in the room.

"If you've got something to say then I suggest you say it." Said Maria. She blinked once but didn't look away. Eve's eyes were stinging from the beating earlier she couldn't hold out much longer and knew that valuable ground would be lost if she looked away first. This was psychological warfare and she had to convince Maria that she was still strong of spirit.

"Oh no Maria, spoil your moment of glory? I couldn't do that, no please carry on. I'm coming round to your way of thinking give me your freaky babies. I want lots of them. Lots and lots and lots of crazy dolls for us all to play happily with together. You can be mother and I'll be the big sister."

"You're crazy," said Maria.

"That's rich coming from you." Eve was feeling stronger by the second; she had Maria jumpy, doubting herself. It would be easier to convince her now. She pretended to tire and wilted into the table breathing heavily. She'd sat with Ellie long enough, as long as she didn't over do it she could pull it off. She let her left ankle spasm just a little bit, and gritted her teeth as though trying valiantly to stop it. "Come on woman, what are you waiting for. Make me pregnant with my clones."

Maria looked more closely at her. '*Atta girl,*' thought Eve, '*you just keep doubting.*'

"Who are you?" Asked Maria.

"You know who I am. I'm Evelyn Erikson, the clone, the freak, the none entity."

"Liar," spat Maria. "You're Eleanor aren't you?" without waiting for an answer she turned on Victor. "You fucking useless idiot, you brought the wrong girl. How could you let them switch on you? Idiot. You're nothing without me you fool. God you couldn't even kill the boyfriend I had to come out in the middle of the night to do that because you were too damned gutless. Victor Khazana the great I am. That's a laugh. Victor Khazana the lily livered idiot is nearer the truth."

"Oh God," moaned Victor, "it's all gone wrong, it's all gone horribly wrong. Everything is crumbling round our heads, police swarming all over the house, the experiment blown sky high. We're finished."

Maria seemed to calm after her outburst at Victor. She had been glaring malevolently at Eve for long seconds.

"Yes we're finished but Victor we can still go down in history, let's go out with a bang eh? I can't be locked away, I can't be locked up Victor, you know

I can't, you know that it's what it's all been about for me. Let's kill her now right in front of their eyes. There's nothing they can do to stop us Victor, by the time they get through that door shooting and screaming she will be dead. Let's do it, let's go out in style. You and me Victor just like it's always been. When they come in firing, if they take us out it'll be a bonus. They can't get us if we've already decided to die. Let's do it. Let's do it now. No more talking no more thinking. We kill her and then in a last act of ultimate power we kill each other. Do it Victor, slit her now. You've got the knife in your hands, show me you've got the balls to be worthy of me at last."

Everything had gone mad in the control room. Rob was screaming at Woodburn to get in there and stop it before he killed Eve.

Victor's hand rose slowly, he looked confused. Scared as hell. His hand was shaking as he put the scalpel to Eve's throat.

"Do it Victor," screamed Maria.

"No," yelled Rob from the control room.

"Wait," said Shannon over and over again. "Let's just talk this through before you do anything rash, let's cut a deal here. Few years in a cosy psychiatric facility and you can be out again. Feeling better with new lives to lead, new identities. This doesn't have to be the way. It doesn't have to end like this."

Woodburn was twitchy, she wanted to send the men in but knew that it would sign Eve's death warrant if she did. Woodburn hated hesitation but all she could do was hover and hesitate. Her hand was half raised ready to flag them in. Every second was crucial now. But all she could do was hesitate.

"Do it you useless piece of shit. I command you to do it. Haven't I always given the orders? Haven't I always beaten you if you don't do exactly as I say? That's the way you like it don't you Victor, me in charge, me telling you what to do? Listen to my voice Victor. Not them, cut them out my clever boy doll. Listen only to me, you know it's the only way. They can't lock me up. You can't let them lock me up Victor. I can't go back into that cupboard under the stairs with the rats. Victor focus on my voice. That's it, that's it Victor. Yes good boy, good boy Victor I'm very proud of you. Now cut her. Cut her." Maria was screeching with her blood lust.

Victor had the scalpel pressed into Eve's throat. A small cut had opened beneath the pressure of the blade, he had madness in his eyes and he was about to slice her throat wide open. He wanted Mother Genesis to be proud of him. He wanted her to beat him because she was happy with him. But he didn't want to die. He was Victor Khazana. He wasn't ready to die.

"Don't do it Victor," said Shannon soothingly. "We can sort this, you and I together can find a way through this. Just put the knife down and walk out of the room. I give you my word that you will not be harmed. My men are ready to just walk you away."

Victor Khazana was not ready to die.

From that second everything happened very quickly. Victor went wild. He ran round the table and plunged into Maria using his bulk to force her hard into the wall behind her. He had the scalpel up to her face. He dug it into her flesh and her cheek peeled away from the bone like an orange.

"Yes Victor. Do it. Do it, let's die. You and me together Victor. Let's die together now."

She glanced up and with one slick movement pulled down hard on one of the huge meat hooks.

Both the perpetrators were far enough away from the woman tied to the table.

"Go, go, go," shouted Woodburn bringing her arm down hard to emphasise her order.

The door to the dungeon was kicked open and six uniformed police officers in protective gear stormed the room.

Maria thrust hard on the meat hook and drove it fiercely into Victor's stomach. She felt it cut through fat and muscle and then she pulled upwards with all her strength. He was eviscerated. His intestines fell out of the hole in his stomach and he stared down in horror at his insides coming outside. He looked up into Maria's eyes.

There was gunfire and Victor's dying body jerked as round after round of ammunition peppered him.

"I am the Creator." He said just before he died.

Maria was fighting with the weight of his body; he swung like a stuck pig on the hook knocking into her. Covering her with his blood and stomach contents. The smell of his intestinal gas and waste products filled the room and one policeman bent to vomit into the corner.

And then Maria was free of his protective bulk. She was running towards the gunmen shouting, "Kill, me. Kill me."

Her eyes locked with Carney's, her mouth was still open begging him to shoot her down. He almost forgot his training, she was bearing down on him, another second and she'd be at too close range to fire a shot into her. Oh my God her hands were coming up. She was going to touch him. He aimed his gun at her midriff and at the very last moment dropped it. The kickback flung his shoulder and he shot Maria's knee out of its socket. Another bullet hit her at the same time it just missed the small of her back and caught her square in the right buttock. She fell to her knees her eyes glazed. Unconsciousness already on its way to claim her. She had no last words to say. She could save it for her trial. She lost consciousness with a smile on her face mistakenly thinking that she would never wake up.

The officers cut Eve free and helped her from the table just as Rob ran into the dungeon. Eve flew into his arms.

"Ellie, Ellie Thank God you're safe."

He had his hands in her hair, he was smothering her face with kisses. His eyes were streaming tears.

"Hello Eve" he whispered softly into her ear. "It's all right now. It's over."

Chapter 40
Epilogue

Every novelist knows that it is the kiss of death to write about window gazing in her opening sentence. Evelyn Erikson, age twenty seven and current resident of Cherry Tree Cottage on top of Beech Hill, didn't know this. In fact Evelyn knew remarkably little about the nuts and bolts of writing, despite having three books hovering in or around the bestseller list. This day held all the promise that only a young day can and the unpalatable, cooling coffee was her reason for remaining rooted at the dining table watching that promise unfold.

Jake padded in from the garden and sat in front of her chair demanding attention. He looked uncommonly girlie, sitting with his great, big head adorned with lavender blooms and cocked enquiringly to the right. Eve laughed despite her mood.

"You've had your nosy snout in that lavender bush again, haven't you?" She said in a mock reproving voice. "Those bees'll have you and then you'll be sorry."

Jake grinned and chuffed at Eve, he was a clever German Shepherd, and he knew the 'Bee' word.

Bees: fat things that don't make sense to a logic seeking dog. They shouldn't be able to fly with that round, furry body and tiny thin wings. It's not right that they should be able to fly and Jake can't. Hmmm they taste good though and it makes his humans laugh when he pulls funny faces as he tries to eat one. Jake forgets sometimes that he only has one human now. He used to have two. Jake mustn't forget that he only has one human, because Eve gets sad when he goes round the house looking. But if Jake could find her, and bring her back, then Eve wouldn't be sad anymore. Jake thinks she's in that hole where they saw a mouse last year. That mouse went in the hole in the skirting boards and never came out again. It is all very confusing though when the whole house smells of her. Eve doesn't smell her everywhere like Jake does. Eve would whine all night too if she could smell her all the time and had an itch behind her ear. Bees shouldn't oughta fly like that; it's not right.

Eve put her hand down and stroked the dog's head. The strawberries were almost ripe. '*She would have loved that,*' thought Eve; she would enjoy picking the first strawberries of the season for their tea. It was always quite an occasion apparently. The first ones would be ripe for picking next week, but it wouldn't be the same and Eve doubted that they would taste as sweet without Ellie there to enjoy them with her.

"Oh well Jakey boy, we can't sit here all day can we? I've made a momentous decision while you've been having fun without a care in the world. I'm going to start writing today."

Jake cocked his head again, deciphering the unfamiliar words from the ones he knew. There was no 'dinner' or 'out' in them, but sometimes humans disguised dinner and out so that they sounded like something else.

Eve got up from the table, and before she was even upright Jake was bouncing around like a puppy.

Oh yes, oh yes, this is it. This is the out. Out, out, out. Oh I'm so excited. We're going out. Do the round and round thing. Eve likes the round and round thing. Make Eve smile. Round and round. Round and round. Out. Out. Out. No Eve that's the study. That's not out, that's Ellie's study. The front door's this way. Eve, Eve. Out. Look I'm wagging, I'm wagging Eve. Out. C'mon Eve, I'll teach you how to catch bees without them getting the ouch thing in you. Eve. Out. Oh sometimes humans are no fun.

Eve walked into Ellie's domain. This wasn't merely Ellie's room this room *was* Ellie. Ellie permeated the walls and infused the very air. Eve hadn't been in here much since… Well, now it was her room and she had to get used to that. Things were different now and she *is* Ellie. It felt strange becoming someone else. Evelyn Erikson had gradually taken the place of Eleanor. As long as Eve was Ellie, Ellie would never be dead.

Lowering herself into the swivel chair she took a deep, calming breath and Jake flopped down beside her. He sighed the sigh of a dog much older than his eight years and rolled his eyes to make his displeasure obvious. Five seconds later his heavy lids gave up the struggle to stay open and he fell asleep.

The computer's sensors had monitored Eve's approach and as she sat down it fired up. Eve envied the computer's ability to come alive within seconds of 'waking'. What the computer could achieve in thirty seconds, she aspired to only after a shower and three cups of strong coffee.

"Good morning Ellie." Said the computer-simulated voice.

"Good morning George," replied Eve. The new name was going to take some growing into.

"It is 8:54 am and the date is the 10th of June Two thousand and forty eight. What can I do for you this morning?" asked the deep though rather tinny tones of the 'sex god in the box.' as they called him.

Eve slumped into the chair. The hairs on her arms began to rise and she was instantly transported back in her mind to another place, another time, another world where every morning an impersonal voice chanted the date and time at her. A place where she was a prisoner contained and controlled, unable even to think for herself. She wanted to run but her legs were leaden. She couldn't do this. She was mad to think that she could just sit here and continue where things had been left off. She raised her head and took some deep breaths. Jake alerted to the change in Eve's mood sat up, whined and cocked his head at his mistress in alarm. She *had* to do this; she owed it not only to herself but also to the only person in the world that she had ever loved. She would do this. She took one more deep inhalation just to check that she was calm and spoke in as reasonable a voice as possible to the computer."

"George, I will be coming in here at roughly this time every morning from now on. I only intend to say this once so I hope your receptors are focused to exactly what I am saying. I like your chirpy 'Good Morning' George, really I do. Sometimes yours will be the only voice apart from my own that I will hear in the course of the day. But, listen up my technological friend. If you ever tell me the date and time when I walk into the room again I will pull every single wire from your circuitry and stuff them so far down your memory hole that you will be choking on techno-spaghetti for a month. Do I make my self succinctly and unconditionally understood?"

The computerised voice was bristling with indignation when it replied "Well there's no need to take that attitude I'm sure, I was only trying to be helpful." It then lowered its voice to a mumble, "Succinctly and unconditionally understood. Huh anyone would think she's a writer."

Having done for the time being with whinging it raised its voice back to the default volume level. "Will that be all for now Miss?"

"Oh George, drop the insulted affront or I'll pinch your emotion chip and use it for a solar token. Oh and remind me George to take a large sub-machine gun and shoot whoever it was who decided to give computers an emotion chip in the first place. It can be highly irritating. Right then George to business. I would like a squeaky clean new document please. Today is the day I begin the new book."

"But Ellie you are only on chapter seven of 'Who Took The Morning Train?' and if I might be so bold as to mention without endangering my delicate circuitry in your present mood, it is desperately in need of a decent edit."

Eve smiled despite herself. Sometimes it was hard to believe that blood and organs formed no part of the make-up of George. "New document please George and then that will be all thank you."

"Very good Miss," said George in his finest simulation of the dutiful servant. "I'll just melt into the background then until the next time you feel the urgent desire to abuse me. Enjoy Ellie it's good to be in service again." George brought up a new word processing document as requested and altered his status. The 'voice activation on stand by' icon appeared in the top right of the monitor screen.

"And George" Said Eve bringing him back online.

"Yes?" he answered in a perfect long-suffering voice.

"I love you." Said Eve grinning, "Save every five minutes please, George."

"Will do Hun. Oh and you asked me to remind you to take a large sub-machine gun and shoot whoever it was that gave computers emotion chips." The screen momentarily went black and flashed with a huge red lips icon. The lips puckered and a large smacking sound crackled from the speakers. They were replaced after five seconds with the document waiting to be written.

This time she laughed out loud, "Bugger off George and let me work." The hardware that produced the voice of the computer seemed to know just when she needed cheering up, and she contemplated the white screen still smiling.

Eve took a great lungful of air and began by writing her pen name in the header. 'Eleanor Erikson'. The next five words produced the title. 'Better The Devil You Know.'

In the body of the document she began the first sentence of the novel that *had* to be written, that *needed* to be told.

She began with the words.

"Every novelist knows that it is the kiss of death to write about window gazing in their opening sentence…"

Eve went into the hospital after Ellie's death and between them she and Rob concocted the story that it was her twin sister Eve who had Tay-Sachs disease all along. Nobody wanted the complications of a woman with no identity so it was convenient to believe Miss Erikson's story. She faced the Press hounds like a trooper, until the next politician slept with a prostitute on the presidential lawn and off they scattered to invade somebody else's life.

Maria Kiltcher is currently seeing out the rest of her life in some fictitious mental institution of the future. She collects porcelain dolls.

And Jake came to love his new mistress almost as much as his old one.

But sometimes truth is stranger than fiction. On 28th December 2002, in real life, in real time when my book was already completely written and in the stages of final edit. A news story broke on British television. A cult has supposedly cloned the first human being. A baby girl …Her name is Eve. It's being hailed as a hoax, but hey folks, just remember. I wrote my story first.